RANDY BLAZAK

THE MISSION OF THE SACRED HEART
A Rock Novel

Randy Blazak is an Associate Professor of Sociology at Portland State University. Past publications include *Renegade Kids, Suburban Outlaws* (with Wayne S. Wooden, 2001, Wadsworth Publishing) and *Hate Offenders* (2009, Praeger Publishing). He regularly publishes in the area of hate crimes. He teaches a variety of criminology related classes as well as his trademark course, the Sociology of Youth Subcultures. He earned his PhD from Emory University in 1995. Blazak lives in Northeast Portland in a house with a lot of records and CDs.

Follow The Mission of the Sacred Heart on Facebook and the author on Twitter: @rblazak

The Mission of the Sacred Heart
A Rock Novel

Randy Blazak

CreateSpace Books
2011

ISBN-13: 978-1460976159
ISBN-10: 1460976150

Printed in the U.S.A.

Cover photography: Salem Victoria.
Cover model: Matthew Lucas

Dedicated to the memory of Heather Hartley

Side one
1. Tightrope
2. Telephone Line
3. Rockaria!
4. Mission (A New World Record)

Side two
1. So Fine
2. Livin' Thing
3. Above the Clouds
4. Do Ya
5. Shangri-La

Author's note: This novel was written in 1999, loaded on Zoloft and the 1976 Electric Light Orchestra album, *A New World Record*. It is about surviving. Reading while listening to ELO and/or on 100mgs of Zoloft will enhance the enjoyment of the book.

Acknowledgements: This book was written in a blur, so I would like to thank the following people and be forgiven for the rest: Jessica Lamb, Bahar Jaberi, anyone who was a bartender in Portland between 1998 and 1999, the homeless old man in front of the Plaid Pantry on NE 16th, whoever took me home the night Frank Sinatra died, the Cannon Beach Police, Jeff Lynne (for writing the lyrics that inspired this story), and a certain young woman from Georgia who broke my heart so I could learn how to fix it.

Chapter One:
Tightrope

He couldn't have known this yet. The city forgets the night. The ancient black night of the gods. The deep memories of stars and their constellations have been whited out by humanity's desire to recreate the night in its own image. There are billions of children, born and dead, who have never seen Cassiopeia or Orion's belt. They have never seen the blanketing Milky Way, their own safe home. It was a slow evolution over the millennia, when the bonfires became torches became gas street lamps and finally became halogen highways surrounded by steel and glass towers that never dim. The American city is a monument to abundance. There is no off switch. And the ancient night suffers. The stars are gone, replaced with helicopters, billboards, and late-night office workers. Occasionally, a nearby moon will shine through the dull sky but the wonder of deep space, of the millions of possibilities, has been erased as humans wall themselves off from the gods and redirect their focus to the streets below.

And they wonder what happened to the magic in their lives.

The change from day to night is really only hours. Tonight Telly Max is not of this world. He walks through the Portland dusk with a glide. Appearing cool and young, he sneaks into a city filled with people who feel like they don't belong. The carefully crafted alien look of the new century; black leather and black bangs and black sunglasses for those who feel the city night is not black enough. He is not distinct. He is MTV, right down to his dour expression. No energy to smile and no reason. Telly's face is wracked with permanent sadness. The shades hide his furrowed brow but his clenched jaw is evident on his lean face. He could be a poster boy of a lost generation if he weren't only a visitor. But in Portland, Oregon he couldn't blend in more perfectly. It is a city that harbors the dark cusp of the soul while it lights up the night.

It is a Y2K Friday night and the streets are filled with pathos, all of which is acutely observed by the newcomer. Teenagers cruise Broadway in cars detailed at the price of their own futures, sending carbon monoxide into the haze and debt into their laps, convincing themselves of a good time. Advertising executives and their assistants sneak out of offices late to catch the last call for happy hour. Commuters shop for a bit of reward and sit in traffic or on the bus, tuned out by their CD Walkmans. There are as many people entering the city energized and hopeful as there are leaving the city tired and burned. Portland on Friday night reaches a homeostasis between old and new blood.

Telly notices this static state and the transfer of energy between waves of urban emigrants and immigrants. He also is aware that amid the transfusion there are those who never leave. They are the homeless, the vagrants and the gutter-punks. The city is their home and they never see the stars. On his first night in Portland, Telly stops his glide to watch a group of vagabond youths in Pioneer Square camped out next to a Starbucks. As professionals and partiers dart in and out of the coffee bar, the kids stay. They have no car to cruise in and no suburban home to return to after a long day of pushing papers. They are sedentary, dirty and unaffected by the plans of the advertising executives, or perhaps rebelling against them. Telly can tell that they are sick and despondent inside and yet they smile and laugh. Their bodies are pierced and many have self-inflicted tattoos that will only become more blurry with age. Two have pet rats and one keeps a rat-like dog on a rope leash. Their punk-rock look is nearly three decades old, but there is something new about them.

Leaning against a column amid the last wave of heading-home commuters, Telly takes in the scene. A mother scolding her hyperactive

2

children on the light-rail platform stands in contrast to the affection of these blackened youths. They are menacing to the straight world but loving to each other. They are polite when asking for spare change and then openly curse their deniers. It could be an entertaining guerrilla street play about the divergence of wealth and poverty or the neglect of a city's children if it weren't for their state of rot. They don't want to be there in Pioneer Square, dirty and homeless, but there is nowhere else they'd rather be. Telly knows this is only an initial observation and he will only truly understand their motivation once he has a home-base, a place to set up his operation. A pad.

Aware of the rules of American urban areas Telly knows he needs an apartment. He could live like the gutter-punks, under bridges or in parks, but that would limit his access to the full range of realities in this world. Likewise, a large suburban home would restrict him to the middle-class ghettos of the city. Telly needs a flat. The type of place that refugees from the middle-class come to escape those suburban limitations and reconnect with an imagined urban past, when only farmers lived outside of Metropolis. There are certain dwellings that are deemed "cool" because of this link. They are not places that the urban poor live but they are like places that the urban poor live. And in these cool pads lies intellectual activity in the form of inquisition, or as it is referred to on the street, philosophy. In these places it is encouraged to ask questions about the nature of things. Theory building is a sport, compared to the stable suburbs and poverty stricken housing projects, where "because" is a sufficient explanation. Telly needs a place where he can ask questions.

Zachary Crisp is certainly of this world, and frankly he's had enough of it. Zak's seen the worst of his generation starving, naked in the negro streets of dawn. And that was just in the coffee shop this evening. The "hipster holocaust," as he sarcastically calls it, has just about lost all its charm. The only thing more vacant being the non-hip world. At least the hipster world offered the promise of emancipation through intense self-awareness, as painful as that may be. Zak's life résumé is something that might as well be thrown into the recycle bin. Maybe someone else could learn something from all the heartbreak and dead ends. To Zak, it was just one big waste. He was sitting in the Starbucks in Pioneer Square when he saw the dark figure that was Telly pass by. "I wear my sunglasses at night," he sang to himself.

The pure fact that Zak was camped out in the Starbucks with a tall hazelnut latte was evidence of how far the cracks in his world had grown. Previously he would never have set foot inside the insidious franchise that threatened to assimilate every American locale into one huge monoculture, along with all the McDonalds, Wal-Marts, Gaps and Blockbusters. Starbucks was the enemy of art and distinctive urban life, turning the city streets into just another suburban strip mall. He supported locally owned coffee houses, boho and funky. Their profits went into the local scene or just trying to stay open in the face of the encroaching franchise hell. Zak often wondered why America didn't have terrorists that bombed Starbucks and yet there he sat. The righteous cultural revolutionary had about as much time for dogma at the moment as he did for the dumbass kids who were cruising Broadway.

This latest tailspin was perhaps the worse he had ever experienced. Tomorrow was supposed to be a special day, a break from his daily number-crunching as a health science graduate student. He was supposed to get married. A week ago his fiancé, Petra Novak, a woman who told him repeatedly how she looked forward to growing old with him, bailed. She left a short note, something to the effect that she was worried about losing herself to the "concept" of marriage (she used that word, concept). He loved this woman with every ounce of life he had. After years of bad relationships, she was his salvation. What made matters worse was that Petra had been living with Zak, so on top of trying to micro-manage the

4

train wreck of his love-life, he needed to quickly find a roommate so he could make next month's rent. Friends knew what a pain-in-the-ass Zak could be and now that he had been dumped by his true-love, they all kept a fair distance knowing that he would be in full asshole mode. Who would want to step into that emotional vortex? He was in a mess and thank GOD for Starbucks.

When Zak stared out of the window at the gutter-punks in the square, his analysis wasn't quite as inductive as Telly's. "Those stupid fuckin' idiots," he thought to himself. "They think they're so free but they're just as enslaved as they were before they escaped from the mall. Street kids grow to be old homeless people." He passed by the old vagrants daily on his way to the university. He'd be on his swift bike and they'd be stuck in a breadline in the freezing rain. Sometimes he wanted to grab them and shout, "Don't you wish you would have tried harder in school?" But he knew that many were mentally ill or had become mentally ill after losing jobs in the local timber industry. Probably many had become alcoholics and drug addicts after having their hearts broken. He had met one homeless fellow who had been a college professor and had turned to the booze after his wife had left him. It was just sad and now he was one rent check away from joining them on the breadline. "Go home," he muttered to the gutter-punks. "Go home and build a way to stay free." Zak was feeling increasingly desperate, like he was drowning, wondering if someone would throw him down a line.

The paper latte cup was empty. At any other coffee shop you could make a two dollar latte in a big porcelain cup last for hours while you sat on an overstuffed couch and discussed Hegel with other twenty-somethings who had read the same *Hegel For Beginners* as you. But at Starbucks the vibe was fast food. Get your drink and go. Turnover, profit and predictability. But Zak didn't want to leave. The depressing commuters had been completely replaced by the Friday night crowd, blankly looking for fun in the city. Some were going to the symphony, others were the early crowd at the clubs and the rest just cruised Broadway, adding another layer of poison to the night air.

Despite its fluorescent lights and pointy tungsten steel chairs, the Starbucks was seeming a bit womb-like. The intoxicating aroma of espresso and the jangly rhythm of the cash register made it hard to head back out into the street, filled with creeps that Zak generally despised. Frat boys in backwards baseball caps dripping with bad cologne and testosterone. Mexican kids with trendy baggy clothes and even worse haircuts. Businessmen who don't realize that they can take their ties off after 5 pm. And of course the hipsters, who thought they were above the conforming ranks while conforming to their own strict codes of conduct. Zak felt like an open sore in their world. He closed his eyes and flashed to Charlton Heston at the end of *Planet of the Apes* when he realizes that he's stuck in Earth's post-nuclear future. God damn you! God damn you all to hell!

A week ago Zak was in a much better place. Same corner, but he was a fiancé then, shopping for gifts for his groomsmen. Somehow true love, that often derided subject of crappy song and lame poem, had found him. He was painfully aware of the appeal of Air Supply and had even caught himself singing that dreaded Titanic song. He promised himself if he ever spontaneously broke into "I Will Always Love You" or "You Light Up My Life" he'd head for the nearest bridge and hurl himself into the Willamette River. But there was no doubt about it, not only was he happy, he was excited about the future. Shit, he was excited about the future of the whole human race. Maybe the new millennium would be OK. Maybe, if all those cheesy love songs were right, we'll be able to work it out. All the people that he had become accustomed to dissing were just poor souls who hadn't yet met their Petra. She was a miracle, a vision of self-confidence, humor and coolness. She loved country music and a good night of drinking and all the drugged out alterna-rockers could fuck off. She had managed to pry open Zak's jagged heart long enough to give him

6

a glimpse of the way the world could be. Then when he lay vulnerable, prostrate before her whims, she had a mood change and destroyed him with one note. If Zak had been a cynic before Petra, he was a complete nihilist now.

Almost as a protest to the fast-food culture within the Starbucks that discouraged loitering, he refused to leave. He just sat in the uncomfortable chair fully caffeinated, tapping on the empty cup. There were more gutter-punks in the square now, getting geared up for their big night of spare changing. Some looked almost angelic in their affection for each other, like a pack of gibbons grooming each other on the Serengetti. There was even a girl with a baby who was passing it around to her friends to fawn over like a new video game. Zak couldn't help thinking about the infant. "There's one fucked kid." From his research at the university on fetal-alcohol children he knew that they were pretty much doomed and if there was one thing these kids knew how to do it was drink beer.

Along with the usual Friday night street parade Zak also noticed Telly parading around the square like he was trying to get kids to follow him to a Marilyn Manson concert. Even though Zak spent most of his free time with hipsters he probably reserved the most animosity for them. It was their potential that he lamented. To rebel from the mainstream was a good thing, but you have to do something with that rebellion besides... shop. But this hipster was more entertaining. He moved like a guy who fell out a 70's sci-fi flick. Maybe he was a runner in *Logan's Run* or a bounty hunter, like Boba Fet. It was surprising that he wasn't wearing rollerblades, the way he slid down the street but Dr. Marten doesn't make rollerblades. What was this guy up to? Maybe cruising for some kid to take into an alley for a quickie. He seemed to be paying a lot of attention to the gutter-punks, possibly collecting fashion tips. But then he looked up at the Starbucks right at Zak and Zak wondered if he was sizing him up from behind those shades. Telly walked into the coffee shop to Zak's table.

"May I join you?" asked Telly in a monotone voice that sounded vaguely European.

"Uh, dude, I'm done, but you're welcome to sit here by yourself." Zak was not a homophobe but on top of all the other drama he didn't want to have to deal with being the object of someone's desire, someone who was trying a little too hard to be cool.

"No, please. I must talk to you. I think we may be able to help each other."

"Yeah, right. Why don't you talk to some other loser. I got enough on my plate tonight, Corey," Zak said trying to get up.

"My name is Telly, not Corey," said the visitor, puzzled.

"Well as long as you wear those sunglasses at night, you're fuckin' Corey Hart and you belong back in the '80's, not bothering me," said Zak impatiently.

"I am sorry, Zak. It was not my intention to bother you." Telly pulled up a chair and took his sunglasses off. The lines around his eyes surprised Zak, who thought this stranger was probably around 20 but now he might even be 40. He had those Paul McCartney eyes that make girls think of koala bears and make guys think they better develop a new angle. How old was he and how did he know his name?

"Right. Do you know me? Are you a friend Lenny's or something?"

"Who is Lenny?"

"He's one of my neighbors. He sings in that band Gurd. Do you know them?"

"No, I do not. I just arrived in Portland. I only know that you have a room in a cool building to rent," he said setting his glasses down on the table and crossing his legs in the way that American men are afraid to. "I need a room and I have cash for you."

8

"Wait. Dude. You walk in here lookin' all Brit-rock and you want to move into my place? How did you know I needed a roommate? You're starting to freak me a bit here. Who are you?" Zak didn't know if this encounter was a blessing or a curse. It could be his economic salvation but it was beyond weird.

"My name is Telly Max. I am not from here. Suffice it to say, I am alien."

Zak burst out in laughter. This was perfect. "You don't look Mexican!" He could be German. A Sprockets-loving Kraut rocker with an Audi full of Kraftwork CDs. But he knew that this guy meant space-alien as in ET phone home.

"I do not expect you to believe me, just trust me," he said staring directly into Zak's eyes. Zak wondered if this freak thought he was putting a space mojo on him.

"Oh, dude I believe you. You must be an alien because you don't use contractions. Everybody knows that aliens and androids can't use contractions. Have you ever met Data?" Zak was fully in the sarcastic mode. It was his weapon. He used it against the high school bullies that beat him up when he was an awkward teenager and now he used it against everyone from bank tellers to hipper-than-thou scenesters who thought that they had some divine right to the blues. "Are you like a *Starman* alien or more like a *Man Who Fell To Earth* alien? Maybe you shaved your alien fur off like in *Earth Girls Are Easy.*"

"In time you will understand. It is true that you need a roommate and you need money for rent. I can give you $500 each month." Telly reached into his leather jacket and pulled out five one hundred dollar bills, setting them on the table. Zak shut up. Since the rent on his downtown two-bedroom flat was only $650 a month he was either being set up for a bad joke or about to room with one crazy fucker.

"OK. Let's go. We can do the obligatory interview on the way. If you like it and I like you, you might have your room. But let's walk. Getting a

9

bus right now is a major pain. Too many freaks. Oh, sorry, no offense."
The two exited the Starbucks and began walking down Broadway, then
Burnside Avenue to the northwest corner of downtown, heading past
swank hotels, then divey bars, bookstores and cafés. They talked amid
the based-up stereos of the Friday night cruisers who were attempting to
annoy anyone not in a car.

"So, how old are you anyway?" Zak asked.

"The same age as you," replied Telly.

"Twenty-nine years, nine months and four days? What a
coincidence! So, what's your home planet?"

"You wouldn't know it."

"Hey, you used a contraction! You aren't an alien! Unless you're
from France. You're not from France are you? I don't want to live with a
guy who never bathes, stinkin' up the place."

"I am not from France," Telly said starting to understand his new
friend's sense of humor.

"Where is all your stuff at? The bus station? The space port?"

"I have nothing. I must purchase what I need," said Telly, giving the
first hint of his deep sadness.

"That's cool dude, you don't need much in this town, as long as
you've got beer money. Aren't you going to ask me any questions?"
queried Zak, beginning to warm up to this completely odd character who
had just dropped into his Friday night and maybe his life.

"Yes." Telly paused. "What compels you to live?" he asked with
complete seriousness.

"What the fuck? Man, like ask me what my favorite Beastie Boys
album is or if I cook Indian food at home, not my reason for existence!
We're almost there. That's a question for when we are drunk on
margaritas with nowhere to go."

"Is there a short answer?" Telly asked, his lanky body seeming to
hover over Zak's equally slight frame. They were walking up Burnside,

past the Allday Music record store, which stayed open until midnight so the music starved Portlandians could get their impulsive fixes.

Zak looked in the window at the shoppers, thinking, "Now those people are doing the right thing on a Friday night." Then he looked up at Telly who was earnestly waiting for a reply. "OK, short answer. What compels me to live. This place right here. I am compelled to live by great records and the completion of the perfect record collection. One that contains every side that Ian MacGlagen has played keyboards on, every record that Steve Albini has produced and every track that has been bootleged from a Springsteen session. Oh yeah, also, every Miles Davis album, it in itself an impossible task. That is what compels me to live. Thank you and good night."

"Is it the music or the desire for completion?" asked Telly feeling like he might be on to something.

"Dude, it's all of the above. Listen I am not in the proper frame of mind to deliver my thesis on the value of record collecting. Presently I'm much more of a space cadet than you will ever be. Ukrainian? There's a lot of Ukrainians in town all of a sudden. Anyway, you must be a friend of Petra's and that's how you know about the room. So you know how fucked up I am at the moment. And if it turns out that you 'know her' know her I'm gonna send you on the next Millennium Falcon into the sun. Dig? I don't need any goddamn Trekkies fuckin' with me right now. I just need a roommate who won't bother me. Have you got a job? Are you on loan from Area 51 or something?"

"I have a job. It is to observe and I will not bother you," said Telly, wanting to please his host.

"Oh yeah, observing. I forgot that's what all aliens do. Observe and then report back to the mothership so they can plot our annihilation. Fine, just don't observe me while I'm taking a shit, OK? That's what we call 'private time' down here on Earth."

11

"Your apartment has a window onto this street. That is all I require," said Telly, forcing a smile, and then looking up at Zak's apartment building.

"Well, I suppose you know that this is it. Maybe you can use your heat ray to fix the radiator." The building was a grand old brick structure called The Eldorado, which seemed more like the name of a gay ranch than a Portland crash pad. The apartment building was on the downtown edge of Portland's chic Northwest neighborhood, where the yuppies came to play and the slackers came to slave. Plenty of cafés and fine dining and boutiques and a guaranteed parking disaster on weekends. Zak's place was far enough away from the trendy area and on the cooler urban side. All that mattered to him was that he was one block away from the late-night record store and one of Portland's best clubs, the Palais. And since Petra had left, the fact that there was a porno mega-store right across the street seemed much more fortuitous than having another Starbucks there (although Zak allowed for the fact that there might be a Starbucks inside the porno mega-store).

Inside, the apartment was spacious and classic, not like the low-ceiling carpeted rat-traps they started building in the 1970s. French doors and a big bay window framed wooden floors and lots of yard-sale furniture. It was decidedly masculine but there was plenty of evidence that a female had recently resided here. Besides the relative lack of dust and the Pottery Barn knick-knacks, the antique dining room table was a dead give-away. Only couples had dining room tables, for "entertaining." Bachelors ate off the kitchen table or off the coffee table in front of the TV. Zak's place was in transition. He was deciding what to keep of Petra's and what to purge. What to keep in case she came back and what to throw out of the window in anger. What Telly noticed was the music collection. Rows of CDs, tapes and LPs lined the living room wall, perfectly organized in library fashion.

"Here we are," sighed Zak. "Pet moved out last week and so she'll probably be taking a few more things out of here. The extra bedroom is through there. Right now it's the music room. I've got all my records in there but I can move them out to... somewhere."

"This is not all your music?" asked Telly, pointing to the extensive collection in the living room.

"No, man. I told you it's my reason for living. I know it's a bit obsessive but there is a method to the madness. I buy around ten CDs or records a week. And now I have to buy all the ones my girlfriend stole. Here's today's booty." Zak lifted up a record and three CDs off a speaker. "I replaced The Police *Synchronicity*, Travis Tritt *It's All About to Change* and Indigo Girls *Strange Fire*. I just hate having these holes in my collection. She took dozens of CDs and tons of vinyl. But in a matter of months, it will be like she was never here. I also picked up this cool old Kiss tribute on C/Z Records. It's got Nirvana doing a wicked version of 'Do You Love Me?' Were you ever a Kiss fan?"

"How much time do you spend here?" asked Telly.

Zak sat down on the futon couch. "Well, not as much as I used to. I'm working on my Masters in Public Health and I'm up at the university a lot. And lately I've been getting back in to going out to see bands and just getting smashed a lot. You'll probably get the whole story at some point. But this place still burns a bit, if you know what I mean."

"I burn," said Telly looking out the window at the Friday night, "but I imagine that you will know this story as well."

"Christ, is this your real schtick? I mean am I rooming with the brother from another planet or the man who fell out of the asylum?" chuckled Zak, looking with a certain amount of disbelief at his new lodger.

"Then you have accepted my offer and I may move in?" said Telly, forcing a smile that only looked strained.

13

Zak wasn't sure what to make of this guy. His entrance was quite amusing. No one had ever used the "Hi, I am from Mars" line on him before. But there was also something incredibly sad about Telly, almost manic, like he was fighting just to keep it together. He seemed traumatized and hiding behind a mask of coolness, but Zak dug coolness as one of the last unadulterated poses left; well, almost. He had worried that any new roommate of his would get sucked into the drama he was having with Petra. Now he wondered if Telly's drama might beat out his own and he'd get drawn into this "alien" cover story only to find something much more sinister. Letting this freak move in could be like walking into a bad *Halloween* sequel.

"The rent's due the first of the month and we divide up phone bills and utilities equally," replied Zak extending his hand to his new flat-mate. Telly hesitated and then shook Zak's hand. Zak immediately noticed how cold and damp Telly's hand was, but then this was Portland and everyone was cold and damp.

Telly sat on the window seat, observing, while Zak put on some water to make pasta. He was half watching this odd bird while he prepared some dinner. What was he getting himself into? Was he going to wake up in the morning only to find himself hacked to bits? Well, alive still, of course, but only barely. This guy had no stuff, which presumably included his medication. Everyone had medication, including Zak. And, of course, there was the inevitable issue of the anal probe. According to popular wisdom, all alien visitors are anally fixated. Or maybe the only close encounters of the third kind are with cosmic proctologists. It's possible. "Hey, man, you want some pasta? I always make too much."

Usually on Fridays Zak and Petra went out for dinner, Italian or Indian or maybe Greek or Mexican. Sometimes American, but certainly never French. There was usually a quiet dinner and then a gig at a nightclub. Petra would get tired before the end of the main band and tell

Zak to stay but they would go home and make love in the living room to Al Green records. On this Friday, there was no fiancé, only Zak and the Watcher. He was planning on eating a plate of pasta and then after some TV, heading out to catch a band at The Palais.

"Thank you, Zak. That would be nice." Telly had found a perch in front of the window and Zak knew he was going to play out this "observing puny Earthlings" gag, but hey, it was a quiet hobby. He really wanted to pepper this guy with questions but was half afraid Telly would actually answer them. He decided he'd get him out with the crew before he tried to pry him open. Zak appreciated being the one who was intent on uncovering someone else's pain rather than spending all his energy covering up his own.

Telly wandered into the kitchen where Zak was stirring the spaghetti in one pot and a jar of Classico sauce in another. In the bright kitchen light Zak thought Telly might actually be a young clone of Rik Ocasek. Rik Ocasek of The Cars who, when he was old and no longer musically relevant, married beautiful Czech supermodel Paulina Porizkova. The Cars were a great band (pre-*Shake It Up*) but Zak had a weakness for Czech supermodels. Petra was Czech and very supermodelesque in her own weird way. Not that supermodels were to be coveted. They were, in fact, evil, mainly because of their horrible power over you. If Elle McPhereson asked you to kill someone, you'd do it without question. Maybe Telly, being Rik Ocasekish, would help to lure his Czech supermodel back. And then Telly'd probably marry her. Zak's mind was riffing and the Classico was bubbling onto the stovetop.

"Shit! The sauce is always ready before the pasta!" Petra had taught him the fine art of timing your dishes so that everything was ready at the same time but Zak was lazy. Usually, when he cooked pasta on his own (which he did a lot) he'd eat the noodles before they were completely soft. He just couldn't wait. Why should he?

"Thank you for dinner," said Telly as Zak used a wooden spoon to push some spaghetti and sauce onto one plate and then another.

"What do you want to drink with that? Beer?"

"I will have what you are having."

"Well, I drink milk with my pasta. Milk is the drink of champions."

"Then I will have milk," replied Telly, sitting down at the kitchen table like a bachelor. Zak poured two big glasses of milk and then joined him. "Why do you like milk?" asked Telly, innocently enough.

"Well Ziggy, I guess because it is the first thing I ever drank. Every glass reminds me of a great big tit."

"Then this is human milk?"

"Yeah, I buy it by the gallon. They've got about 200 maidens hooked up to machines down at the dairy. No, rocketman, it's COW's milk. It's from the breasts of fine Oregonian bovine. Moo juice, y'know?" Zak was willing to play along with the puzzled visitor bit.

Telly then had the sense to ask, "Do you drink the milk of any other animals?"

"I like goat cheese but not goat milk. Who else makes milk like cows?"

"All female mammals produce milk. You could drink the milk of dogs, sheep or otters."

"Dude, I'm trying to eat not uneat! Maybe the French wash down their snails with a glass of otter milk, but not me. That's just way too gross."

"My friend, do you know what milk is?" asked Telly with a raised eyebrow.

"Um, mucus from the stomach of a big dumb animal that's shot up with hormones? I'll have another!"

"I just find it curious that humans prefer cow's milk to their own." It was a valid point but as much time as Zak spent thinking about it he couldn't imagine that there were enough eager lactating women on Earth

16

to supply all the needs of the ice cream sandwich industry let alone the dairy world in general. He'd have to think about it some more. Breasts. Milk. Breasts. Milk.

"Speaking of breasts, it's Friday night and I'm going to go out to a show later. This band, Hair Eater, is playing over at The Palais. You're welcome to tag along. It should be cool. Lots of Earth girls. It's just across the road there." Telly had noticed the building on the walk up Burnside. It seemed to be a center of activity but he was feeling a lack of energy. It wasn't your standard I'm-too-tired-to-go-out wane but a deep soulful ache. Telly knew that he wasn't ready for the crowds and multi-level social interaction. He just wanted to be alone.

"Again, thank you," he said finishing his pasta. "I am very tired and will require rest before tomorrow's activities."

"You don't sleep on the ceiling or in a cocoon or anything, do ya? If you want to sleep on the futon until you get a bed you can. There are some blankets in the closet in the music room, I mean your room. Make yourself at home, just don't beam anything of value out of here before I get back."

"Your home will be safe, my friend," said Telly with his Paul McCartney eyes.

After some typically banal TGIF Friday TV, Zak threw on a suede jacket and headed out the door to the club down the street. A block away he looked back up at his apartment. There was Telly in front of the window, watching cars and couples cascade up and down Burnside. "I might have to double my happy pills with this guy around," Zak thought. "He's one sad song."

At the Palais Zak tried to lose himself in the rock world that had sustained him throughout his twenties. When he was a teenager at punk shows he'd be pressed up as close to the stage as possible, sometimes leaping off it into the arms of his sweaty peers. He was moshing when it

17

was still called slam dancing, long before people began moshing at Hootie and the Blowfish concerts. It was always the frat boys who took something pure and turned it into a cartoon. He remembered slamming at a Fishbone show in the late 1980s and feeling like he was part of a huge generational orgasm. Amid the anarchy was a beautiful sense of order.

As the pit became increasingly populated by high school wrestlers and as Zak moved into his twenties, the distance between him and the stage grew. Where he once couldn't get close enough to the band, now he settled for the second row of viewers who stood back and let the kids do their thing. Occasionally, he would play the role in the buffer zone, dividing the moshers from the hipsters, getting out his aggression by pushing the very un-punk punks toward the stage.

But now that Zak was staring down the double barrel of 30, he rarely made it anywhere near the stage. He usually remained in the bar letting the band serve as background music while he talked to his friends. He couldn't remember the last time his hands had touched a stage instead of an endless succession of micro-brews. Extrapolating from this trend Zak predicted that by age 35 he'd only get as close as the parking lot of any given gig, listening in through the air vents with a bottle of Mad Dog. The scene had a nice way of putting old hipsters out to pasture. They just keep moving farther and farther away from the music until it just made more sense to stay home and die.

Tonight Zak had his spot at the bar, peeking at the Hair Eaters over the various age-graded zones of rockdom. If Petra was here she would already want to go home, which was okay because that meant sex to Al Green. But Zak didn't even know where Petra was, hopefully not in a bar like him. Zak had no fiancé but he still had the Al Green collection. Maybe he should cash in on his newfound freedom and scoop up a hot rock chick. That would show her. If she thought he was going to spend months wallowing in self-pity she was sadly mistaken. He was back on the market and all the girls better beware.

Zak scanned the bar, where all the other aging Gen Xers hid from the loud music. There were numerous possibilities, including a few former near-flings. It would be easy enough to talk his way into a night of meaningless sex and then make excuses in the morning. When he was engaged, the women seemed to be appearing out of thin air in a near-successful attempt to keep him single. He was weak to their seductive poses, intellectual and stylish at the same time. The girls with the creative tattoos pulled on him the most, but he loved Petra. Petra was his salvation, a woman who loved the unlovable man, and he resisted. So now where were these tattoo love girls?

The whole game was just too hard at this point. Unless some goddess was going to float down and carry him away, he might as well be home listening to records. He was too wise to the after-effects of cheap sex. And what if Petra decided she had made a mistake and came back only to find him in their bed with a randomly selected death rocker? He couldn't chance it. Wallowing in self-pity was easier.

Just as Zak was deciding to bail, his friend Lenny caught his eye. Lenny was the definitive millennial Peter Pan. He never left that sacred spot in front of the stage. His method of accommodation was to start a band that would allow him to leap into the pit at will. The band was called Gurd and it fit Lenny's demeanor. His version of cool was the upset stomach variety, slumped over with messy hair and just-woke-up-and-threw-on -some-clothes clothes.

"Hey, man what do you think of this band?"

"They're OK for a bunch of hair eaters."

"Dude, I'm really sorry we're not at your bachelor party right now."

"Don't remind me. I'm trying to drown my sorrows in this micro-brew but I think some sneaky bastard at the bar has been giving me O'Doul's instead." Zak hadn't figured out how to handle these types of inevitable conversations. Should he play up the pity angle or come off more like she did him a favor? Pity might get him some comfort love but he was too angry for that bullshit. It was easier to dis. "You haven't heard where my lovely ex-bride-to-be ran off to, have ya?"

"No. Neither has Cozy." Cozy was Lenny's fabulous girlfriend, a stunning aspiring opera singer and only if she was Zak's girlfriend the world would be fine. "Dude, don't spend too much time thinking about where she is. First, you'll think she's alone and then you'll think she's not alone and then you'll think that she's with some specific person, even though you can't see his face and pretty soon you're getting into drunken fights with every guy because he might be the one. I've been there and believe me, you don't want to go there. It fuckin' sucks."

It was too late, Zak was there. Not as deep as Lenny's warped world, but he had wondered if it was all about another man. But he was not thinking about it at that moment, until Lenny reminded him.

Lenny wasn't done. "Like, what you need are some serious distractions. Why don't you start a new hobby. You could grow Bonzaii Trees, like Arnold in *The Karate Kid*. Stamps. Stamps are good, too. Are you still gonna get a roommate?"

"Well, it's an economic necessity. Actually, I got one tonight. He just sort of, fell out of the sky. You'll meet him and tell me you don't immediately think 'Rik Ocasek'."

"Why, is he dating a beautiful Czech supermodel?"

Argggh.

Zak was about to launch into his tale of the unlikely roommate who thought he was from the cosmos but into the bar zone walked Mia McZane. Mia was the local rock queen. She played keyboards in the band The Pop Art Express and had it down, the ass-shaking, lip-pursing, cool haircut-having, right clothes-wearing thing. She was a vision and Zak had coveted her for years. He and every other rock dude in Portland. Besides Mia's hipness, she looked like Drew Barrymore, but with better tattoos.

20

And as much as Zak hated the hipsters, Mia was different. Often when he and Petra were having fights, he'd quip, "Well, I can always go out with Mia McZane," even though he didn't even know her. Well, he knew about her and about how much he had fetishized her, but until now he hadn't had the nerve.

"Oh, there's Zak's favorite rockstar," said Lenny, fully aware of the obsession. "Why don't you go ask her for an autograph. Or a fuck." It was entirely possible. While The Pop Art Express had gained some renown in Europe and even scored a video on MTV, they were still relatively small beans at home.

"Dude! Maybe I should. If I want to forget what's-her-name, with, man... Mia!" Zak had been on a tightrope for the last week. Each step had to be carefully planned. The unthought out action is probably what had sent Petra running. Now he was just one mis-step from falling into a pit of depression. He had vacillated hourly between sobbing and wanting to punch holes in the wall. And then there were the endless sessions sitting on the end of his bed wondering what had happened to his life. Was it some big karmic payback for the way he had treated women in his life? Each day he walked the tightrope to the next day, hoping he wouldn't fall. The anti-depressants helped but he knew he had to maintain the vigilance of his emotions. Few returned from the downward spiral intact. Maybe Mia was just what the doctor ordered. "OK, watch my back."

Mia was her usual glamorous self, in a big white fake fur coat right off of the corpse of Brian Jones. She was surrounded by all the hangers-on, the worst vermin in the rock world, the ones who hang out with anyone who is famous, like the fame will rub off on them. Zak waited until Mia made a break for the restroom, and away from the embarrassment of pledging his love in front of the posse. "Hey, Mia?"

"Oh, hi!" she said, thinking that she might have known him. She should have known him since they had been traveling in the same circles for years. She should have at least recognized him, after all, the only time

21

that Zak ever returned to Zone 1 was when The Pop Art Express played and he would dance in the crowd right in front of her.

"Hey, my name is Zak and you've been a mysterious force in my life for the last three years and I just really wanted to finally meet you." He though this line was golden. It just came to him from the ether. Mysterious force? Odds are she would be powerless to such a line. He was about to begin his relationship with Mia McZane.

"Oh, that's nice. Have a good night." And she disappeared into the restroom.

"Sometimes you're gonna win. Sometimes you're gonna lose," said Lenny who had been watching the attempt and had come over to comfort his neighbor.

"Rockstars," muttered Zak, not realizing that that golden line could be a bit frightening and stalker-esque to normal thinking humans.

"Man, don't worry. Cozy told me that she's gonna fix you up with some high-class broad from the orchestra. She knows all these chicks, totally private school. They wear glasses and go to Europe and read poetry and all that shit you like."

"Don't do me any favors. I have no doubt that Pet will be back and begging to reschedule the wedding. And if not, there's always hookers." The brush-off from Mia had Zak wobbling on his tightrope and he needed to get back to stable ground. "Len, I think I'm gonna split. This is a day I'd like to put behind me. I'll give you a ring tomorrow."

"Right on. I want to hear about this new roommate. Keep it between the ditches, my friend!"

Zak's love woes had made him forget about his new flatmate. Now he had two tough situations to explain, that his fiancé had left him suddenly and he was living with ET. But he was glad that his apartment wasn't empty anymore. No matter how weird this guy was, he was replacing the silence that had filled the place the past week.

When he got home Telly was no longer at the window, nor was he asleep on the futon. He was in the music room, lying on his back on the floor in his clothes, sound asleep. "At least he's not in a cocoon," Zak thought.

The change from night to day is really only hours. When Zak awoke, Telly was back at the window with a cup of coffee. In the morning light he looked like a lost boy who had misplaced his mom at the bus station. Maybe he was looking for a specific person. He was probably a stalker. The act of stalking had crossed Zak's mind recently. He was dying to know what Petra was doing. He wanted to track her down, find out whom she was with. He wanted to tap her phone calls and learn what she was saying about him and her reasons for leaving. He was willing to travel long distances to confront her, but somehow he knew that it would only make matters worse. If Telly was a stalker, he would be conflicted. "I hope you don't mind, I've made coffee," said Telly, using contractions again.

"Great. I can't begin life without it."

In the kitchen Zak's favorite coffee cup was set out. It was a souvenir mug from the Osmond Family Theater in Branson, Missouri. Zak and Petra had stopped there on their drive across the country from Birmingham. Zak had read an article about it in *Details* and decided to make it the main pit-stop on their trip, being a good Donny & Marie child. There at the theater they ran into Jimmy Osmond and Zak was tempted to tell him about how when he was seven he'd pretend that he was an Osmond. He'd put an Osmond Brothers album on in the living room and go into his bedroom and pretend that Donny, Wayne, Merrill, Jay and Alan were in the living room rehearsing and he was the youngest Osmond that no one ever talked about, Zak Osmond. He was going to tell Jimmy, the lovable lad from Liverpool (via Odgen, Utah) this when an aunt called him to the office. "Jimmy, Merrill is on the phone!" It was a pivotal rock 'n' roll moment.

Now in the kitchen the mug was just a reminder of one of the many Zak and Petra adventures that had made him so happy. No more adventures. Just coffee, his favorite drug. He poured a cup and went out and plopped down on the futon.

"How's the world look this fine morning?"

"Life is slow at this hour. The rain is coming."

"Well, welcome to Portland. It should clear up around late June. Doesn't it rain on Planet Claire?" Zak could feel the caffeine kicking in.

"Tell me Zak, about your music collection. Why do you own so much music, more than you could ever listen to?"

Realizing there was a brief moment of morning sunshine and nothing playing on the stereo, Zak grabbed the *Revolver* CD off the rack and slid it into the player. "Because, my friend, music is the soundtrack to life. All this music is there to capture specific feelings of a specific moment." The Beatles chimed in with "Good Day Sunshine" right on cue.

"You see Beldar, we humans are complex creatures, emotional mysteries. We contain thousands of states of mind, many occurring simultaneously. But we are also inarticulate, at least our hearts are. 'Inarticulate Speech of the Heart.' That's a Van Morrison record. We have a hard time expressing how we feel. Women are much better at it but guys suck. That's why most music fanatics are male, women don't need it as much. So the more music I have, the better I can communicate. Sometimes I feel like a Nine Inch Nails song, some times I feel like a Tammy Wynette song. If I have the right song I can adequately express myself, but if I'm feeling Leonard Cohen, 'Suzanne' and all I've got is Tony Basil's, 'Mickey', I'm fucked."

"That is quite a useful explanation, but how do you communicate your feelings to others who are not near your collection?"

24

"Well, obviously I can't drag everyone up to my apartment and say, 'Listen to this. This is how I really feel.' Or tell them, 'Hold on a minute I've got to go home and get you this record.' That's not the point. I'm not trying to communicate to others. I'm trying to communicate it to myself." Zak had spent a lot of time thinking about this, thus the quick response.

Telly took all this in, processing it methodically. "I am not clear. What is the point of communicating something to yourself, that you already understand?"

"Look, you don't get a lot of affirmation in this world. Very few people are going to tell you, 'Oh, yeah, I know how you feel,' and mean it. But I know that if there's a song, that Percy Sledge or Kurt Cobain or Lauryn Hill are saying what I'm feeling, then I must not be crazy. Besides, there are ways to communicate with songs. Don't you guys get Casey Kasem on Mars? Ever hear of the long distance dedication?" Zak wondered what Top 40 songs they'd be dedicating from Mars, besides Chuck Berry.

"And of course there's always the compilation tape. That's the best way to send a message." A message of love. He had sent Petra dozens of compilation tapes that were filled with songs that tried to express how he felt about her. He even proposed using a tape of songs about getting married: David Bowie's "Be My Wife," and Nina Simone's "Marry Me," and John Lennon's "Grow Old With Me," and of course Al Green's "Let's Get Married." A lot of good it did. Now he was going to have to send her heartbreak tapes filled with Chris Isaak and Linda Ronstadt tunes.

"It sounds very efficient," said Telly, thinking everyone thought this way.

"Well, it's not really. It starts simple but then gets complicated. I mean that's why number one songs are number one, because they express something universal. It could be something as cheesy as Boyz II Men's 'Til the End of the Road' or as cool as the Stones' 'Miss You.' There's something about it that millions of people key into and say,

25

'Yeah! This is how I feel, too!' All great songs are based on universal truths. Look at the durability of Christmas songs. 'Have Yourself A Merry Little Christmas' is the saddest, truest song ever written." Zak was speaking like the graduate student that he was, full of well thought out theories that existed perfectly in the abstract and had little use in actual intimate relationships that required listening more than professing.

"But then what happens is those great songs get turned into something else. People love them so advertisers think they can use them to sell their crap. It started to get bad once Michael Jackson began selling Beatles songs to Nike and light bulb companies. It gets very confusing. You don't know if this great Arlo Guthrie song is expressing the way you feel about America or the way you feel about laxatives. Tell your home planet that if they want to move in without having to use their death rays, just turn all our favorite songs into Burger King ads. People will get so depressed because they won't have any way of expressing themselves that hasn't been ruined. Then you can send Elvis down and clean house."

"Elvis?" Telly didn't get the references, but he grasped the concept. People were cynical because something that they loved had been turned against them. It was a common tactic of warfare, for the enemy to co-opt local culture and use it for its own agendas. Locals no longer know what they can believe in and begin to turn on each other. Trust was the basis of civilization. Without it things began to crumble.

Zak was pleased with his off-the-cuff dissertation. He didn't care if Telly was a crackpot. It would be fun pretending that what he said would be relevant to some far off world, even if it was the Evil Empire. Zak needed distractions to stave off the creeping depression he felt from being such a loser. Telly had thrown him down a line. Of course, it *was* from outer space.

Chapter Two:
Telephone Line

Portland might as well have been another planet. Most of those planets you know, Venus, Saturn, Jupiter, you never actually see the planet itself. All we know about them is their thick layer of clouds. On Jupiter you have to descend through 200 miles of ammonia clouds before you ever get to anything you can stand on, and then it's muck. Same thing with Portland. Of all the astronauts and cosmonauts (and whatever they call French astronauts) to gaze down at Earth, it is doubtful that any of them have actually seen Portland, Oregon, unless they were in their spaceship on a good day between July 5 and September 27. Portland is the Rain Planet.

Like the Eskimos and their snow lexicon, Northwesterners have dozens of words for different types of rain: rain, showers, downpours, heavy humidity, drizzle, washouts, mist, cloud bursts, mizzle, gushes. It's all very Forrest Gump. They send the worst meteorologists on Earth to Portland because the forecasts are dead easy. "Here's the five day forecast, rain." And they come up with exciting ways to talk about the momentary respites from the rain; sun-bursts and cloud breaks and so on.

That Oregon has the highest suicide rate in America is a myth (it's Nevada), but make no mistake about it, people are close to the edge. Of the seven Portland bridges that cross the Willamette, every one has a suicide hotline number posted on it to head off jumpers. A local news station did a report on which bridge was the deadliest as far as suicide attempts went (the St. Johns) and immediately the numbers leaping off the other bridges dropped. Suicide is a way of life in Portland. If you don't want to get your feet wet, you and your significant other can make a double noose and hang yourself off a bridge or take a flying leap off of any of Portland's taller buildings. Zak was riding his bike down 4th in rush hour one day when a body bounced off a hood of a car in front of him. Some sad sack had leapt off the adjacent parking deck. No one was phased.

And of course there's always heroin.

That nine straight months of rain don't give everyone the official Portland mental health problem, Seasonal Affect Disorder (SAD), is a miracle. The only explanation is the large amounts of coffee that people in this region consume. While Italians have been sipping cappuccinos in sidewalk cafés in the Roman sun, Northwesterners have been gulping down double tall mochaccinos in travel mugs out of necessity. There are coffee shops on every block in the city, sometimes one on every corner. Zak used to joke about the Waffle Houses in Alabama, how there would be two at each highway exit. Well, in Portland it is not uncommon to get two Starbucks a stone's throw away from each other. The caffeine is people's hedge against the rain, the only guarantee that they won't be on the bridge by mid-February. There never was a better tasting anti-depressant.

The result is a madcap balance between downers and uppers. If it's a drizzle, you go with the single tall vanilla latte. Showers? Double it up in a Grande! Gusher? Go for the straight shots of espresso and take a couple of chocolate covered coffee beans for later. By mid-winter you can see Portlanders' eyes spinning around like Saturday morning cartoon characters. The balance can unbalance very quickly and that pleasant pseudo-midwestern demeanor can turn deadly. Yeah, Portland has a low crime rate because everyone is stuck inside watching retarded weathermen on TV. But when there is crime, it's savage. The Northwest breeds serial killers like it breeds mold. Bundy, Manson, all your favorites are from here. People don't just die, they are dismembered and hidden in septic tanks or rented storage spaces. The cause: rain and coffee, it's a deadly combination.

You'd think the rain would keep the street people off the street. Of all the places to run away to, Portland, Oregon? Yet the city is teeming with homeless souls creating a twenty-first century mix of high tech capitalism and feudal peasantry. Lucinda often wonders what the fuck she is doing on the rain planet. Almost 20, she's been on the streets for about three years, living in shelters and halfway houses and under bridges. Her hometown is equally rainy. The house where she grew up in Seaside was in a bonafide rainforest on the Oregon coast. Maybe that's what drove her parents mad. They drank a lot of coffee, too.

Most people think that being a teenager and living on the coast would be a real deal. All beach blanket bingo and surf parties with Moondog and the gang. Lots of frugging and beach volleyball with the occasional Baywatch rescue. Not the case. The only surfers are the nutjobs who can brave the frigid Alaskan current and the sharks. It's raining on the beach, just like everywhere else. The coast is a cold and desolate place that broke the hearts of Lewis and Clark. Beautiful, but not if you are seventeen and dream of rays of sunlight.

Lucinda had to leave. She was going out of her skull in the small town. Her parents had some fear that if she had any fun, she'd turn into a drug addict. So she ran away from home and became a drug addict. Well, actually it's a bit more complicated that that. First of all there was her dad. He never abused her or anything, but he looked at her like he wanted to. Especially when she got breasts. It was always uncomfortable with him. Maybe it was all in her mind but she felt like, at any moment, he would make his move, when she was coming out of the shower or asleep on the couch. Just creepy. And her mom knew and resented her for it. She became an unwilling wedge between her parents. It was a

29

downhill slide and she had to escape before it all blew up and ended up in a family bloodbath, which happens.

So at seventeen, with a Jansport backpack filled with clean underwear and a Walkman, Lucinda hitched her way to Portland because that's where things happened. A job, an apartment, a cat, they were all just waiting for her. Instead she fell in with a gang of gutter-punks who taught her "the system." The system was the network of shelters and social services that tried to help homeless youths, and the fine arts of hustling, spare changing, camping, and getting dead drunk on cheap beer. The shelters were filled with kind-hearted volunteers who urged her to go home and rescue herself. It was tempting on cold wet nights but the streets had more freedom to offer than she could ever find in Seaside. And if things got bad she knew that a quick fuck would land her in a nice warm hotel room for the night.

That's how she got Polly. The guy pretended to put on a condom, but didn't. His name might have been Frank. Frank or Hank or Tank or Sam. He said he worked on one of the grain ships that hauls America's oatmeal from Portland to China. When she realized she was pregnant she was excited because now she could take care of someone. She could love them and have complete power over them, just like her own parents had. Polly was born one week after Lucinda's nineteenth birthday and seemed to be OK, given the fact that the first time Lucinda had seen a doctor since leaving home was when her water broke. The motley crew from under the bridge were all in the waiting room. After the birth they erupted into a drunken brawl over what to name the kid; Snake, Death Ray, Vampira. Lucinda chose Polly because she thought her baby looked like a little parrot.

When Polly arrived, things changed. The romance of the street faded. Nursing the baby in damp, dirty squat was in no way a healthy thing. Polly gave Lucinda a new status in the vagabond world: homeless mother. This entitled her to programs and welfare subsidies that the

30

gutter-punks couldn't get. She was admitted into a job program that provided training while her baby was watched in a government daycare facility. But, fearing the loss of her friends, Lucinda used that time to hang out with the gang in Pioneer Square or get drunk under the highway overpass. It wasn't long before Lucinda got kicked out of the program. If she got an actual job, she worried that her friends would think that she was a traitor to the world of the street.

It didn't matter anyway. The gang began to treat her like an adult after the baby came. Sure, they loved to hold Polly and make up fantasy futures about her, like how she was going to be a rockstar or a great philanthropist. But Lucinda's need to mother extended to the gutter-punks. She began to criticize their wild behavior and scold them, chanting, "You need to get a fuckin' life!" And they'd all respond, "Yeah, just like you."

On one specific occasion, seven of them, plus Polly, were sitting on the east bank of the river drinking some 40-ouncers they had lifted from a Plaid Pantry. Once they emptied the last drop of beer, some of the boys started smashing the bottles against the rocks. Lucinda shouted out, "Fuckin' quit it! I've got a baby here, you assholes! You need to get a fuckin' life!"

"Yeah, just like you."

Lucinda was in a bind this Saturday morning. The night before she had blown her friends off. They wanted to get drunk by the river. The last time she got drunk with them she left Polly on a cross-town bus. The busses are free downtown and the kids were trying to get into a shelter before it closed. Almost missing the stop they all bounded off the bus and then realized that no one had Polly. The sight of a dozen drunken kids in ragged leather and dreadlocks chasing after a bus screaming for an oblivious baby must have been quite a sight and they all laughed after the bus driver stopped and Polly was back in her mother's arms, but it was a sobering event for Lucinda.

That Friday night she told them that she didn't want to get drunk with them and they gave her lots of grief. Lots of, oh, you're so much better than us now. She felt like she was very old. Too old for wallet chains and sagging pants and cheap beer and no future. Too old for punk rock. She went to her homeless mother shelter and left them to their freedom and 40-ouncers.

The problem was that she was supposed to hook up with them the next morning. Saturdays were golden for spayngin' shoppers downtown. The kids would roam Pioneer Square and the bus stops around the old courthouse, wearing their saddest faces, and play on the guilt of suburbanites who had a vague notion that this was how the French Revolution got started.

Instead of groveling before those homeless children, she spent an hour or two sitting in a bus shelter on Burnside, out of the rain. The Tri-Met busses would begin to stop, but she would just wave them on. She just sat and stared at Polly's parrot-face.

A hip-looking couple on their way to post-sex Saturday brunch noticed her not getting on the bus. Since they were in love or lust and the world was beautiful and full of love, hope, faith and charity they gave her a few bucks and told her to get out of the rain. Lucinda shoved the bills into Polly's blanket and headed toward coffee.

Telly was up and out, walking the wet sidewalks of Northwest 23rd Avenue, known locally as NW Trendythird. He made several passes over the thirteen block strip, waiting for the boutiques to open. If Telly had really understood the concept of cool he would have gone to the Goodwill and done some thrift shopping.

It was a curious cultural irony that the poor kids were willing to kill each other to have the right overpriced clothes. A human life was only worth an ugly Tommy Hilfiger jacket or a clunky pair of Nikes. Their hardworking parents spent any spare money on gold jewelry or gold hubcaps to prove they had a little capital in a cash-poor society. Meanwhile the kids with money were doing whatever they could to hide it. They wore vintage clothes, listened to rap, and drove around in gas-guzzling '86 Oldsmobile Cutlass Supremes.

Like most Saturdays the Northwest Goodwill was filled with hip kids looking for that perfect find, but Telly was oblivious to them. He window-shopped until he found a place that might allow him to fit in with his target audience. It was a little shop called There & Back and the shop girl was just opening for business. "Good morning," she said all fresh faced behind her vintage horn-rimmed glasses.

"Good morning," said Telly, "I need to purchase clothing."

"Well, come on in. Y'know, you're in the right place." Telly walked in as she propped open the door. The shop was one large room filled with color. Some jazz was playing and he had to stop to take it all in. "What are you looking for today?"

"I need a wardrobe."

"Yeah, I know what you mean. Once a year I say to myself, 'Y'know, it's time for a new wardrobe' and I go on a binge." She didn't realize that Telly had no wardrobe to replace. He needed the whole damn thing. Checking out his standard black rocker get-up she held up a brightly colored Hawaiian shirt. "How about something like this? It's very lounge."

Telly raised his eyebrow the way Mr. Spock would when he wanted to say, "What the fuck are you talking about, Bones?" but the censors wouldn't let him.

"No? How about this shark skin suit for your next big swing dance?"

"Do you have anything that is... cool?" Telly didn't understand that there are many types of cool, in fact so many that the word is absolutely meaningless. Eight-year-old boys think car crashes are cool. Computer geeks think high-speed modems are cool. Homemakers think self-cleaning ovens are cool. Stockbrokers think Roth IRAs are cool. Guys in the military think biological weapons are cool. Everything is cool by somebody's standards.

"Well, y'know, everything is cool in my shop," she said with an irritated look. "Let me guess, you mean 'rock cool.' You want to look like a rock dude."

"Yes, a rock dude."

The young clerk surmised that Telly was Euro-trash in the Great Northwest looking for some souvenir rock-wear, about ten years too late. She saw a chance to unload some old post-trendy merchandise. "Well, I've got some really gnarly gear over here. Here are some flannels and these skater pants are all the rage in Seattle and these long johns were once worn by the original bass player of Soundgarden," she said holding out an armload of clothes. But Telly was oblivious, staring at a sharp vintage white leather jacket. "I would like this. I also require shirts, pants, socks and shoes."

"Well go crazy finding the shirts and pants. As far as the other stuff goes you're going to have to go to Target." She pronounced Target, "Targé," thinking he might think it was another hip boutique instead of a place in the suburbs where you go to get good crap cheap. "We don't sell undies."

Combing the racks, Telly pulled out every item that had black stripes on it: a black and red striped pullover, a black and tan striped T-shirt, a pair of black and green striped jeans, a black and purple striped top. Each time he stepped out of the dressing room he looked like a different test pattern.

Taking a half-dozen items he had picked to the register the salesgirl rolled her eyes. "Oh, this stuff will look great with that white jacket." But Telly knew the look he wanted. He wanted to start conversations. He wanted to fit in but not too much. He wanted to get his job done and go home. "That comes to six-hundred dollars even. So where are you from?"

Setting six one hundred dollar bills on the counter and picking up his shopping, Telly slid his sunglasses back on and said, "France."

"Oh, cool. Au revoir, then." That explained a lot, she thought.

Across the street from There & Back sat Lucinda, trying to make the rare luxury of a mochaccino last as long as possible. Long enough to legitimate parking herself and her baby in a busy coffeehouse. She set a paper in front of herself and pretended to read the Metro section. But her eyes roamed from Polly to the street scenes.

Twenty-third was filled with burning pockets, burning with cash and credit cards and debit cards and the power that went along with them. Other girls her age were spending their Saturdays at the mall maxing out Daddy's Visa at The Limited and listening to the new N'Sync CD at Musicland. Lucinda was trying to concoct a scam to get free diapers.

The more she thought about it the angrier she got. Why did she have the baby? Why did she have parents who were so fucked up? Why did it always rain? Why did Polly look like a parrot? Why do these people spend tons of money on stuff they will hate in a month? Why is coffee so expensive?

She noticed Telly walking out of the shop and scowled. "Fuckers." Watching him glide down the street and into another boutique she caught a glimpse of a couple of wannabes. Every subculture has its wannabes. Wannabe gang bangers. Wannabe hip-hoppers. Wannabe Satanists. Wannabe bikers. They all want the pose but not the values that go along with it. They skim the style off of a group and its attributed coolness with none of the risk. Wannabe gang members don't have to slang cane, gun in hand, to survive. Wannabe hip-hoppers don't know what it's really like to grow up black in the ghetto. Wannabe Satanists don't understand the dark power of Lucifer. And wannabe bikers have never wagered their old lady in a roadside brawl. Wannabes only wanna be different from their yuppie friends.

For some God-awful reason the Portland gutter-punks had their own group of wannabes. These kids weren't runaways and didn't have abusive parents (unless you count being told not to max out the Visa at The Limited as abuse). They romanticized the life of the street kids, often hanging out with the hard-core punks, sometimes even spending the night under the bridge or at the squat just to freak out their parents. The gutter-punks served as a warning to their parents: "Give me that Visa or I'll run away and end up like these losers!" Lucinda hated them for thinking that any homeless kid wouldn't trade places with them in a second.

These two were particularly annoying. Two high school girls who thought it was very "alternative" to snort heroin and ask for spare change in Pioneer Square. One girl, Virginia, staked her claim on rebellion by fucking one of the gang and then telling her shocked friends back in the suburbs about it. Lucinda called her "Vagina."

Vagina and Clarissa were cruising 23rd, trying to look menacing in their $200 Dr. Martens and $400 leather jackets with lots of eye-liner and moused hair. Lucinda tried to hide behind the newspaper but they saw Polly and tapped on the window. "Shit!" she thought. "Hi!" she said.

The bell on the shop's door tinkled as they bounded inside, turning heads. "Lucy!" they shouted in unison. "What the fuck are you doing here?" said Vagina, being obvious. Nobody was shocked by "fuck," but to a kid that was a big deal.

"Having a mochaccino and reading the paper, of course." She thought she'd fuck with them, which is what she always did. Their opinion of her was inconsequential, as was their existence.

"Why aren't you down at the square with everybody else?" asked Clarissa, who was interchangeable with Vagina, except she hadn't given up her cherry to a runt. Well, it's possible. Anything is possible when you are smacked out in a dark squat. The only thing more common than lice on the street was rape.

"I don't hang out with those kids anymore. I've got a nice place up in the West Hills now. Things have really turned around since my father died and left me all that money. I'm dating the drummer of Everclear and we have a nanny for Polly." She knew that they would find out the truth as soon as they got downtown, but it was worth it to see the look on their faces. Their eyeliner formed four perfect circles, she thought.

"Holy shit! No way! You mean you're not gonna hang out with us anymore?"

"Nothing personal, but I have a life now."

"She was always saying, 'Get a life,' and now she's got one," said Clarissa, almost sadly. "Can we crash at your place now?"

"Hell no!" Lucinda's brow was furrowed. "You have a fucking home, already. Why don't you guys stop pretending and leave the spare change to the kids who need it." She could tell that the girls were put off but she didn't care. She was almost twenty with a baby and they needed to get a fucking life. Of course, so did she.

"Bitch! You never were as cool as the rest. At least not since you had that ugly fuckin' baby. C'mon, Virginia, let's go get a slice."

"Bye, Vagina. Bye, Claritta. Don't take any butt plug nickels."

Score. The wannabes were gone but so was the coffee. It wasn't even noon yet and Lucinda had a whole day to fill up. Babies were boring 99% of the time, once you got over the cute effect. They just ate, cried, slept and shat. It was kind of hard to meet boys at the food court with an eating, crying, sleeping, shitting kid under your arm. It was pretty much hard to do anything, so she just sat tight.

It was moments like this that Lucinda thought about calling home. She knew that her father had come to Portland once to look for her, but only once. Things were too messed up to go home. They could all never get past the anger. Plus she'd have to decide who she was going to ally with, Mom or Dad. They didn't live together anymore and probably had gross lovers who would judge her as a wayward problem child. She was an adult now and didn't need that shit. But she couldn't pass by a phone without having these thoughts.

"Mom, it's Lucinda. I know it's been a long time. You want me to come home? OK, but I have a surprise to bring with me. You have a granddaughter. Oh, I'm glad you're so excited. You're gonna come and get me? OK, meet me at the coffeehouse on the corner of NW 23rd and Flanders. I love you too, Mom." It always went something like that, but then Lucinda would convince herself that she hated her parents and that Seaside was hell on Earth. She would still be alone and left trying to fill up a whole day with nothing.

Zak spent most of the morning, sitting by the telephone. He wanted to call Pet. He wanted to be free of her grasp. He wanted to track her down and cry at her feet. He wanted to never see her again. In the weeks leading up to her flight, Zak found himself increasingly angry at her. Initially she had been so enthusiastic about getting married, then she pulled back. Zak got scared. His anger at not being able to control the situation was expressed through his sarcasm and manipulation. Petra took that as sign that he didn't respect her feelings, when actually he was just trying to deal with his own swirling emotions. She pulled way farther, which made Zak even more unstable. He thought of Butthead's great quote (or was it Beavis?), "This sucks more than anything has ever sucked before."

The past week he had spent a lot of time doing nothing. Incapacitated. The best place to do nothing was on the foot of the bed, next to the phone. In case she called. She could call at any minute and tell him that she had been a huge ball of confusion. After a week alone she knew that she couldn't live without him. Zak wasn't ready to be thrown on the scrap heap of love. Not yet. Maybe he should call her.

Petra was either at a motel or at their friend Lisa's apartment. He knew that she hadn't gone back to Alabama because, well, that's leaving the state and you have to let your betrothed know when you're leaving the state.

Zak was afraid to call Pet's parents because somehow they would blame him for their daughter's schizophrenia. They loved him but they were also blind to Petra's unstable side. It's a long story that always made Zak think of William Shakespeare's *Taming of the Shrew*. He had never read *The Taming of the Shrew*. He only had vague images of an out of control Elizabeth Taylor being calmed by Richard Burton.

When Zak had met Petra she was wild like Elizabeth Taylor, and he loved it. She was a first generation Alabaman whose family had left foreign horrors. There are three classes of white folks in Alabama. The poor, who need to vent their depression and anxiety on the nearest target. The aristocracy, who cling to their racial status by reliving the rituals of the Confederacy, like tea parties and cotillions. Then there's the "New South," the people who flooded the sun-belt in the seventies and eighties to cash in on the economic boom. For their children, life was one endless party.

The party circuit was centered around the university system; Tuscaloosa - Auburn - Birmingham. The fraternity system created a mafia more powerful than any crime mob or Klan klavern. Petra's father was a political science professor at the University of Alabama - Birmingham and she grew up in party central.

The night that Zak met Petra she was drunk and two frat boys were trying to take her shirt off. He was just about to graduate from sex camp and it was the last sight he wanted to see. With only a flash of violence he was able to rescue her to become her knight in shining armor. That she had a reputation was not an issue. She was beautiful and stacked and

39

every guy wanted her and after a few drinks they probably would. On their first date Petra told him that she was a sex-addict without blinking an eye. His response, "Right on!" If he only knew what hell lay ahead.

Her parents didn't know about her drunken whoring. Zak admired them too much to let them know what their girl was up to. He was in love. In love with her sexual energy and her need for action. They were birds of a feather. She had survived her wild days without catching AIDS (she had caught every other STD, but not the fatal one). And now both could be redeemed through love and monogamy.

If he called her parents, Zak would have to tell the whole story, which included the parts about their daughter not being a perfect angel, and then it would be his fault for not giving her a good enough alternative to the single life. Besides, her folks were supposed to be in Portland for the wedding. All three were probably held up in a swank hotel downtown, talking about what a loser Zak was. God, he hated her.

He could call Lisa's. She worked Saturdays so if Petra was there she might answer. But what should he say? Should he reveal his anger or his love? How could he keep his sarcastic tone out of the conversation? Should he forgive her and invite her back into his waiting arms or browbeat her for fucking up his life? Everything he would say would be wrong. Or right. Zak stared at the telephone from his bed trying to restrain his impulse.

"Hello. How are you? Have you been all right through all those lonely nights?" That's what he'd say but there was no one answering Lisa's phone. Please, pick it up, he thought.

As the phone continued to ring, Zak's thoughts turned to technology. Maybe Lisa had Caller ID allowing Petra to see that it was Zak calling and not pick it up. But why would someone have Caller ID and not an answering machine? Everyone had an answering machine. It was the twenty-first century, for chrissake. If you called someone and there was no human or recording of a human you assumed their machine was broken or they hadn't paid their voicemail bill. Even homeless people had pagers these days. What was going on?

"Hey! How ya feelin'? Are you still the same? Don't you realize the things we did were all for real, not a dream? I just can't believe they've all faded out of view." The phone rang for about the hundredth time and Zak knew he should hang up, but he couldn't. The ringing was a connection to another place, one where she might be. If he hung up he would be alone again. If he just let it ring a little longer she would know that he wasn't going to give up. He laid back on his bed with the ringing receiver next to his head and fell asleep.

It wasn't long before Zak was in deep REM sleep, dreaming. Dreaming of his beautiful Petra. She was standing in the street in the rain outside the window. She was stunning. Even though Zak had seen her almost every day for the last three years, he was still taken aback by her beauty. She was the woman he fantasized about as a boy reading Marvel Comics. In Marvel Comics all the women were incredibly beautiful; Red Sonja, Gwen Stacey, The Invisible Girl, even She-Hulk. They were all shapely and pouty and strong. Petra was a supervixen straight out of the comics, or at least a Russ Meyer flick. There she was outside the window.

In the Portland rain she looked sad and sexy. She was shouting at Zak that she was sorry and wanted to be buzzed into the flat. He was glad to see her but couldn't find the button to ring her in. Where was it? It was his goddamn apartment and he couldn't find the button to buzz people in through the door! What kind of cruel trick was this? Maybe the landlord didn't like his friends and took out the buzzer. And where was the door? He couldn't get out of the apartment to let her in! There she was looking so sexy and sad and he couldn't get to her! Suddenly his teeth began to fall out. One by one. How could he reunite with Petra with all his teeth falling out of his gums?

He was startled out of the dream by a banging on his apartment door. "I do have a door!" he thought. The receiver was still ringing next to his head. In that disoriented state, he hung up the phone and looked around the room. The door rapped again and he leapt out of the bed. Petra?

It was Cozy from down the hall. Cozy, as in Lenny's girlfriend. Cozy, the opera singer. Cozy, the girl who made Zak think that love was a blanket to be laid over many women.

"Hi Zak. I thought I'd come by and say hi. I know it's gonna be a rough day for you so if you want to do something fun, I'm free."

"Hey Cozy. Come in. Welcome to my wedding day."

"I don't know what that girl is thinking but she's crazy to give you up." Zak immediately felt a twinge of guilt. Guilt because Lenny was his friend and any of Cozy's effortless affection made him want to kiss her. And guilt because he was so in love with Petra and here he was wishing he was marrying Cozy. Maybe it was a case of transference.

"I really don't know what I'm supposed to do in a situation like this. Maybe I should call Dr. Laura. Is it too early to get drunk? It feels like a bad dream."

"Are you taking your pills?" Cozy was worried because when Zak found Petra's note his first impulse was suicide.

"Yeah. I called my shrink and upped my dose to 100 mgs. It makes me wonder; if my insurance covers my Zoloft, why doesn't it cover my lattes? They do the same thing."

Cozy looked at Zak in an adoring motherly kind of way. She was thin but seemed to fill the room with nurturance. "Life's just not fair, sweetie. Just be glad you don't need a prescription for coffee."

"Oh Coze, I feel like I'm living in twilight. I don't know if I'm living or dying. I'm so angry and sad and everything. I've got that damn Leanne Rimes song stuck in my head and it's killing me."

42

Cozy, being the music mate, knew the reference and launched into the aria version, "How can I live without you, without your love? How can I ever, ever survive?" It was so serious that they both laughed out loud.

"Zak, my man. Your problem is silence. I've never been in your place when there was no music playing. Put on something rockin'! It's Saturday. Let's kick out the jams, brother!" She didn't wait for him and grabbed a CD off the stack on top of a speaker and plopped it in. It was a great compilation of the sixties garage band The Shadows of the Knight. Track One was their hit version of "Gloria." E-D-A - those chords felt like heroin and Cozy pulled Zak off the futon and began to dance.

I'm gonna tell you about my baby! The music was magic. No wonder every band had a version of this song. The clanging rhythm gave Zak energy and he danced around the living room with his lovely neighbor. If she could see him now. G-L-O-R-I-A, Cozy!

"Hey Zak, how's your research going?" she asked as they danced around the room. A month ago he entered the last stage of his master's work, coding interviews with parents of fetal alcohol children. It was heartbreaking work taking the crushing stories of people who unknowingly wiped out their kids' futures with a few well-intentioned drinks and turning them into frequency variables. He was trying to find the role of fathers in mothers' drinking habits. Bad mothers were the ones that got blamed for Fetal Alchohol Syndrome and Telly knew that the fathers had a hand in the damage. A month ago it seemed very important.

"I haven't done shit with it for two weeks. First I was too busy getting ready for the wedding. Then I was too busy trying to kill myself."

"Not funny, boy. If you kill yourself I'm gonna have to kick your ass!"

Zak laughed at the thought of this recovering anorexic kicking his lifeless corpse while singing Wagner's "Ride of the Valkaries." "I haven't even been up at school this week. I just don't want to face anyone. It's

43

just too pathetic. I e-mailed them to let them know that the wedding was cancelled and that's it. Besides, I'm too busy drinking to be very academic."

"Yeah, Len said he saw you last night and you were OK enough to hit on Mia."

"Yeah, now she thinks I'm a psycho fan."

"Well, you are. He also said you got a new roommate. Where is he?" Cozy stopped dancing and began looking around the flat peering into the music room. "Is he shy?"

"Now we get to the real reason for your visit, eh? Well, sorry, he's out shopping for supplies. I think you'll find him quite interesting."

"You mean, weirdy?"

"No! He's just, well, um..." Zak wasn't sure if he should spill the beans on his interstellar roomie. Maybe it was supposed to be a secret, for the sake of mankind. "Coze, have you ever had a totally random person show up at just the right time? Like it was for some reason. I mean, I really don't know what the fuck I'm talking about, I just met this guy last night. But it's like his shit is so deep that I don't even think my drama matters."

"What is he, a philosopher?"

"No, just a guy with some dark mystery. I think he's running away from something. I just get this vibe from him that something is gonna happen. Maybe I'm just hoping for a distraction."

"Maybe it's a love connection."

"Not my type. Too tall. All I'm saying is I'm open to any new influences. Nothing is working at the moment. I'm ready for a new paradigm."

Cozy wasn't sure if this state was much better than the suicidal tendencies. It sounded like the thing that people said right before they joined a cult. And then they ended up under a purple blanket with their

Nikes sticking out. "And you think this guy is going to hand you your new 'paradigm' on a silver platter?"

"No. I just think he's probably been through some shit that I could learn from, that's all. I don't have much faith in things at the moment. I gotta figure out what the hell happened to my life."

"Why don't we start with coffee and scones?"

In the middle of his shopping spree (he didn't have to go to Target for socks and underwear), Telly watched a man in black open the gates to an odd building. It was the Cathedral of the Sacred Heart and the priest was opening the doors for noon mass.

A handful of people had been waiting to enter and Telly followed them in. He wanted to see what was going to happen. They all seemed serious and anxious, the opposite of last night's gutter-punks. It was about time to start getting some clues.

Inside the cathedral was larger than he expected. The high ceiling was much different than the low ceilings of the shops and Zak's apartment. He stood in the entrance and immediately felt a sense of peace. He also felt a sense of embarrassment as he and his shopping bags were blocking the way of an older couple.

"Excuse me."

"Come in and make yourself at home," said the old man.

Telly looked around the candlelit room and was hypnotized. It was silent even though a dozen people were sitting in the wooden benches on the left side of the hall. A few more lit candles and dropped quarters into a jar. The gray stone was framed by colorful glass windows with images of a woman and a baby glowing from the noon sunlight. Maybe she was the one they had come to see, he thought. Telly took a seat in the last pew so he could observe. He noticed that some of the people were lowering to one knee and bowing or crossing their chests. He knew

45

nothing of religion. He knew that it existed here but he knew nothing of
the experience of religion. He had a feeling that this was a religious place
and he began to cry. He lowered his head to hide the tears, reminding
himself of his promise to keep up a neutral front.

The main hall of the chapel was dark and empty. Everyone was
sitting in a chapel within a chapel on the left side of the cathedral. While
Telly wiped the tears away, two men in black and white robes walked
before the people, entering from a rear door. One was carrying a candle
and the other a metal cross. People crossed their chests again and Telly
tried to mimic them. The men began to say things about Mary Full Of
Grace and our father and some of the people sitting said the things with
them. He had studied this type of ritual before coming to Portland but it
was fascinating to see it in person.

He struggled to keep up with the group who at random points
stood up or got on their knees. The older couple that he had blocked
earlier occasionally looked back at Telly and the woman snickered at
seeing Telly one step off, like a chorus line dancer who had missed a
practice.

The man with the cross was saying some things that seemed to
have been said many times before. It was about the love of the mother
and the father and the power of the heart. The heart. The organ that
pumped blood, that's what they had been crossing. It was something that
he hadn't heard before. Yes, it is well known that some people put a
mystical relevance on to their body parts. Their stomachs talked. They
lost their minds. They found their backbone. They got a nose for news.
But this was different, as if the heart was a source of something. The
words of the priest gave him the impression that the heart was believed
to be some type of separate being within a person, to be listened to.
Perhaps like a computerized guidance system in a missile.

As he listened he felt his own heart, a blood-pumping organ,
sinking in his chest. He was embracing an emptiness that he knew kept

46

him far removed from these people who had come for something that was beyond him. He put on his sunglasses to cover his eyes.

Eventually the men stopped saying things about Mary Full Of Grace and her father and went back into their little room. Slowly people began to leave. Telly didn't quite understand his sorrow. He had just come in to the room to observe and had been caught off guard by this emotional outburst. It was just a sense of loss, of what he wasn't sure. These people seemed as clueless as him, many just getting out of the rain. But they had something, something to do with the heart. They had someone inside them telling them what to do and he was alone in the universe. How could something or someone that lives completely inside an internal organ have any useful knowledge of the external world?

Using one of the new striped shirts he had bought to wipe his eyes dry, Telly noticed the older woman trying to approach him but not being able to navigate his shopping bags. "Are you from far away?" she asked, too knowingly for Telly's comfort (although he felt only comfort from her).

"Yes. From very far away."

"Well, you are always at home in the arms of the blessed Virgin." She grabbed the cross hanging around her neck, winked, and walked away with her man, hand in hand.

Lucinda was still in the coffee shop on 23rd. It had gotten pretty obvious that she was overstaying her welcome after the barrista came over and took the long empty cup from her. But the baby gave her some extra time. It was easy to bounce loitering teens out into the rain, but a bit harder to eject a "mother and her baby." She grabbed Polly and headed into the restroom to wash up, eyed by the barrista. Public bathrooms were the sanctuary of the homeless. Most people take having a nice clean place to take a shit for granted. They don't ever think about needing to pee like Niagara Falls and having no place to go other than between two

47

parked cars. The public restroom was a place to wash the dirt of the street off your hands. It was place to drink clean water without having to ask. It was a place to hide from people who wanted to roll you. It was also a place to have sex.

Sitting on the toilet, she thought about all her hormonally disadvantaged friends, discovering their sexuality under the damp bridges of Portland. While the kids of the suburbs played spin the bottle while their parents were away, or groped in the back seats of BMWs or got hotel rooms on prom night, the street kids fucked in dirty toilets. In fact, the men's room of the Burger King on Burnside was known as The Bridal Suite because of the considerable amount of coital activity that went on there.

A smile crept across Lucinda's face as she thought about a moment of passion with Valiant, another punk, in the bathroom at the youth shelter. They were discovered by a shrieking volunteer and sent packing. The whole encounter was a laugh, especially since neither of them had gotten off. She always promised Valiant, called that for his wavy blonde hair and bright smile, that she would let him finish someday, when he got a fucking life.

She flushed the toilet and stuffed half a roll of toilet paper in her old army jacket. Polly was crying and needed to be changed. She set the baby in the sink and undid her diaper, thinking about how nice it would be when Polly was potty trained, about a million years from now. She wiped off her baby in the warm sink water and fastened the last diaper around her waist. Looking up from Polly she stopped to study her reflection in the mirror.

Sure, millions of moms change their babies in public restrooms, but how many were tired of begging for diaper money or were just plain tired of carrying their baby? Lucinda's face was round and tired. She looked and felt older than her almost twenty years. Her long brown hair, once the recipient of endless conditionings and treatments was oily and limp.

She had bleached the strands that surrounded her face, but that was half-grown out already. She had thought of just shaving it completely off, like some of the other street girls, but that made it harder to spaynge. You needed to look like the girl from next door to get the cash.

Motherhood had aged Lucinda into a beauty that she wasn't old enough to recognize yet. She just thought that she looked old. Older and more like a woman. She looked at her eyes and lips in the mirror and imagined them covered in the make-up that the twenty-somethings on NW 23rd wore. For now, the make-up counter at Meier & Frank would have to do.

The bathroom door was banging and the coffee maker was asking what was going on in there. There were customers who needed to use the facilities, she said. "Just a minute. I was just changing my BABY'S diaper!" She opened the door and handed the dirty diaper to the barrista and headed for the exit. Out on the street Lucinda knew that she was going to have to beg for some money for diapers and headed for Pioneer Square.

Zak and Cozy never got scones and coffee. They got crepes and coffee. That seemed to be more special. A special treat on a special day. Maybe even French. They walked through Trendythird like most Oregonians, oblivious to the rain. Zak was hoping a member of the PLF (Petra Liberation Front) would see him parading down 23rd on his former wedding day with the tall raven-haired beauty and report back to Petra, who was hiding in a cave somewhere. "He looked pretty happy to me."

They had no plan other than to meet Lenny for a drink at the Blue Moon Tavern around one. "Hey Zak, let's go into this bookstore. I'm trying to find this book," said Cozy, pulling on Zak's arm.

"OK! OK! Why don't you go in and I'll be across the street at the record store," he said. Record shopping was a Saturday ritual and today was no exception. No wedding or no no-wedding.

"Man, come on. I want you to see this book." There was no point in resisting, even if Zak had wanted to. That Cozy wanted him to see something, that anyone had wanted him to do anything, was a warm feeling in the cold rain and they ducked into the store.

The shop was one of those rare independent bookstores that hadn't been run out of town by Barnes & Nobles or Wal-Mart or Starbucks. They didn't have the discounts that they did at Borders or the other chains, but Portlanders loved their ambiance and this place had it in spades, right down to the urine stained carpet in the kids' section.

"Have you ever read any books by William Styron?" Cozy had read a lot of books in her attempt to have cultural capital.

"Yeah, I read *Sophie's Choice* in college. He's great. No one makes a concentration camp survivor more sexy than Styron."

"Oh, stop it. He had this book out in the late nineties. It's sort of an autobiography. It's supposed to be killer. I'm gonna buy it for you as an un-wedding present!"

"Gee, thanks. Hey, is that that book about depression? All about his wonderful triumph over depression that got him back on *60 Minutes?*" His eyes squinted in distrust.

"Zak?" said Cozy, mom-like, as in don't go there.

"C'mon, Coze! I don't need to read any weepy tome about how life gets better and we've all had a hard time but not as tough as the prisoners of war in Vietnam or Stalin's starving peasants who had to eat their own shit."

"I heard that the pilgrims were so hungry that they dug up dead people to eat," said Cozy trying to steer the discussion away from any denial.

"Yeah, then the Indians taught them how to plant corn so the pilgrims just killed the Indians and ate them."

"Yeah, but they served them with corn."

"And pumpkin pie. Cozy, I'm not going to read some depressing book about depression! If I want to listen to the trials of the suicidal I'll put on a Morrissey record."

Cozy was having none of it. "Tough shit, I'm buying you the book. You can use it to smash roaches with it for all I care."

"We don't have roaches here." Zak remembered how he and Petra had discovered that they had left the roaches of Alabama somewhere in Missouri. There aren't roaches in Oregon, just ants and spiders. Millions of ants and spiders.

Cozy found the book in the psychology section and before Zak could say anything about using it to squash spiders she had her debit card in the hand of the clerk. It was touching really, the concern.

Cozy had been the recipient of Zak's "cry for help." A week ago when he found the letter, he flipped. His excitement about spending his life with Petra turned into panic. How could he go back to square one? It had taken him years to find the one great love of his life. If he just responded with an "Oh well," then that ruined the foundation of his very romantic ideology. It either meant that since his one true love had beat a hasty retreat he would never have that intimate joy again. Or it meant that he would meet another one true love, which meant the whole one true love thing was bullshit. All the songs were about "the one." There weren't any songs about my "dozen true loves" unless they were by Willie Nelson.

Zak's response to the note was overblown and dramatic and existential. True love is supposed to be the force that guides lovers together, like Robin Wright and Daniel Day Lewis in *The Princess Bride* and *Last of the Mohicans*, although they weren't in love with each other. I will find you, no matter what the cost! As you wish. And poor Leonardo DiCaprio, willing to die in the frozen North Atlantic to save the woman who he had only been in love with for thirty minutes. If love wasn't enough then the premise of Zak's whole life had been a lie and life in a world without love as a basis was a crock. All you need is love went down the toilet.

That's what he was thinking when he started drinking straight Jim Beam. He'd had his joy and didn't want to go on as the guy who lost his true love. He didn't want to see her in the arms of another man, or be in the arms of another woman, but be thinking of her. It just seemed like a lifetime of pain that could be avoided through a romantic exit.

It wasn't the first time he had thought of suicide. At the age of seventeen he stood on the edge of a kudzu shrouded pond and thought about drowning himself to escape the war zone that was his family, only to discover later that every family was a war zone. At twenty-one he stood on Pont Neuf over the River Seine after a day of drinking at Jim Morrison's grave and contemplated his rejection by his French girlfriend and the immortality that comes with dying young in Paris. The plan this night was to drink and go for a swim in the Willamette River and die like singer Jeff Buckley, in an unexpected undertow.

Soon after moving to Portland and getting on the student health plan Zak began to see a psychiatrist who identified his suicidal tendencies and put him on a mild anti-depressant. Most people would have never guessed that he had regular thoughts about killing himself, always by drowning. He was full of energy and creativity. He loved his volunteer work with at-risk kids and trying to solve the world's problems. His music collection gave him the resources to transcend any emotion. He was basically very happy, except for the fact that he was depressed. He loved to tell his psychiatrist, "I didn't realize how crazy I was until I paid you to tell me."

On the day of the note he was frantic and then bombed. He tried calling friends but all he got were answering machines. As the Jim Beam bottle emptied his messages got more desperate. The drunken last one was to Lenny and Cozy's apartment. "Hey guys. I just can't do this. I just can't live in this fucked up world. It's the fuckin' Twenty-first Century and we're still stuck on this god-forsaken planet. I want off. I'm going down to the river." He began to sing a slurred version of Bruce Springsteen's "The River." "I went down to the river and into the river I died..." Then he sang a few verses of "Take Me To The River," but not the hopeful Al Green version. He was doing the quirky Talking Heads version. Finally, for some reason, he riffed into "Islands in the Stream" and began to laugh at himself. "Oh God, do I suck. Just give my records to the library or the university. Thanks. Goodbye Cruella Deville."

Lenny and Cozy got home not long after the message and thought it was a joke at first. But when they couldn't find Petra they got worried. Lenny jumped back in the car to comb the streets and Cozy headed down Burnside toward the river. As she passed All Day Music she noticed a small crowd inside. There was Zak on the floor. Apparently he was going for one last record shop and passed out in the country section with a Kenny Rogers CD is his hand. He better be glad that he didn't die, not with Kenny Rogers anyway.

Back at The Eldorado, Lenny and Cozy nursed Zak's aching head but were at a loss as what to do about his breaking heart. They were as shocked at Petra's leaving as he was. She seemed like she was madly in love with him and just two days earlier Pet had told Cozy how excited she was to be marrying Zak. She told her that she knew that she had found the right guy; that Zak would take care of her. It was exactly the wrong thing to do to a happy depressed guy.

So it wasn't surprising that Cozy had cast herself as Zak's guardian angel. Stopping short of removing all his shoelaces, she kept a close eye on his moods and his drinking. And buying *Darkness Visible* by William Styron was just part of her angel duties.

From the bookstore they headed over to the Blue Moon Tavern to meet Lenny. Cozy and Lenny were an odd pair. Lenny was a street-wise rocker who looked like a young Charlie Sheen, who looked like a young

Martin Sheen, who looked like a young James Dean (well, there was no "old" James Dean). His religion of cool meant giving up on career tracks and health care. He was happy making pizzas and spending any surplus on clothes, guitars, or Sean Penn videos.

Cozy was a stretched-out goddess whose thinness gave her the illusion of Audrey Hepburn-style elegance. Where Lenny's demon was youth, Cozy's was acceptance. She had spent most of her teens and early twenties battling anorexia, on more than one occasion coming close to death. There was always some image to internalize: Kate Moss, Gwyneth Paltrow, Calista Flockhart. Some standard of what men wanted. She finally broke out of the starvation cycle after reading Naomi Wolf's *The Beauty Myth* and seeing it all as a huge plot. She really just shifted her obsession from her weight to opera. Opera would gain her acceptance. When opera singers walked into a room people said, "Oh, there's that opera singer." People rolled their eyes when you said Celine Dion or Whitney Houston was a diva, but not Leontyne Price. Cozy was studying to be a real diva. How that big voice came out of that narrow frame was not understood.

It was probably those demons that kept Cozy and Lenny together. They reinforced each other's weaknesses. Lenny loved Cozy's dream of musical stardom and Cozy loved Lenny's love. He was the first guy to say nice things to her that had nothing to do with her looks. At Gurd shows she would stand on the side of the stage, staring at Lenny, thinking, this guy actually loves me. But if you asked Zak, Cozy was easy to love.

"Oh, it's nice and warm in here," said Cozy, glad to be out of the freezing rain.

"I don't see yer boy. Let's grab that table near the fireplace. It's after noon and I need a god damn drink!" Zak wasn't an alcoholic but he had upped his drinking this week with license. When your woman leaves you, you are allowed to drink yourself into the gutter. It's a clause, written by Charles Baudelaire or Frank Sinatra. You are allowed to be pathetic and

54

incur sympathy. You are allowed to play Trisha Yearwood or Hall & Oates on the jukebox. Most importantly, it is the one time in life when you are allowed to vomit on yourself.

"He'll be here. Would you be a nice future drunk and buy me a beer?"

"You got it, sister." Zak and Cozy put their wet leather jackets (both brown) on the back of their fireside chairs and Zak went to the bar to get Cozy's beer and a Jim Beam and Coke for himself.

As he leaned over the bar, Cozy thought, "that boy is heading down, he's too romantic to survive in this shallow world."

"Here we go. I had too many beers last night. I'm sticking with God's whiskey. So how are things going with you and Len? We've been so wrapped up in my shit that I haven't been paying attention to much else. Are you guys doing OK?"

"You know, Lenny is Lenny. I love him, but I wish he would grow up. But then I think that if he grew up, I wouldn't love him as much. It would be cool if Gurd happened and he could quit flipping pizzas but it doesn't seem very important to him. He's an 'artist' which means he's broke."

"We're all broke. But we're supposed to be. *La Boheme* and all that. Broke and happy."

Cozy loved the fact that Zak knew about opera. He knew about all kinds of music. Lenny only knew about four-four rock 'n' roll. "Well, Puccini made some money and so did whoever owns *Rent*. I don't mind, really. We're young, but I just wonder where it's all going to end up. If I get this job with the Portland Opera, we'll have a shot and I'll be able to get to know the whole symphony scene a lot better."

It was Verdi's *La Traviata* that Cozy had been rehearsing for over the last week. In Zak's misery he would lie alone in his and Petra's bed listening to her sing while Lenny was at band practice. He didn't understand the Italian but the melodies held him close. In all the pain on

Earth, there was beauty. It was Cozy's beautiful singing that made him realize that suicide was a bit too final of a choice. No more Verdi, no more Beatles, no more pure moments that seemed completely unique and completely universal simultaneously.

"Oh, you'll get it. It's about time for a young opera star to bring all us Gen X types into the world of long hair music."

"They don't still call it that, boy. I think that death-metal is the present 'long-hair' music. I just wish it was Wagner. I can sing the shit out of some Wagner. It's my Aryan roots. Oh, hi Lenny!" Lenny had slid in, chair and beer in hand.

"How's my groovy posse? I'm here to assure all concerned that Planet Earth is still in its heavenly orbit."

"Hey, Len!" said Zak, looking at Cozy and thinking, what the hell are you doing with this lunatic. "Are you working today?"

"Yes, yes, but not until three so I have a valuable window of opportunity to get drunk with my favorite bachelor. I predict that today is the first day of your career as Portland's most sought after love-hound. In fact I'm willing to wager that in six months you are dating a TV reporter, if not an actual anchor woman." Cozy laughed since Lenny's frame of reference was the frame of the television. To date a local anchor would be about the highest romantic plateau he could imagine. Fortunately, Portland was filled with attractive newscasters.

For a moment Zak thought about which anchor was the most attractive. "Dude, I don't think any clear thinking female is going to want to get near my mountain of baggage. I'm better off just jacking off to the five o'clock news."

"I'm looking for baggage that goes with mine," sang Cozy from *Rent*, knowing Zak would pick up on the connection.

"My man, let's look at the facts." Lenny was going to make sure that Zak didn't leap off of a parking deck today. "You're The Man, right? Highly intelligent. Number two, you are going to have a Master's Degree soon. Three? Pretty damn good-looking for a hick. On top of that, you got the best record collection in town. I'm tellin' ya, all the ladies are gonna line up when the word gets out."

Zak, already feeling the whiskey, slung his head over to look at Cozy, who just gave him one of those motherly smiles. How could he tell them that a love affair with Katie Couric herself couldn't mend his broken heart? He wanted Petra. Petra was the other half of his sky. No string of "hot dates" could replace his love for her. She was it from the first moment he first kissed her. It wasn't rational, but it was real. He didn't want to grow old with Katie Couric (although a fling would be nice). He wanted to be sixty-four with Pet. She was the most beautiful woman in the world, even if he was the only man who thought so.

"Did you tell him about that girl in the orchestra, Coze?" Lenny was trying to keep Zak focused but Zak was flagging down a waitron for a refill.

"Well, I don't have any one person in mind. But I'm sure there is some swank girl in the symphony who loves music as much as you." Zak was shaking his head, wondering why no one understood him. "But you're not in any shape to date now. You need to wait awhile. It's not definite what's going on with Petra. Maybe she just got cold feet."

"Exactly!" said Zak, who had been waiting for someone to offer hope. "Why is everyone so eager to bury this thing? We've been together for over three years. It's not over, not yet anyway. I just have to be Mr. Cool. I'm just gonna stay drunk until she comes home."

"Well, I hope you've got a spare liver," said Lenny, giving Zak a look that said, be real. "My friend, take the journey into the drunken well of sorrow, but come back strong. I want to see the phoenix arising out of that well to terrorize the city like the dragon in *The Hobbit*, breathing fire on all the fair ladies of the land. Your best revenge on that woman is to become The Man. Let her live with the regret while you plow the fields of the new dawn."

"Len, Zak doesn't need to be thinking about plowing any fields..."

"Hey, there's Telly!" interrupted Zak. Telly was walking by the tavern window with his shopping, headed back to the flat. Cozy and Lenny looked at each other with shrugged shoulders, not knowing who Telly was. Zak ran over and knocked on the window and Telly, black sunglasses dripping with rain, turned and recognized Zak who was waving him in. He stopped and headed into the bar. Heading back to the table Zak said, "That's my new roommate. Get ready."

Telly came into the Blue Moon and approached the table, removing his sunglasses and setting his bags down. "Hey, y'all, this is that new roommate I was telling you about. His name is Telly Max and he's an alien."

"He doesn't look Mexican," said Lenny.

Lucinda and Polly got down to Pioneer Square on the light rail, which was free downtown. She was half-dreading having to face the gang, but they knew that emotions were transitory in this crowd. There wasn't much use for grudges when you might need someone's surplus luck on any given rainy day. They would probably be glad to see her and want to borrow Polly for spare changing.

But when the electric doors of the train slid open she didn't see the gutter-punks in their usual spot next to Starbucks. She looked around the square but there were only weekend shoppers and a few old bums. Maybe they were on the next block, spayngin' by the courthouse, she thought.

She sat on a courthouse fountain, one with metal beavers playing in the water. No sight of the motley crew. "Fuck!" Lucinda said out loud, causing some suburbanite to frown at the uncivilized act of cursing in front of a baby that couldn't even say "mama" yet. Lucinda's mind was trying to work it out. They were here every Saturday afternoon. It was prime time for hitting up shoppers who were already feeling a bit guilty for their weekend orgies of crass consumerism. And it was only a light rain, which brought twice the usual winter crowd.

Then Lucinda remembered how the kids had been chased out of the square during Christmas by the cops who were tying to make a "homeless-free zone." It seems that some starched matriarchs were being intimidated out of shopping downtown by the presence of hordes of unwashed youth, so the cops started threatening the gang with loitering citations if they didn't move along.

If that was the case they could be in a drop-in shelter or getting a meal at the Krishna temple or hanging out on the park blocks or getting drunk under a bridge or down by the waterfront. The thought of lugging Polly, who was getting heavier everyday, to all the old familiar places did not excite Lucinda one bit. Besides, she was too old to waste her time with those jokers.

Lucinda decided to head back to Northwest and hit up yuppies and upwardly mobile hipsters. She still had to buy diapers and soak up the rest of the day. She could stop at a bookstore or a record store along the way and maybe run into someone new.

Telly had sat down at the table with Zak, Cozy and Lenny, setting his bags on the floor. "Looks like you scored some serious goods on your spree. Did you buy lots of Gortex? That's a fabric, not a planet," joked Zak.

"Yeah, definitely Rik Ocasek. Hi ya, Telly-caster. I'm Lenny and here for all your juvenilia."

"Don't mind him, he's on drugs. Hi, I'm Cozy. Welcome to Portland. Are you sure you're up for living in our drama-plagued building?"

"It makes *Melrose Place* seem like *Father Knows Best!*" added Lenny.

"Melrose? Yes, the building is quite adequate. I will settle in nicely there. Cozy is a very interesting name. Is it foreign?"

"It's because she's so cozy!" chimed in Zak, knowing that that should have been Lenny's line.

"Well, when people hear that I'm an opera singer they think my real name must be Cosima, after Franz Liszt's daughter, the one that Wagner married."

"Yeah, that's exactly what I thought!" shouted Lenny. The only thing that Lenny knew about Franz Liszt is that Roger Daltrey had played Liszt in an obscure seventies rock film, directed by Ken Russell.

"Actually, my parents were big fans of Victor Hugo and named me after Cosette in *Les Miserables*, so I grew up having to sing 'On My Own' a million times."

"Well, I knew there was something French about you!" interjected Zak. No one knew if his Franco-phobia was just a running gag or an expression of something deeper. "You wouldn't want to be named after Cosima Liszt Von Bulow Wagner anyway. She was supposed to be a real dog."

Cozy just stared at her friend. "You never cease to amaze me, Zak."

"Hey, I got the music in me."

Telly was picking up none of these historical references. They might as well have been speaking French. But he knew that in the information age, knowledge of detail empowered the powerless.

Lenny worried that if he didn't step in he might be wedged out by a classical music name-dropping-fest between Zak and Cozy. "So, Telly, my man, where exactly do you come from? What's with the alien thing? Are you a Jedi warrior?" He had noticed Telly's emotionless demeanor but wasn't ready to concede that he was a little green man.

"That is my roommate's sense of humor. He just means that I am not from here. I am from... Kosovo." He had noticed the name on the front page of an *Oregonian* in a newspaper box on 23rd.

This was news to Zak, but didn't surprise him. Telly had probably learned that he couldn't go around introducing himself as a space man.

The Kosovo thing would be a good cover as no one really knew much about the actual people of Kosovo, other than they were gun-happy. Maybe he really was from Kosovo and been tripping last night on some stardust. But Zak still held out that Telly's alien status may be one big secret that only he would be privy to.

"Are you a refugee? Things have been cool there for a few months. Man, did you escape?" Cozy had vaguely followed the news of Kosovo's civil war since 1998.

"Yes and no. I wanted to escape my country but I also wanted to come to America and learn about American culture. I am here to study."

"Well, dude, welcome to the land of milk and honey." Lenny was gearing up for one of his America-Is-Too-Rich diatribes. "We got more shit here than we know what to do with. More time, more work, more TV, more poor people, more rich people and just more crap in general. If you want to know what this country is really about go to the grocery store and stand in the cereal aisle. One day I just counted. Sixty-seven different types of cereal! In other countries you get maybe five. There are eight types of Shredded Wheat alone! Do we need eight Shredded Wheats? I don't think so. We got kids starving in the streets of Portland and more Shredded Wheat than we can digest. It's an embarrassment of riches."

"I will go to the grocery store and see the Shredded Wheat." Telly meant it.

Cozy loved when Lenny got passionate about silly things. He had soul. "You need to write a song about that, love. 'Shred the Wheat!' Anyway, you like Shredded Wheat."

"That's not the point, is it, Coze? I don't need the abundance of Shredded Wheat or Cheerios or Raisin Bran. It's just a symbol of overkill."

"Well, at least we know who is the most regular at this table," chided Zak. "Hey Tel, what did you buy, man?"

Telly began pulling clothes out of his various boutique bags and handing them to the three at the table. Almost all were striped articles,

61

black stripes. Cozy, Lenny and Zak held up the clothes, looked at each other and then burst out laughing.

"I think I see a pattern here!" chortled Cozy. "I didn't know there were this many stripes in Portland!"

"They are all from shops on NW 23rd Avenue. I like stripes." He said it without even cracking a smile. Maybe it was the drinks or the coffee or the Nth day with no sunlight but the three couldn't stop laughing and Telly just sat quietly until they stopped.

"OK, dude," said Zak, getting up off the floor. "We're going to play Where's Waldo? with you then. Hey, Lenny, can you see Telly in this crowd?"

"Yeah, man, I think he's that cat over by the bar in the stripes."

Cozy jumped in, "No, those are brown stripes. He's that cool looking guy over by the stage. Or is that Charlie Brown?" More laughter and Telly tried to grin. "Sorry, man. I think it's cool that you have a sense of style. Like Elton John and his sunglasses or Marilyn Manson and his fake eye. Telly Max and his stripes."

"Thank you, Cozy," said the newcomer, appreciating her compassion for the outsider.

Zak was now on to something else. "Hey Len, do you think there is any connection between Sammy Davis, Jr. and Marilyn Manson, with the fake eye thing?"

"Oh yeah, most definitely. Both broke down major barriers of their time, Sammy as a black Jew hanging out with a bunch of white guys and Marilyn was a transsexual Satanist hanging out with MTV veejays. I could see Manson singing, "This Is My Life" and I could see Sammy singing, "The Beautiful People," if he wasn't dead. I might have to make a CD matching up their songs."

"If Marilyn Manson is Sammy Davis, who is Frank Sinatra?" asked Cozy, taking the musing a little too seriously.

"Courtney Love, of course."

"Dude, no way!" Zak had serious Sinatra issues.

"Look, who else is a part of the same scene as Marilyn, parties more, been in more fights, had more lovers, made movies? Courtney Love is Frank Sinatra."

"It makes sense to me," said Cozy, sticking up for her man. "Why does it have to be another guy? It's a new age, boy!"

Lenny was excited about having a theory that Zak might actually buy. "Yeah, and Billy Corgan is Joey Bishop and Trent Reznor is Dean Martin."

"Got it. And Beck is Don Rickles." Zak could play the game.

Once again, Telly was lost but enjoyed the enthusiasm of his new friends. They obviously cared about these personalities and thought this was important information.

"Hey guys," Lenny interjected, "I almost forgot. We got a last minute gig headlining at The Palais next Friday!"

"What?"

"Yeah, The Cramps were supposed to play but canceled the tour. I think one of them got a cataract or something. Anyway, Bill called and asked if we'd pitch hit. It's a rather big deal for us little pipsqueaks to get top billing on a Friday, but we are fully prepared to rock the fucking house!"

"That kicks ass, Len!" Zak loved Gurd. The band was just five guys who loved five decades of rock "n" roll. *The Oregonian* had described them as "Sha Na Na on dope" but they were much more. They studied the best of rock, the Fifties abandon, the Sixties experimentation, the Seventies anger, the Eighties pomposity and the Nineties fear. Lenny was a regular Iggy Pop on stage, wild and charismatic. Jim Morrison without the agenda. Gurd shows were always an excuse to cut loose.

"Oh, that's so great Len. We'll get everyone to come. Between your gig and my audition, we're headed straight to the top." Cozy stroked his arm and fantasized about the grand marriage between the soprano and

63

the rockstar. They talked about designing a stage as Telly listened, but Zak began to tune out.

The past week might have brought a lot of down time for Zak, but not a lot of sleep. He had suddenly become an insomniac the day Petra left. For the past seven days he basically just lay in bed, unable to drift off, his mind spinning, full of what ifs and how could shes. The only thing that helped was Cozy's distant singing. He had resorted to over the counter sleeping pills washed down with Jim Beam. When he did finally pass out he would awake by 5 am and spend another three or four hours motionless in bed, occasionally looking over at the whiskey and pill bottles next to his bed. It seemed romantic somehow.

"Zak?" It was Telly.

"Huh?"

"I was speaking to you and you appeared to fall asleep. Are you OK?"

"Yeah, I'm fine. I just phased out. It's the whiskey."

"Dude!" Lenny noticed Zak's glazed look. "You've only had two. You're getting old, man! Garcon! Another round!"

"Sorry, Telly. What were you saying?"

"I went to a mass today."

"Jesus Christ! Why'd ya fuckin' do that?" Zak had religion issues, along with his Sinatra issues.

"Zak! Kosovo is a Catholic country. Be nice. No raving!" Actually Kosovo was a Muslim region of Serbia, but Cozy meant well.

"Oh, sorry. I just meant why would you go to Mass in the middle of a shopping spree?"

Cozy, Lenny and Zak were now all staring at Telly and Zak tilted his head at them as if to say, I told you this guy was weird.

There was silence and Telly looked down at the floor. For a second Cozy thought he was going to cry, homesick for his Catholic homeland. He crossed his legs and folded his hands on his knee, looking out the

64

tavern window at the rain. "It seemed like an interesting building and something pulled me in."

"That's the Lord," said Lenny, sarcastically. Cozy smacked his arm.

He continued. "There seemed to be something happening to people who were going in. They were gaining hope just by entering the cathedral. I went in to witness this attraction but saw only ancient rituals. The people seemed to be orphans or children of the same mother and father. It was strange and I envied them for deriving something from this event. What were they deriving?"

"Good question!" Zak was the wrong person to ask. If anything can sour a person on the majesty of faith it's growing up Southern Baptist, where God mandates a series of unholy restrictions. Religion becomes something that prevents people from having a religious experience. "Look, Tel, you're not going to find any answers in a church, just obfuscation. Religion is the worst drug of all."

"Zak, religion can be beautiful. You need to listen to some Bach some time." For Cozy religion was the romantic factory that generated the sacred canon of classical music, lots of angels and hallelujahs.

Puzzled by Zak's sudden anger Telly said, "But there was something happening there that I could not identify. A process by which those inside were gaining energy or calm. I'm not sure and I will return."

"Dude, be my guest. I mean Catholic churches are always 'nice,' like the ones in Europe. That's from exploiting all the peasants and the raping and pillaging that went on in the Crusades. It's just a bit too patriarchal for me," said Zak thinking about the arguments over religion he had had with Petra.

"The Pope smokes dope!" shouted Lenny out of left field. "Being a man, I know that God is a woman. The thing that bugs me is the Church's stance on birth control. There's too many freaks on this planet. The Pope needs to come out with a consecrated holy condom. Maybe a little picture of Mary on the tip. Anyone that gets pregnant using it can claim

65

'immaculate conception' and win a prize from Rome!" It actually made sense.

Confused about the gendered nature of Christianity, Telly asked, "There is a difference between this holy mother and father? At the cathedral I heard more about the mother than the father."

"Yeah, Telly. God is the father. The mother is Mary, the woman he raped."

"Zak!" Cozy disapproved of that image.

"Oh, let's face it, Cozy, Mary was raped! She had a husband already. How was she going to say "no" to God? If it wasn't rape it was a serious case of sexual harassment. Anyway, the reason they talk more about Mary in Catholicism is the early church had to sell Christianity to a lot of goddess worshipping pagans. They would say, 'Where's your Goddess?' and the Catholics would say, 'Oh, we've got something even better, Mary, the mother of God'."

Now Telly was twice as confused. "I thought Mary was the victim of God. Was she also his mother?"

"Well..." How do you sum up the whole ideology of Christianity into one drunken image? "God gave Mary the holy roll in the hay and she had a little brat who was both the son of God and God Himself. I know, it makes absolutely no sense at all, but this shit wasn't written for the logical, just the faithful sheep."

"Telly, you've never heard the story of Jesus before?" Cozy was reevaluating her Catholic Kosovo statement. Maybe he was Jewish.

"This is new information for me and I wish to understand."

Leaning back in his chair with a drunken sneer, Zak said, "Well if the Lord really had loved the world, She would have given her only daughter!"

"Dude, don't harsh the Lord!" Lenny was referring to the son Lord, not the father Lord. "He did many fine things. He healed a lot of fucked up people, he raised hell with the capitalists, and let us not forget the turning of the water into wine. He was a seriously righteous hippie!"

Zak was not in the mood for faith in the unknown. "Maybe, but we don't really have much evidence that the guy even existed, except for the Roman arrest record, which said he looked more like the hunchback of Notre Dame than Willem Dafoe. All that shit that he supposedly said and did was written decades later."

Telly was again fascinated by this spirited discussion. "Is he revered for turning water into wine?"

Lenny laughed. "Well, that's why *I* revere him. He ended up getting executed because he was such a rebel and a threat to the Roman pricks. And then when they went to check on his tomb, he was gone, supposedly up into heaven."

"Or kidnapped by aliens," smirked Zak. "He supposedly died for our sins, but I never asked him." Zak began to sing the Patti Smith version of "Gloria," hoping that Cozy would pick up on the connection. "Jesus died for somebody's sins but not mine. Melting in a pot of thieves, wild card up my sleeve. Thick heart of stone. My sins are my own, they belong to me." The "me" sent Zak's mind to the image of Jimmy the Mod in the film *Quadrophenia*. The Who song "Love Reign O'er Me" plays and Jimmy screams "me!" before hurling himself over the white cliffs of Dover. That scene had been playing in his head the night of his suicide bender. The daydream distracted him from the fact that Cozy had burst into the "Gloria" chorus.

"It's a good thing they killed Christ on a cross. If they had done it in the Twentieth Century, the symbol of the Christian Church would be an electric chair," joked Lenny.

"Oh, who would want to wear a chair? Can you imagine trying to chase vampires off with a little Barbie chair?" Cozy was always brilliant after a few drinks, Zak thought.

"Yeah, instead of the bloody crucifix in churches with Jesus looking down you'd get a bug-eyed Jesus with his hair standing on end and choking on his tongue." Zak loved the idea that all the sacred imagery was just a historical accident.

The four spent another hour talking about religion and Lenny's gig and Cozy's audition and Telly's plan to observe. There was never a sense of wasting a Saturday afternoon because there never is any sunshine on Portland Saturdays in winter to waste. Sooner or later they all stumbled back to The Eldorado and made plans to meet up later and spend Zak's un-wedding night getting really drunk. Cozy and Lenny peeled off with plans of getting some housework done and Zak opted for a nap, hoping the booze would get him to the much-needed REM state. Telly took his spot on the windowsill.

The light rain continued. Men raced into the porno store across the street with newspapers over their heads. Tri-Met busses splashed pedestrians. In the bus shelter Telly noticed the homeless girl with her baby who had been with the group in Pioneer Square the night before. Lucinda was killing time, waiting for her life to begin.

Chapter Three:
Rockaria!

Any city that has ever been deemed "cool" has an underground. Not a real underground, like the French Resistance or the White Rose in Germany in the Forties. A musical underground. A collection of hipsters who have one primary function, to fertilize culture. In any given city there are between 200 and 2000 young adults who live by the ethic that if it's popular, it sucks. They were the kids in 1966 Haight-Ashbury who turned their paisley backs on the Beach Boys. They were the kids in 1977 Lower East Side Manhattan who gave the big punk finger to the Eagles. They were the kids in 1985 Athens, GA who told Huey Lewis to fuck off. They were the kids in 1991 Seattle who threw their flannel in the faces of Roxette.

The kids of the scene play a crucial role; to love a style of music until it becomes mainstream and then despise it. Bands that once had street credibility lost their hip factor once their music was played on commercial radio or bought by suburban teenagers. The scene chants, "Sell out!" in unison. This world is full of people who wax nostalgic about seeing The Velvet Underground/Sex Pistols/U2/Pearl Jam/etc. in a small club before they became mass marketed icons, dumbed down for popular consumption. Of course these same veteran hipsters are the ones who put on the classic rock station when no one is in the car.

For all the posturing of "I liked them before they got big," it ultimately helps new artists. If you have to abandon your favorite band once they get on MTV and frat boys start listening to them, you're going to have to find a replacement real quick. The scenesters scramble to get the low down on the next big hip thing. They put their ear to the ground and listen for the buzz. They tune into college radio stations. They badger indy record store workers. They inspect opening acts.

Once the word hits the street it happens quickly. Zak remembers how the Portland band Sleater-Kinney was playing tiny venues and got a mention in the hip bible *Spin* and soon was selling out the largest halls in town. They suddenly became the favorite band of every third-wave feminist rock grrrl, and rightly so. And bands have mixed emotions about being caught in this star machine. On the one hand it means that bigger things are ahead, but on the other... Well, basically the people you love will hate you. Who was it that we said we hate it when our friends get famous?

It's basic selfishness that propels the rock scene. That's *my* band! And if everyone is going to like them then I won't! Trendophobia. Portland was awash with trendophobics. Worried that their stake in cool might be discovered and turned into an overpriced fashion spread in *Jane* magazine. Seattle never truly recovered from that horror.

Lenny often said he would never sell out, but that didn't mean he didn't want to be huge in Japan (and everywhere else). There was a buzz brewing about Gurd. It could have gone either way.

Nap time ended with a blast of the stereo. Cozy and Lenny were over and Len had thrown on some Ramones to get the vibe going. The sound of the pounding punk shook the windows and distracted Telly. It was the music that Lenny and Zak had grown up on, loud, fast and ruling. The two neighbors bounded into Zak's bedroom and jumped up and down on his bed, shouting, "S! A! T-U-R! D-A-Y! Night!" over and over, causing the sleeping Zak to think he was being abducted by alien Bay City Rollers.

"Christ! What time is it?"

"Get up, boy!" shouted Cozy, shaking Zak's shoulders. "It's after eight and time to party."

"Yeah, old man! You can't sleep your life away. We've got a city to rape and pillage. This night must be remembered as the night Portland was turned upside down by the spirit of Bacchus. Let's go, mon fro!" Lenny was standing on the bed, playing air-guitar in the low-slung Ramones style.

"OK, OK!" Zak pulled himself out of bed, stood up and scratched his head. He had been sleeping in his shoes and was ready to go, except for his hair, which was also standing up.

"Dude, you look like such a rocker. You've got the whole Keith Richards just-fell-out-of-bed look happening," said Lenny. "Shit, I have to work hours for that exact effect!"

"Yeah, I'm such a wild man," he replied deadpan as possible. He wasn't feeling too wild on this wedding night. He had planned to be in a tuxedo and impressing everyone with how much he had grown up, taking the plunge and all that. But he was still just a typical disheveled rock boy about to hit the bars on a Saturday night. He started to wonder where Petra was again when Cozy grabbed him by the arm and pulled him toward the living room.

"C'mon, I've got someone I want you to meet." On the futon talking to Telly was an attractive woman with long curly blonde hair. She looked like a girl from a Noxema commercial, too young to be hanging out with this group. "Zak, this is Daisy. She's in the orchestra. I invited her to come along tonight. I hope you don't mind."

Zak was not in any place to be fixed up with a young thing. This was his un-wedding night and he needed to wallow. He was at least allowed one night of being supremely pathetic, as long as it didn't end in suicide. But she was cute and might distract him for a moment. "Hi Daisy. Welcome to my world."

"Hello, Zak. I like your apartment. What a great location. Your roommate was telling me about your music collection. Do you like any of the classics?"

"Oh, yeah, The Yardbirds, The Small Faces and, of course, The Beatles." Zak knew he was being a dick. "So what's the plan y'all? Where should this raping and pillaging start?"

Telly was caught up in the excitement. He had gathered from the day's discussions that Saturday night was something special. He had planned to walk the streets of the city seeing how people acted differently on a Saturday night in Portland, but now he hoped that he would be invited along for an inside view. Spending time with these people had begun to lift his spirits. He wasn't sure why but they seemed to become excited by the most irrelevant things.

Lenny was ready with an itinerary. "I thought we'd start at The Annex. They've got the best jukebox on this side of the river and a new bar maiden who is under the correct, but unpopular impression that all cocktails should have the maximum amount of alcohol in them. I thought we should take advantage of the lass before the evil management sets her straight."

The Annex was a basement bar complete with candles burning in Chianti bottles. It was a "Zak and Petra" place, but any decent place was a "Zak and Petra" place. It would be nearly impossible to escape her ghost in this town.

"Yeah, that sounds fine. But let's try to go to someplace new tonight. I need a new memory, even if I'm too drunk to remember it. Are you coming with, Telly?"

Saturday nights weren't much different than any other night for Lucinda, just sadder. The world seemed to come alive for people her age, looking to the city streets as a road map to the type of anything-can-happen fun that only happens when you've got a bit of money in your pocket. While the kids were hitting the streets, she was worried about making it into the shelter before curfew. Nothing was more boring than a shelter on a Saturday night with women drinking coffee, smoking and watching crap TV, amid a dozen screaming babies. What kind of fucked reality was that?

She had wasted enough time at the Burnside bus shelter and managed to spaynge enough money for a generic box of diapers and some pizza. She had also noticed Telly sitting in the window across the street and recognized him from earlier in the day. He seemed sad, like a lost soul, but one with a comfy Northwest apartment.

Tired of the damp, Lucinda packed up her baby and backpack and walked up the street to the Fred Meyer store to buy the diapers and marvel at all the wonderful grocery items that people were willing to buy. $4.80 for a box of cereal! The horror! The sliding doors and warm fluorescent lights always lured her in. Even in her economically screwed state she recognized that the grocery store was a symbol of normality. Everybody went to the store, even on Saturday nights. Here the pleasure is priced. Something for everyone including the lowly one banana buyer and the food stamp mama. The chiming of the scanner was an approval of the system. You are normal, you may choose paper or plastic. God bless consumption and the American love of stuff. If only she could afford some of it.

Roaming the isles she fantasized about shopping for her nonexistent rockstar husband. Maybe she would make him a nice pasta with fresh mushrooms and Paul Newman sauce. A bottle of wine, a cherry cheesecake, some of those big French breads, all loaded into an SUV with a state-of-the-art baby seat.

Lucinda remembered how she used to shoplift from this particular store regularly. She would take candy bars and hairbrushes and fruit, anything she could slip under her jacket. She got busted at a nearby drug store boosting some make-up shortly after Polly was born and the welfare worker told her that one more arrest and the state could take her baby away. But being a mom removed some of the never-ending suspicion that shopkeepers cast down on street kids, so it was always tempting to re-offend.

But the cash in her pocket gave her legitimacy. She didn't have to steal, the diapers at least. Lucinda stopped at the check-out lane to look at the covers of the fashion magazines. All the women seemed so perfect and clean. In their glow she felt imperfect and moldy.

Outside the Fred Meyer and on her way for a slice of pizza, she noticed the forlorn guy in the window coming out of The Eldorado with four friends, laughing and singing. Their Saturday night was just starting. All she had to look forward to was feeding and changing Polly and *Walker, Texas Ranger.*

The quiet mood at The Annex was shattered the moment Zak, Telly, Lenny, Cozy and Daisy walked down the stairs. It was too early for the drunken crowd, just the drunks. The basement bar smelled like the yeast from the brewery across the street and was on the verge of feeling like a dank dungeon.

"Where the hell's the music?" Lenny shouted and made a dive for the jukebox before it could dawn on Zak that there would be no waiting to hear your songs for the one that got to it first. While the others put their coats at a table and went to order drinks, Lenny put two crisp dollar bills in the machine and tried to pick the best seven Saturday night songs; 9701 - "Green Onions" by Booker T. and the MGs, 9905 - "What Is And What Should Never Be" by Led Zeppelin, 3201 - "Maybellene" by Chuck Berry, 6606 -"Big Time Sensuality" by Bjork, 1702 - "It's Tricky" by Run DMC, 5904 – "Shooting Star" by Bad Company and, as a joke, 4401 - "Larger Than Life" by The Backstreet Boys.

The Annex changed complexion as the groovy organ of "Green Onions" kicked in and Lenny came to the table quite pleased with himself. "Right on. That's all this place needed. A little Steve Cropper. You can have the next seven, birthday boy."

"You and Zak are always fighting over the jukebox. It's so silly," said Cozy, with that "boys are another breed" tone.

The jukebox was a big issue with Zak. "Hey, the ability to select from hundreds of songs allows you to set the mood of a bar. We can give these sorry asses some of the best tunes they're gonna hear in this dive. The CD jukebox is the only contribution the compact disc has made to our culture."

"Oh, here we go," said Cozy to Telly, sensing a monologue. But he was interrupted by Daisy.

"I can't believe I've never been here. This place is way cool!" Daisy was looking up at the wooden rafters and the stone bar.

"Is it because you're not old enough?" Zak wasn't planning on being too nice.

"Hey, I'm twenty-three! I just look young."

"Noxema," Zak said under his breath as the waitress brought the cocktails over from the bar. As the bourbon touched his tongue, Zak sat back in his chair and sank. How could she have done this to him? He was going to have to become an alcoholic now. Telly was watching him drift away from the energetic group.

"Zak? Would you tell me about the compact disc?"

"Oh, Daisy, Telly is from Kosovo. They don't have things like CDs there." Cozy wasn't sure what they had in Kosovo.

Knowing it would push a big button and reel Zak back in, Lenny shouted, "CDs revolutionized the music industry in 1984 by improving the quality of records while increasing the amount of actual material that could be placed on one disc. And they're handy dandy as well!"

"CDs are crap and you know it." Despite his hundreds of CDs, Zak belonged to the Vinyl Church. "CDs are killing music with digital bullshit. OK, Telly, here's the spiel. Number one. CDs are too long. Who has seventy-five minutes to listen to one record? One album is maybe forty-five minutes tops. Those riot grrrl albums were only thirty, fifteen a side. You can digest it. All these fucking bands think that because they have seventy-five minutes they have to fill it with whatever wanking they can come up with."

"But isn't that just like free music?" asked Daisy, all wide-eyed.

"It's free crap! If someone said to you, 'Here is a big plate of shit. Take it, it's free!' Would you take it? No. Give me a 20-minute side to listen to and take those last seven Soundgarden songs and flush 'em!"

Zak was becoming his old animated self. When it came to records he was a fascist. Ever since he was six and diving into his parents' platters, the things have always been sacred to him.

"Number two. CDs don't have as much ritual. You just slide them in and push a button. With records you have to carefully slide the sleeve out of the jacket and then gingerly slide the record out of the sleeve, being careful not to get your fingers on the grooves."

"Zak holds his records like they're made of the most fragile Bohemian crystal," laughed Lenny.

"Shut up. The ritual continues when you put it on the turntable. You can look at the grooves and see which songs are long and which are short. You can look at the label and see who wrote the songs you are about to enjoy. And you can tell when that side is almost over. With a CD, you don't see anything. You have been removed from sharing the experience by that which is giving you the experience."

Cozy and Lenny were rolling their eyes in amusement but Telly and Daisy were listening intently.

"Number three. Records give you art. That nice big square has been the canvas for some of the best art of the twentieth century. Has there

76

been a cover equal to *Sgt. Pepper's* since the CD came out? Who looks at a CD cover, anyway. Usually it's something stupid stuck behind a cracked piece of plastic. And with albums you can get stuff inside. When I was a kid, half the fun of getting a Wings albums was getting the poster inside. Kiss used to cram their albums with all kinds of shit, posters, stickers, pop-guns."

"Dude, my parents used to listen to Chicago and they'd come with these massive posters. We had them up in the rec-room." Lenny was a true Seventies child.

"Exactly, what can you fit in a CD?"

"Crap?" Daisy was catching on.

"Crap. Number four. CDs are overly technological. Do you know how they work? No, no one does. It has something to do with lasers. But records are simple. You can see the music in the grooves. You can see where it gets loud. All you need to play a record is a needle and a paper cup, but on a CD, again, you are alienated from it. Archeologists will be able to understand human culture up until around 1989, because the data on vinyl is so easily retrievable. They'll think CDs were coasters or something. I mean, why do you think they put a record on the Voyager and not a CD? Because any dumb alien will be able to figure it out."

"But CDs sound better," said Daisy, honestly, to which Zak just sat dumbfounded.

"There is music in space." Telly knew about the record on the Voyager space probe with it's Bach and Chuck Berry. He didn't want to give away too much, but he knew about it.

"Yeah, it's floating around like a lost Columbia House Record Club order. The Martians owe Carl Sagan for that one." Zak, didn't want to become too vitriolic. "Yeah, Daisy, I know CDs are supposed to sound better, but all that digital shit sucks the soul right out of the music. Vinyl is so much warmer. You're a musician, you must understand what I mean."

77

"Well, I've never owned a record player. I just remember that they skipped a lot."

"Well, not if you take care of them. Besides, those skips are from your life. The record ages with you."

Cozy turned to Telly. "Telly, what do you mean? What did you mean when you said, 'there is music in space'?"

"Zak is correct in that the Voyager carries Earth music to the cosmos, but there is already music in space. It is not the vacuum it is believed to be. Gravitational waves, black holes, supernovas, cosmic rays, all have their own frequency modulations."

"You sound like you've been there," said Cozy, resting her hand on his arm.

"He has," said Zak, knowing it would be taken as a joke.

Telly was drifting, thinking of the distance from where he had come from to this unique cellar bar. He had no idea the exact distance in miles, but it was a long way from home. His mind sank into the cocktail. The bubbles in the cola were streams of supernovas, living too quickly. A world gone in a second. Maybe his home was already gone, just another bubble that had outlived its own kinetic energy. He knew his new friends held some compassion but he risked their friendship and their insights by telling them why he was really sitting in The Annex, in Portland, Oregon, USA, Earth. There would be time, if he survived. The key was fighting off the demons. They were the forces inside him that told Telly the odds were he would never make it home again, and if he did, it would probably be too late.

Lucinda lasted about an hour in the shelter. She couldn't handle the other women there or the volunteers. The volunteers were either there to ease their own guilt or told to work there by some judge who thought a few nights in a homeless shelter would stop them from driving drunk again, which, of course, made no sense whatsoever. But the homeless women were worse. They'd tell her that she was too young to be there. They'd tell her to go home if no one was beating her. Then they'd cough up a lung as they'd tear into their tenth pack of smokes. Who were they to judge her? Unless they were her in ten years. The endless moralizing was just too much.

"Hey, Bren, would you do me a favor?" Bren was one of the cooler shelter workers. She seemed to have more in common with Lucinda than the other do-gooders. She had allowed Lucinda to sneak in after curfew once and always was ready with an ear or two. "Bren, would you watch Polly for about an hour. I really need to sneak out of here. These bitches are drivin' me crazy."

"Um, well, you know, you're not supposed to leave after you check in."

"Yeah, I know. But I've got to find my friend Wally. He's supposed to give me some money so I can buy some new baby clothes." There was no Wally. "Please, I'll be back as soon as possible and Polly's asleep. I just can't carry her anymore today."

Bren knew that young Lucinda just wanted to hit the electric streets on a Saturday night. She had been in a similar place not that long ago. "OK. One hour! You've got a baby here to take care of. It's your job, not mine."

"Thanks Bren, you rule!" Lucinda handed Bren the sleeping baby and a package of diapers just in case and snuck out the back door.

Out on the street she headed straight for the river, oblivious to the rain. She needed some life and her friends should be in full swing down by the river. A little camaraderie from the gutter-punks would make going back to the shelter a little more tolerable. She had never gone for a whole Saturday and not hung with them.

At The Annex, the wrong pairs were connecting. The Backstreet Boys song had Zak lunging for the jukebox to play some downbeat sad tunes; Otis Redding, Modest Mouse, John Coltrane. Daisy and Cozy were talking about some of the upcoming special concerts by the orchestra and Lenny was trying to explain how the gay discos weren't really for gay people to Telly.

"Play more Chuck Berry!" shouted Telly to Zak, not quite sure how to process the alcohol soaking into his brain.

"There you go!" said Lenny. "There are few things greater than a Chuck Berry tune. 'Up in the morning and off to school...'." Lenny was playing the air guitar again and Telly looked at him like his hands were transmitting some secret code, or were epileptic.

"The teacher is teaching the golden rule." Cozy often worried that Lenny thought she was being a snob with her opera obsession and occasionally tried to remind him that she grew up on the same music that he did.

"Cozy, when you sing rock 'n' roll you sing it like Brigitte Nielsen!" laughed Lenny, enjoying the Berry aria.

"That's Birgit Nilsson. And I can sing rock as good as you!"

"Uh, oh!" rolled Lenny, sensing a turf battle. Daisy laughed even if she didn't know why. "You better stick to *Carmen*, my sweet lover, and leave the rocking to me."

"Dude, rock singing is totally easy. You just need to scream and writhe. It's all about screaming and writhing." It was challenge that wouldn't have been made within the constraints of sobriety.

"Look, I'll admit that I can't sing that opera shit, but there is a real trick to singing rock music. It's not just karaoke."

"Teach me lover, 'cause I'm ready!" Cozy's drunken pale blue eyes were impossible to resist.

"Yeah, teach all of us!" chirped Daisy.

"OK, let me load up a good song. Zak is over there playing melancholy baby." Telly got up and loped over to the jukebox. The girls and Telly watched Lenny push Zak toward the bar and push a dollar bill into the CD machine.

Zak leaned against the bar with orders to buy the next round. "So you're the special new bartender?" Zak said to a sweet woman in pigtails, feeling drunker than he was. "Give us five of your favorites." He returned to the table with five sidewalk lemonades, some sickly sweet drink with more vodka than anything else.

"I like these songs, Zak," said Daisy, trying to be nice.

"Yeah, this is music to kill yourself to." He now had the excuse of strong drinks to be a prick.

"Zak, you're a prick!" Cozy always kept him in line. "Lenny is going to teach us how to be rock singers."

"Robert Plant is quite nervous, I'm sure."

Telly should have been more interested in this issue of rock and roll versus opera singing, but he was lost in a daydream about the depth of space. Zak's jazz selection blasting from the bar PA made him dream of star clusters and the path home. Lenny returned to the table, took a sip of the new drink and made a horrid face.

"Christ! Are you hoping for a group Technicolor yawn before midnight, Zak? Jeez, you need to stick to the straight shit. As soon as Zak's weepypalooza songs are done, rock 'n' roll high school kicks in." As the Coltrane played out, the table was a maze of transfixed faces. Cozy lovingly stared at Lenny, who was eying the bartender. Zak angrily and lustfully stared at Daisy, who was staring into her drink and Telly stared off into space.

Eventually Zak's blue selections gave way to The Blues. "Now this is the shit," said Lenny, rocking back in his chair. "We start at the beginning. You can't sing rock and roll if you can't sing the blues!" Etta James was wailing in The Annex. It was "In The Basement," an unofficial theme song for the cellar bar and a few hipsters began to dance. Lenny leaped out of his chair and burst into the first verse, shaking and shimmying. The first

81

smile of the night crossed Zak's face. Suddenly he was in a wacked out version of *Beach Blanket Bingo*. Telly just looked confused as Daisy and Cozy clapped along.

"Now tell me where you can party, child, all night long?
In the basement! Down in the basement!
Oh, where can you go when your money gets low?
In the basement! Down in the basement!
And if a storm is taking place, you can tell it's gonna be safe
In the basement! Down in the basement!
Where can you dance to any music you choose?
In the basement! Down in the basement!
All the comforts of home and nightclub, too.
In the basement! Down in the basement!
There's no cover charge or fee and the food and drinks are free,
In the basement! Down in the basement!

"Go, cat go!" shouted someone from a neighboring table, realizing that he was suddenly in a teen exploitation musical. The vibe was shared as strangers joined in the chorus. "In the basement! In the basement! That's where it's at!" If you thought those scenes were never very real, how every one would break into song, with full backing tracks and the gangs would burst into a highly choreographed routine without a single rehearsal, then you never hung out with Lenny and Cozy. They were Sandy and Danny.

Zak lost his blues at the sight of rockstar Lenny hamming it up. "Oh, man, this is rich! Take note, Telly. Typical Earth behavior!" As if those movie scenes happened all the time in Portland.

The song was a favorite and Cozy took the cue to play Ann Margaret to Lenny's Elvis. She jumped up with a little Sixties watusi shake and took over the second verse.

Nobody's gonna check your age at the door,
In the basement! Down in the basement!
Do the Barracuda and Jerk 'till your feet get sore,
In the basement! Down in the basement!
Do any dance you wanna do, there's no one under you,
In the basement! Down in the basement!

The place was falling out with people dancing and clapping. Zak half expected Eric Von Zipper to ride in on his wayward Harley sidecar and bust up the joint. If only Pet could see this. What a scream! There was skinny little Cossette belting out some serious barrelhouse blues like it was 1962. What a perfect woman. Things like this just don't happen in the real word.

On the other hand, Telly was studying the event like they did happen. It seemed so well prepared, as if Lenny and Cozy had known this Etta James. Fun was something that seemed so distant to him, yet it's appeal was intoxicating. He couldn't wait to see what would happen next.

The song began to fade and Lenny hugged Cozy as the room applauded. "Yeah, I guess you can flow. I must have been wearing off on you." They headed toward the others when the opening guitar riffs of Lenny's next selection kicked in.

"Oh, hold on boy. I'm not done yet." It was "Roll Over Beethoven," Telly's Chuck Berry request, but Cozy took it as a challenge from Lenny to her classical sensibilities. Blaming it on the Sidewalk Lemonades she jump on top of the table and hit the very un-opera guttural tone, "Well, I'm gonna write a little letter and mail it to my local DJ..."

The place would have probably continued rockin' Frankie and Annette-style but Cozy's over-enthusiastic twisting sent her head over heels, crashing into the next table. After seeing that she wasn't mortally wounded, Zak sat back down. "Fall over Cozy and tell Tchaikovsky the news."

The new barmaid, who had waited all her life to see a room break into a musical number, brought over a tray of free drinks. "Man, that was so *Xanadu*! Here's a round on the house. Just stay off the tables, hun. OK?" Cozy rubbed the back of her head and thanked her.

The five spent the next round talking about Elvis movies, Daisy's oboe playing, and whether or not Cozy should sing with Gurd. Telly enjoyed himself, but the alcohol repeatedly sent him into moments of deep despair. When he mentioned that he should probably retire the gang picked him up and insisted that he come to the next bar. So the five, along with Bacchus, stumbled out into the street looking for adventure.

An adventure for Lucinda would have been nice, as long it didn't involve any old winos, the police or any agents of the State. The boredom of homelessness was numbing. The hours of walking around and not having anyone to talk to. And no one wanted to talk to her anyway. She went through a phase of being very chatty to waitresses in coffee shops and then they'd find out that she was a street kid. They'd throw each other sideways looks and make excuses to interrupt the conversation, never to return. It was humiliating, but better than the silence. If only Polly could talk.

Tonight the gutter-punks would suffice. They never really had anything insightful to say when they were sober but at least they didn't treat her like a fucking loser. She found them across the river, under the Hawthorne Bridge, which meant that she spent half of her one hour furlough just tracking them down. "Lucy!" they shouted out, seeing her walk out of the shadows.

"Hi, guys. I busted out of the fucking women's prison to find you."

"Where's fucking Polly?" asked Dean, the kid with the lopsided mohawk who loved playing with the baby.

84

"One of the shelter workers is watching her. Don't worry, she's fine. What's going on tonight?

"Same shit, different millennium." There were six teenagers, ripped on Ranier beer, in various stages of deterioration, facing the river. The rest of the gang was scattered across the city. "Have a beer."

Sometimes Lucinda missed the care-free ritual of getting drunk and passing out. It was a good way to pass time and the hangover was no worse than the sober reality. Since Polly showed up she had tapered off for fear of dropping the baby in the Willamette or leaving her on another bus. But she was free and lonely tonight. Glad to see her forgiving friends, she cracked open a can. "Ah, this is the life," she smirked. She guessed that she should be happy to be dry under the bridge with her drunk friends but it wasn't exactly the ideal Saturday night. While the gang talked about which cops, shelter workers and yuppies sucked the most she thought about the group she saw coming out of The Eldorado, on their way to debit-carded drinks and conversations about things that mattered. Conversation.

"Hey Lucinda! Are you just going to drink our beer and space out?"

"Sorry. Don't you guys ever get sick of this? I mean, it's great not having to deal with parents or teachers and not having to wait until you're 21 to get wasted, but, I mean, like aren't you bored?"

"Oh, shit, here comes the 'Get a fuckin' life!' speech," said one of the girls.

"No, really. I'm in the same fucked up place you are, just with a baby, which is ten times worse. I just wonder where it will end up."

"Look, Lucy," interjected Dean. "What's the fuckin' point? Do you want to work ten hours a day and then spend the next ten shopping or cooking or watching fuckin' TV? Any of us could die at any minute. There could be a shooting on a bus, or an earthquake or a fuckin' bomb. You gotta enjoy life now!"

"Yeah, you enjoy life?"

85

"Damn straight. No one tells me what to do. I'm the king of the street." That line sent the group into drunken laughter. "Well, you know what I mean. I'm not punching a clock at Burger King for slave wages. We are refusing to be wage slaves. That's a righteous fucking thing. We live off of the garbage of the richest people in the world, which is better than working your ass off in 99% of the countries on Earth."

"That's swell Karl Marx, but aren't you fucking bored out of your skull?"

"I'm bored in my skull!" shouted one of the kids.

"No, I'm not bored. Who has time? Being a scavenger is a full-time job. And if there's nothing to do, you can always roll a bum or fuck with the Mexicans. Remember how you used to sneak into the movies with us? I mean we can do anything they can."

"Except get out of this town." Lucinda realized that it was pointless to crack through this rationalization of a life misspent and opened another can of beer, forgetting about Polly.

The Eldorado gang invaded a few more bars that night. Both Zak and Telly lost their melancholy in the booze and conversation. Zak stopped thinking about Petra long enough to start being nice to Daisy and ended up with her phone number. Cozy asked Lenny for some more singing lessons and managed to convince him to let her sing with Gurd on Friday. Just on one song, if the guys said yes. They all cabbed back to The Eldorado around 2 am. Daisy slept on Cozy and Lenny's couch, leaving Zak alone on his wedding night.

Of course, Lucinda was gone from the shelter a lot longer than an hour. She got back around 6 am to find the doors locked. She had to wake up several people by ringing the bell before someone would open the door and let her in. Polly was sleeping next to Bren in the office and before she could get yelled at Lucinda snuck her baby out from under

Bren's hand and found a cot to crash on. She pulled the covers over her head and wished it was ten years from now.

The rest of the week was filled with busy distractions. Lenny was busy rehearsing with Gurd, including a new song with Cozy. Cozy was helping to publicize the show and build a stage design. She also was working on her Verdi for the audition. Zak got back to his graduate work up at the university and was happy to see that no one acted differently after the canceled wedding. He resisted the temptation to call Petra once he found that she was, in fact, staying with Lisa. It was her move. He busied himself with analyzing his research data and teaching Telly the history of rock 'n' roll, enjoying the alien fantasy. Telly explored the city, observing life on both sides of the river, watching gutter-punks beg for change, bicyclists and motorists yelling at each other, and a gang of skinheads attack an Asian man. But he spent most of his time at the window, watching the world roll by. There, on a few occasions, he spotted Lucinda sitting at the bus stop, waving busses by, cradling her baby. He wondered what kept her going. For Lucinda, it was a typical week spent trying to soak up time and scrounge for basic survival resources, like tampons and pizza. She had a brief flirtatious encounter with a clerk at the Plaid Pantry that lasted for three days. Then he tried to rip her bra off and she slapped him and ran off, cursing the fact that she couldn't go into that convenience store during his shift anymore.

It was a hard week for Zak, maybe the hardest. He bounced between manic levels of energy and deep depression. He was crippled, emotionally and socially. Socially because he felt like he had let everyone down by shattering their illusions of love and driving this wonderful woman screaming into the night. There were hours that he couldn't move, sitting on the floor with the phone in his lap, praying she'd call. There he found a napkin that Petra had used to dab her lipstick. He kissed it and put it in his jacket pocket.

The turntable was featuring gut wrenching dirges like Bob Dylan's "Man of Constant Sorrow" and Billie Holidays "Why Was I Born?" or some Etta James whenever he was home. He called Daisy once but she claimed she was busy "making food" which Zak took as a blow-off in reward for his assholenss. Lenny and Cozy were too busy with their project to babysit but occasionally popped in to make sure Zak wasn't hanging from the door with a belt around his neck.

He'd drag himself out of his bedroom after a good cry to Hank Williams' "I'm So Lonesome I Could Cry" and see Telly sitting at the window with the same pained expression on his angular face. Telly seemed to hide his tears, but he definitely wept. Zak knew he too had a great sense of loss to overcome but he was in no position to play psychologist, especially if Telly was a leaver when Zak was the left.

By the time Friday rolled around Zak's jaw hurt from clenching it. He was trying to come to grips with the fact that he wouldn't be marrying and growing old with his one true love, proving that the concept of love was a bourgeois crock. His head hurt from thinking about it and drinking about it. All the number crunching couldn't distract him from the reality that he had been abandoned. She had completely abandoned him, just like his father had abandoned him years earlier, without a simple courtesy call. It was as if he no longer existed in their world. Zak fought off the daily impulse to throw himself in the river and return to the water. Something about the idea of his floating body, drifting north to the Pacific, seemed comforting. One breath and he would again be a fetus in amniotic fluid, waiting for a loving womb to be reborn in. Waiting for a world that wasn't quite as vicious as this one. He tried to stay away from the end of the bed, but there he was, praying for the end of the world. He read the book that Cozy gave him and kept the madness at bay. Who would want to end up like William Styron, after all?

88

Lenny and Cozy had been very secretive about the hurried plans for the show at The Palais. He and the other four members of the band had been practicing furiously, realizing this gig was a shot at the high dollar Friday night crowd. In Portland people just needed an excuse to go out. You can only spend so much time cooped up. If you wanted to go to the movies on a Friday night you had to buy tickets hours in advance because even the dumb Adam Sandler movies would be sold out. People would line up to see cheese turn green on a Friday night, as long as there was booze on tap.

What Cozy the Diva's connection to the show was unclear. She popped down to Zak's around seven to tell him that he was on the guest list plus one and made sure that Telly was the plus one.

"Dude, you are going to be blown away," she said coyly.

"Come on, Coze, what's the skinny? Are you singing with the band?"

"You'll see. Telly, get prepared for your first definitive American rock 'n' roll experience."

"I am quite prepared, Cozy. Zak has fully explained rock 'n' roll to me. I am anxious to experience it first hand." Indeed Zak had given Telly the complete class, explaining how the white boys in the South visited the black tonks and used the blues to create their own "honky" tonks, eventually giving birth to the avatar Elvis Presley. Zak explained how Dylan turning The Beatles on to pot led to the psychedelic explosion and how The Ramones and The New York Dolls coming to England allowed Malcolm McLaren to create the punk rock movement. He played him ska and explained its connection to hip-hop via Kool Herc. He explained to Telly the essentials of uncool, citing Pat Boone and Michael Bolton, Anita Bryant and Celine Dion. And Telly absorbed it with rapt attention, seeing rock 'n' roll as a lifeline.

He had also picked up on the lowdown on Gurd, from Zak and a few street conversations he had eavesdropped on. Gurd was the music

89

lover's band. The kids outside The Palais referred to them as a living jukebox, appropriating the best of the fifty year history of rock music. They were as likely to play riffs from Fats Domino, The Stones, David Bowie, U2 or Fat Boy Slim. They *were* rock 'n' roll, the kid said. So Telly greatly looked forward to experiencing this phenomenon in person. It seemed to be such a powerful force in this world.

Around ten, after a few shots of Jim Beam, Zak and Telly walked down to The Palais. Telly was in his usual stripes and Zak was in black with his blue CBGB's hoodie on and just glad to be out, hearing live music. For Zak, it was like going back to the world of Friday night fun, before the drama, only without his sidekick. Telly might make a good sidekick, but he wouldn't look as good in a tank top as Petra did.

Both Telly and Zak's spirit picked up as they joined the crowd feeding into the front door of the hall. Zak was quite amazed that so many were coming to see his friend's little band and realized that Petra would probably be there, somewhere and he would have to decide how to react.

Before he could think of a plan, Telly asked, "What is this marking?" The bouncer at the door had stamped his hand unexpectedly. The stamp read, "Joel's bitch."

"Oh don't worry, man, that's just to show that you didn't sneak in. Joel is the door man and I guess we're all his bitches."

"His bitches?" Telly still didn't understand.

"It's this bullshit rock 'n' roll thing. It's sexist crap, using slang for 'female' as a put down, I hate it, even if it is funny." Zak was guiding Telly up the stairs into the main ballroom.

"But if you love rock 'n' roll so much, how can you disagree with something associated with it?"

"Look, rock is like society. It's got a lot of diversity woven into it. Like those assholes who mosh to the wrong kind of music, they give us boundaries. I can't love all of rock 'n' roll. I just love what I think is the

90

most important. There's a lot of shit in rock that's very anti-woman. Remind me to play you some Guns N' Roses or Eminem. I don't agree with all its manifestations, just its basic premise and 90% of its manifestations." Zak was becoming skilled at explaining things to the alien boy.

Once inside the venue Telly was struck by the noise. The opening band, Quasi, was on stage and the music was similar but much louder than that coming from Zak's stereo. Telly could feel every note shake his body. He had to stop and step back, as if the beat was knocking him down.

"You OK, my main man? Let me buy you a drink." Zak pulled Telly toward the bar, scanning the crowd for his ex, with no idea of how he would respond if he saw her. He should have gotten Cozy to convince Daisy to come with him so he would have a bit of armor. "Two whiskey cokes," Zak told the barman. "This is it, brother. This is what it's all about. They come to rock, they come to drink, the come to fuck, they come for fashion tips, but most importantly they come."

"It is like the cathedral, only louder," shouted Telly. "These people are drawn together by a common ritual."

"Yeah, it's called TGIF. That's an Earth saying. It means, 'Thank God I'm Fucked,' and everyone here is."

"Fucked?"

"Yeah, or fucked up or a fucker or, like me, fucked over." Quasi was finishing their set and there was a crush toward the bar. Telly noticed many faces that he had seen around town during the week. The occasional person smiled at him and he nodded back. He had hoped to see the girl from the bus stop but it didn't seem like a good place to bring a baby. Zak was leaning over the bar, doing his Sinatra imitation. He didn't want Petra to catch him looking. Instead he put on his best pathetic barfly look.

The music coming from the PA was a trippy montage that Andy, the Gurd drummer, had put together. It was a swirling mix of jazz samples, muzak, third world chanting and big band drumbeats. Telly was confused by it and was unsure if he was hearing it correctly. He had not gotten used to Zak's constant alcohol flow and felt a bit off balance.

After about a half hour of Zak leaning on the bar waiting to be seen looking like Dean Martin and Telly trying to figure out if he was drunk or just listening to drunken music the lights went down. Andy's tape was turned off and people began moving toward the stage. "C'mon Telstar, we go Zone One for this one." Zak took Telly to the front of the stage, with the kids.

There was some special staging set up but it was hard to see in the dark. Once some spotlights hit the stage four chairs were evident. Out walked four women in tuxedos with string instruments. Some of the crowd was confused, thinking they were at the wrong gig, but others cheered knowing that Gurd was full of tricks.

It was a string quartet! They sat down and tuned for a bit and a booming classic rock voice announced, "Ladies and Gentlemen, Symphonic Gurd." The four women broke into the unmistakable bars of Beethoven's Fifth Symphony and the audience roared. Telly looked at Zak with the Mr. Spock eyebrow and Zak lifted his hand up to say, just wait.

After a few passionate bars of Amadeus, Cossette walked on stage to more applause and stood behind the center mike. She was also in a black tuxedo, with her long black hair up and looking damn fine. The violinist then changed tempo with a familiar if unsymphonic riff. The others launched into the piece and the crowd went nuts. Here was the beautiful Cosette onstage at The Palais on a packed Friday night singing an operatic version of "Roll Over Beethoven"! Telly suddenly got it and Zak was jumping up and down. Some of the kids were even moshing, to opera! She was stunning in the spotlight and Zak was happy to just be in her presence.

92

While the crowd was distracted by Cozy, the members of Gurd slipped on stage and suddenly joined in on the backbeat, giving the song the Chuck Berry meets the Boston Pops attack it deserved. With the addition of the electric guitars, Cozy untied her tie and ripped her hair down and began to wail, "Roll over Beethoven!" It was a moment. Lenny and his diva, rocking the house.

With all the lights up it was clear that the stage was designed to look like a millennial dance. All the icons of the last 50 years were behind the band, posters of 70's cop shows, disco balls, plasma balls, turntables, even a guy dressed like Michael Jackson and a woman dressed like Marilyn Monroe dancing. It was like a surreal Beatles album cover.

After the crowd's shouts died down, Lenny took the mike. "Good evening, we're Gurd and we're here to rock. This first one is a brand new one and it features the next great star of the Metropolitan Opera, Cozy Daniels!" The band then kicked into a rollicking number that the string quartet helped fill out. Lenny was singing about an opera singer who couldn't sing rock 'n' roll, obviously inspired by that night at The Annex. Cozy was dancing and clapping and happy to be sharing the stage with her rock boy. Through parts of the number Gurd would break it down and Cozy would sing some of her favorite Wagner riffs. It fit perfectly. The perfect marriage of rock and opera. Pete Townshend would have been proud.

As the song ended, Lenny and Cozy, both sweaty, kissed deeply and the crowd cheered. Cozy and the quartet took their bows and ran off the stage and Gurd jumped into one of their more well-known rave ups. It was obvious how much this odd couple loved each other. It made Zak smile and then Telly grabbed Zak by the neck and shouted, "That was fucking brilliant!"

"You're drunk, you bastard!" yelled Zak, getting back into the thunderous music. The band looked great, a tribute to post-modernism. Lenny was all glammed out, looking like Marc Bolan with a boa. JE, the bassist had the whole slick fifties thing happening. Jeff, the sampler/keyboardist had on a leisure suit. Andy was very nineties with his shaved head and the funniest of all was Buren, the guitarist who has some kind of crazy Spinal Tap/Parliament Funkadelic outfit on, playing a double-necked guitar that looked like the one used by Jimmy Page.

The crowd was wild for them. Too many rainy days with noses in books. These people were busting at the seams and Zak was one of them. This was high decibel escape from his hourly contemplation of death. He defied the age rules and moved toward the center of the pit to mix it up with the kids. The adrenalin was flowing and every elbow in his side or slam into his back made him feel a bit more alive.

It was the usual cross-section of Portland moshers, young, dumb and full of, spunk. Portland had set the benchmark for making sure that women had an equal voice in the scene, and that included moshing. In most cities the mosh pit was a cesspool of testosterone, jocks and off-duty Marines seeing how many people they could knock down. But in Stumptown the pit would occasionally achieve it's potential, a throbbing organism of generational harmony. In the pit the individual and the collective became synchronized, perfect anarchy.

It was in this utopian state that Zak saw her. Not Petra but some vision of the Great Northwest Goddess. She was a beautiful Japanese girl in a tight black T-shirt, short choppy hair and a ring of thorns tattooed around her left bicep. She had glitter on her perfect round cheeks and was lost in the music and strobe lights. She moved to the beat like a Cadillac, full of power. He stopped moshing just to get a good look at her. She was one of those legendary BBA's (Big Boobed Asians) that white boys only dreamt about or spied on the Internet. She dripped cool while dancing furiously, in a high-powered trance. He tried to get closer since there was no "personal space" in front of the stage. Maybe he could defend her against some groping stage diver.

He looked to see if Telly was OK in his spot and when he turned around to make his move she was gone. Lost in the chaos. Zak was frantic. He loved her, how could she leave so soon? He headed back to the bar in hopes of finding her. Telly followed him.

"What is wrong, fucker?" Telly still hadn't got the hang of multi-tasking "fuck."

"Dude!" Zak sounded pissed. "Did you see where she went?" But Telly looked confused. "That bomb girl with thorns tattooed on her arm. I think she was Japanese."

"No. Do you know her?"

"No, but I love her. She's my salvation, the girl of my dreams."

"I thought Petra was the girl of your dreams."

"Petra had her chance. Besides, what better way to forget about the girl of your dreams than with a new girl of your dreams? I have to find her."

"It sounds like you can dream of as many females as you like."

"Dude!" Zak scanned the crowd like a conning light on the tide, looking for the sparkle of her eyes, but it was just a sea of chaos. Usually Gurd shows were in venues the size of your living room. They finally get a huge Friday gig and look what happens. His eyes crossed a female coming toward him. A momentary panic told him, Petra! But it was Cozy excitedly tracking him down.

"Hi guys! So what did you think? Can you believe Lenny wrote that great song for me? Wasn't it killer?" But Zak was still half-searching.

"Zak is looking for a big boobed Asian."

"Telly! Just this amazing girl I saw in the pit. I've got to meet her."

"Zak, you're hopeless!"

"Your thing was totally cool, Coze. Telly and I were hugging each other we thought it was so kick ass. I can't believe you guys pulled that together so quickly, with the strings and all."

95

"Thanks! Yeah, the girls were really into doing some rock. Now who's the chick?"

"A fucking mosher!" said Telly, still drunk.

"Look, I don't know her."

"But he loves her!" Telly wasn't helping.

"She is just, it. She's the it girl. I tagged her and now she's it."

"God save her. Why don't you go look for Cousin It. I'm going to drag Telly backstage. He can watch the rest of the show from back there. C'mon Telly, I'll show you what Gurd looks like from behind."

"Groovy, soul sister!" Cozy led the stumbling Telly back toward the stage and Zak dove back into the crowd hoping to find his new love before he ran into the old one.

For the street kids of Portland the excitement of a packed weekend rock show where people drank cocktails and went out for 3:00 am breakfasts afterwards might have as well been in another time-space continuum. Sometimes they hung around outside the shows, like the time they all got drunk on the roof of The Palais when Fugazi played there. Some of the girls might get in on the blow job pass, but the best things got on a weekend night was a party at the squat with a boombox blasting Korn and a supply of free smack stolen from a dealer.

This Friday Lucinda was not at the squat or drinking and smashing malt liquor bottles under a bridge, high on carbon monoxide. She was sitting in the shelter nursing a cold. She and Polly were both snot factories. Fortunately Polly couldn't complain but Lucinda complained enough for both. The older women were tired of the snotty kid and her snotty kid and sent them away from the TV. Bren gave her some Nyquil and she fell asleep before 10:00.

Zak never found the girl of his dreams. There were just too many people at the show. The crowd was a confusing mess of moshers and

96

swing dancers. Half of Portland had black hair making it impossible in a dark club to tell the Asians and Hispanics from the Goth Rockers and Greasers. After the last encore, a tongue-in-cheek version of T. Rex's "20th Century Boy," Zak headed backstage to find Telly.

Telly had been roped into a bit of roadie work. He wanted to see the tools of rock 'n' roll up close and was helping Andy load his trap. "Zak, I'm a roadie, motherfucker!"

"That's fine, Telly. Just don't break anything. Where's Cozy?"

"She's out in the back with Lenny."

Zak headed out to the loading bay, expecting to see Lenny and Cozy greeting their new legion of fans in the alley. Instead they were alone behind the dumpster, making out furiously against the brick wall. Based on the fact that Cozy was strangely taller than Lenny, Zak figured they were doing more than just kissing. An embarrassed smile brushed his face and he went back inside. It must be nice, he thought, to be with the one you love.

Chapter Four:
Mission

An incredulity to metanarratives. That's what Francois Lyotard called the post-modern condition. Sometime around the time Marcel Duchamp painted a moustache on the Mona Lisa things began to cave in. The Twentieth Century was born in the promise of modernism, the belief that, with the right paradigm, all society's problems could be solved. Marxism, capitalism, technology, religion, populism, all offered the agenda of emancipation.

That century ended in a whirlpool of nihilism. Marxism produced the slave labor of Vietnam. Capitalism produced the corrupt war machine of the Pentagon and declining safety standards in the name of profit. Technology was the Mir space station crashing into Northern France and rampant cloning experiments. Religion was the bloodshed of Central Europe and India and the malevolent agenda of the Christian Right. Populism became racist militias arming themselves against the urban hordes who were too busy killing each other to notice. Suffice it to say there wasn't much to believe in.

After the Clinton sex scandal every small time emperor was revealed as nude. Without an arc of hope people sank into the solace of consumerism, trading community in for Internet shopping and debt maintenance. Homeless people with cell phones and 12-year olds with credit cards were the new symbols of the end of the American Century.

That there was fear and trepidation about the new century and millennium was an understatement. But the sigh of relief that came after the Y2K bug whimpered and scurried away didn't immediately usher in a golden age of Aquarius. The first year of the new era looked pretty much like the previous one. The buzzword was nostalgia. The last years of the nineties and the first years of the zeros were like the week before New Year's Day when everyone compiles their Top Ten lists. There was comfort in looking back. Everyone was eager to create a mythological Good Ol' Days. The Big Band Era. The Hippie Era. The Depression Era. The Disco Era. The Spanish Inquisition Era. It was comfort food. Something that didn't quite happen like the way you remember it. Just like *Happy Days* didn't really have anything to do with the 1950s. But you couldn't tell people that their memories were as bogus as Disneyland. People really believed that the barbarians of the dark ages spoke like Xena and Gabriele.

Nostalgia was a guilty pleasure. A few hours of Nick at Night prevented you from having to think of anything new. Hollywood was right in the thick of it, turning old TV shows into modern movies, *The Flinstones*, *The Avengers*, *The Mod Squad*, *My Two Dads*. Zak eagerly awaited the full screen version of *Charles in Charge*. Gurd's success was built on mining this backward orientation and they did it well, juxtaposing some of the most unlikely things, like their combined tribute to The Sex Pistols and Mariah Carey. But the guys in the band knew that the schtick couldn't last forever. Sooner or later they were going to have to come up with an original idea. They were going to have to take a huge gamble and think of something completely new. The thought kept Lenny up at night. Everything had been done. All that was left was to recycle.

There was the usual post-gig scramble at The Palais. The gear had to be loaded, kids had to be greeted, Gurd T-shirts had to be sold and everyone had to get paid. Lots of friends were there to tell the guys how amazing they were and how amazing Cozy was and how amazing the stage and strings were. It was a wonderful stroke that had Lenny strutting around like James Cameron.

"Dude, that fuckin' rocked!"

"Awesome Lenny! Gurd kicked my fuckin' ass!"

"You guys are gonna be fuckin' huge!

"Jesus fuckin' Christ, I crapped in my pants!"

The whole time Cozy was an ear-to-ear grin, seeing the night as Lenny's great triumph. Of course, Zak saw the night as Cozy's great triumph. The rock aria had been pulled off to perfection. He went to find Telly who was shirking his roadie duties, sitting on the stage about to pass out.

"Ground control to Major Tom! Are you with us, Major?"

The excitement, the hour and the drinks had Telly teetering on the edge of consciousness. "This hall looks much different when all the lights are on. It's so beautiful," he slurred.

"Yes it is. Get up, space boy. The rockstars have invited us to breakfast. We could all use some coffee and eggs. There will be no upchucking in our happy home."

"Is he OK?" Cozy was hanging on Lenny and looking like Jerry Lewis on the day after Labor Day.

"Yeah, he's good to go. It's just been a big night for our little foreigner. He'll be much better once we get a big greasy cheese omelette inside him."

Lenny and Cozy gave their last thanks to the sound crew at the club and then the four hopped in a cab and headed across the river to the Hot Cake Hideaway, one of the few places you can get a good breakfast at three a.m.. It had all the things you needed after a night of rocking: eggs, a surly cook, endless coffee refills, and a jukebox.

The place was packed with nightclub refugees not ready to end their evening. Grease soaked the air and the smell of coffee was intoxicating. "Damn, I'm in heaven!" shouted Lenny upon entering and a few of the patrons recognized him.

"Dude, you fuckin' rocked tonight!"

101

Lenny loved it. The four grabbed a booth and immediately ordered coffee and menus. While they waited to order Zak loaded a few bucks into the jukebox, which was blasting Foghat.

"Oh man, that was fun!" said Cozy, squeezing Lenny's neck.

"Yeah, you were just incredible, a regular Shirley Manson. If the opera thing doesn't work out, you can always be a rockstar. Wasn't that Pat Benetar's deal?"

The coffee was waking Telly. At least enough to announce, "Hell is for fucking children." Zak rejoined the booth mid-laughter in time to catch Lenny's rare transfer to serious thought.

"Yeah, tonight was super cool. But man, what do we do next? I mean should we continue to do this until we break out nationally? What if people get sick of us and our crazy tribute to rock cabaret? I always loved how The Beatles had a completely different vibe every year. A new look, a new sound. Just between 1965 and 1968, what a transformation!"

"Yeah, but the Beatles were playing the same Carl Perkins and show tunes for years in Liverpool and Hamburg before they ever got out of their leather jackets. You gotta pay your dues." Zak was a Beatles scholar.

"Yeah, I know. It's all about credibility. But it just seems like everything has been done."

"Well I had that same thought when I saw Gary Numan play 'Cars.' I never would have predicted Public Enemy or DJ Shadow. It's a new century dude, anything could happen." But Zak knew the sentiment. Anything could happen that was the problem. Mass murder, anthrax bombs, genetically engineered fruit flies that bred in your ass. There was nothing beyond the realm of possibility ever since Dolly the cloned sheep and Pixar computer animation. Technology had pretty much stolen the copyrights to the most childlike dreams.

"Whatever."

"Lenny is having one of his confidence crises. You just can't be happy, boy. You just rocked the biggest crowd of your life," said Cozy, smiling.

"Yeah, but you gotta admit, it's getting harder and harder to be creative. We're all just stuck doing shit that's already been done. I'm mining rock history, you're singing two hundred year old opera songs, you spend all day listening to old records. Telly?" Telly was listening. "Dude, what was the newest thought that you've had?"

"That I am afraid to eat eggs?" He was watching plates of eggs, scrambled, poached, over easy and in omelets being carried by and thought better against a "Do you know what eggs are?" speech.

The four ordered their food (Telly had pancakes) and Zak's songs began to play on the jukebox. The conversation continued.

"I don't know. Sometimes I just think it's all bullshit. That I should go live in a cave so I can block out all the distraction," said Lenny pushing around his eggs with his fork.

"God, Lenny, you're fucking bipolar. First of all every cave is taken by those nuts that think Armageddon starts when the Dow Jones hits 20,000. And secondly, everything is bullshit. You know that. Everything is a huge fucking lie. We're just in on the joke, you and I. Since when has there been anything to believe in?"

"Zak, have you taken your Zoloft?" Cozy was concerned but not immune to this feeling.

"C'mon Coze, when was the last time you were excited about a politician? We know that they are all going to fuck us eventually. Democracy is a lie, manipulated by special interest groups and rich lobbyists. And what about the family? Another lie. All that bullshit about family values back in the Nineties. What crap! Yeah, I want to trust families that molest their kids and belong to a gang or the Klan. If blood is thicker than water then why are you more likely to be robbed, raped or murdered by a family member than a stranger?"

"Well if everything is bullshit, then why do you keep playing these love songs?" Aretha Franklin was singing, "Until You Come Back To Me" to the diners.

"God, love is the ultimate lie. I'm just trying to purge it out of my system. You know how people complain about violence in the media? They should be complaining about love in the media! How many people go see a movie and then commit a crime? Very few, my friends. Now how many people believe in the happily ever after of the love story? Millions! More people have been hurt by *Shakespeare in Love* than *Taxi Driver*. You see the boy get the girl and then ride off into the sunset and the assumption that it's just bliss from then on out. You don't see them a year later when he's an alcoholic and she's fucking her boss and they can't fuckin' stand each other. That's what happens with love. That's why I like *Romeo and Juliet* and *West Side Story*. Because they die. The only way that love lasts is if you die very quickly after you say, 'I love you.' I'm getting out of love."

"Isn't that a monologue from *Dawson's Creek*?" joked Cozy. "Was it you or Pacey that said 'romantic' is just another word for loser? Besides, what about that girl you saw tonight? I believe the word 'love' came out of your mouth."

"Lust, I meant lust."

"Dude, you've been burned, bad. Love will come your way again and you'll fall all over again." Lenny knew the drill.

"No way. Like the song says, love stinks. I'm going to embrace my cynical side and fend off any illusions to the greatest love of all. It's just a set up for pain. If you don't fall in love you never have to suffer. All those assholes getting divorced. More than half! That's a pretty good kill ratio. They should have just said, 'fuck you' instead of 'I love you.' Besides, it's not normal human behavior. Most cultures have arranged marriages that don't have anything to do with romantic love and they're just fine."

104

"Zak, love has always been around," said Cozy, the romantic/loser.

"Not true, chicky. It's all started in the middle-ages with the troubadours and the fable of Tristan and Isolde. This whole idea that you could love a person more than you could love God was just a gimmick. The original Latin, amor, is Roma spelled backwards. The inversion of agape. It was just a crazy gimmick that fuckin' Shakespeare turned into a 400 year fad."

Cozy was getting pissed at the wet blanket bit. "Well, you can intellectualize it all you want. Shakespeare was just writing about something that already existed. Don't project your bad luck onto the rest of us."

Another, more modern, song came on the jukebox. "Hey Telly, I played this song for you. It's called 'Planet Telex' by Radiohead. OK, Cozy, I'm going to say a really shitty thing right now. Do you really think you and Lenny are going to be so madly in love five years from now?"

Lenny grabbed his head and Telly just stared down at his syrupy plate. "Yes, Zak, I do. I think we will love each other twenty years from now." Cozy understood Zak's bleak outlook, but it was out of place.

"OK, but do you think you'll be happy?"

There was no response to Zak's question, just stares and silence. It was a pointless discussion. Everything is bullshit and love fades away. There was nowhere to go with this, until Telly began to cry. At first it was just a tear and then he began to sob.

Zak felt bad, even though he wasn't sure it was his fault. "Telly, man. Are you OK? I'm sorry about this argument. I'm just being an asshole."

"Telly, hon, are you alright? Are you homesick? What's wrong?" asked Cozy.

"This planet is so beautiful from a distance," he said, wiping his eyes.

"What?" Lenny thought he was going to start singing that Bette Midler song.

"The Planet Earth from way out there is beautiful and blue, but when you touch down things look different here."

"Uh oh." Zak sensed that the booze and drama and lack of sleep had sparked Telly's big alien story. He wasn't sure he was prepared to hear it in front of his friends at the Hot Cake Hideaway. Besides, he had enjoyed the fantasy that his roommate was an ET not an HC, head case. "Telly, you don't have to say any more. We know what you mean."

"Speak for yourself. I'd love to hear this." Lenny was rapt.

"You are my friends. You have shared much with me this week. I owe you the truth. I am not from Kosovo. I am from another world."

"France?"

"Quiet, Cozy!"

"I am from a planet called Elo. You don't know it because it is not in your sky."

Zak rubbed his eyes as he thought, "Oh shit." Cozy and Lenny looked at each other. "Telly, did someone give you some drugs tonight?"

"No, this song and your discussion about love made me want to tell you, even though you may not believe me. Elo is a very desperate world. It is not plagued with disease or war, but cynicism and emptiness. We reached a place several generations ago where we stopped believing. Our scientists disproved the gods and extended life indefinitely. All the mysteries of life were explained empirically. Emotions were replaced by medications. Trust gave way to doubt and then indifference. Our culture became skeptical and passive, apathetic and uncreative. Our philosophy was reduced to two words, why try. Soon the drugs could not ward off the waves of depression that began to drive us further away from our past. The birth rate dropped to far below replacement rates and suicide became the norm."

"I saw this film!"

"Shhh, Len!" Cozy was interested in the drama, even it was a psychotic fiction.

Telly continued as the tears dripped down his cheeks. "No one made any art. No one made any music. There were no political innovators or spiritual leaders."

"Why try?" said Zak, sounding like one of them.

"Yes, why try? Except for the fact that our narcissism meant the destruction of our entire race. A culture cannot survive a whirlpool that is sucking the whole world down to extinction. The value of life on Elo is next to nothing. The masses believe we might as well be extinct if there is no magic left to life. People are often murdered only because they looked at someone the wrong way. We in our last days."

Zak really wanted to believe this incredible story. "OK, Telly, let's just say, for the sake of this story, that everything you've told us is true, what are you doing here in Portland?"

"It was clear to some of us that something had to be done. You cannot continue to deconstruct your reality and hope to survive. Rituals were abandoned as futile, beauty was abandoned as bogus. There was nothing left. But we knew about Earth. We new about the culture of Earth that for thousands of years has leaked into space, despite ice ages and plagues, global wars and holocausts, a spirit of life."

"You mean from radio waves and TV and stuff like that?" asked Lenny.

"No, those things travel too slowly, but your energy, your life force spreads instantaneously. We knew that the culture of Earth faced many of the same philosophical battles that we fought and lost on Elo. And it's such a beautiful planet, floating softly through the rainbow of your galaxy. Environmental degradation has turned our world into a gray hell. Four of us were selected to come to Earth and learn how you have survived. What is it about the human spirit that survives when there is no real reason to survive? Eloians and Earthlings are not lower life forms, breeding out of instinct. There is some learned survival mechanism that we have forgotten. I saw a homeless man today covered in open sores laying on the sidewalk, half conscious. Why does he choose to continue this life?"

"Jeez, that's heavy. Where are the other three Eloians?" Zak was beginning to buy it.

Telly took several deep breaths before answering. "We traveled for many days to get here, but separately. As I got closer to Earth, I could begin to feel the feeling of hope as a real emotion, not an abstract concept. I assumed the others did as well. We were to meet, discuss our plans, and then begin our mission in separate cities, Portland, Paris, Pretoria and Pusan. We just liked the 'P' sound. And they were places known for their culture in less than ideal situations."

"I'll say!" interjected Lenny.

"There was to be a celebration once we arrived, but something went horribly wrong. Somehow, somehow I am the only one that arrived. The others did not survive the journey. One of the travelers was my mate, Bev."

Cozy was near tears listening to Telly tell his painful story. "Oh, Telly, I'm sorry. That's horrible. Did you love her?"

"I am not sure that I understand love. I had wanted to know what love is, with Bev."

"Zak, they got any Foreigner on that jukebox?"

"Lenny! Let him tell the story."

"We were sure that the Earth held the answer. From a distance it seems like such a perfect world. But the perfection disappears up close. I have walked the streets of this city for a week and seen much of our horrible past. I have seen scores of homeless children ignored by those with homes. I have seen beautiful public art covered with ugly graffiti. I have seen people with disease and poverty treated with indifference. I have seen people beaten for the color of their skin. You are infected with the same hopelessness. But then I also see beauty. People happily reading and going to art galleries and singing music. I can't reconcile these two realities. You have fun, despite yourselves."

"Well, when you figure that out, you can write a book and go on *Oprah!*"

"You three have shown me that the image of desperation on the surface is not the reality. Your excitement about things is a form of kinetic energy that we lack. Your love of rock 'n' roll is proof of some transcendental power. It makes you happy to be alive. I have never seen anything like it. When I watch you listen to music I think there is some strange magic there, like the people in that cathedral. I don't understand it, but it is real."

Zak liked this idea of rock 'n' roll saving the world. "There you go, Telex. All you need to do is ship a crate of Led Zeppelin records back home and your planet will be back to it's old self."

"I wish it was that simple. It is more than that. I felt as though I was beginning to understand the power of music as a lifeline but then you began to tell us how everything is bullshit. Religion, politics, family, love are bullshit. All of the songs I've heard this week are about things you consider bullshit. Therefore, music is bullshit. I am more confused than ever."

"Oh, Telly, we're just a moody bunch." Cozy had discussed this same topic in her music theory class in college. "We are perfectly happy to hold two completely contradictory ideas in our little heads. There's a thin line between love and hate. I love Lenny, but sometimes I hate him."

"Hey!" Lenny would have preferred another example.

Cozy continued. "Yeah, love can be bullshit, but love songs express the hope that love can not be bullshit, too. OK, maybe it is a lie, like Zak says, but believing in the lie is better than believing in that reality."

Zak was right there with Telly. "Yeah, it's called mythology. Little kids believe in Santa because if they don't they won't get any toys. It's a form of extortion. That's how religion works; Believe in the Church or fry in hell. It's a lie we willingly buy into because we're afraid of thinking for ourselves."

"What does that mean, thinking for ourselves?" asked Telly.

"It means that we stop just accepting everything that is spoon fed to us by those that have power. It's like that John Lennon song, 'God.' 'God is a concept by which we measure our pain.' I don't believe in all these concepts, I just believe in me."

"Yoko and you," added Lenny.

"And where does that leave you, only believing in yourself?" Telly wanted to know and so did Cozy.

"Fuck. I don't know. It just protects you from getting let down by the myth."

"Fear," said Cozy.

"No, it's not fear, it's fucking intelligence. And when did this discussion become about my issues. I thought we were talking about Telly's crazy science fiction tale."

"You do not have to believe me, Zak. But I do wish to believe you."

"Well, don't assume that I know anymore about the meaning of life than any other dumbass Earthling. We're a race of fucking idiots."

"Thanks, pal!" smirked Lenny.

The four felt drained by the weight of the conversation. It was after 4 a.m. and another night on Earth had been survived. Zak, Lenny, and Cozy liked Telly too much to leave him at the Hot Cake Hideaway. They'd entertain his fantasy for now. On the ride home Telly assured Lenny that he had no interest in anal probes. They wearily dragged themselves out of the cab and back into The Eldorado and the world of dreams. Cozy hugged Telly and whispered, "Maybe she's OK."

Needless to say, no one made it up for cartoons on Saturday morning. When Telly awoke, he wasn't quite sure which world he was in.

He couldn't see anything or feel his arms. He was floating disembodied through space. He had passed out with his head inside his pillowcase and spent the night in an odd contortion causing both of his arms to fall asleep. He stood up, pillow over his head and arms limp and stumbled around his bedroom, crashing into things and then finally finding his way into the living room.

Zak was sitting on the floor, watching TV, when Telly stomped in, like a pillowheaded version of Frankenstein. "Christ," Zak muttered. If Telly was trying to prove his alien status, he was going to have to think of something a little less goofy.

Telly fell over the back of the futon and the pillowcase flew off his head, revealing the bright Earth world to him. "Oh, good morning, Zak." He tried to push his hair back but his arms were still not working properly and he only managed to slap himself in the face.

With a laugh, Zak went back to his TV. He was watching a video of a scene from a film over and over again. The scene was about two minutes long and then he'd push the remote to replay it. It was of a young man on a scooter riding along a white cliff. He screams, "Me!" and then the scooter crashes on to the rocks below.

Feeling the feeling coming back to his appendages, Telly asked, "What is this you are studying?"

"It's *Quadrophenia*. It's a movie from 1979 based on that Who album I told you about. This is the end. That's Jimmy the Mod. He's stolen Sting's Vespa and he's all suicidal on the white cliffs of Dover."

"Why are you watching it over and over again?"

"Well, it's sort of one of the great rock mysteries. This kid, Jimmy, is totally fucked up. Schizophrenic. Just a mess. The whole movie is his spiral downward. So here at the end, this amazing song about wanting love and not getting it is playing. 'Love Reigh O'er Me.' And Jimmy is riding toward the cliff, obviously about to off himself. But then you just see the scooter go over the edge. So the question is, did he kill himself? Is

111

the scooter symbolic of his youth? Did he jump off at the last minute and grow up?"

"And what is the answer?"

"That's what I'm trying to figure out. Apparently, Pete Townshend refuses to tell. It's just suddenly become very important for me to know." Zak was staring intently at the image of the scooter bouncing on the rocks in slow motion. He had felt very close to the edge of the cliff the last two weeks. He wondered if he was going to go over.

"Zak, how often do you think of suicide?" In the context, it was not an odd question.

"Oh, every hour or so, not counting sleepy time." Not really every hour, but it felt like it.

"Like Jimmy, you wander the fields of your sorrow, obsessed with death, yet you continue to live. Why?"

"Jesus. 'Fields of sorrow'? Have you been listening to my Metallica records again, Telly? Look, I don't have the answer you're looking for. I have no answer. I just think there's hope. Hope that Petra will come home. Hope that that girl last night will turn out to be my real 'real love.' Hope that the Prize Patrol will knock on my door with an oversized check. Any straw I can grasp will keep me around."

"Interesting."

"Well, I have to tell you my friend, that tale you told last night was pretty fucking depressing. Elo sounds a little too familiar, you know? Like Earth circa 2095. That story alone was enough to push me over the edge."

"I am sorry. That was not my intention. We believe that your world will be much stronger in 2095 than ours is now. That's why I was sent here. To understand hope." Telly looked out the window at the rain as Zak let the video play out. It had rained continually since he had arrived in Portland and he wondered if the other destinations were as bleak. "Zak, do you know what the other cities are like? Pretoria, Paris and Pusan?"

"Two things. It probably doesn't rain as much and people aren't as fat."

"What do you mean by that?

"Americans are just fat as hell. We eat too much and we eat a lot of crap. I've been to Europe and whenever you see a fat person, it turns out they're American. Most of the world eats small amounts, but since we think we rule the world, we have to devour as much as possible. No one produces more garbage than us. We probably shit more than the whole rest of the world combined. In Pusan, they probably just have rice and a little fish. In Paris you have a baguette and some wine. Who knows what they eat in Pretoria, zebras probably. But we go to the McDonald's and shove double crap burgers down our throats like tomorrow was the apocalypse."

"And this is a bad thing?"

"Hell yeah. Gluttony is a sin, not because fat people are gross, but because it's selfish and wasteful. I'm sure you know about the huge ozone holes. They were caused by fast food containers. Look at all the trash in the street. It's Big Gulp cups and candy wrappers."

"So there are no fast foods in these other places."

"Oh, there sure are. We have infected the world with our bad habits. There's a Burger King right on the Champs Elyse in Paris. But those French fuckers deserve it. They all deserve it for wanting to be like this shitty country. They think that by eating KFC they'll have democracy, but it's the exact opposite."

Zak continued his tirade about the inverse relationship between democracy and fast food franchises but Telly lost him. He was staring out the window at the rain when he saw the homeless girl and her baby, sitting at the bus stop across the street. "There she is. Zak, excuse me. I must go talk to someone." With the full use of his arms, Telly went back into his room to put on his boots.

Saturdays could be perfect. Perfectly beautiful or perfectly miserable. If the sky was warm blue and the birds were singing, things could seem like heaven. But this was another cold, wet perfectly miserable Saturday. The freezing drizzle prevented lovers from promenading down Burnside on their way to brunch, happy to share the wealth. Those that were on the street darted and hunched and looked at their feet, not at the pathetic homeless mother on the dirty worn-out sidewalk.

And Saturdays gave way to Sundays. Sometimes on Sundays when it was cold Lucinda went to the Presbyterian church downtown. The people were generally friendly and the sermon was never overly preachy and the furnace heat came right up through the floor vents under the pews. She loved to look at how people dressed, much cooler than back in conservative Seaside. She felt connected to the images of Christ suffering and thought he looked hot up on the cross, like one of the guys at the fetish club. But sometimes she fell asleep or got a rude stare and when Polly cried she had to leave. If this cold kept up and she and her baby were sneezing up a storm she'd probably not go to the church tomorrow. She'd probably be right here.

That bus-stop had become her spot, right between the gritty life of downtown and the clean living of Northwest Portland. And there was the free entertainment of dirty old men sneaking out of the porno mega-store. Sometimes she pretended she lived in an apartment of The Eldorado and this was her bus-stop. This was her bus-stop, even if she rarely ever got on the bus. Her fantasies about living in Northwest filled up the minutes until something happened.

She had no plan for this day. She was tired of feeling sick at the shelter so she thought she'd feel sick at the bus-stop and watch traffic. She and Polly needed some fresh air, she reasoned. When she saw Telly crossing the street toward her she recognized him as the guy from the

114

window. He must be catching a bus for brunch, she thought. His hair was a spiky burgundy-black and he had a green scarf tucked into his white leather jacket and skin-tight red and black striped trousers. He looked like he had just gotten off the tour bus.

"Hello," he said.

"You just missed the bus," Lucinda said, with a bit of a sneer, to give herself some upper handedness.

"I don't need a bus, thank you. I need to speak to you."

"Excuse me?" She admitted to herself that this guy was cute in a rock-scene sort of way, but with the mucus pouring out of her sinuses she wasn't in any state to be picked up.

"Yes, I live across the street and I have seen you here many times. I would like to talk to you. May I buy you lunch?"

"About what? And yes," she said, wiping away some snot from under Polly's nose.

"I am studying life in Portland and I was hoping to interview you."

"What are you, a fucking writer?"

"My name is Telly. We can go right up the street."

"OK, but stay way from me. We have a cold. I'm Lucinda and this is Polly."

"Like the Nirvana song?"

"Dude, you think I'm going to name my child after a song about rape? It's my grandmother's name." The gutter-punks always sang the Nirvana song, while passing Polly around and Lucinda thought it was seriously fucked up.

Lucinda grabbed her bag and the two headed west up the street. She hoped he would take her to one of the swank cafes on NW 23rd but he led her into the McDonald's, which was fine.

"I thought you hipsters hated this fuckin' place!" she snarled.

"But I know you like it. I mean, I thought you might like McDonald's."

115

"Why, because I'm a dirt bag?" She resented all the baggage that went along with being a street kid. She could enjoy some of that haute Northwest cuisine, if she knew what the fuck it was.

"No, it is very popular with young people." She hadn't known this guy for 15 minutes and he was already patronizing her. She couldn't wait to see what bullshit he was going to ask.

Zak had moved from his *Quadrophenia* obsession project to another when Lenny walked into the apartment, looking no worse for wear.

"Good morning, professor. What are you doing?" he asked, plopping down on the futon.

"Chance Meeting."

"What?"

"Chance Meeting. I'm writing a Chance Meeting!" said Zak, impatiently.

"No fucking way! For who? That girl from last night?"

The chance meetings were the most pathetic part of the personal ads, the proverbial message in a bottle. Lonely hearts ran them after meeting the boy/girl of their dreams and being too stupid to ask for a phone number. They were always sad to read because the odds of the target reading the ad were about a billion to one. But still, they were incredibly romantic, fueled by hope. "The Refectory, 2/10. You: blonde, very petite. Me: short guy seated by the bar, we talked about your Geo Metro. I'm losing sleep, call me."

"Look, how else am I going to meet her? If I get this in Wednesday's paper we could be hooked up by the weekend."

"Zak, if she even sees it she's just gonna think you're the biggest dork in the Rose City." It was obvious that Zak was obsessing on the mosh girl to push Petra out of his head. "Fuck, OK, what is this magical message going to say? It better be fucking good or I'm going to make you start over."

Zak slid the short blurb out of his laser printer and brought it over to Lenny who studied it very closely.

> Asian rock goddess moshing at Gurd's Palais gig. I was there too but mute due to the voodoo spell you put on me. I'm not insane just crazy. We have to meet for sonic living and public indecency.

"You get 25 free words. That's 38. Too goofy?" Zak knew this was evidence that he was rapidly falling out of even the broadest definition of "cool."

Lenny just shook his head. "Brother, you are fucked up twelve ways to Sunday."

"Where's Cozy? I should get her opinion on it."

"She's resting. She's worried that she strained her voice last night. But I know her and know exactly what she'd say."

"What?"

"Brother, you are fucked up twelve ways to Sunday." But this time he said it with loving puppy eyes.

Zak was in no mood to have any Doubting Thomases stand in his way. "Just wait, you'll see. When me and this chick link up, it's going to be a new chapter in the Book of Zak."

"Keep telling yourself that. Speaking of nut cases, where's your roomie? Is he taking a walk on the moon?"

"I don't know. He tore out of here a little while ago. He's on a mission, you know."

"Alright, Zak, you gotta give me the skinny on this alien bit. I mean, do you think he's dangerous?"

"He already told you he wasn't going to give you an anal probe!"

"No, I mean he could be psychotic. Like being an alien is his excuse for killing people. He's not bound by Earth laws."

"He's harmless. I just think he's a stranger in a strange land. He's from some fucked up central European country. He was probably ethnically cleansed and totally traumatized and this little alien act is his way of dealing with it." Zak didn't want to let on that he wished Telly was from somewhere besides this God forsaken planet.

"Maybe he is an alien. He sure looks like one. Man, this is just like *My Favorite Martian*! The TV show, not that shitty movie."

"Yeah, it's nothing but wacky hijinks around here." Zak was staring at a VH-1 special on the TV. It was a behind the scenes rockumentary on Menudo.

Lenny slowly pointed his index finger and brought it slowly toward Zak's face. In a slow creaky voice he said, "Elliot."

"God, you're a fucking comedian," huffed Zak.

"Hey, man, here's a question for you. If I watch ET and get all hot for Gurty, knowing that she turned into Drew Barrymore, does that make me a pedophile?" These were the issues that weighed on Lenny's brain.

"I feel like it's raining all over the world," sniffled Lucinda as she opened up the Big Mac that Zak had bought for her. "Careful with the coffee. It's way hot."

"Thank you. How is Polly?" Polly was quietly laying on the orange seat.

"She's cool. They gave her some baby medicine at where I stay and it makes her sleep, which is a fucking blessing. So where are you from?"

Telly's eyes cast down. He didn't want to unload the lengthy explanation that he had with his friends the night before. "I'm from a very far away place that is ugly and violent and I don't really like to talk about it."

118

"Kosovo?" she asked with a mouth full of meat.

"What made you say that?" Telly was struck by the coincidence.

"I don't know. You just have that look. The Kosovo-look."

"That's interesting, I would like to ask you why you sit at the bus stop almost every day? Why don't you go to your home."

"Well, at the moment that is my home. I like that corner. You know what they say?"

Telly looked confused. He wasn't sure what they said.

"Location, location, location, dummy! That corner has been good to me. Besides, some lady sings opera in her apartment. I don't really like that shit, but it's fun to listen to her when her window is open."

"Yes, that is Cozy Daniels. She is very talented."

"No way, dude you know her? That bitch can sing! Anyway I'm on the street. I have a baby. Big fuckin' deal. There's a million of us. What don't you get?"

"You are young. Could you live with your parents?"

"No way," she said with disgust.

"Why not?"

"Because they fuckin' suck! They live in a shitty town and they'd drive me out of my fuckin' skull. I know what you're gonna say, 'But isn't that better than living on the street?' Hell, no. I mean it really sucks, so Polly and I just roam, waiting for something good to happen."

"And you don't worry about your little girl?"

"Naw, she's fine. My friends love her. The people at the shelter love her. Even the pigs love her. She's golden." But Lucinda did worry about Polly all the time. She worried that some other homeless girl would steal her and claim that she was her baby. She worried that she would get hurt in a drunken fight. She worried the State would take her away and put her with a family of child molesters. She worried that Polly would get sick and she wouldn't know what to do or be able to buy the right medicine.

119

Worrying about Polly took up a big chunk of Lucinda's expanse of mental time.

"When you say that you are waiting for something good to happen, what do you mean?" This was the crux of Telly's query.

"Well, you know, anything! You know, I could get a really cool job, or win a big scratch-off. Maybe the government could have a new program for single moms. Or maybe some bohunk dude would fall madly in love with me and shower me with love and cash." Lucinda stopped herself. Was this very un-bohunk guy her ticket? He was tight and he had a great apartment and cool clothes. Most importantly he listened to her. No one ever listened to her. Even with her gross cold, he listened very intently.

"Do you ever imagine that none of these things will happen?" OK, he was an asshole.

"You mean do I ever wonder if I'll be a fuckin' homeless bum all my life?" She didn't give him time to answer. "Yeah, sometimes, but it's not going to happen," she said angrily. "There's no way I'm going to end up like those toothless street hags with the big saggy tits, selling blow jobs for a hit of crank. No fuckin' way. I got a cousin down in California. I've been thinking about going down there and getting out of this rain. But I'd kill myself if I had to spend too much time out here. I'd put Polly in a basket in the river and they could think she was fuckin' Moses. But I think things are gonna get better soon. They already are. I'm in a great job training program now." She was kicked out of a great job training program.

"Interesting."

"You look like Dr. Spock when you say that." It's possible that Dr. Spock and Mr. Spock said, "interesting" the same way. Who knows? "Yeah, big things are gonna happen."

Lucinda stared out of the McDonald's window at the street. A poor elderly woman walked very slowly in the rain down the sidewalk. She was a local bag lady on the hunt for bottles and cans. What perfect timing. "The good part of the all the rain here is the rainbows we get afterwards," she said misty-eyed. But you need the healing sun to break through the wall of clouds for that to happen. Telly knew that through her veil of tears she saw no rainbows.

Lenny had gone back to his apartment to tend to Cozy, bringing her lemon tea and kisses. Zak was left with his dumb Chance Meeting ad on the futon. It wasn't working. He was thinking about Petra. It took every ounce of strength not to call. He didn't want to give in to his anger and become a beggar. The Zoloft was like a little devil on his shoulder, urging him, "Do it, do it!" The stuff might have kept him alive but it also made him more impulsive. Since the doc upped the dose he noticed an increase in his assholeness, snapping and putting people down without thinking. She was turning him into a psychotic mess. Between the anti-depressants, the sleeping pills, and the juice it was only a matter of time before he went on his killing spree.

Right, he thought, gotta get out of here. The auto-pilot in Zak's brain sent him to the record store whenever there was more than fifteen minutes of cranial inactivity. Saturdays were always good because you could have first dibs on all the stuff that came in on the weekend, when most people sold their records and CDs to pay for their drug habits. He grabbed his jacket and headed off for the utopia that was All Day Music.

Out on the street the rain stung the back of his neck. He wanted to shrug his shoulders and watch his feet on the wet sidewalk but he didn't want to miss Petra if she was driving by. Lisa didn't live far from his hip corner and she could be circling the block, deciding if she wanted to come home or not. He had to keep an eagle-eye out. Portland was a small town, he didn't want to be caught off guard bumping into her. He clenched his cold wet jaw and made eye contact with motorists.

Once inside the busy store he had the frightening thought of finding both Petra and mosh girl there. Which one would he approach? If he chose Petra, there would be an ugly scene in his sacred record shop. If he chose mosh girl, it would be seen as an obvious ploy to anger Pet. Besides, mosh girl might think he was a Grade A creep.

All this fear and trepidation caused Zak to completely lose his mental list of needed recordings. Well, anytime he walked into a record store he forgot what he wanted. The overwhelming possibilities jarred his mind.

As usual, the browse reflex kicked in. With no female trouble yet, he dove into the "A's" in rock-soul. His stomach tensed a bit. He hadn't gotten to Aerosmith before he realized nearly all the CDs were leaning forward. Some butt-wipe had flipped through the discs without pushing them back into the proper "display" mode. This was one of Zak's most irrational peeves. It looked messy, he thought. He used to gripe, "There are just a lot of selfish a-holes in the world who think everything exists for their benefit. These are the dicks that throw their trash out of the car window. It's just too much effort for them to push the CDs back. It is the spoiled brat generation." And on and on.

Somehow he suffered through it. He tried to find some angry punk rock to keep his rage in the forefront. He couldn't buy any country music as much as he wanted to sink into some Patty Loveless or Clint Black, that was *her* music. At the moment he wanted to free himself. He needed something to stop him from driving by Lisa's apartment building, The Greenwood, hoping to catch Petra. Hopefully not catch her with another guy. So far so good.

He thought about what Cozy had said at the Hot Cake Hideaway. How we humans are damn happy to hold two contradictory thoughts in our smallish brains. How could he love Petra so totally and get all weak-kneed around Cozy? And how could he have his sights set on the Asian rock goddess? Maybe he didn't really love Petra. Maybe it was just a convenient emotion that was like a kickball kicked up on the roof of the school. As soon as you get a new kickball, you forget about the one you lost. No, he knew he loved her, down to the marrow he loved Pet. It's the love thing that's the problem. If ever there was a situation meant to bring hell to Earth it was love.

He had a handful of obnoxious Saturday afternoon CDs, Anthrax, Bad Religion, Corrosion of Conformity, the ABC's of loud, fast rules. The Zen of flipping through the plastic cases had him in a comfortable place. Clack, clack, clack. Then he got to Elvis Costello, specifically the *Painted From Memory* album that he recorded with Burt Bacharach in 1998. Zak had to stop and hold the CD. "God Give Me Strength" was perhaps the most gut wrenching pop song of the 1990s. A tear welled up in Zak's eye. Fuck! How could even the thought of a song have such power over him? What was this strange magic, as Telly had called it?

Zak had done his damnedest to not think about his matrimonial situation. He'd tried booze, yoga, masturbation, Internet chat, sitcoms, sleep, obsessive fantasies about big boobed Asians. But, like Burt Bacharach said, there was always something there to remind him. Maybe he should just give in. It had been two weeks. Maybe it was time to be a man and get her back. He put the loud fast rules CDs back and took Elvis to the cash register. It was time to make a mix-tape.

Against better predictions, Telly and Lucinda were having a wonderful time. She was enjoying trying to shock him with things she'd done to survive on the street. He was taken with her spirit of independence. Things could be so much easier for her. Polly was awake and bouncing up and down against the table with only the occasional sneeze. She had her mother's smile, which crept out of both at odd moments. Telly even held the baby, wondering about the hope that she represented.

123

"Dude, you do not look like a baby person!" laughed Lucinda. "You don't have to hold her so tight. She won't break."

"She is a beautiful child, Lucinda."

Lucinda liked the way he said her name. Very European, she thought. He seemed more like a therapist than a writer. He asked the same questions she asked herself on a daily basis. Sure, he dressed like a freak, but watching him awkwardly holding her baby, he seemed very sweet. "So were you in the war in Kosovo?"

"I'm not from Kosovo, actually. But I am from a similar place. Lucinda, may I ask you something? Do you like your friends?"

"They're a bunch of shitheads! Oh, I guess they're alright. They just need to get a fucking life. Getting drunk all the time gets boring. Some of them live on the streets because they think it's fun. I figure they must have been really bored at home because few things are more boring that being homeless." Then Lucinda noticed the back of Telly's right hand. "What is that on your hand? Joel's bitch? What the hell?"

"It is a sexist rock 'n' roll thing. The doorman at the Palais stamped this on my hand last night to prove I had the right to enter."

"Joel?"

"I assume so, yes."

"I've never actually been in that place. Who was playing?"

"Cozy Daniels and Gurd."

"I've never heard of them. But that place is always packed on a Friday night. I can't wait to turn 21. It sucks being under-age. You can't do anything." Of course the reason Lucinda couldn't do anything is that she had no money and a baby. Polly had taken to Telly for some reason, further messing up his hair with her little hands. The sight caused Lucinda to burst out laughing, which made Telly smile. "You have a nice smile, Telly."

"Thank you. I think you should meet my friends. They would like you and Polly. Maybe we could meet for dinner this week."

"I'll have to check my day-runner and see if I have time in my schedule. Are they also foreigners?" Lucinda felt her foot wedging in the door.

"No, they are Portlanders. Two are musicians and one is..." What was Zak? "One is a graduate student."

"That opera lady? Yeah, I'm really sure we'll have a lot to talk about."

"Cozy is very cool. Here is my telephone number." Telly pulled a pen out of his jacket and wrote "TELLY PHONE" on a McDonald's napkin and handed it to Lucinda. "Call me if you would like to join us."

Lucinda guessed this is how it happened when you were an adult, but in a wine bar, not a McDonalds. A lot of guys hit on her but 99% of them had crabs and smelt like beer soaked barroom floors. She looked at the napkin and smiled at the joke. "Can I have my baby back now?"

An hour later Telly finally made his way back to the apartment. He found Zak on his own mission. The living room floor was scattered with albums and CDs. Zak was making a tape to win Petra back. To prove that true love would survive. Zak was drunk with the idea that the right song would strike a primal chord in her soul. That just the right phrase and melody would convince her not to turn her back on love. He was almost done filling a 90 minute cassette with messages of love that she would not be able to resist.

Side One
"God Give Me Strength" by Elvis Costello
"Waiting For Charlie" by Etta James
"When Something Is Wrong With My Baby" by Sam and Dave
"Come On Home" by Tammy Wynette
"Better Be Home Soon" by Crowded House
"I Say A Little Prayer" by Dionne Warwick

125

"The Difficult Kind" by Sheryl Crow

"All Apologies" by Nirvana

"Singing In My Sleep" by Semisonic

"You Can't Lose A Broken Heart" by Billie Holiday

""Oh My Love" by John Lennon

"Nothing Takes The Place Of You" by Kelly Hogan

Side Two

"Something" by Frank Sinatra

"We're Stronger Than That" by Amy Rigby

"I Will Buy You A New Life" by Everclear

"Who Would've Thought?" by Rancid

"I Know We Could Be So Happy" by Jeff Buckley

"Learning How To Love You" by George Harrison

"Until You Come Back To Me" by Aretha Franklin

"Train In Vain" by The Clash

"Ex-Factor" by Lauryn Hill

"Anyone Who Had A Heart" by Dionne Warwick

"This Guy's In Love With You" by Herb Alpert

"Don't Be Sad" by Dwight Yoakum

He resisted the temptation to load the tape with just Burt Bacharach songs. Suddenly the cheese of Bacharach had become transcendental in it's complete truth. He also stayed away from the obvious Beatles, Carpenters or Captain & Tennille tunes. He wanted to create the aural equivalent of a neutron bomb. It would reduce Pet to dust but leave the buildings standing. Every song had to have the right balance of detachment and desperation. The Temptations' song, "Ain't Too Proud To Beg," was out, but the smarmy Stones version was a consideration.

"Hello Zak. What are you doing?" Telly was a bit more animated than when he left.

"Nothing."

"You look like you have a project." Very observant.

"OK. I'm on a fucking mission. I'm making the perfect mix tape. I'm recording some songs for my 'true love.' I told you about the compilation tape. This is for my estranged un-wife." Indeed the compilation tape had been a key factor in Zak's wooing of Petra, so he had every reason to believe it would work now. "Where have you been?"

"I have a new friend. Her name is Lucinda and her baby is Polly," said Telly sitting on the floor with Zak, picking up a George Harrison album.

"You've already fathered a child, how nice. I can't even talk to my supposed fiancé." His sarcasm sailed over Telly.

"It is not my child, Zak. Lucinda is the girl who spends so much time at the bus stop across the street."

"That little street urchin? Why would you hang out with her? She's what we call 'the dregs of society.' Are you trying to learn about the white trash of Planet Earth?"

"She is a very decent person, Zak!" Telly was a bit pissed at Zak's classicism. "The troubles of her life outweigh yours greatly. She is an interesting case study. I want to know why someone like her, a homeless woman with a baby, continues to have hope."

"Oh yeah, that's a great line. You're interested in her life energy so you can save your world. Fuck, I should try that one. Did you tell her you're from Planet Claire?" Zak was trying to write the songs down on the tape sleeve. He had cut a picture of John & Yoko out from an Apple ad for the cover, hoping Pet would make the connection.

"No, but I imagine I will."

"That's nice. Chicks love insane men. No, that's wrong. Men love insane chicks. Either way you should be very happy together." The Dwight

127

Yoakum song was playing out and Zak hit the pause button. "So Telly, about all that last night. Do you really want us to believe all that shit. About Elo and all that? I mean, who are you?

Telly looked straight into Zak's eyes. "Believe what you choose. I told you the truth. Who are you and who am I?"

"Fuck, dude. First of all, I really don't know why everyone doesn't just kill themselves. Secondly, can you replicate some fine cognac? I'm thirsty." Telly squinted his eyes in response. "Ah, shit"

"What's wrong, Zak?"

"I forgot Al Green! I need some Al Green on this tape. Obviously, 'Let's Stay Together' but maybe 'Call Me' or 'Here I Am.' Bye-bye Dwight." Zak rewound the tape to gap between Herb Alpert and Dwight Yoakum and then stopped. He was sitting cross-legged on the floor with his face in his hands, rocking back and forth. "I hate her. I hate her. I hate her," he muttered.

"Zak?"

Zak pushed his wet hands back through his hair. He was sick and tired of crying. He wanted to be a badass who couldn't give a fuck about women, any woman. Love 'em and leave 'em. But he couldn't. His soul was fused to Petra and he couldn't pry it loose. He resented her for doing this to him. For letting him fall in love with her. For saying yes to his proposal. For sharing a dream of a life together. For leaving with only a fucking note.

Telly knew this was the moment where it was normal to offer words of encouragement, but he didn't really understand the concept. How do you give someone hope without reason? All he could muster was a hand on Zak's back and these strangely comforting words, "She must be an evil woman."

Before things could get any more awkward, Lenny walked in. He never knocked because no one ever knocked on soap operas or on *Friends*. So he just burst into Zak's like Kramer. "Am I too late for the pity party?" he cracked, sensing something unnecessarily heavy going down. "Christ, you two are like a commercial for Prozac!"

"Right, Lenny," agreed Zak. "What's up?"

"Andy and I are going to this party tonight in Southeast and I wanted to see if you two losers wanted to come."

"How is Cozy?" asked Telly, who hadn't seen her since her kind hug the night before.

"She's just taking it easy tonight. Unlike the rest of us nocturnal emissions, she doesn't feel the need to come out just because it happens to be Saturday night."

"A party, huh? Yeah, Tel, let's go. No more moping today, right?" said Zak.

Telly had moved back to the window seat and thought to ask Lenny if he could invite Lucinda and Polly, but they were not at the bus stop. Maybe they had found something to do. "Perhaps," he responded.

About two hours later Zak and Telly climbed into Zak's car to go to the party. It was a black 2000 VW Bug. Ever since he could remember Zak had dreamed about having a year 2000 car, so for Christmas 1999 he walked into the bank and got a loan and joined the mass of Americans who owe more than they own. Yeah, everyone had a VW Beetle but his dad had driven him around in his own '74 Bug when Zak was a kid. It was a logical choice. Besides, in all the past images of the 21st Century, there was only ever one type of car. You didn't see a thousand different types of vehicles when the Lost Saucer landed on another world. Just one white bubble-mobile that Jim Nabors and Ruth Buzzi would inevitably crash while trying to escape robots. There was something comforting in the modernist conformity of so many Bugs on the street.

The party was in a big Victorian house in an ex-hippie neighborhood that had gentrified all the stoners out. The rain had stopped and there were hipsters in the yard, on the porch and dancing to

The Red Hot Chili Peppers inside, in the living room. The two made their way up the crowded stairs, Zak already wishing he'd stayed at home.

"C'mon, Tel. The only way we're going to survive this is with some vodka." Zak felt like Captain Kirk leading Mr. Spock into a strange version of Earth culture that he would never be able to explain to a Vulcan. Telly quietly looked at all the people and noticed how much they looked like the people at The Palais and deduced that these probably were the people at The Palais.

On the porch they saw Lenny who came out of the front door to greet them. "Hi guys! There's booze inside." He was holding bottle of micro-brew. "What's up, Telly? How's life on Earth?"

"It appears to continue, in spite of itself, Lenny," said Telly, thinking that he was achieving sarcasm.

"Hey Zak, guess who was just here?" grinned Lenny.

"Christ. Who was she with?"

"No, not Petra, you're little heart-throb punk rock girl. That Asian chick you've been pining over. She just left. I almost talked to her but Andy gave me the dope. Her name is Lynne and she's from Astoria. She left to head back. Apparently there's some big beach clean-up tomorrow."

"Fuck!" Zak was mad at himself for spending time putting his mix tape together and not leaving earlier. "She's an eco-babe. God, I need a drink. Telly, I'll bring you something." And Zak plowed through the entry to the house in search of liquor.

"That boy is one big drama," said Lenny, taking a gulp of his beer.

"He is confused about the meaning of love," replied Telly, as if this were a rare condition.

"Yeah. That's a big club." Lenny wanted to change the subject. He was having his own doubts about the strength of love but wasn't prepared to articulate it on a loud party porch. "I'm so glad the rain stopped. You can actually see the sky tonight."

130

They both looked up at a growing fissure between the moonlit clouds. It was the first time Telly had seen the night sky since arriving in Portland. "When all the stars above point their fingers down on me I feel closer to home."

"Yeah, that was some story you told us last night. Cozy and I have been talking about it all day. What about your friends? Could they be here somewhere?"

"I don't think so. We feel life energy the way you hear sound and I cannot feel them." Telly's eyes fell from the heavens to the dirty porch floor.

"Dude, that sucks. What were their names?" Lenny wanted to be sympathetic even if it was the story of a delusional schizophrenic.

"Bev, Fennel and Ryan."

Lenny didn't think that Ryan sounded like a very good alien name. Not as good as Gort or Calgon. "I'm sure they're OK. They probably just went to the wrong planet by accident."

Zak was returning with bald-headed Andy in tow. He handed a glass filled with ice, vodka and orange juice to Telly and kept one for himself. Andy recognized Telly as the drunk drum roadie from the night before. "Hey Dude. Glad to see you survived!" Telly nodded, thinking that that was a more suitable greeting on Elo.

"Man, Len, Andy's telling me that you guys are gonna change the name of the band. What's up with that?"

"I don't know. 'Gurd' just sounds so 1990's. Like we're a noise band. It's limiting. We were thinking about Fun Explosive! but then Andy pointed out that people might not take us serious as artists."

"Yeah, serious artists. We're serious," chimed in Andy.

"And what is the name of your band now?" asked Telly, anxiously.

"Sort Of," answered Lenny.

"Sort of what?" asked Zak.

"Yes."

"Who?"

"The band."

"Who?"

"Sort Of."

"Who?" Zak was more confused, but Andy picked up on the classic rock Abbott and Costello.

"Guess who?" he shouted out.

"Sort Of," answered Telly, correctly.

"The band?" said Zak with a smile.

"Yes!" said Lenny.

"Third Base!" shouted out Andy and Zak in unison.

"Oh, they broke up ages ago," laughed Lenny. "See? Isn't it a fun name? It's the ultimate qualifier in our non-committal society. Right up there with 'like' and 'you know?' I can see the reviews now, 'Sort Of sort of kicks ass!'"

"Yeah. Actually it's brilliant. It will look great on T-shirts," proclaimed Zak.

The four stood on the porch and drank their drinks, talking about all the fun things they could do with a band name like Sort Of. They didn't talk about Petra or Cozy or Bevan or Andy's ambivalent sexual stance. Zak did manage to find out that Lynne was at the party alone, which could've meant anything. The vodka loosened him up enough to entertain the thought of driving to the coast in the morning. It was just a thought, but if he was going to do it he was going to have to get a good night's sleep. After the drinks were done he told Telly that he could probably get a ride with Lenny but he was heading home to crash but Telly wanted to stick with his friend.

On the way home Zak switched the radio to the oldies station. The opening strains of "Brother Louie" by The Stories slid out of the system. "Oh, man you have to hear this song!" said Zak pulling over the car in front of a large apartment building.

132

Telly listened to the song about inter-racial love but also recognized the building they were parked in front of. Zak had taken an indirect route to the party so he could slowly drive past it. He understood. "Is this where Petra is staying?"

"Dude, are you mind-melding me?" Zak knew that Telly wasn't getting any of these *Star Trek* references. "OK, yeah. That's where Lisa lives. The famous Greenwood. There on the first floor. I'm not stalking. I just want to drop off this tape." But Zak didn't get out of the car. He just sat listening to The Stories and wondered if he'd see his love coming out of the building on the arm of another man. "Brother Louie" faded into "Rock On" by David Essex. The deep bass line made his stomach quease even more.

"Zak?" Zak was just staring at the front door. "Zak, would you like me to drop off the tape?" Telly was coming to the rescue as the sick feeling in Zak's stomach was becoming an incapacitating ulcer.

"Yeah, OK. Thanks man. Just put it in the mail box for apartment 10." He didn't want to get caught dropping the neutron bomb. Let Telly be the bombardier, which he did quite calmly.

Hopping back in the car, Telly gave Zak a nod just as the song growled, "James Dean." Zak knew he had a good ally in the space boy and sped off.

Back at the apartment, Zak threw his jacket on the floor and Telly sat down at the window seat. "Man, I'm going to bed. I've got to figure out what to do with my life tomorrow. Are you going to stay up?" which is what Telly did.

Telly noticed that the space between the clouds was getting greater, revealing a few stars that hadn't been obscured by the remaining city lights. He followed them down to a fight on the street between a drunken couple. "My orders are to sit here and watch the world go by," he said with his chin on his bent knees.

133

"Right. I forgot. OK, dude. Good night." And he disappeared into his bedroom to dream of Petra or Lynne or Cozy or Ashley Judd.

Lenny's question stuck in Telly's head as he stared out of the window. How is life on Earth? How is life on Earth and what is it worth?

Chapter Five:
So Fine

What was the connection between artists and tragic death? Why did a great painter or writer or musician have to burn like a supernova and then explode in some act of self-destruction and leave a huge hole where their art should be? It's better to burn out than to fade away, Neil Young sang and Kurt Cobain put in his suicide note. The belief that creativity is a young person's job is a potent myth. Compare the product of the 25 year-old Paul McCartney or David Bowie to the 45 year-old Paul McCartney or David Bowie. We'll never have to experience a 45 year old Cobain or John Belushi or Janis Joplin. They will forever be young and vibrant.

But the Tin Machine isn't an inevitability. Amid the young Turks that became middle-aged and irrelevant, like Dan Akroyd or Billy Idol, there were those who hung on and refused to diminish; Bruce Springsteen, Tom Wolfe, Joni Mitchell, Iggy Pop... They didn't kill themselves with drugs, booze or guns. They broke the cardinal rule of bohemianism, they lived. Zak often thought Kurt Cobain could have been more like a Bob Dylan than a John Lennon, loyally putting out an album every year or so until old age. Sure, some would suck, but most would be brilliant as he reinvented himself a few times a decade. Like Dylan, he would have shed that "voice of a generation" burden by the staunch independence of his own art. Every April 8, on the anniversary of Kurt's big cop-out, he'd try to imagine the Nirvana records or solo records that would have been released since 1994.

It was the suicidal streak that was the most troublesome. Ever since Henri de Murger penned *Scenes in the Life of the Bohemian* in 1848 there on the Left Bank, artists from Hemingway to Hutchinson have been taking themselves off of this Earth. Something about having to suffer for your art. The vague notion that you have no right of self expression until you've woken up in the gutter, looking up at the stars, and been a breath away from eternal damnation. That was the ultimate poetic license. How many Plaths and Baudelaires and Morrisons and Hendrix's had to join that stupid club? Who has more claim to the mantle of "artist", Brian Jones or Keith Richards? (OK, maybe Keith isn't the best example.) But the essence of the romantic myth is that the true artist just wasn't made for this world. That Kurt was just too sensitive to survive in this harsh reality. The price you pay for opening yourself up as a vessel for the world's pain is self-obliteration. One day you are translating the language of the heart into art for every inarticulate clod in the world, and the next you are floating face down in a swimming pool. Next tortured poet, please.

Zak was laying in bed thinking about Kurt Cobain, Artist of the Decade. He had forgotten everything about how stupid that club was and how angry he was that he wasn't getting any more new Nirvana records, ever. He was thinking about how Kurt got out before it was too late, before he became a cheap caricature of himself. There will never be a vote on the "young Kurt" versus the "fat Kurt" postage stamp. The James Dean, Marilyn Monroe and John Coltrane stamps all had the stock youthful iconographic portraits. We didn't have to see Kurt ravaged by heroin or divorce or bad artistic decisions. No one will chuckle about his misjudged 1998 rock opera about slam dancers who turn into giant cheese sandwiches. He will always be pure, teen spirit. Maybe William Styron would have benefited from that impulse. Suicide was a sure route into the canon. You could do it quickly with a blast or slowly with booze or madness. Where would Jack Kerouac or Karen Carpenter be on the hip-meter if they hadn't purposely turned their internal organs inside out?

He had visited Jim Morrison's grave in Paris, there with Edith Piaf and Oscar Wilde, and seen how death makes a man into a god. You make a dramatic exit and let everyone else clean up the mess and design the stamp. He didn't want to think of his slow grind into ruin, as the man who Petra left. Suicide served multiple functions. Like Kurt, it froze his memory in youth and vitality. It relieved him of the duty of pulling the shards of his existence together into a reasonable facsimile of a meaningful life. And it allowed him to punish Petra for leaving, forever. The last reason was the weakest because obviously she didn't care enough about him to stick around, so she probably wouldn't care that much if they dragged his body out of the river. Oh sure, there might be some tears shed and she would feel a bit bad, but ultimately she would move on and fall in love with some guy who was more "stable." If he was going to be suicidal, he had to do it to save himself from life on Earth, not to punish her. He had to save himself and Kurt.

The Sunday sun was creeping into his bedroom as he laid there arguing the merits of suicide in his head when he remembered that he was going to try getting a life instead. "Oh shit!" he thought as he remembered his renewed optimism from yesterday.

He had a line on the mosh pit girl! The best strategy was to mount a battle on two fronts. The compilation tape was the first sortie in his campaign to win Petra back. And then there was Lynne. He had a name and a hometown. She was probably already out on the coast picking up oil globules. She could be his hedge against failure with Petra. Maybe she would turn out to be even more amazing than his redneck Czech babe.

He had meant to get an early start but it was already almost noon. Zak leapt out of bed in an old Drivin' N' Cryin' t-shirt and boxers and went to rouse Telly. A trip to the coast would be good for him. There's more to life than the city. The road out of town was always filled with promise. But the apartment was empty. Telly was somewhere on his mission, looking for the secret to life.

Grabbing a half empty bottle of cranberry juice from the fridge, Zak went to sit on the window seat. The sun was shining and it was blinding the mole people of Portland, Zak included. A beautiful sunny Sunday. He immediately felt guilty for wasting so much of the rare day laying in bed thinking about the joys of death. Taking another sip he noticed a note left for him on the window seat. "Zak, I have gone to church. Back soon. Telly."

Sitting toward the back of the Presbyterian Church were Telly, Lucinda and a sweetly cooing Polly. Telly had garnered a few stares with his striped trousers and leather jacket, but this was a downtown church and fairly hip to the colorful street life that found sanctuary behind the big wooden doors. In the next to last pew they settled in and Telly observed. Religion just seemed so alien to him, he had to figure it out. The speaker addressed the congregation in more informal manner than in the Catholic church. He didn't mention anything about Mary or Blessed Virgins. He told a story about the son god and a prostitute, which made some of the teenagers giggle.

Telly was not confused about the metaphorical value of the story. All members of a society are valued, especially the hookers. It was a sentiment that he wished existed on Elo, and on Earth. But he was confused about this person, Jesus, the father/son lord. If this God was powerful, why could he produce only one son? And what about God's daughter? And since none of the Presbyterians actually knew Jesus, who probably didn't speak English or have an assistant, how do they know that he said any of these wise things? They surely could not claim that he died for their sins if he was executed unwillingly 2000 years ago. It didn't make much sense, but he liked the music.

After the services and songs were over, Lucinda gave Polly a bounce and turned to Telly who was looking around the church. "So, what did you think?"

Telly had no immediate impression. "It was interesting. There is much less ritual than at the Catholic cathedral. I noticed many people who were asleep. I did enjoy the singing."

"Yeah, it's so funny how everyone sings even when they don't know the tune. It's like drunken karaoke. Like I said, I like to come here just to come. All that stuff about Jesus is bullshit. I mean, who is helping all the suffering now? I just like to come and Polly likes it too. Right, pretty Polly?" Polly was blowing a spit bubble.

Beneath the tone Telly detected a feeling in Lucina that she wanted to believe. Her life had been a series of disappointments and her disbelief was a mechanism of self-preservation. As they walked out of the church the sun was blasting through the clouds, causing many of the parishioners to comment on the glory of God.

"Jesus fucking Christ, it's bright out," said Lucinda, shielding her eyes. Polly was squinting too and buried her face into her mother's neck.

"It is the first time I have seen your star from Portland," said Telly, staring straight at the sun, then putting on his black sunglasses.

"Star? You mean the sun? We don't see it very often around here. Whenever we get sun breaks everyone goes completely blind. I could make a ton today selling shades."

"Every sun is a star. This one is beautiful and warm. Your city seems very different when the clouds do not obscure its rays."

She loved the way Telly talked, with his European accent. Like a poet. "Well, winter should be over soon. I'm sure your friends have told you how our summer here is three months long and winter is nine. It sucks out loud. I gotta move to California." Lucinda was letting some of the churchgoers "oo" over Polly who had adjusted to the bright light with a big smile. "OK, Tell, what are you doing for the rest of the day?" She had no plans as usual and was hoping that her new friend would help her use up some of the day's hours and maybe sponsor a brunch.

"I don't make plans. I prefer to allow things to happen. Would you like to come back to my apartment? Perhaps my roommate is there. He might have plans."

"OK, but no funny stuff. This baby can be used as a deadly weapon."

Telly nodded in amusement and the three headed towards the Northwest corner of town, looking like just another dysfunctional hipster family.

Lynyrd Skynyrd was blasting out of the stereo. Zak was climbing out of the shower and singing loudly, "Ooh that smell! Can't ya smell that smell?" Now that he was out of Alabama it was safe to love Skynyrd. Back home he would have been lumped in with the Klansman and dirt farmers if he had given into his butt-rock tendencies. But far away in Oregon, the Southern boogie-woogie was like a loving postcard from home. "Freebird" or the right Allman Brothers song could set his punk heart to whimsy. In fact he'd drive his Northwestern friends crazy by playing "Freebird" on the jukebox back to back with The Verve's "Bitter Sweet Symphony" and going on and on about how they're really the same song. "It's the same chorus, man, 'I can't change.' It's a universal theme," he'd profess.

And then someone, usually Lenny, would say, "Yeah, but the Verve can't change their mode. Skynyrd can't change their minds!" It was one of those inside jokes that only got more stupid with time.

Zak let out a big "Hell yeah!" just as Telly came in to the apartment with Lucinda and Polly in tow. Lucinda laughed at the site of another skinny rock boy, hair mussed in just a towel. "Telly!" he yelled out, startled. He had been caught half-naked and mid-Skynyrd.

"Excuse us, Zak. This is my friend Lucinda and her daughter Polly."

140

Zak smiled silently for a moment. So this is her? She was in traditional street-kid wear; army pants and a blue hooded sweatshirt over a black t-shirt, clunky boots. She had some punk rock patches on her clothes of bands that broke up before she was born; Black Flag, Dead Kennedys, the Circle Jerks. Her big round eyes just smiled at Zak and so did Polly's. Zak saw the appeal of Telly's new friend. Under the two-tone hair, she was a little cutie.

"Oh, sorry," Zak finally said. "Welcome to our pad. Telly, be a good host and get her a drink and let me get dressed." And he darted into his bedroom.

"Would you like something to drink, Lucinda?"

"Yeah. You got any beer?"

When Telly returned with two bottles of beer Lucinda was sitting on the futon and Polly's head was under her black t-shirt, nursing. Telly paused in confusion.

"I hope you don't mind. She was getting fussy. She's gotta drink too, you know." She lifted up her shirt to show Telly Polly latched to the breast like a vacuum. Polly grabbed the beer and took a swig just as Zak walked back out, dressed and caught the scene.

If Telly was concerned, Zak was intent. All his research on fetal alcohol syndrome tried to shield mothers from all of the blame of the booze-brain damage connection and here was the quintessential bad mom. She might as well have been pouring the micro-brew straight into the kid's mouth. Why do all the wrong people breed? Why isn't there some kind of test? He and Petra should be having a beautiful Polly, not this clueless gutter-punk. "Hey Lucinda, if you want, we can get you a non-alcoholic beer," he said.

"Why?" This was nothing new to her. The beer-milk seemed to help her baby keep calm. "Oh, that. Don't worry about Polly. She's a tough kid."

What could he do? The two roommates looked at each other with that "whatever" look. Both had bigger things on their minds. Zak plopped down on a stuffed chair and began to put his sneakers on. "So how was church? You're becoming a regular zealot, Tel."

"Very interesting. I got the distinct impression that most of the people didn't want to be there."

"Well, shit! The sun is out. They'd probably all rather be on their jet boats on the river."

"I really don't get it," chimed in Lucinda. "If I had to work 9 to 5 every day. I wouldn't be dragging my ass out of bed on the day of rest to go to church." She looked quite comfortable with her suckling child and beer. Zak was waiting for the inevitable cigarette to pop out.

"So why did you go?" he asked.

"Well, I sleep in all the other days, so it's like, OK for me to get up on Sundays, if I'm not way hung over. It's not that bad." Lucinda was looking around the apartment at all the "stuff." Stuff that she could never have if she continued to live in shelters and street corners. She was thinking about how much she could sell the stack of CDs on the floor for at All Day Music. Several meals.

"Zak, do you have plans today?" Telly figured he must since he was putting on sneakers instead of lounging in his socks, as usual.

"Oh, dude. Yeah! Do you wanna go on a road trip with me? I'm headed out to the coast to meet, um, to hook up with Lynne. You gotta come, the sea air will do you good. It's a perfect day for getting out of town."

"Who's Lynne?" asked Lucinda. She had a brief thought that these two might be gay and what was the point of getting stuck on Telly if he wasn't about the ladies.

"Lynne is Zak's chance meeting," said Telly, trying to be clever.

"Dude, did she run an ad?" asked Lucinda, excitedly sitting up, briefly shaking Polly loose from the nipple. She loved reading Chance Meetings in the weekly, confident that some totally together richy would have spotted her in a coffee shop and fallen.

142

"No, she's just a girl I like. She's out in Astoria today and I thought it would be fun to drive out to the beach." At the thought of the Oregon coast, Lucinda sank back into the futon.

"Maybe, Lucinda and Polly could come along with us." Telly knew that the pair were lacking much adventure in their monotonous existence. But Lucinda nervously responded by biting her nails. Zak, as well, wasn't too keen on loading the trip down with a stinky street kid and her drunk baby. The Bug wasn't that big.

He sensed that there was some issue here that he didn't have time to wade into. "Look, you guys can talk about it. I need to run upstairs and see Cozy. We were gonna go book shopping today so I need to let her know I'm bailing. Back in a few." And Zak leapt up, shoes tied, and headed out the door, leaving Telly, Lucinda and the baby alone in the sunny apartment.

Lenny and Cozy lived up on the fourth floor. The jaunt from 110 to 401 usually took seconds but when Zak hit the stairs everything seemed to slow down. Some weird conversion of thoughts. Star-lost Telly and his homeless girl, Cozy and Lenny rapt in the blind love of young souls, this complete mystery in Astoria that was likely a dead end of hope and, of course, sweet Petra. He crashed on to the steps like he was falling down a well. The gravity of the world pulled at his gut and then his arms, legs and head. Not another step up.

"Petra, where are you?" he suddenly thought. Why couldn't he get her out of his head? Maybe she was listening to the tape that he and Telly delivered last night. But why hadn't she called? Why hadn't she called her lover? Before this, whenever the two were apart for more than a day there would be long phone calls and reunion loving. They hated being apart. In every picture of them together she was staring up at him with adoration in her eyes. What the hell happened?

His head hurt again. His eyes hurt from scanning the streets and the bars for her. His ears hurt from listening for the phone to ring. His heart hurt from missing her. She was gone. Why didn't anyone kick his ass and force him to just fucking accept it?

"Oh well, " he sighed and started back up the staircase, realizing that nothing was going to happen camped out there.

It was curious to Telly that Lucinda finished her beer at the exact same time that Polly let go of her nipple. "Polly looks content," he said quietly.

"Well, wouldn't you?" Lucinda said, winking in mock sexuality. "So Tel, I'm not gonna go to Astoria with you guys. I've got some shit I have to take care of, so you guys have fun."

He knew she didn't have any shit that needed taken care of. "Is it because of your parents? Are you afraid you will see them?" He struck a nerve.

"Dude! They live in Seaside not Astoria." But she knew that they often went into Astoria for Sunday meals. Lucinda's mom would take her antique shopping there on weekends and they'd watch the ships entering the Columbia River from the Pacific. Her dad loved to tell her how it took Lewis & Clark weeks to get from Astoria to the sea and it only took him ten minutes. The odds were that she would run into them.

"Burp!" That was Polly's addition to the discussion.

"I just don't like going out there. It's probably all rainy and cold. I don't want the baby to get sick again. Besides Astoria smells like rotten fish. It's all fishermen and tourists and shit out there. God, I hate it."

"There will come a time when you want your mother and father to meet Polly."

"Well it ain't fuckin' now. Maybe when I get some money. If they find out I'm still on the street, they'll give me so much shit. I know my Dad. He's all family values and shit. He'd probably try to take Polly away. When I get an apartment, they can come and visit me."

Telly wasn't going to force her, especially since Zak didn't seem very enthusiastic about the idea. "OK, Lucinda. Can you tell me about Astoria?"

"Beer-battered fish. It's all about beer-battered fish."

Zak finally made it to the door of apartment 401, feeling a bit more winded than normal, and knocked. There was a minute of silence and then Cozy's voice. "Hold, on I'm scrolling!"

After another minute Cozy opened the door dressed in a tank top under a flannel shirt and a pair of Lenny's jeans. "Why is it whenever I copy something that's in Times font, it becomes New York when I paste it? It drives me fuckin' crazy." Cozy was cutting some reviews of Verdi operas off of websites and pasting them into a Word file to study later.

"It's a fuckin" conspiracy, I tell ya."

"Come in, boy. Did you just get up?"

Cozy was dazzling in the few rays of sunlight that slid in between the blinds. Her gentleness was like a blanket around Zak's out-of-hand bullshit. "Oh, Coze, am I a high maintenance friend?"

"Oh God. What happened?"

"Nothing. I was all up and at'em and then I just crashed on your steps on the way up, like I weighed a million tons. Like I can't fuckin' go on."

"It's called 'depression' you butt-head. You're totally DSM-IV. But don't worry, Nurse Cossette is here. Lenny told me he got you a line on your mosh girl. Why aren't you on the beach makin' sweet love to her right now?"

"Fuck. I was going to get up early and head out but I spent about four hours laying in bed thinking about Kurt Cobain."

"Well, he ain't making love to no hot Asian chicks on the beach unless it's in the sweet hereafter."

"Oh, c'mon, Coze. No mystery girl is going to help me deal with this fucked up situation with Petra. I just can't function until she explains to me what the fuck happened. It's like everything was dreamland and then, poof! I know that she's over at Lisa's. How fucking cruel to let me just die here."

"She knows you're OK, Zak."

"How? Have you been talking to her?"

Cozy looked away knowing that a friend's secret was about to be revealed.

"Yeah, we've had coffee a few times. She wanted to know how you're holding up."

"Fuck! I'm going crazy, that's how. I'm spending all day laying in bed thinking that Kurt had the right idea. I'm two shakes away from shoving a syringe full of black tar in my arm."

"God, you're over dramatic. The closest you'll ever get to doing heroin is listening to The Velvet Underground drunk on Jagermeister. You're doing fine, Zak. You're on the Zoloft. You're back at the university. You've got a crush on some scene chick."

"Oh, great. Did you tell her about that? It's all tears of a clown, my friend. Tears of a fuckin' clown. So what's the skinny? Why did she do this? It's gotta be some big misunderstanding."

"Dude, she's going to have to tell you that." Cozy was torn between her loyalty to the two. She knew that behind Zak's daily hysterics, he was holding it together and in time it would all make sense. "She just wants you to take care of yourself."

"What about her? I'm sure she's just fine, probably having a grand old time in the Zak-free zone. It's so obviously some guy. Goddamn, this sucks. Who is it Coze? Anyone I know?" He was clenching his jaw again and running his fingers back through his hair.

"Zak!" Cozy wasn't going to say much more. She put her arm around him. "She's not OK. Don't think she's enjoying this. Her heart is breaking too."

"What the fuck? Then why is she doing this?" It made absolutely no sense to him. "If she needs me, I should just go over there!"

"No, don't. Just give her some time, OK?"

Zak just shook his head in disbelief, eyes red from holding back tears. "Fuck!"

"Alright, I want you to do something for me. I want you to take that freaky roommate of yours and get out of this town. The sun is seriously out, brother! Go to the beach. Have an adventure! Climb on the rocks and eat some beer-battered fish. It will be good for both of you. Who knows what will happen."

"Yeah, we'll probably get hit by a logging truck. What are y'all doing? Do you wanna come with?" He was trying to pull himself out of his state.

"Sorry, Charlie. I really need to get ready for this audition and Len's rehearsing for the debut of Sort Of. They're going to try for a weekend gig at RJ's. I think I might go to the park. Do you think people will think I'm strange if I'm singing Verdi?"

"This is Portland, you'll start a sensation. Fuck, I was hoping you guys would come so I didn't have to take Telly's new friend." Zak looked out the window to see if there was an army of street kids headed for his flat.

"The homeless girl? Shit, what's she like?" Cozy had to know what kind of woman caught the stone-faced alien boy's fancy.

"She's a mess. And her kid's gonna grow up to be an ax-murderer."

It was after one when Zak and Telly finally loaded their gear into the Bug and hit the road out of town. Lucinda was off taking care of her "shit," Cozy was singing in the sun and Lenny was sort of rocking out.

147

Once on Highway 30, Zak popped in one of his custom-made road tapes. The opening chords of "Helen Wheels" were cranked to full volume, the windows were rolled down and Zak let out a big "wahoo!" into the warm air and stepped on the gas. Of course, Telly did the same. "Wahoo!"

The tape was loaded songs about the journey being greater than the destination and it gave both a sense of the thrill of the unknown. The Doobie Brothers, The Donnas, Steppenwolf, Wilco and the rest would push them all the way along the Columbia River to the Pacific. If only Lewis and Clark had Sonys in their canoes.

As the city faded into the valley, Telly's eyes grew wide at the change of scenery. Fir covered mountains to the left and the broad river and its barges to the right. The black Beetle sped between the trees and tugboats and the promise of the West lay straight ahead. With the wind at their backs they followed the afternoon sun into the unknown.

"Two drifters sailing wide and high!" shouted out Zak, the wind tousling his hair. "This is your quintessential American experience, my friend. This fine nation of ours was built on thousands of road trips!"

"The Oregon Trail!" said Telly wanting to show that he got the point.

"Dude, studying your history, I see!" Zak turned down the Wings tune. "So now that we're out of it, what do you think of Portland? Are you glad you came?"

"It is a powerful place. The people are quite well-mannered. The bus patrons thank the driver when they get off the bus, the citizens are friendly and many people have invited me to their home."

"I told you, Telly, that's a gay bar. I don't know why you keep going back there."

"I like the music. Friendliness is something we've lost on Elo. It is viewed as superficial and pointless. We are more likely to just state what we want without the pleasantries. I never realized how powerful a simple smile or a 'thank you' could be. It is very intoxicating."

148

"It's because everyone is so caffeinated. They aren't being friendly, they're fucking wired. I get a little tired of people talking to me all the time. It can be a bit much when the check-out guy at Fred Meyer wants to have a convo in the express lane, but you're right. The opposite would be even worse. You know what they say."

"Mean people suck?"

"Mean people suck."

Brunchless and with no real shit to take care of, Lucinda hit the street. The young couples with their baby strollers just pissed her off. Polly was getting heavier every day. Too heavy to carry. Soon she would be able to walk, but not at a pace to roam the streets with her wayward mom. The bright sunlight was making her hips and breasts sweat. She decided to head for the shade of the park blocks where the gang was likely to be.

She glanced over her shoulder at Telly's building, The Eldorado, and wondered what would become of this relationship. Her eyes scanned it from bottom to top, and rested on an open window with a pretty girl in it. It was the opera lady. What was her name? Cozy! Maybe she would be Lucinda's new girlfriend. Opera reminded her of her dad, but this chick might be alright.

Cozy was letting the sun stroke her face. Her eyes were closed and she looked like she was stretching her neck. She was a beautiful goddess to dirty Lucinda on the street. So fine in her top-floor perch. And then she began to sing. Not words, just sounds, sounds that bounced down between the traffic on Burnside, muting carburetors and exhaust pipes. Even Polly looked up to hear where the pretty music was coming from.

The singing stopped and Cozy shrugged her bare shoulders, smiled and opened her eyes. Down on the street she saw a tattered girl with a baby staring up. That must be Telly's little friend, she thought and waved.

Caught staring into someone's window, Lucinda nervously spun around and walked away, feeling foolish.

Ten streets later she was at the South Park Blocks and sure enough a handful of gutter kids were taking refuge from the sun under the trees, smoking and skateboarding. "Lucy!" they cried out.

"Lucy, you have to see this!" shouted out Dean. When Lucinda got to the group she noticed a small pink dog barely standing in the grass.

"What the fuck?" Lucinda wanted to laugh but the poor thing looked like it was on the verge of having a heart attack.

"Oh, dude, get this. Roxy found her. Someone dyed her pink and shot her full of smack!"

"Jesus Christ, Dean! You fucking asshole!" It had all the signs of a Dean prank.

"It wasn't me. I fuckin' swear!"

The dog was now foaming at the mouth causing the group to move back a few steps. "Gross!" shouted out Clarissa and Virginia in unison, causing Lucinda to sneer.

"Here, hold Polly," said Lucinda handing her over to Dean. She slowly approached the dog and bent down to pet her head. "That's it. Good girl. It's gonna be alright, puppy. What did these fuckers do to you? Just keep breathing. That's it." She was as gentle as she was with her pet baby.

"Careful!" yelled out Virginia. "She's probably got AIDS now!"

"And you don't?" snapped back Lucinda.

The pink dog laid down on the grass and nodded off, the foam serving as make-shift pillow. Lucinda grabbed Polly away from Dean and snarled, "You guys are so fucking juvenile. That dog is probably going to fucking die now."

"It's a fucking dog, man. No one cares about it," defended Dean.

"And you're just a fucking punk and no cares about you." Probably not the best thing to say as these street kids were always a gram away from suicide. But the point was made.

"We'll take care of her, Luce." Dean looked over at two of the boys standing on their skateboards. "Hey, why don't guys carry her over to the animal hospital on 10th. Just leave her on the front steps." Happy to have a mission, the two lifted up the dog and wedged her into a backpack and rolled off down the hill like a rescue squad from hell.

With the pink puppy gone, the group broke up and Dean put his arm around Lucinda and walked with her through the trees. "Where you been, Luce? You never hang out with me anymore." His wallet chain was banging against Lucinda's thigh and she pulled away.

"I've been with my new boyfriend."

"Yeah, the guy from Everclear? That was a good one."

"No, this guy's fuckin' real. He's from Kosovo and cool as shit. We went to church this morning." Polly was struggling to get free so Lucinda sat down on the grass to let her play.

"Sure. So where is he now?" Lucinda was Dean's dream punker. She was sassy and sure. He wasn't going to let her just get whisked away by some outsider. "Where is this foreigner? I'll fuckin' jack him."

"Don't be such a fuckin' Nazi. He'd beat you down in a second." That might have been true. While Telly was skinny as a rail, Dean was usually drunk or high. "He's going out to the coast with his roommate. They're doing some beach clean-up out in Astoria."

"Sounds like a fuckin' hippie. What does he do?"

She stopped, realizing that she didn't really know. Maybe he was a visiting student or an artist. "Um, he's a writer."

Dean and Lucinda didn't talk any more about Telly. They talked about their little scene and how hard it was for any of the kids to find space in the shelters and how great it was that the sun was out. Watching Polly transfixed on a squirrel scaling a tree made them laugh. The gang

151

was headed off toward Riverfront Park to watch the pleasure boats and with a little prodding from Dean, Lucinda and her child tagged along.

"What's it like?"

"What's what like?"

"The vast expanse of outer space."

"Vast."

"Oh, come on Tell. Just for the sake of discussion, let's say you are my favorite Martian. Tell me about space." The two were trying to keep up the pace by stopping at a Quickie Mart in St. Helens for snacks instead of a proper sit-down lunch. Zak had lemon ice-tea Snapple and a bag of Cooler Ranch Dorittos and Telly had two Dove Bars. High on sugar, they kept westward.

"OK, Zak, I will make you a bargain. I will tell you about space if you tell me why you love Petra." Telly's concerned eyes were hidden behind his dark sunglasses.

"Right on, that's fair. I'm sure you'll be able to glean some insight into the human condition out of that mess. Well? Beam me up, Snotty."

Wiping the Dove Bar off of his face with the sleeve of his leather jacket, Telly looked out the car window at a huge cargo ship coming toward them on the Columbia. It was proceeding against the great current, throwing waves of resistance up into the air. "See that ship?" and Zak nodded. "See the turbulence that it is causing in the water? That is what space is like. It is a not a silent smooth vacuum as many Earth people believe, where one just drifts. It is an ocean of massive storms and waves. The pull of all objects interacts with multiple levels of energy from billions of sources."

"Billions and billions? It sounds violent," said Zak, taking it seriously.

"It is sublime. The way you can watch a lightning storm in awe, we look at space. When you look at space you focus on the points of light, we watch the blackness."

"So do you fly around in it all Silver Surfer and shit? I mean if you wanted to go to Venus tomorrow could you?" Zak wanted to see the flying saucer.

"Our travel is similar to surfing, but more like a flame following a trail of gasoline. We follow trails of energy to the source. The life source. There are no ships."

Damn, not very Star Wars, Zak thought, but just as well. The last thing Zak wanted was to end up in some star cruiser with that fucking Jar Jar Binx. "So how did you get here and how do you get home?"

With a distant gaze toward the sun Telly replied, "I was sent here and when my mission is complete they will deliver me home."

"How convenient," said Zak in his best church lady voice. "C'mon, you've gotta have some special fucking powers. Levitation? Heat vision? Can you make the end of your finger light up?"

"Zak, you live with me, you would know if I could levitate."

"Not if you put a Vulcan mind meld on me!"

Telly shook his head and sighed. "I am here in human form. I have the powers of a human. I have told you about space, now you must tell me about your feelings for Petra."

"OK, give me a minute." Zak turned up the stereo. It was the Modern Lovers singing, "Roadrunner."

"Roadrunner, roadrunner. Drivin' a hundred miles an hour..."

The song played out before Zak said anything.

"Fuck, I can come up with a hundred reasons I love her without trying. The thing that sticks in my head is the way she listens to music. She could be listening to Sinatra, The Beatles, L7 or Trisha fuckin' Yearwood and pull the essence of the feeling out of it no matter how uncool it might be. It was like we both speak this mysterious language

153

when it came to music. Watching her listen to a Bad Company song is better than sex."

"Again, music is the connector."

"Yeah, well it doesn't hurt that she's so fine. I could never get tired of looking at her, even if she was 70. I was definitely marrying up. She is way out of my league in the looks department. Maybe she figured that out. And that body, God. I drove her crazy because I couldn't keep my hands off of her. It was like a giant magnet pulling me in."

"But there are many beautiful women in the world, my friend."

"None like that. None that ever told they loved me and meant it. It's more than her looks anyway. It's her spirit. We just automatically had fun whenever we were together. It was like striking matches. I guess she just burned out before me. At least it happened before the wedding."

Telly reached over to turn down the music a notch. "Are you positive there will not be a wedding?"

"Shit. I don't know. It doesn't seem like it at the moment. But maybe after some time. Maybe she'll figure it out. Maybe..."

"Maybe the tape will work?"

"Yeah."

What was the folly of chasing after the girl from the Gurd show when all he wanted to do was get Petra back? What must Telly think? Or did he understand the need for silly diversions for the sake of sanity. It was today's life-line to bide time until the world made sense again. He was crazy, he knew. But the sun was out, the music was on and anything could happen.

Further down Highway 30, after a lecture from Zak on why *Star Trek Voyager* was better than *Star Trek Deep Space Nine* (*Voyager's* endless journey and Six of Nine), something strange happened. The VW had been following the road, which alternately brushed against the river and then climbed into the edge of the Siskiyou Mountains. Heading back toward the river Telly suddenly grabbed his head in pain.

"Dude, what is it?" asked Zak.

Telly's cool demeanor dropped as he winced. "Ugh!" The sunglasses fell off of his face as he grabbed his head and Zak, worried, began to pull over.

"No, Zak! Keep driving! Please get past this point. Get past this radiation!"

"Huh?" But then Zak looked to the North and saw that they were about to pass the abandoned Trojan Nuclear Plant. Zak's first thought was, wow, he really is an alien! His second thought was, he could have seen that on the map and worked up this bit. Either way he felt the need to comment, "Tel, they shut down that plant ages ago. They got rid of the dead reactor in '99. There's no radiation there."

Regaining a bit of composure but still tight jawed, Telly replied, "Believe me, there is still radiation there."

"Well, isn't there nothing but radiation in space, cosmic rays and all that?"

"Yes, I just was not expecting this much along this highway."

They drove a bit farther, reaching Ranier. Emerging out of the trees into the riverside town allowed both to get a simultaneous look at the Washington side of the Columbia. Longview, Washington was the home of a huge timber processing plant. The massive facility dumped plumes of white smoke out of its dozens of smokestacks. The rare blue sky was obliterated by the pollution.

"Fuck."

"Yes, it is not good. Can you smell the sulfur?" Telly rolled up his window. "I know this is a common thing on earth. It is more common on Elo. The long-term costs of such activities have been ignored in favor of the short-term profits. Many of our people are very sick because of the

155

impurities in our air and water. People die slowly, but business is business."

"It's all about the Benjamins. The rich get richer and all the poor people have to breathe this shit to make an honest living. It's bullshit." Zak was going into his worker's vanguard mode.

"But you have a democratic process to change this. We lost that will generations ago. People just stopped voting. We let the industrialists have power. You have something to protect you from this." Telly was trying his best to offer this thing called hope.

"It's too late for us my friend. The corporations run the world and the only thing they let us vote on is whether we want to eat at KFC or Taco Bell, which, of course, are owned by the same huge company." They continued on toward Astoria, each wondering which one was more cynical about the world.

The rich were having their day in the sun on the Willamette River, far from their industrial barges. The yachts sailed under the drawbridges as jet skis bounced around in their wake. Whenever Lucinda sat by the river she imagined Polly's dad on a tugboat floating up the Willamette to meet his daughter. But there was nothing but pleasure boats out today and she doubted she would see Frank, or whatever his name was, on one of those.

The gang was sitting on benches in the Waterfront Park, sneaking sips of beer out of brown bags. They looked decidedly out of place in the sunlight in their ragged black clothes, multi-colored hair and various chains. They shouted obscenities at the yachts and wrestled in the grass like the children that they were. The park was crowded with Portlandians suffering from cabin fever and desperate to soak up the sunshine. The gutter-punks were just part of the crowd and unsure of their momentary normalcy.

156

"I'm gonna a have a boat like that someday," said Dean, pointing to a white and blue cruiser with two bikini clad women on the bow. "A hundred-footer complete with the bitches." The other kids nodded in agreement. They were all convinced that they would be rich one day. They would become rock stars or movie stars or win the lotto. It was a fantasy that made another night under a bridge a bit more bearable.

Lucinda shared in the fantasy. "Like, if I had a boat like that, I'd sail right out of this town. I'd take it out on the ocean and go down to California." Polly was transfixed on all the brightly colored boats bobbing on the black water.

Dean had heard the California dreamin' before. "Luce, you ain't goin' to California. What would you do there that you wouldn't be doin' here, except for compete with Mexicans for the same scraps?"

"Dean, why don't you go hang out with your skinhead buddies? Anything can happen in California, that's why. There's more of everything."

"More Mexicans."

Lucinda remembered one of the reasons hanging out with this group got her down. Even though she was guilty of the racist scapegoating herself, it became increasingly obvious that some of the kids used bigotry to make themselves feel like they had a bit of power. It was silly because there were Hispanic homeless kids and black homeless kids and, especially, gay homeless kids. But every time someone used the word, "beaner" or "nigger" or "fag," they imagined themselves one step up on the ladder. It was bogus.

"I'm going to take Polly over to the Saturday Market. Are you guys going to be here for a while?" It was signal that she'd maxed out her "hanging with the gang" time and needed to break free for a bit.

"We'll be here just working on our tans and waiting for our ship to come in," cracked Dean with a wry smile.

Throwing Polly on her hip, Lucinda headed off through the crowd to the Saturday Market, where local artists sold their funky crap. Located under the west bank of the Burnside Bridge, it was a weekend mecca for suburbanites and spare-changers alike. Lots of candles and birdhouses and jars of marionberry jam. Along the way Lucinda saw the opera lady. Cozy was sitting on a park bench with a beautiful brunette, both were sipping coffees very seriously.

"He's really hurting, Petra."

"I know. But he's strong. He'll survive. He just likes things to be dramatic as possible." Petra's shoulder length brown hair blew around her beautiful face as she looked down at her latte. Her voice was soft with a strange mix of Eastern European and Southern accents. Even in rumpled Sunday afternoon casuals she was stunning. Beautiful and sad.

"You're going to have to talk to him soon. I'm worried he's going to drink himself to death." Cozy's allegiance was split right down the middle, but Zak seemed to have dangerous plunges downward into depression. He had been drinking a lot at home, which was a new thing. He seemed proud of his drunkenness, telling Cozy that Jim Beam was his new lover. Some of it was obviously done for effect. "Look at how much I've been hurt." That sort of thing. But Zak's self-medication unleashed some of darker parts of mind and the current obsession with suicide had Cozy on edge.

"He's young. His liver can take it." Petra seemed almost callous as she stared out at the boats.

"Petra! This is serious. He fucking kills himself and you're gonna wish you'd done something."

"That's what he wants us to think. It's part of his manipulation game. He's not going to kill himself. He's just being a baby, trying to be the tortured poet. Just keep him away from me for a few more days. I'm going to talk to him."

The two sat silently, watching the roller-bladers and the Sunday sunshine parade. Petra knew she was being harsh, but she felt like she had no other course. Finally, Cozy muttered, "poor Zak," and walked away. Petra sipped the last few sips of her latte and remained.

They weren't on Route 66, or the A-1 motorway, or the New Jersey turnpike, but they were living those roads musically. Telly often watched Zak listen to music, which made Zak uneasy at first. But watching Zak listening to road songs on the road made everything that much clearer. It was both an escape and a journey to a mythical destination. In their movement was the chaos of the heart, the "madness in the soul" that Springsteen was singing about. What was around the next corner? Would they make it to Astoria at all? Would they find Lynne or something much bigger? Would there be Dove Bars there?

Just past three they rolled into Astoria with it's Victorian houses and gaping bay that fed the Columbia into the Pacific. The quaint town was founded by a fur trader, John Astor, in 1811. At the time Astor was America's wealthiest man. Now his town was coastal getaway for young lovers and sea-food freaks. Instantly romantic in its beauty, it immediately set Zak's mind on Petra. Angry at the thought, he replaced it with an image of Lynne in a hillside bed and breakfast. They were having post-sex coffee on the porch.

"This is it!" shouted Zak, his face out the window trying to catch the sea air. "Welcome to Astoria."

"How will we find the big boobed Asian?" asked Telly as he spied the downtown pedestrians.

"Dude, you're gonna have to stop saying that. You're gonna get me seriously busted. Her name is 'Lynne,' OK?"

"Lynne, yes. Are we near the beach?" All Telly could see was the river and the Oregon and Washington banks, lined with fishing boats.

"It gets really confusing around here. Why don't we stop for lunch and see if anyone knows where the clean-up is. I don't want to spend all day roaming the coast like an idiot."

Highway 30 had slowed down as it became Main Street, Astoria. Zak pulled the VW off the road at a cafe called Andrew & Steven's that advertised "fresh chowder" in flashing neon letters. The trip had barely been two hours but Zak and Telly looked like they had just driven across the Nevada desert, as they stretched their limbs in the parking lot. The windows had been rolled down the whole way, except for the stinky parts. With their hair tousled, dark sunglasses and thrift-store finery, they were probably mistaken for a low-rent rock band when they walked into the small town cafe.

"Smell that goddamn fish!" proclaimed Zak as he threw open the swinging door.

"Beer battered, I believe," finished Telly. His timing was beginning to fit in with Zak's sarcastic sense of humor. All that observing.

They sat in the bar of the restaurant where a Trailblazers game was on the TV and a couple of drunks shouted for more Portland baskets. Zak enjoyed playing Telly's role of the stranger and left his sunglasses on when he ordered for both. Two plates of beer-battered halibut, chips and two Hefeweizens. Telly kept his shades on too and the kind waitress rolled her eyes when she turned away.

"Tel, my man, we are out of town and about to see the big wide ocean and the beautiful women it attracts. Love on the rocks, ain't no surprise."

"Your oceans are still so blue and full. Their beauty reaches deep into space."

The comment made Zak think of Apollo 8. It was Christmas of 1968 when three men sailed around the dark side of the moon and saw the first "earthrise." In a world torn up with violent revolution, the televised images of the pale blue ball, devoid of geographic borders, gave

160

humanity a powerful moment of hope. When Zak was a kid, he was sure he would be living deep in space by the beginning of the twenty first century. Portland, Oregon was a long way from Moon Base Alpha.

As Zak dreamed of space life and Telly studied the basketball game on the bar TV, the waitress brought out two heaping, steaming plates of fish and chips.

"Christ!" exclaimed Zak. "You could feed the Blazers with all this food!"

"You're a big boy," she said.

"Why thank you, ma'am. Hey, can I ask you a question? Do you know anything about a beach clean-up today?"

"Oh, yeah. They're out at Fort Stevens. They've been out there all day. There's a big party so they can trash the beach after they've cleaned it up," the waitress said with a crack.

"Right on." So maybe they weren't too late to find the mystery girl. Maybe they wouldn't even have to pick up any disgusting trash. They could just sit around the bonfire and beat on bongos as Frankie and Annette watusied barefoot in the sand. And Zak and Lynne could sneak away for a moonlit kiss.

"Good fish," mumbled Telly, his mouth full of fish.

"It doesn't get any better than this, my boy," smiled Zak, gulping on his lemony Hefeweizen.

After finishing half of their food but all of their beer, the two drifters got back on the road. Fort Stevens was just a few miles further on the peninsula that protected Astoria from the sea. Built for the Civil War, it was the only spot on the mainland to be attacked by Japanese submarines in World War II. Now it was a grassy park surround by stark beaches.

It wasn't long before the two found the beach parking lot filled with hippie vans and painted cars, a sure sign of a rainbow warrior gathering. Zak parked his 2000 Beetle next to a pale blue 1975 Beetle, thinking it made a small statement. An "I'm not a hippie" statement. The blue sky had disappeared somewhere along the way, and the ocean wind blew strongly. A wall of sand and grass separated the parking lot and the Pacific.

"Ready to see that ocean up close?"

Telly knew that Zak was hoping to see more than water. They headed up the trail of the dune, feeling a bit like Christmas morning.

At the top, all they saw was gray. The gray sand and the gray sky divided by the black-gray ocean. A clean but empty beach.

"Fuck!" Zak said, sliding down the hill toward the barren beach.

"Perhaps we should head north." Telly was right. It was a huge beach and the low clouds meant visibility was only about two hundred yards. The party had to be nearby.

The waves slid up the sand and Zak got as close to the water as he could without getting his Converses soaked. "Come sleep on the beach. Keep within my reach," he sang to himself.

"Quadrophenia," answered Telly, as if he were on *Rock 'n' Roll Jeopardy.*

The mythic sea surrounded by the gray loneliness put Zak on a melancholy track. The sea. The sea. So dark and unknown. The waves were godly manifestations of the tug of war between the Earth and the moon. The waves existed long before man and will certainly outlive life itself. The waves are the taught rope of God. At least the local God.

Framed in cosmic push and pull, the two walked up the beach, silently. For Zak, the desolate scene made him feel like he had crossed the Styx into a world of death. For Telly, the teaming life under the waves made him high with massive energy.

"You know we came from the sea," Zak finally said. Somewhere along Highway 30 he decided, privately, it would be OK to talk to Telly as if he really was an alien.

"Are you so sure?"

162

"What? You believe in Adam and Eve?"

Telly knew the importance of myths. He knew because all his myths had been destroyed. "There are other explanations for your race. Perhaps humans came from other planets."

"I don't buy that *Chariots of the Gods* crap. Look, you can see evolution happen. You can see fruit flies evolve to fit their environment. The chimpanzee is genetically, like 99.9% the same as man. It's so obvious." Zak was beginning to get into that space, where he had to make the point.

"Be careful of the obvious, my friend."

"Hey, you're into studying religion, right? Doesn't it make sense that they made up all that bullshit because they didn't understand anything scientifically? They actually thought that the sun went around the Earth and the Church would kill anybody that said otherwise."

Telly just stared out of the ocean, and understood how its size could inspire generations of legends.

"Here's a perfect example. The dudes that wrote the New Testament had no concepts of genetics, right? They didn't know what a fucking chromosome was. So if Jesus Christ really was the son of God, he would have his DNA, right? All you would have to do is get some of the blood off of the Shroud of Turin and separate Mary's DNA from the male DNA and you could clone God. Everyone could have their own fucking God. Mini-God. Of course it wouldn't happen because Mary was probably just raped by some asshole and put it all off on God. 'Gee, Joseph, I got knocked up by Jehovah, deal with it.'"

In Zak's rambling they hadn't noticed that they'd come across a group of twenty-somethings dragging some driftwood up the beach. There were more ahead. As they got closer, they saw several coolers, blankets and a few guys desperately trying to start a fire.

"It appears we have found the party," dead-panned Telly.

One of the fire starters was crumpling up some newspaper for kindling when Zak approached him. "Hey, man. Did we miss the clean-up? We came out from Portland to help out. We're all set to make the beaches clean." "Clean" fell out of his mouth without the slightest bit of sincerity.

The dude looked at the two, dressed more for a Ramones reunion than any serious beach work, and shook his head. "Sorry fellas, we just got done. But you can stick around for the party. You can have some beer if you can help me get this fire started."

Telly took the wadded up paper and something that looked like a lighter out of his leather jacket pocket and reached under the logs. Suddenly bright yellow flames jumped out of the pile and the wet wood began to crackle.

"Right on, dude!" said the dude. His flannel and gortex friends began to throw more wood on and Zak smiled.

As they walked away from the growing fire Zak whispered, "You *can* make your finger light up. Now, let's find that beer."

About twenty-five young people were on the beach, along with a few small kids and older hippies. Most were smoking, which struck Zak as typical. Environmentalists always smoked. 3M was guilty of polluting the world, but they were just enjoying an herb. Soaked in cancer-causing poison. Before he had a chance to go off on another rant, Zak saw her. Lynne was cracking open a bottle of beer. She was wearing a jeans jacket over a tight, faded Hole t-shirt, baggy army shorts and Doc Martens. Even on the beach she was cool as shit.

"Uh." Zak stopped his trajectory toward the beer.

"Should I say something?" prodded Telly.

"Uh, no. Let's just go get a beer. That's all. Just gettin' beer."

Lynne was talking to a few of the less crunchy beach cleaners with one booted foot on the beer cooler. Zak, with Telly in tow, trudged up in the sand to claim his prize after a hard day's work, picking up Styrofoam and dead sailors from the beach. "Um, mind if we get a couple of beers?"

164

With a squint, she tried to recognize the two faces. "Yeah, have you guys been working farther up the beach?"

"Well, actually we just got out here. We got out of Portland late and missed all the fun." Zak was transfixed on the curve of her eyebrows and cheeks and the breasts hidden under the jacket.

"Portland, huh? Well, the fun is just about to start, guys. So drink up."

The flames roared as the sky began to darken and clear. The winter day became a summer night as the clean-up crew made a drum circle around the bonfire. Guitars were strumming Beatles chords and lovers were walking hand in hand down the beach. As the sun set, the sparks mingled with the first stars.

Zak had gotten in his well placed, "Hey, weren't you at the Gurd show?" conversation and impressed her with his inside information. Lynne was a bartender in a coastal karaoke bar who took frequent trips into Portland for fun and adventure. Bartender was a plus. Karaoke was a plus. Not wanting to appear too infatuated, Zak broke away from the object of his affections. Telly was being pulled toward the drum circle, so Zak quickly grabbed him and a few bottles of beer and headed up the sand dune. From the top of the grassy hill they could watch the scene from a safe distance, with no risk of being forced to hippie dance.

"Look at that sunset, would ya Tell? Our sunset is the rising sun in Japan. The land of the rising sun."

"So you are pleased we came?" Telly was already half-lit.

"Oh, yeah. She is so fuckin' rockin. She likes all the cool music and she's got a crazy sense of humor. All that energy. She put this whole thing together. Hey, man, she has a cute friend, Erica. That other non-hippie over there. Why don't you go talk to her?"

"I am OK here, Zak."

Zak, leaned back on his elbows. "Uh oh, I think Telly is smitten with the sweet peasant girl," he laughed.

"Lucinda is not a peasant. Peasants work the fields. I am not in love. She is a contact."

"Right, you are 'studying' her. I think it's all about the milk."

Telly wasn't sure he heard Zak right.

"You're the one that asked why we don't drink human milk. Now you've got two big jugs of it!" Zak was laughing drunkenly.

Shaking his head between his knees, Telly replied, "That is just for Polly. I mean, I guess it is. Isn't it?" Zak laughed even harder.

Telly and Zak both laughed and drank their beers. Once the bottles were empty they stood up to take in the huge horizon of the Pacific that was fading into the darkness of space. "Look around, Telly. The world is in our hands."

"Hey Zak! Telly! C'mon down!"

Once the sun set the bonfire brought the park police who asked the kids to put it out. They picked up their trash and tried to be Earth friendly by launching the burnt logs into the surf. Zak and Telly came down from their stargazing to get the lowdown from Lynne.

"The cops busted up our shin-dig," she said, pulling on her jacket as Zak's drunken eyes spun around her chest. "What are you two doing tonight? Not going back to Portland."

With his arm around his roommate's shoulders, Zak said, "Oh, we're thinking about a little karaoke. Know any good bars?"

"Not on a Sunday night! A bunch of us are going to my apartment. You wanna ride with Erica and me?"

The two drifters looked at each other. "Well, I don't want to leave my car out here."

"You're not gonna drive tonight. We'll come get it in the morning. It will be safe."

166

The slot machine in Zak's head flipped, "Joker, joker, joker!" It was an invite to sex and a new life with the goddess of the seaside. He resisted the urge to do a Pee Wee Herman dance in the sand and kept cool. "Yeah, that sounds fun. Let's go."

After the clean-up of the clean-up everyone bounded into different cars and sped out of the park. A few vehicles belonging to drunk drivers were left behind, including the 1975 and 2000 Bugs. A tipsy Telly, Zak and Erica climbed into Lynne's badass '74 Dodge Dart and headed back toward Astoria.

Lynne's apartment was in an old Victorian on a bluff near Coxcomb Hill, above a place in the bay where the Columbia and Pacific met. The westward flow of the river and the east moving tide of the ocean made the water crash and swirl. It was perpetually windy and dramatic. The rocky cliffs and the violent white foam were scenes from the Creation.

The apartment itself was a wreck. Trashed. Lived in by two young women who were too busy living. There were cigarette packs, clothes, deodorant canisters, CDs and unidentifiable bits of trash all over the floor. Beer bottles, candles and dirty plates sat on the window sills. It looked the party had just ended instead of just started.

"I knew there was a reason we didn't clean this shit up," said Erica, who seemed to be Lynne's Caucasian twin. Bypassing the mess, she went straight to the fridge and pulled out a bottle of cold gin.

"Cool," muttered Zak to the room and the gin.

"Is this a typical Astoria apartment?" asked Telly, in all seriousness.

"We're not exactly Martha Stewart and Suzy Homemaker," replied Lynne, shrugging her shoulders.

More like Laverne and Shirley on cocaine, thought Zak.

Three more from the beach entered the scene with bottles of bourbon and rum and a two liter bottle of Surge. "OK, let's get this party started right, c'mon!" The obligatory Beastie Boys went onto the CD player and the switch from beer to liquor was made.

167

"Here Telly, this is a typical Astoria drink, rum and Surge. Where are you from anyway?"

"He's an alien," interjected Zak.

"He doesn't look Mexican," said Lynne.

Before the conversation could go much farther, someone knocked over some empty bottles sending Lynne to pick up the pieces. Telly looked at the tumbler of rum and highly caffeinated pop and proceeded to drink the whole thing down. Zak's eye's widened and Telly nodded in approval. Then he passed straight out onto the dirty floor.

"He's had a lot to drink tonight," apologized Zak, as he propped Telly up in the corner, with the cup still in his hand. In a way it was fortunate. Zak wasn't sure that his friend knew the meaning of "make yourself scarce." He needed room to have some solo time with Lynne.

After making sure that Telly wouldn't choke on his tongue, Zak got Lynne away from the rest by asking her for some more ice for his drink. They were alone in the kitchen and he felt the drink was going to make him say things that he would later regret. She was so alive and beautiful. He wanted her to press her body against his. He wanted her to whisper things in Japanese in his ear while they made love. He wanted her to make that Astoria to Portland drive in the Dart with his tapes playing. He felt like her lips were begging to be kissed. How could he get that close?

"Lynne, I'm going to have to warn you of something." No, Zak, don't.

"Are you about to pass out, too?"

"No. Do you ever read the *Willamette Week*?"

"Well, when I'm in Portland. We don't get it out here very often."

Shit. Why did he open his mouth? She probably wouldn't even see the Chance Meeting, especially way out here. Why embarrass yourself even further? Play it cool, boy.

"Oh. Uh. Yeah. Well, I was just going to tell you that there's probably an ad for the next Gurd show, 'cept they're called Sort Of now."

"Sort Of?"

"Yeah, Sort Of. I just wanted you know that that's Gurd."

"Why did they change their name?"

"They just thought Gurd was too Nineties sounding. One word band names were last decade. The O's are all about two words."

"Right on. Two words. Thanks for that important piece of information, Zachary."

Damn, had he blown that one. She was headed back to the living room and all he had was a few extra ice cubes.

The little party went on for another hour. Zak did his best to send the love vibe without looking like a drunk asshole. She was just playing hard to get, he thought. Finally a fed-up neighbor banged on the door and asked for some peace and quiet, sending most of the guests crashing out into the street and disappearing into the night.

Erica and Lynne were in a pile on the floor, cackling and wrestling and Zak was enjoying the show, wondering when it was going to be his turn.

"OK, Zacharia. We're going to make a little bed for you and your comatose friend on the floor."

Zak squinted in confusion.

"We'd let you guys sleep in our bed but you might barf." The comment sent Erica into hysterics.

Then Zak looked around the small apartment and realized there was only one bedroom and one bed. No. Fuck. Really? He usually could tell.

"Here you go." Lynne flapped out a blanket over the debris-covered floor and Erica brought out a few pillows and tried to roll Telly on to the blanket. Zak just sat on the love seat. "OK, good night. We'll get your car in the morning." Lynne gave Zak a wink, turned off the light and pulled Erica into the bedroom, shutting the door.

169

Fuck. Zak just sat there in the dark. Fuck, fuck, fuck. How could he get it so wrong? All that energy and fantasizing. All those miles and erections. That fucking Chance Meeting. Maybe she was bi-sexual. Well, it didn't matter. She was serious enough about Erica to be sleeping in the same bed with her. Fuck.

He suddenly began to get mad at Petra. This is the shit pool she had dumped him in. He was in Goddamn Astoria, drunk on Surge and rum, in a trashy apartment, thinking he might score with a punk rock lesbian. Thanks a lot. He should be happily married right now, not hoping his deranged roommate doesn't drown in his own vomit. Petra.

Feeling like his one life-line to hope had just snapped, Zak walked out of the apartment and down to the bluff. The stars danced in a liquored ballet and confused themselves with the moonlight, dancing on the ocean. The salty wind blew his hair in all directions. It would be so easy. A short fall and then washed to sea. Back to the water from where we came. There he teetered between all the unanswerable questions and the answer to the unanswerable question.

Chapter Six:
Livin' Thing

What is the issue with suicide, anyway? How did it become a cardinal sin? In medieval times they would drag the bodies of suicide victims through the streets until they were dismembered as a warning. They put Death Row inmates on suicide watches, reserving the satisfaction of taking a life for the State. If you kill yourself you lose out on heaven and insurance claims. Why is it OK for NATO to bomb innocent civilians, yet we've lost the right to blow ourselves up? How many courageous police officers and firefighters have risked their valued lives to bring someone down from a ledge? Someone who no longer valued their own life.

Suicide is what separates us from the animals. But long before the "self-murders" of Pythagoras and Socrates, the sanctions were heavy. Suicide was an insult to God, or the gods, who gave us life, and was dealt with accordingly. Those committing suicides were denied religious burials and their families were denied inheritance. Momentarily, during the Enlightenment, suicide was viewed as the ultimate act of free will and was, briefly, fashionable. God's gift, the soul, was immortal. The body was merely transitory.

Since that time we have dissected the act and tried to rationalize the, at least from an animalistic point of view, irrational. Emile Durkheim, the first sociologist, found cultural patterns in this very individual act. For example, Catholics had lower suicide rates than Protestants. With all those "Hail Marys" and "Our Fathers," and all that confessing and genuflecting, they just didn't have any time to do it. In 1897, Durkheim broke suicide down into a nifty typology: egoistic, altruistic, fatalistic and anomic. The egoistic suicide is the guy whose wife left him and just got laid off from the bank and can't cope. The altruistic suicide is the soldier in the movie who throws himself on the hand grenade to save his buddies. The fatalistic suicide is the slave who would rather die on her feet than live on her knees. And the anomic suicide is just the product of a confusing society. One filled with quick changes and mixed messages. More questions than answers, like "What's love got to do with it?"

Oregon had a special relationship with suicide. The deprivation of sunlight on the rain planet made melancholy the regional pastime. June 27 is a cold, dark, wet depressing as shit day. With all the incredible accomplishments of the Lewis & Clark expedition, enough to make them America's greatest heroes in 1806, Meriwether Lewis ended his own life three years later. At the age of 35, in an inn in Tennessee, called the Grinder's Stand, on the way to Washington DC, he put one bullet in his head and a second in his heart. What is there to accomplish after you've discovered the route to Astoria? In 1998, Oregon was the first state in the union to legalize doctor-assisted suicide. Despite external efforts by the Catholic Church, Oregonian voters overwhelmingly supported the idea that sometimes the silence of death is nobler than the pain of life.

Maybe that was why Zak felt so immediately at home when he arrived in Portland. The ghosts of Meriwether Lewis and all the poison takers, bridge jumpers, heroin users and wrist slitters that came after let him know that death is not the end. Even people who have only been there a short time know. Back east, idle chat of suicide would ring bells and whistles and someone would call the hot line or the men in white jackets. In Oregon, every word and action is a "cry for help" from October to July. Like Camus wrote, "The worm is in man's heart." Since Portland has no major league baseball or football teams and no one wants to talk about the rain, suicide chat becomes polite. Fortunately for the tax collectors, most of the people who talk about it never actually do it.

Zak stood on the cliff, feeling gravity's pull. It was so romantic, dying for love, his body on the rocks, like Jimmy the Mod. Shakespeare had infected us with this poison and now the price must be paid, again. The sound of the waves crashing was a soothing white noise that allowed him to dissect all the spinning thoughts.

He knew that he'd lost her. It wasn't just a case of cold feet. She was just a few blocks away from their apartment, letting him twist in the wind. The love she gave was a high he would never again have. She took him higher and higher. Every single day would be filled with regret. If he had only done something different. That damn Cher song popped in his head. "If I could turn back time..." No. He didn't want a Cher song to be his last musical thought. He didn't believe there was life after love. "Yesterday, all my troubles seemed so far away..." Yeah, a little better.

He was thinking about how he couldn't face each day solo. He loved being a couple, with her. He loved watching her sleep. He loved making love to his best friend. She was like a drug that only got more potent with time. There was so much ahead. It just wouldn't be worth a single day without her. He could momentarily distract himself with this girl or that, but they'd know. They'd all know that he was wishing that they were her.

Of course, things could go horribly wrong. He could hit the rocks and not die. He could end up like Christopher Reeve, trapped in a chair and making the people on the bus wait while they lowered the handicap ramp. Or he could die and find out there really was a Hell, or worse, get reincarnated as a blind hunchback in Calcutta or a telemarketer. And there was his mom. His mom would be stuck with the void and that line, the one about how parents aren't supposed to outlive their kids. If he thought about them too much, he wouldn't do it. This was a selfish impulse.

His therapist tried to convince him that suicide was an inherently immoral act. Suicide solved nothing and caused more suffering for those

173

left behind. But it was a bit like abortion. In of itself, an abortion can seem like a vastly immoral act. An innocent fetus with no chance to stand up for itself, gets snuffed out before it is even aware of its own existence. On the other hand, abortion is an incredibly moral act. What is worse than unleashing another unwanted human into the world, filled with assholes that probably should have been aborted? At best the kid can hope for two resentful parents. The more typical pattern is, Dad splits and the overburdened mom gives up her own dreams and can never properly supervise the kid who becomes a gang or cult member and kills some decent dad who bothered to stick around. Like abortion, suicide could do the world a favor by removing those who were no longer productive members of society. Wouldn't the Republicans be happy if all the poor people just killed themselves? Of course then there would be no one to work in the shitty low wage jobs they kept creating.

Zak was thinking that he was done. He had no more in him to give society. Not at least that would balance out what he would take by being this drunken blight. He could feel the booze pulling him down and he couldn't halt the slide. It was pretty stupid to treat depression with a depressant, but he liked it. It was the only thing that eased the aching in his heart. Southern comfort. But he was beginning to feel like he was stuck in a slick walled well. And we all know the only people who get saved from wells are cute blonde kids named Ashley or Jessica.

It would be so easy. Just one step. Take a dive and float downstream. He would probably die before he hit the ground from a heart attack. That's what happened when the Green Goblin threw Gwen Stacy off of the Brooklyn Bridge. Spiderman caught her just before she hit the water, but it was too late. His woman was dead. Painless. Blameless.

The creeping madness in his soul swirled all the black and white into a nauseating shade of gray. All that was left was gray. No direction, just one gray day after another. He didn't tremble, but stood firm in the resolution that this was that moment. He reached into his jacket pocket and pulled out the napkin, the one Petra had pressed her lipsticked lips against. He gently kissed her lips and let go of the napkin and it floated out to the dark sea.

It was the first clear night in months and Lynne couldn't sleep. She was craving a cigarette and climbed over Erica who had conked out straight away. In the living room she saw Telly asleep on the floor, cup still in hand. But Zak wasn't in the room. Maybe having a smoke, too, she thought.

She stepped outside and lit up a Marlboro and looked up at the stars. The breeze felt good and the horizon was marked by the moonlight on the sea. In front of the silver ocean, there was a ghostly silhouette. She squinted to make out what was down on the bluff. Shit, it was Zak, standing right on the edge of the cliff! She ran down toward him, trying not to hurt her bare feet on the rocky ground.

"Zak? Man, what are you doing? Be fucking careful. That's a huge drop."

Zak was lost in thought about doing the world a favor. He was swaying over the precipice and then back, as if in a trance.

"Dude, you are drunk! Just step back." Lynne was starting to panic. She didn't really know Zak or what his scene was, but she didn't want her front yard to be a diving board into oblivion. "Zak!"

With no response she turned tail and ran back to the apartment to get some help. She crashed on Telly. "Telly! Telly! Wake up, man. Your friend is seriously fucked up!"

Telly was sleeping like a vampire, with his folded hands on his chest, holding the empty plastic cup. His eyes opened as if he had just been rebooted.

"Is Zak in trouble?" he asked.

"I don't know, you tell me. He's down on the cliff looking like he's about to jump. Does he have any issues we should know about?"

Sailing away on a crest of a wave. Zak was thinking about his body magically disappearing into the vast sea when Telly and Lynne ran up. He knew they were there, but he didn't want to look them in the eye. This was a selfish impulse.

"Zak? What are you doing so close to the edge?" asked Telly, calmly as Lynne nervously wrung her hands.

"I'm taking a dive. I can't do it my friend. I can't live without her." "Yesterday" had been replaced as his melody line. Now it was Brian Wilson singing, "I guess I just wasn't made for these times..." "I just can't stand it. It hurts too much."

"Shit! Do something, Telly!" screamed Lynne. The wind was strong and a sudden gust could carry him right over the edge. But Telly did nothing. He had seen many suicides and they always went the same. Whenever you tried to reach out to them, that's when they panicked and jumped or pulled the trigger or swallowed the pill.

"He controls his own fate. He has a right not to exist in this life, Lynne," said Telly. That was the party line, but Telly didn't believe it any longer. Things are different here. That's why he came. He just couldn't figure out exactly why Zak shouldn't jump.

"You're as crazy as him! He's your fucking friend!" But Telly stood motionless. "Shit, I'm calling 911!" and she scampered back to the apartment.

"I'm sorry, Telly. You picked the wrong guy to room with if you were looking for the secret of our resilient spirit. I'm tired of being resilient. Hope is a four-letter word. I'll never be able to live up to the fantasy of my own life. I'm tired of being shit on by people who supposedly care about me. I'm tired of everyone just looking out for number one. I'm just tired of living." The waves were rolling over the rocks as the tide began to slide out. It seemed so enticing to Zak, like a heavenly cloud.

"Your world is so much different than mine. There is beauty here. Many times I wanted to end my life. But if I had I would never have had the opportunity to stand on this beautiful spot and see this view. I would never have gotten to drink alcohol with you, Cozy and Lenny, and listen to music. I would have missed out on so many things that I could not have even imagined at the time. I will not stop you from jumping, but you must be prepared to give up all the things you love or could ever love."

That made Zak think of Kurt Cobain again. Actually a poem that Jim Carroll wrote about Kurt. He said something like, "Didn't the thought that you would never write another song, a feverish line or riff make you think twice?" But Kurt knew the soul demons were like a poison. They would contaminate anything that was left. Zak's love of a Beatles song would remind him of their shared passion for music. A wonderful meal that could have been eaten with her. Cuddling with someone who was not her. All the light of life would be blackened by her absence. He was a smart guy, he knew he couldn't just paint over his memories.

"What did loving something ever get you but sorrow?"

Telly was not prepared to answer that. He only had second-hand information about the joy that love can bring. From watching his friends listen to music, from the people in the church, from Lucinda and her baby. The two stood silently while the wind decided which way it wanted to blow them.

Silently, an Astoria police cruiser drove up to the bluff and Lynne and Erica followed behind on foot. The lone officer climbed out of the car but did not move any closer to Zak.

"Son?"

Zak thought that was ironic. It was ironic how his dad had left him and now here was this stranger coming to save him, calling him son.

"Zak. We're gonna get you some help. Things always seem worse than they really are, especially after as many drinks as you've had tonight." Lynne had told the 911 operator as much as she could about the situation. "Once you get over your hangover tomorrow you're gonna be really glad that you didn't jump."

The cop seemed kind enough, but he really couldn't stop Zak from taking that one step. What was he going to do? Shoot at him? Suddenly a big gust of wind pushed the tottering Zak toward the sea. Everyone took a step forward because they thought he was going over, but Zak managed to get his balance back. The instinctual move away from the last inch of the ledge made him think he wasn't exactly ready to die. There was something inside him that wanted him to survive, buried deep, but there. He turned around to make sure that no one had accidentally dived over the cliff to save him. Lynne and Erica were holding onto each other in fright, the cop was pleading to Zak with his eyes and hands, and Telly was nodding, knowing that Zak would choose the right move.

His face contorted in anguish, Zak stepped away from the cliff. He turned to Telly and shrugged his shoulders and shook his head. The police officer walked up and put his hand on Zak's shoulder. "It's going to be alright, son. You did the right thing. I'm going to have to put the handcuffs on you, just to transport you to the hospital. We've got someone there who can help you out, OK?"

"Great," thought Zak, "now on top of everything else I'm going to have a police record that says I'm a monster-raving loony." "Yeah, that's fine," he said. The officer snapped on the cuffs and Zak got into the back of the squad car without making eye contact with anyone.

"I think you'll be able to pick him up in the morning at the police station." And the car backed down the driveway, Zak looking out at the sea from the back. On the way to the hospital the cop looked at his dour passenger in the rear view mirror and said, "Life is a gift, son. A livin' thing is a terrible thing to lose."

Zak was thinking that the terrible thing was livin'.

Lenny and Cozy were still up having their Sunday night "the weekend isn't over until we say it is" party for two. They were sitting on their bed, listening to *Astral Weeks* and drinking Oregon wine. The bedroom was filled with the obligatory posters of Keith Richards and Kurt and snapshots of Lenny and Cozy being a cool couple. Cozy was just beginning the process of getting ready for bed when the phone rang.

"Cozy? This is Telly. Please excuse me for calling so late." Telly was back at Lynne's, who was having serious second thoughts about letting these two strangers into her life.

"Hey, Tel. It's cool. We were still up. Where are you?"

"I am in Astoria. Zak has been taken away by the police. I believe I need your help."

"Oh my God! What the hell happened? Is he OK?" This is exactly what Cozy was afraid of, a meltdown.

"He was on a cliff and said he was going to jump. He was drunk and talking about Petra. Someone called the police and they are taking him to a hospital and then a jail. He should be out in the morning. I think someone is going to have to drive him home. Can you come out?"

"Yeah, of course. Fuck. Yeah, we'll be there." Cozy and Telly made plans to meet at the Astoria police station at 7 a.m. and retrieve their suicidal friend.

"Shit. He tried to do it, Len."

Lenny knew that she meant suicide. It had been a running concern of hers the last two weeks, since the failed trip to the river. "But he's OK, right? No gunshots or slashed wrists or anything."

"No, he was on a cliff in Astoria, saying he was gonna jump. They have him in custody. We have to go get him in the morning." Cozy got off the bed and began to pace around the room. "That cunt! I told her this was going to happen! Zak's a fragile boy. You can't just leave him at the altar without a fucking explanation. I told her that this is what would happen."

179

"Yeah, but Pet also said he wouldn't actually do it. That it was all a show." Lenny was on Zak's side but he did have a flair for the dramatic. He was, in fact, not dead.

"I know, but he was drunk and could have. The guy is spiraling. That bitch just rips his heart out and then splits. It's inhuman!" It was like an Italian opera to her. "I'm gonna call her."

Lenny wasn't about to stand in the way of this. He just got under the covers and watched.

"Hello? Can I talk to Petra? Yeah, I know, but this is an emergency. A serious emergency."

There was a minute or two while Lisa woke up Petra and got her to the phone. "Yes?"

"Pet, it's Cozy. I just thought you should know that Zak is in jail in Astoria. He tried to jump off a cliff."

"Oh, God." Then there was silence as Petra tried to figure out what to say. "Is he OK?"

"I guess so. Telly is out there. We're going to go out in the morning and try to get him." Cozy was hoping for a little bit of compassion from Petra, the woman who loved Zak enough to move across the country with him and agree to marry him.

"Maybe, I should come too," she said softly.

"I think you should."

The emergency room of the hospital was blindingly bright and empty. Not a lot of action on the coast Sunday after midnight. Zak felt like a murderer in his leather jacket and matching handcuffs. He stood alone as the cop talked to the attending doctor about the situation. Apparently, jumping off of cliffs was fairly common around these parts and there was a whole routine.

"OK, Zak. I'm going to take these handcuffs off of you now. They're going to talk to you and make a recommendation. I'll probably be back later to pick you up."

"Am I under arrest?" Zak was getting nervous about what he had gotten himself into.

"Well, I could. Suicide is illegal, you know. But I'm just going to ask that you do what the doctor says, OK? We want you to come back to Astoria many times. So I'm just holding you in custody. Understand?" The officer was very kind and even had admitted in the car that he had thought about suicide once when he was having problems with his wife, and was very glad he stuck it out.

Zak nodded and a doctor led him back to an examination room and told him that the county psychiatric worker was coming in to interview him. If he'd just wait in the room. It was a stark patient room with no scalpels, pills or nooses.

Sitting on the white paper of the table, Zak thought this absolutely had to be his worst day. Going back in time as far as he could remember, he couldn't have conceived of a more depressing event. Failed in love, failed in death.

He laid back and listened to the sound of the sterile paper crackling underneath him. He kept motionless and wondered if he could will his heart to stop. After all, yogis and escape artists could slow their heartbeats down to appear dead, right? How hard would it be to go from involuntary to voluntary? Zak closed his eyes and begged his beating heart to knock it off and release him. But it didn't work. The fucking meat pump kept right on working. If he had been in the hospital in Birmingham, there would have been a half-decent chance that some crack-crazed gunman would have burst into the room and just shot him. No such luck in Astoria.

Finally, after several failed attempts to stop his heart, hold his breath and switch off his brain, the psychiatric worker entered the room.

181

She was another goddamned caring individual that didn't seem to mind that Zak's drunken impulse had gotten her out of bed in the middle of the night. Zak got an immediate Woodstock vibe from her, a baby boomer who put all those hippie ideals into practice. The practice of trying to save the children from the shrapnel of society, like the Catcher in the Rye. Lots of luck.

Her bright smile and flowery jacket lit up the already bright room with a warm motherly glow. "Hello, Mr. Crisp. I heard you took a trip to one of our more scenic cliffs this evening."

"It was a lovely view. I was just having a look." He desperately didn't want to be branded with the label "suicidal," or worst, "attempted suicide survivor," at least not until he actually had done it.

"That's not what I heard, young man. Now, Zak, tell me why you were on that cliff telling your friend you were going to jump." She was a caring individual and therefore hard to resist.

He rubbed his hands on his face and listened to the paper crackle. "Oh, I know, it was a pretty stupid stunt. It's the same old story. My girlfriend left me. She is the most perfect girl and we were about to get married and she just split. So I was drunk and sad and listening to too many love songs. I blame it on Air Supply."

"We had two of those last week. Not Air Supply related suicides, but dumped lovers. They were both teenagers. You're 29. Shouldn't you know better? There's more fish in the sea."

"Well, what do you think I was doing?"

She realized the pun and laughed out loud. "Unless you're looking for the Little Mermaid, you're not going to find anything down there but cod. Look, you're a sharp guy, Zak. I need to figure out what to do with you. Have you ever been in therapy?

"Yeah, I go sometimes. He's got me on Zoloft, but sometimes it makes me feel really caffeinated and impulsive."

"Maybe you just need another medication."

"Maybe. Maybe I just need to figure out how to get Petra back." Zak was thinking about Petra ending up with some schlep after he was dead.

"Well, I can tell you one thing, you will never ever get her back if you die." True enough.

Zak and the psychiatric worker talked for another half hour about the reality of suicide and the other strategies that were there to deal with life. She was impressed with his honesty and clear headedness and put the attempt down to the drink and maybe the drugs and made her recommendation. Zak was to be held in custody until the morning and then he was to see his therapist immediately to discuss the event and alternative medications. She made him sign a pledge that he would do this and not kill himself. He was relieved not be headed for a padded cell.

The police officer returned to collect Zak. He let him know that Petra called and that she, Lenny and Cozy were coming out in the morning. The thought of finally seeing Petra, but in this situation, made Zak want to puke. It would just reinforce whatever the reason was she left him. He tried again to make his heart stop.

Once at the Astoria jail, the cop asked him to take off his Doc Marten boots. It hadn't crossed Zak's mind, but he could hang himself with his boot laces. But hanging seemed way too painful to him. As the metal bars closed and locked he laid down on the cold metal bed. The walls were white painted cinder blocks. There was a stainless steel sink and toilet. What a punishment to have to shit while the free men and women of Earth watched. He tried to sleep, unsuccessfully.

The rest of the world didn't stop spinning on its axis because Zak tried to end his life. Fishermen fished, policewomen policed and lovers loved. Telly went back to sleep at Lynne and Erica's who agreed to give him a ride to the police station in the morning. Petra, wracked with internal conflict, never made it back to bed. She walked around Lisa's apartment and then around Northwest Portland, trying to figure out what

183

she was going to say to Zak. Around 5 am she knocked on Cozy and Lenny's door to rouse them for the trip out. They made coffee and shook their heads. Petra knew Cozy wanted to say, "I told you so," but the looks were enough. The silence was enough.

The three got into Lenny's Corolla before the Monday morning sun was out. No one said much. Lenny put on NPR to distract them from their own inarticulateness. All they knew was that 100 miles away was Zak, either the most heartbroken or the most manipulative boy in the Northwest.

At some point he managed to fall asleep. He wouldn't remember his dreams, but they were what you would expect. He got home to his apartment in the Eldorado and there was Petra and some dude moving things out. Carrying out furniture and stacks of CDs that they had bought together. Her sewing machine and mother's china. They were taking out anything that would remind him of her and he couldn't stop them.

The sound of a drunk shouting in another cell woke him from his dream. He looked around at the white walls, reached by some nearby daylight. Daylight comes to those who live, he thought. He took a look at the bars on the door that held him in. What had he done? Sitting against the wall across from the cell was a girl with her knees pulled up to her face. Her brown hair fell over sweatered arms and her blue jeans, as she slept. It was Petra. Maybe it was a dream. Perhaps she was his angelic guide. His beautiful Petra, finally.

"Pet?"

She looked up and gave a loving smile. For a moment, they just looked at each other as if it was that moment when she had accepted his marriage proposal. But they weren't in her bedroom in Birmingham with Al Green crooning, "Let's Get Married." They were in a cold jail in Astoria, Oregon. She didn't know what to say but she had to say something.

184

"You. You and your sweet desire." The words rolled out her mouth like a song.

"Oh, Pet. Where have you been? I just couldn't take it anymore. The thought of living in this world without you was just unbearable." Zak's eyes hadn't been open for two minutes and they were already filled with tears. Just the thought of her made his heart light. The sight of her was a moment of joy in the middle of all the agony.

She put her face close to the bars. "You nut. You didn't have to do this to get me to talk to you. I just needed some time to think things out."

"But you're here now. Let's just go home and try again. We're in love. We need to be together." He was getting that pleading tone that was hard to recover from.

"No, Zack. No. I'm still trying to figure things out. I'm sorry I just ran away, but I knew you wouldn't understand. I do love you. But it takes more than love. Marriage is a big thing, and I'm not sure that I can do it."

Zak didn't know what he expected to hear from her, maybe she was in love with the postman, or she couldn't marry him because she was actually his sister. But this just confused him. "What do you mean? Love is all you need. Everything else is built upon that. We have our whole lives to work it out."

"That's just in movies and Beatles songs. I just don't think I'm ready to get married now. I'm too young and I've got this new job. I need to work on me before I can become an 'us.' Does that make sense? I'm not doing this to hurt you. I'm doing it to help me."

Oh, it made sense to Zak. Petra had recently landed a job with a local advertising firm. The place was filled with color-by-numbers hipsters who had sold their creative souls to the satanic gods of commerce. They rationalized their corporate cock-sucking by partying like a bunch of frat boy Hell's Angels wannabes. Everybody was getting drunk and fucking everybody else. Portland was filled with flotsam that had been kicked out of the firm. All were more than willing to talk about

185

how accusations of sexual harassment were laughed at. No one wanted to rock the boat. There was a lot of money and status to be had by everyone as long as you didn't mind blowing one of the partners and some of the boys in the creative department. The place destroyed marriages like Mark McGuire destroyed baseballs.

Zak hated advertising. It was the cancer of a superficial consumer society. And he hated this place even more for all its bogus hip posturing. But he loved Petra. He was glad when she finally found a job in Portland. He bit his tongue about the Beast. She was making her own friends and feeling more at home. But the stories about the non-stop bacchanalia at this place made him nervous. The employees were expected to drink together as well as work together. It would be a great place to work for a single person, but Zak knew that his beautiful young fiancé was on every oversexed creep's hit list.

"Pet, I don't get it. You can't have that and me? We don't have to get married right now. I can handle that. It's losing you that I can't deal with. Cool jobs come and go, but I'm going to be here for you forever. I swear that. We don't need a piece of paper for that. Our love is whole." He really wanted to marry her. He really wanted to pledge before all that was deemed holy that he would honor her until death. He really wanted to have a baby with her. But he didn't want to lose her over it.

"Oh, my love. You have to let me go. I will probably come back, but I have to be on my own for a while. I need some space. You're smothering me." There were now tears in her eyes and she was grasping at his hands through the bars.

"What? What are you talking about? I only tried to love you." Now Zak felt like his heart was really stopping.

"That's the problem, Zak. The way that you love me. I moved out here to be with you, but I feel like I lost myself. I have your friends, your car and your Saturday nights. I don't know who I am anymore separate from you." She didn't know how to explain it any more simply.

"That's what happens when two people fall in love. They become something new. A synthesis." To Zak, everything was Hegelian.

Petra pulled away from the cell door. "No, it's not healthy. It's not even. I became more like you than you became like me. You think you're such a feminist but you don't know how to listen to a woman. Really listen. You just take everything I say and try to fit it into your plans. You wouldn't disregard a real friend the way that you disregard me."

He had heard this before, but it was too challenging to think about and he just, well, disregarded it. "OK, well, we've got the problem isolated. Now we can fix it."

"It's too late, honey. I've been too damaged. I've got to get strong and find myself."

Both's eyes were red. Their hands were wet.

"God, Pet we have so much ahead of us. So much joy." His head was reeling. The pain of her words won out over the pain of his hangover.

"I can't think about that right now. Please forgive me. All I know is I have to do this. Just trust me, please." She reached into the cell and pulled out his hand and kissed his palm, which made it hot.

"Petra..."

"Telly, Lenny and Cozy went to get your car. Cozy and I are going to drive it back and you and your roommate will ride back with Lenny. The police said they would release you if we drove you back. You silly boy."

"Pet, what about us?"

"See? You haven't been listening to me!" She resisted the temptation to be angry at the attempted suicide survivor. "Zak, I just need some space. I need to be on my own for a while, OK?" She wiped her eyes and went out of the station to see if the others were back with the cars.

Lenny, Cozy and Telly were standing next to the VW, talking to the cop that had brought Zak in. He had told them how impressed he was

187

with Zak. That he was a smart guy who, if he stayed away from the booze, would be alright.

"Is he awake? How's he doing?" asked Cozy.

"He's OK. Just being Zak." She didn't want to say how worried she was in front of the police officer for fear that he wouldn't let him leave. Zak was making that face. The one Jimmy Stewart makes in *It's A Wonderful Life* after talking to his mother, when he realizes that Clarence is right and nobody knows who he is. It's a face of the pain of psychic war. "He's ready to go home with us."

"Fine. I'll go send him out," and the officer went in to unlock the cell door.

Petra didn't know how much Telly knew about their situation. She turned to Cozy and in a soft voice said, "He didn't take it so well. He won't accept it."

"Well, can you blame him? He's just had a major blow. It's going to take him a long time to get over this." Cozy wasn't trying to guilt-trip Petra. Petra was already guilty.

Lenny and Telly pretended they weren't listening. All four hoped that this was as bad as it got. They just stood there in the parking lot, waiting for Zak.

Out he came, over compensating his shame by strutting like Jim Brown, in *The Longest Yard*. The badass ex-con attempted suicide survivor. It made Cozy laugh. The gall.

"Hello, kiddies!"

"Oh, Zak. When I get you home, I'm gonna kick your fuckin' ass," said Cozy, acting more like Zak's girl than Petra was.

"Hey, it was all a big misunderstanding. I was out by the cliff and said, 'I've gotta take a dump.' Someone just thought I said, 'I'm gonna jump.' Big misunderstanding, right, Telly?"

Telly's Mr. Spock eyebrow popped up from behind his sunglasses.

Lenny was glad he was driving. Ferrying a suicidal maniac and a self-proclaimed space alien back to Portland would be easier than riding with Cozy and Petra. Both loved Zak, in different ways, perhaps. Maybe Petra would be able to make her understand and then she could help Zak. But who would explain it to Telly?

"OK, gang, let's get on the road. It *is* Monday morning." This wasn't exactly the rush hour crowd, but they did work for a living. Lenny had to open the pizza place up for lunch. Petra had only voice-mailed in that she needed the morning off from the ad firm. Cozy had to go to the symphony office in the afternoon and sell tickets packages over the phone. The undead Zak probably had some grade spreadsheets to do, and Telly? Well, Telly didn't really have anything to do, besides save his planet. Cozy climbed into the Bug with Petra. It was officially Pet's car, too, and she had already missed it. She missed Zak's road tapes. Telly squeezed his long legs into the back of Lenny's Corolla and Zak got shotgun, a special privilege for those who spent the night in jail. "Dude," said Lenny, pulling out of the parking lot, "you are one crazy motherfucker."

"All I wanted was a Pepsi," cracked Zak.

The mood in the two cars was not exactly the same. In the Bug, Petra began to make inroads with Cozy. This little stunt was a pretty good example of the lengths he would go to get his way. Any communication gap was due to the fact that Cozy would give anything to be loved so completely, without reservation. It was like Tristan and Isolde, no suffering was greater than being apart from the one you love. If Lenny threatened to throw himself into an abyss, she would be putty in his hands. Who could turn their back on a love like that?

But Petra was a different kind of woman. Less romantic, more utilitarian. She could be loving and full of kisses, or she could be a cold calculating robot, whichever suited her mood or needs. She could see how

189

Petra might get a little worn out by Zak's passionate attack. Zak thrived on conflict. Everything was a fight. A fight against straight society and its mirror equal, the hipsters. Fights against racism and sexism and stupid people who brought their children to R-rated movies or drove in the bike lane. But there was a time to not fight. Cozy could understand how Zak hadn't figured that out yet.

It was a hard sell, though, because Zak's love was so sincere. He was willing to emasculate himself to any point to be a good partner. He was just a little slow. Guys aren't ever taught how to be with women. They spend so much time segregated from them, on little league teams, in Indian Guides and Boy Scouts, in fraternities and on submarines. They can only objectify the idea of woman because they've never actually listened to one speak. Oh sure, girls say things to boys, but it's usually something the boys want them to say. "Nice touchdown." "Pick me up at eight." "Would you like another beer?" "Blow jobs are fifty bucks." Stuff like that.

If the male gender was collectively in the dark about women, Zak at least had a clue. He had embraced feminism as ideal. He had read Greer, Daly, Friedan and Eisler. He saw the weapon of sexism on magazine covers and in classrooms. He was a much better woman man than the guys at the sports bar. He was just a little crazy, that's all. Petra should take that as a bonus. Cozy suspected it was more than that. She knew Pet's weaknesses. She knew that being the new hottie at the hip advertising firm was a big ego stroke. Maybe she thought being wooed by some hot-shot executive was more exciting than marrying a health care researcher. Some people were deathly afraid of those words, "settling down."

Petra was still young. She would figure it out one day. Real love is rare, you don't throw it away. But she had to learn that lesson on her own. And she was right, she couldn't marry someone when she wasn't 100% sure about it. They just needed time.

In the Toyota, Zak was torn between defending his masculinity by bashing Petra and just coming clean and admitting that he'd just done the stupidest thing in his life. Surely he'd fucked things up more by this little performance. He really should have jumped. This would always be held against him. But he couldn't get her comment about the job out of his head. He obsessed about it. Her leaving had something to do with that job, he knew it.

The sun was up in the eastern sky and their shades protected them from the new day.

"Len, remind me to get that ring back from her. Four little dimonds. I'm goin to hock it and invest in porn."

"Oh, my brother. Invest in prisons! This is America! There's one thing we do better than anyone else, and that's incarcerate ourselves. They can't build those fuckers fast enough."

"God, Petra looks good. Destroying me really agrees with her." Zak's brain wasn't going to break out this loop anytime soon.

"Dude, she's not trying to destroy you. She's just a mixed up little girl. Give her some time."

"Time, while all those guys at her job devour her?"

"Oh, come on. Have a little faith, they're all dumbfucks. Those guys come to our shows and act like idiots. Give Petra some credit. She can see through those fake pricks." The stories about Drake & Campbell were legion. They employed some bullshit Gen X management technique, like company scavenger hunts and zines, which only alienated them from everybody else in Portland.

Telly sat in the backseat, trying to make the connection between Petra's job and Zak's attempted suicide. Jobs were a good thing. Being with members of your own age cohort was a good thing. What was the problem? He hadn't triangulated the power of jealousy and mistrust and Petra's past.

There was much to figure out, but one thing was sure. That moment when Zak backed away from the edge of the cliff was the key. Telly had to find out what it was that stopped him from jumping. Even if there wasn't a word for it. Even if it was an unknown brain chemical. Whatever it was, it could be the thing that saved his world.

"Man, I just wish I could get this out of my head," Zak said, shaking his head. "Like, what did I think about before all this happened? 'Cause all I know is that I spend every moment thinking about it. It's like the static between stations. If I'm not thinking, is the pasta done yet? I'm thinking about this fucked up situation. I must have had thoughts in my head before this. I just can't remember what they were. You know how when they tear down a building that you rode by everyday and you can't remember what the building looked like, even though you passed it every fucking day? I know there was this building there every day, but know all I can think about is the fucking hole that's there now."

"You thought about songs, Zak" Lenny remembered the Zak of a month ago. "You thought about what was the coolest Rancid song. You made top ten lists of the best records of every year you've been alive. You imagined what it would have been like if Stanley Kubrick had directed the Spice Girls' videos. Shit like that."

Zak looked at Lenny like he was talking about someone else. "I did? Really? I guess I thought about grocery lists and student loans and my research, which has gone to hell. And I thought about what being married to Petra would be like." He drifted off to the image of her pretty face. He knew he should have been listening to her instead of fantasizing about the life he would invent for her.

"Love has to be God's cruel trick. Like toothpaste and orange juice. You think, tooth paste tastes good and orange juice tastes good and then you get them in your mouth at the same time and you want someone to fuckin' beat you with a baseball bat, it tastes so bad."

"Did they do a full psych evaluation back there, dude?"

192

"No, I'm serious! Love lures you in like it's supposed to be the greatest thing on Earth, but once you're inside its tender trap it goes bad. You think it's going to be that first kiss bliss forever, but then it gets weird. And guess what? Too late, fucker!"

"I know, I know, Romeo and Juliet got it right. Zak, my brother, you're letting that woman have too much power over you. You need to just chill. Just kick it with your N's and have a good time. Life is too short, dude. Portland is filled with beautiful babies and wild nights. A lot of dudes bust up with their girls just to make the summer more like a smorgasbord and less like a sack lunch." Lenny knew all the standard rationalizations for his generation's need not to take relationships too seriously. He had been tempted to dump Cozy and exploit his growing rock stardom, but he knew it would break her heart.

"Pet ain't no sack lunch, she's the prime rib."

"Dude, you don't eat red meat."

"OK, she's the delux Garden Burger. The one with feta cheese in it."

In the lead car, Cozy's attempt to keep the discussion light with chatter about the beautiful sunshine (which was losing ground to the returning gray clouds) and the goings on of Zak's band didn't quite work. The two women were having mirror opposite relationship problems. Petra was trying to break free and Cozy was trying to get a commitment.

"I wonder what they're talking about back there," Petra said, looking in the rear view window. "Probably how horrible I am."

"I doubt it. They're probably having a debate over who was the best lead guitarist in the Stones. Besides, Zak knows he fucked up. He's just hiding it. I'm sure he's really embarrassed by this whole event."

"Telly sure is a strange fella. Is he a dope-head? I hope he's not a bad influence on Zak." She hadn't heard the whole spiel on the roommate, just that he was "foreign" and a bit odd. She noticed him silently staring at her from behind his black sunglasses and it made her a little uneasy.

"Oh, Telly's great. You just have to get him drunk and he starts talking. I think he's good for Zak. They talk a lot about philosophy and stuff." Of course, there was a danger. Telly's morose outlook on life, his whole "dying planet" thing, could just push Zak over the edge.

"I still haven't figured out what they were doing in Astoria at this girl's house."

"They just took a road trip, that's all. You know, nice Sunday. I guess they just found some party to get trashed at." Coze didn't know if it would be a good idea to dump Zak's mosh girl into the drama.

"My life is such a mess, Cozy. Sometimes I wish I had met Zak five years from now. Am I so bad to want to just play?" Highway 30 was getting more congested as commuters began to hit the road.

"Well, I think it's what you mean by 'play.' Being married to Zak doesn't mean that you can't play. It just means you can't go around fucking everybody." Cozy wasn't from Birmingham, so she couldn't really know that she was hitting a major chord.

"I'm not a slut! C'mon, Coze, you know that being single is more than just sex. It's the feeling of possibilities. That that guy who is making eyes at you from across the café might ask you out. But it's also just being free to do whatever you want. You don't have to worry about anybody's feelings or schedules. You can just go."

Cozy knew what she was talking about and the thought briefly brought a grin to her face. "Yeah, but you know what? That gets old really quick. I was single for a long time and that was fun for about a month and then I just wished I had someone. Someone to share my life with. Lenny is my best friend and I can have sex with him. That's a million times better than being single. Being single means being lonely."

"Well, I've never really been lonely. Maybe I need to experience that." It was a valid point. She had always had a boyfriend or just boys. She and Zak had been inseparable the past three years. She had never really lived alone as an adult.

"Well I've never jabbed a hot poker in my eye, maybe I should try that."

In the Corolla, Zak and Lenny were discussing how the Rolling Stones career would have evolved differently if Brian Jones had never been fired and drowned in that swimming pool in 1969. Zak was convinced that *Sticky Fingers* and *Exile of Mainstreet* would never have been recorded without Mick Taylor's blues licks. Instead, Jones would have dragged the band into hippy-dippy world music with Tibetan flutes and Ukrainian yodelers. Lenny added that The Faces would have become bigger than the Stones since their later sound was all about Ron Wood's chugging guitar style. The general consensus was that after "Jumpin" Jack Flash", the Stones would have gone the way of Jefferson Airplane. "We Built This City On Rock 'n' Roll."

Telly was fascinated by this highly animated musicological discussion, but the burning question still remained. How could Zak go from the edge of death to this? He remained silent as the wind from the front windows blew his dark hair around.

"You alright back there, Tel?" Zak didn't want to alienate his roommate with all the rock talk.

Finally the dark figure spoke. "Why didn't you jump, Zak?"

Zak laughed. He knew that Telly didn't mean that he should have jumped. Telly had his own suicide issues, but Zak didn't really have an answer.

"I wanted to stick around so people could say, 'There goes a loser.' I thought it would be good to really humiliate myself."

"Dude," was Lenny's input.

"Oh, I don't know, man. I guess I need to go to the edge and see if it was me that went over or my scooter."

"And it was your scooter?"

"Yeah, I guess so." Zak knew that that meant that something had to have died, crashed against the rocks: his youth, his impulsiveness, his relationship with Petra, his love of frozen waffles.

"What fuckin' scooter?" Lenny missed the *Quadrophenia* reference.

"I just realized how stupid it was. Another heart breaks. Big fuckin' deal. All over the world people are breaking up. When that wind almost blew me over I had this moment of clarity where I just laughed. Like, what the fuck was I doing? It's like that scabby homeless guy in our neighborhood. Why doesn't he jump? Does he know something that I don't? Fuck, I need to find out! He'd probably be pissed as shit to find out someone like me jumped into the ocean and he's laying on the street, peeing in his pants."

Telly wasn't convinced. "What about all those things that you said about how life would be less valuable without her?"

"Dude," Lenny had to put his two cents in. "Look at it his way, at least you had her. For a couple of years you had this beautiful girl."

"Yeah, but that means that everything is downhill from here."

"But your mountain was higher than the rest of our hills." Lenny wasn't using a very good metaphor.

"Well, it's still downhill. But don't worry my brother, " he said in his best Martin Luther King voice, "I will return to the mountain top!"

About thirty miles from Portland the two cars stopped at a quicky-mart in St. Helens to make sure everyone had gas and a plan for reentry to reality. Zak slid out of the Toyota and shuffled up to the VW. He crouched down by the driver's side window. She was so beautiful. How could he let her go? How could he ever find another like her?

"Oh sweetie, how are you doing?" she asked.

"Well, you know, I'm alive. So, are we gonna get a chance to talk when we get back?"

196

"I'm going to drop the car off and catch a bus into work. I just left them a message that I'd be late. I hope they're not mad."

"Gee, I hate to do anything to slow down the mighty advertising machine. You can blame it on your crazy boyfriend, who you're dumping. The fact that I was going to kill myself because of you should raise your stock with the boys at the watercooler." Here he was, digging himself another hole, spoiling the show.

"Zak, I'm not going to listen to this shit right now."

Zak knew that he shouldn't say shit like this. He should be a good boyfriend and accept that Petra was having doubts like we all do. He should be supportive and patient, but there was something deep in his brain that was fucked up. It was somewhere near the memory of his father leaving, some suppressed abandonment phobia. And just at the wrong moment, the shit would zip out, straight past the part of the brain that says, "Should I say this?" and fly right out of his mouth.

"Besides, those guys don't even know I exist. I'm just another worker bee. Only a few of the girls even know I'm engaged."

Zak tried to get some confirming eye contact from Cozy, who was watching the morning traffic. Then he looked down at Petra's left hand on the steering wheel and got a bit teary. "Well, um, I see you're not wearing your engagement ring. Is that for the guys in the executive washroom?

"Stop it! It's for me, OK? If I decide that I want to get married, I'll put it back on."

"But you decided when you said 'yes' to me and started planning the wedding." He was trying not to whine.

"Zak, I can't have this conversation right now. I'm going to drop Cozy and the car off and you can get the keys from her."

"Meet me out front, so I can kick your ass!" Cozy said and the Bug speed back on to Highway 30.

In a cloud of dust, Zak stood up and walked back to Lenny and Telly, both who were leaning against the driver side of the Corolla.

"Give her time," Lenny said. "No one knows which side the coin will fall."

"She appears confused," commented Telly. "As do you."

"Oh yeah, we're all confused. It's one big fucking ball of confusion."

The three got back in the car to make the final stretch back into the city. They missed the last of the morning rush hour and sailed smoothly along the highway. The last bit of morning sunshine was now obscured by clouds. Portland always seemed to have a dark cloud hanging over it. Just outside of the city, north, south, east or west you could find sun, but Stumptown was perpetually a gloomy Gus. Usually, driving into a big city with the morning sun would stir a feeling of elation. Today there was just a feeling of dread. Trips to pick up suicidal friends will do that.

"Well there she is," Zak said as the tall buildings and bridges came into view. He suddenly realized that if he had jumped he would never have that experience of returning home again. What was even better were the clear days when you could perfectly see Mt. Hood and Mt. St. Helens. Their snow peaked capped against the blue sky always took his breath away.

"Home, sweet home!" shouted out Lenny.

"Yep. New day rising," added Zak, hopefully.

"New world rising, Zak," said Telly.

Lenny flicked the radio on to KUFO, the Portland rock station. It was the opening vibes of Kid Rock's "Bawitdaba" and Zak quickly turned up the song to full volume. The car instantly filled with kinetic energy as the metal/rap/punk beats blasted out of the Corolla. Lenny and Telly thrashed back and forth like Wayne and Garth on crank. Even Telly had to move inside the rolling mosh pit. As they moved onto the city streets, pedestrians had to laugh at unlikely Monday morning site.

"Now get in the pit and try to love someone!" Zak shouted out of window, along with Kid Rock.

The song was still blasting when the car pulled up in front of the Eldorado. There was Cozy. She shook her head at the sight of the three rocking out, having a great time and thought, yeah, really suicidal.

Zak jumped out of the car and left the seat up for Telly. "There's our Cozy! OK, yer boy did a good job. I'm not going to kill myself this morning."

"That's nice, Zak. I'm not getting up at daybreak again. I'm no daybreaker, OK?" She was so sweet, living in the same building as her was reason enough to live.

Lenny parked the car and joined Telly, Zak, and Cozy in front of the building. "Well that was an adventure. Can we all get back to our lives now, please?" Lenny was no daybreaker, either.

Zak realized the trouble that his friends had gone to for him, getting up so early and all. "Listen guys, I just wanted to say that it really meant a lot to me that you came out to get me. I'm really sorry you had to. I'm just a dumbfuck. I miss her so much, I just let it overwhelm me. Plus I was wase-ted."

Cozy gave him a soft hug. "Oh, boy. It's OK, just don't do this to us ever again. I'm still going to give you that ass kicking. Now here are your keys. Why don't you just go in and relax for a bit. Listen to your favorite CD and be glad you're fuckin' alive."

"But Zak, if you do die, I get your record collection," joked Lenny.

"OK, I now have a reason not to kill myself," scowled Zak. "OK, Tell, let's crash in the crash pad."

Telly ran his fingers through his hair and said, "Go ahead, Zak. You may want some time to be alone. It is a new day and I would like to go for a walk."

"Observing," said Zak, Lenny, and Cozy in unison.

Zak gave the happy couple hugs and headed inside to #110. Lenny and Cozy stayed on the sidewalk for a minute to recap. She wanted to know how stable her charge was. Telly headed down 16th. Turning the corner on to Burnside, he saw Lucinda sitting by herself at the bus stop looking very sad.

Once inside the apartment, the whole trip to the coast seemed like one disjointed dream. Road songs and disabled nuclear power plants. Beer battered fish and bonfires. Lynne's t-shirt under her jacket and grassy dunes. Surge and a trashed apartment. Crashing waves and the big drop. The psych ward and the jail cell. Kid Rock. Just a bunch of thinly connected movie scenes that he happened to have lived.

When he left the flat was filled with sunshine and hope. Now the rain was returning and things couldn't be gloomier. Not only did he not have a distraction from his drama, the actual drama itself was much more serious than he had thought. Some unmanageable communication breakdown was pushing them apart. He couldn't even find the inspiration to put a record on the stereo. He just sat on the windowsill and began to cry. Zak's dreams of life and love had been given a serious jujitsu kick. Love wasn't all you needed, John.

Sitting in the dark made sense. All he needed to complete the scene would be some Johhny Hartman songs and a bowl of chicken soup. He looked down onto the street and saw Telly at the bus stop by the porno store talking to his friend, Lucinda. She was crying, too.

"Telly, where have you been?" cried Lucinda, who always seemed odd without Polly.

"You knew we were going to Astoria. We spent the night and just got back. What's the matter? Where's Polly?" He was concerned for his young friend and feared the worse. But then again, if Polly had died, she probably would be spared an unhappy life as a homeless child.

"I've been banging on your fuckin' door all fuckin' morning! I thought you'd get back last night." She was sucking in her cheeks, trying not to bawl. "Oh, Polly's OK. They're watching her at the shelter. It's Dean."

"Dean?" Lucinda had mentioned Dean in passing. He was a gutter-punk that she was more than bonded to."

"My friend? Dean? He's dead! Dean's dead. It happened early this morning. Fuck! He took a bunch of acid and freaked out. He ran all the way to the top of the Marquam Bridge and had all the fuckin' traffic stopped." The Marquam Bridge carries the I-5 interstate over the Willamette River and, since it opened in 1966, has been another jumping off spot.

"What happened?"

"He was screaming about the fucking graveyards. About how there's not enough land left in America to bury everyone and there's just going to be more people so we're just going to start sending the bodies to the dump. Crazy shit like that. This cop tried to grab him and he just bolted over the edge. They said he looked just like a bird trying to take off. Poor Dean." She began to cry loudly.

Feeling the irony of having survived Telly's aborted flying leap, Telly could only reach out and take Lucinda's dirty hands into his.

"I fucking hate this city," she said. "I hate my fuckin' life. All my friends do is die. They take too many drugs or get drunk and fall asleep on the train tracks or they get murdered by some fuckin' serial killer in Forest Park. I can't take it anymore. Telly? Tell me you're not going to die on me. You're not going to get shot or kill yourself. Please?" Her big eyes were lakes.

How could he tell her that his time in this place was only temporary? "No, Lucinda, I will not die. I promise."

She smiled and hugged him for a long time. Lucinda didn't want to let go. She just wanted to know that Telly wasn't another freak. Telly let

201

her hold him. He looked up at the apartment window and saw Zak nodding with a faint smile.

Chapter Seven:
Above The Clouds

There are over two million homeless kids in America. Runaways and castaways. An estimated 70% of them are on the streets because of abuse at home: physical, emotional, sexual. These are the "family values" that conservatives celebrate in their flag-waving campaign ads: violence, terror and rape. Father knows best. Some of the kids have good parents who have no idea how to help their troubled children. Some have evil parents who repeatedly beat and fuck them. Some have yuppie parents who are too wrapped up in their own dramas to listen to their kids and can only threaten their miscreants with boarding school. Some have poor parents who can't manage their own bad habits, let alone the needs of an American teenager. Some have homophobic parents who would rather turn their queer children on to the mean streets than love them. All would have done the world a favor by not breeding.

For the street kids, escape is salvation from the hell of "family values." Most are only on the run long enough to slap their moms and dads into parenting mode. But 16% of runaways run away more than five times. They feel safer on the street. A quarter of homeless youth are homeless for years, the new Skid Row.

Survival on the streets is a hustle. How are you going to eat? Where are you going to shit? How are you going to not get beat down? Where are you going to score some meth? In a capitalist society there is always cash at the intersection of supply and demand. There is always a marketplace for sex. There are half-a-million juvenile prostitutes in America. The gutter-boys of Portland can always pick up a quick $40 on Stark Street, also known as Vaseline Alley. They sell their asses for pot and beer.

For gutter-girls it is a matter of survival sex. While many practiced survival sex at home, at least on the streets they can pick and choose. It isn't always daddy. But the constant dehumanization takes its toll. The girls of the street are at the greatest risk of rape and violent attack. They are fodder for serial killers and abusive police and all the scum on the street. They are surrounded by death and as a result kill themselves. The futility and fear of life on the streets pushes them to suicide, drug-abuse and self-mutilation. The beloved daughters of America who choose this life over father-knows-best.

America values it's children as long as they act like Bud, Princess and Kitten. As long as their problems can be solved in thirty minutes, minus commercial time. As long as they don't have to be respected as humans. As long as we don't have to raise taxes too much to imprison them.

Lucinda knew that the father-knows-best trip was over. She didn't have to take it anymore. When she landed in the middle of Portland's gutter-punk scene, she saw that she wasn't alone. The fifty or so kids (not counting the wannabes and weekend grommets) couldn't take it anymore either. They would build a new family, built on street family values.

But the dream of the gutter-punks and the reality were two separate things. Despite their post-apocalyptic hippie utopianism, life on the street bred more of a watch-your-back philosophy. The street's hardness forced the kids to become abusive and dishonest. They had to be selfish and learn how to play the system, which often meant screwing their fellow travelers out of a bed or a meal. It was a schizophrenic existence.

Telly wanted to invite Lucinda in to get her off the street and the world it represented. But Zak was inside, coming down from his failed suicide attempt. Likewise, Lenny and Cozy were wrung out from the trek to the coast. They were standing in the returning rain, silently looking at each other.

"Oh, Telly. I'm such a mess. I don't want you to see me like this." Lucinda wiped the tears from her big eyes with the sleeve of her army jacket and made a Mona Lisa smile.

"I have an idea," said Telly, who wanted to take Lucinda somewhere. "We could go to the movie theater and see a matinee. That might take your mind off of things." He had his hand on her shoulder in a friendly way, not a lover-ly way.

On any other day Lucinda would have jumped at that chance. A movie with all the previews and commercials could use up a good three hours of her day. Everyone was always so up on the latest films. She missed going to the multiplex, even to see the crap her family used to drag her to. Like when she wanted to see *Pulp Fiction* and her Dad took her to see *George of the Jungle* instead. She didn't even recognize any of the people on the cover of the celebrity magazines anymore. If it weren't for catching *Entertainment Tonight* occasionally at the shelter, she would be completely out of the loop.

On any other day she would have jumped at the chance to go on a movie date with her new boy, but today she actually had something to do. "Oh, thanks, Tel. That's a nice offer but the gang is meeting down at the square to figure out what to do about Dean. It's so fucking sad, we really need to hang out. As much as I hate those fuckers, they're like my family. Why don't you come along? I want you to meet my friends."

Telly wanted to meet Lucinda's support network. He wanted to know if they were like her, dark and angry. He needed to know if they helped each other survive or if they just exacerbated their own fatalism. "Sure, I'd like that." And they headed downtown.

205

Zak was back in his bed, staring at the ceiling, listening to a Jeff Buckley CD. "It's over, it's over and what can I do?" he thought. He was trying not to be paralyzed and sat up. The fact that she had come out to the coast to collect him was a good sign. The fact that she wasn't wearing her engagement ring was a bad sign. But the fact that she said she just needed some time was a good sign. But the fact that she went straight back to the advertising firm after getting him home was a bad sign. He lay back down on the bed.

There was certainly a proper course of action here. He had to be careful about what he said and did. Ragging on Drake & Campbell and the advertising world in general wasn't helping, neither was threatening to throw himself off of a cliff. Maybe calm conversation would do it. No hysterics. Maybe he should go off the Zoloft for a few days and just smoke pot.

Zak couldn't exist without a plan. Even at his most catatonic, he was scheming. There was always something that could be done. The hardest thing to do was nothing. Just let it go. Not possible.

Of course, most of his impulses got him into trouble. For such a romantic, he had the worst instincts, at least where Petra was concerned. He often thought about that old episode of *Seinfeld*, where George realizes that his instincts are always wrong so he decides to do the exact opposite of what his gut tells him to do and things start going great. Unfortunately, in reality that's a lot harder to pull off. How do you know that the exact opposite of the impulse isn't actually the impulse you should do the exact opposite of? See? Zak might have an impulse to graffiti a message to Petra on the sidewalk in front of Lisa's building and then counter that with an impulse not to do any graffiti at all. But maybe his mind would try to trick him by throwing out bogus impulses that would be easy to resist, like running naked through Portland with "I heart Petra!" written on his ass. Then the instincts and the counter-instincts would get all mixed up and you'd ultimately end up doing just what you would have done before, just without all the mental back-flips. It's inevitable, because ultimately the subconscious wants you to do stupid shit.

But the easy thing was identifying the things that got him in trouble. Acting "crazy" got him in trouble. So he decided to wait a day or two, giving her the space she requested, and then calmly talk to her and try to really listen this time.

Petra was back at work trying to act like nothing had happened. But that was hard. She hadn't seen Zak since the night she left the note and slipped out and away from their wedding. To see him next in a jail cell was really difficult. She knew she should bury her anger at him and at herself if she could just focus on work. But it just wasn't happening.

Zak's concerns about Drake & Campbell weren't unfounded. Despite the company's "pro-social" front, the place was run like a big frat house. Since they had gotten the big macro-brew account, it even smelled like a frat house with spilled free beer every Friday. The fact that Ben, her boss, was always hitting on her made things even more confusing. Confusing because she was considering giving in to his advances even before she decided to call off the wedding. He was smooth and successful and didn't care that she was engaged. He was an entree into a whole new world.

It wasn't the reality of an affair with her boss that excited her; it was the idea of the affair. She wrote about it at length in her journal. It was taboo on so many levels, she just had to do it. As long as Zak didn't find out. But now that the marriage was on hold, Ben seemed more like the sleaze that he was. It didn't matter. The whole thing was evidence that she had no business getting married. She looked at the picture of Zak on her desk for a few minutes and then un-tacked it and placed it in a drawer, under some labor contracts.

The dreary Monday clouds weren't dreary enough to push the gutter-punks out of Pioneer Square. In fact, the day of sunshine was a bit much for them and their weak eyes and they welcomed the return of winter. They were used to being cold and damp and the warm weather just made them stink.

Lucinda and Telly found them on their usual perch, next to Starbucks, getting ready to spaynge the lunch crowd. They were a bit less rambunctious than normal, in the wake of their comrade's death, but still obnoxious, giving the finger to anyone in Columbia Sportswear rain gear.

Roxy saw them approach from behind the light-rail train. "Hey, Lucy. Who's that?" Any newcomer to the group was viewed with suspicion, especially one whose clothes came from a boutique.

"Hi Rox. This is my friend Telly." Telly nodded.

"Oh yeah, Dean told me about him. What's up, rockstar?" she asked, squinting her heavily mascaraed eyes.

"I am fine. I am sorry about your friend," said Telly sitting down on a bench next to Roxy with Lucinda.

"Yeah, it fuckin' sucks. We're all hella bummed about it." She tried to run her fingers through her tangled purple hair, but they got stuck.

"That fuckin' Dean. He should have stuck to the zip," added Lucinda, referring to Dean's love of methamphetamines. "Where did he get this acid anyway?" LSD wasn't rare on the street, just out of character for Dean.

"Oh, we were doing a little car-shopping last night in Southeast and he found it in the glove compartment of some fuckin' SUV. He must have done four hits. We still have the rest of it. Dean's death doses."

"Shit, he was a fuckin' idiot," exclaimed Lucinda.

"Well, you know he was all fucked up about you going on and on about your new boyfriend," said Roxy, shooting Telly a sideways glance. Lucinda became flustered and Telly just looked at the sidewalk, not sure how to interpret the multiple meanings of the statement.

"Oh, don't start that Rox. Dean didn't kill himself because of me. He was an idiot who took too much acid and jumped off a bridge. Don't fuckin' try and lay it on me just because I'm trying to get a fuckin' life." She hoped her bluster would deflect the "boyfriend" issue.

"Yeah, Dean was a fuckin' idiot, but we loved him," said another punk who came over to bum a smoke off of Roxy. A couple of the others came over, knowing that Lucinda occasionally served as the matriarch of the scene. "We loved him, even though he was full of shit most of the time."

"What do you mean?" asked Telly, sensing an opportunity.

"Fuck. Like half the time he was into everybody, and the other half he was a fuckin' Nazi, just sayin' crazy shit," the kid said.

"He would say some pretty funny shit," said Lucinda to Telly.

"Like, remember when he said this, 'If black guys like to go out with white girls and white guys go out with Asian girls, why don't Asian guys go out with black girls? Because they both suck!' Like, where did he get that shit from?" the punk asked.

"Dude, those boneheads were always trying to get them to join their little Nazi gang," said Roxy. "Didn't you ever see those flyers he had?" A local chapter of the Aryan Front skinheads regularly targeted white boys in shelters for recruitment. Homeless kids were easy. "My favorite Dean saying was when we'd like just be kickin' it and he'd see some fat chick and he'd yell, 'Look how fat her ass is! She must be a dyke! Only dykes have asses that big!' And we'd all have to look away we were so fuckin' embarrassed. What a dumbass. I already miss him."

Telly was a bit confused. "I'm sorry if I seem confused. You think he was a dumbass, and a Nazi, and an idiot, and yet you still cared for him?"

"Well, duh!" said Roxy, wondering who this weirdo in the white leather jacket was.

"Roxy, Telly's from Europe. He's just trying to understand." She took Telly's hand, hoping to give credibility to the boyfriend claim. "It's like this Tell, Dean may have acted like a Nazi, but he really wasn't one. He wasn't going to kill any Jews or anything. He was just being obnoxious to get a reaction out of us. Out of society, I guess. It's like those Columbine kids or Sid Vicious. Some people just talk that Nazi shit because people will listen. Dean wasn't too bright. He was pretty fuckin' dumb, actually."

"Hey!" shouted Roxy. "Some respect for the dead!"

"Whatever. But Dean was OK. He just wanted someone to pay attention to him. He knew that there was a lesbian with a skinny ass somewhere. It's like being stupid is more fun than being smart." Lucinda was well aware of the drill. Anyone who tried to appear book smart instead of street smart was seen as a crab trying to crawl out of the barrel, and we know what happens to them.

"I understand," said Telly. He knew that Nazism was viewed as the great evil of the last century. He had heard Hitler's first television broadcast, along with most of the film, *Contact*. The accusation would be a serious one if Lucinda hadn't explained it so well. "Thank you," he said and pulled his hands away from hers.

"So what are we gonna do for Dean, then?" said the punk.

"Let's get wasted!" said another.

"Let's do something he would want," proposed Roxy.

"Gee, why don't we all get ripped on crank and go beat the shit out of some Mexicans," said Lucinda, straight faced. "Just kidding!" She looked at Telly with a smile, hoping he got the sarcasm.

"I know," said Roxy, slyly. "Why don't we do the rest of that acid he found? There's enough for at least a hit for everyone."

"Right," said Lucinda. "And then we can all jump off of the Marquam Bridge."

"No dude, let's go up to Mt. Tabor and just fry as the sun goes down. It'll be the perfect tribute to Dean. Who's in?"

Several "I ams!" came from the group. Lucinda had to admit that it was a perfect idea, as much as she was sick of the drugs. Maybe Telly would trip with her and it could be a bonding moment. She looked at his face but couldn't get any clues from behind his sunglasses. It was a gamble and she'd have to make sure that Polly was safe for the next 24 hours.

"OK, I'm in."

Zak was having one of those, "I'd get out of the bed if I actually had a reason to" days when there was a buzz from the front door that gave him a reason.

"Package for Petra Novak and Zak Crisp." Shit, maybe it was a bomb.

"OK, hold on." Zak ran down the hall and signed for a big padded box. There would probably be a few of these. Wedding presents from the uninformed and the found-out-too-late. He brought it back to the apartment and set it on the floor.

There were several possibilities he had to dwell upon. He could write "Return To Sender" on it, with a little note, and put it back in the mail. He could take it over to Lisa's and let Petra deal with it, since wedding presents are the property of the bride (and presumably the should-be bride). He could open up the box and enjoy the contents himself. After all it could be packed with CDs or something electronic. Or he could take the box up to Cozy and Lenny's and, in the spirit of *SCTV* and all the fucked-over, hurl it out of the window, enjoying the symbolic value of shattered dreams on Burnside.

He opted for Option #3. The parcel package was from a Novak but it came to his apartment. Zak pulled at the packing tape until he got the

211

box open. Under the foam paper was a stack of china plates. The Lenox Cosmopolitan Collection to be exact.

China was one of those last meaningless rituals. Granted, rituals were important, as Telly would say, but china? That shit was expensive! Zak and Petra, the young newlyweds, would be cash poor and could use gifts like actual plates that you could eat off of, or gift certificates to Target or Tower Records. They wouldn't be entertaining too many Royals there at the Eldorado. Apparently, they wouldn't be entertaining anyone at all.

Feeling like a boy who found his Christmas box full of Underoos instead of Atari cartridges, Zak pushed the box into a corner and climbed back into bed. Perhaps the gift gave him an excuse to go and talk to Petra. He fantasized about heading over to Lisa's and bumping into Petra, headed over to the Eldorado. They would both look at the ground, realizing how silly they'd been. There would be an awkward silence before he reached for her hand. Then there would be a hug, followed by a soft kiss, followed by a passionate kiss, followed by Al Green.

Zak began to feel hopeful again. He put on a Superchunk CD and danced around the apartment with his air guitar, planning his strategy. He'd have to wait until she got home from work. The sun would be down and she might not be with some other guy. Things could only go his way.

Right before all the commuters poured out of their office towers onto their tax-funded mass-transit trips home, the gutter-punks climbed on a bus and headed out of the Fairless Zone. The #15 would take them up Belmont Ave. to Mt. Tabor Park. The dirty dozen (plus Telly) would have to hike to the summit. Mt. Tabor was a supposedly extinct volcano in the heart of Southeast Portland. It was a haven for big thighed cyclists, wine smuggling lovers and lesbians with dogs.

The half-rainy day had enough cloud-breaks to promise a decent sunset over the valley. The motley crew slogged up the hill, their beer

212

bottles, wallet chains, baggy clothes and safety pin armor conspiring with gravity to prevent the ascent. Telly followed a smiling Lucinda, unsure of what would happen, but feeling that it would be important.

Lucinda had pulled another fast one with Bren over the phone, convincing her that she would be just a little late. She could tell that Bren didn't buy it and that the scam would wear out soon. But this was important. It was for Dean. Maybe it was for her, too. A symbolic farewell to these lords of the flies. How could she and Telly not fall in love on acid? She sensed the excitement and trepidation in him that had "virgin" written all over it.

"You've never done this before, have you Telly?"

"No, but Zak explained the importance of LSD to the evolution of rock music. Have you ever heard of *Sgt. Pepper"s Lonely Hearts Club Band*?"

"Oh, God. That's like one of my dad's favorite fuckin' records," she said with a snarl.

"Man, The Beatles fuckin' rule!" shouted one of the kids. "That's the best fuckin' music to trip out to. Those fuckers invented the head trip!"

"I'd rather listen to some Cowboy Junkies or Morcheba, myself." Lucinda was hoping to impress Telly with her sophisticated music tastes that had come mainly from hanging out at All Day Music where she looked and listened but never bought.

"I don't know what to expect," admitted Telly. "I have listened to 'Lucy in the Sky with Diamonds' so I believe I know the effects of this drug.

This sent some of the punks into a fit of laughter. "Oh, yeah, dude, you know that 'Lucy in the Sky with Diamonds' stands for 'LSD,' don't ya?" said one of them.

"Isn't that an Elton John song?" quipped another.

One of the gang was toting a beat up guitar and turned to Telly. "Dude, when we're fryin', I'll play that song for you and you can tell me if you see any newspaper taxis."

"Thank you," said Telly, kindly.

The thirteen reached the summit and looked around. As usual, it was pretty dead on a Monday night. A few joggers and lesbians with their dogs circled on the paved path. The gang found a spot on the west-facing slope and sat down on the wet grass. The city lights were just beginning to pop on, but they had a good hour before the full-on sunset began.

"We should have got up here an hour ago," said Roxy, who had become the ringleader, since she held Dean's death doses.

"Well, we're here," said Lucinda. "Let's get this show on the road."

"Hold on a second!" Roxy wanted the mass acid drop to have more ceremony. "We should do some kind of ritual, like the Indians do before they get loaded on shrooms." Everyone looked at Telly, since he was the only one in the group who might have been to college. His cold eyes remained behind the sunglasses.

"Dean's life energy still exists," he finally said. "Perhaps we can take a moment to send him a message."

"You mean like Luke Skywalker?" asked one of the kids.

"That was Obi Wan Kenobi, dumbass," cracked another.

"I know what he means." Lucinda stood up. "Let's make a circle and hold hands and send our thoughts up to Dean."

"Oh, goody! Holding hands!"

"What should we think about?"

"How about, Dean, don't be a Nazi up there in heaven!"

"Hey Dean, send us down some good bud and nice pussy!"

Lucinda was trying to stay above the juvenile antics. "Look, just have a simple thought. Like, Dean, I miss you."

"Dean, you fuckin' idiot. Thanks for leaving us this dope."

214

Roxy stood up next. "No, you guys. It's a good idea. Come on lets do it. And then maybe after we drop, he'll answer us."

So the group formed a circle and held hands. The boys that had to hold hands with other boys made the obligatory "fag" comments but then noticed Telly. He seemed to be taking it very seriously for someone who didn't even know Dean. They calmed down and became silent. The wind blowing through the trees on Mt. Tabor was framed by the faint white noise of the rush hour below. Each thought of Dean doing something stupid and felt sad that he was gone. Telly felt like he was already in touch with the homeless boy. He pictured him as lonely and cold, clinging to anger as a lifeline.

"Amen," said Roxy. "OK, one hit each and we'll save the others for a rainy day."

"Like tomorrow?"

Roxy quietly gave each kid their lysergic communion. She was the priestess to the lost flock. She handed the last tab to Telly who examined the small plasticky paper carefully. He thought, "how tiny" and looked to others for the next step of the ritual. Each gutter-punk placed the tab on their tongues and quietly sat down on the grassy hillside. Telly followed suit. The drug made his tongue numb and it quickly dissolved.

"You're gonna just love this," said Lucinda, grabbing his hand. "I'm going to make sure you're OK." She was thinking that it might end up the other way around, given her hesitance about the whole thing.

The thirteen looked out over Portland, the Rose City, framed by green hills and sewn right up the middle with seven bridges. The lights on the west side of the river were coming on first, in the downtown office towers for those working late and the West Hills mansions of those who don't work at all. Then the more dispersed east side lights followed as commuters got home to neighborhoods with names like Ladd's Addition and Laurelhurst.

"It ain't working!" shouted out one punk. "This shit is crap!"

215

"Jesus Christ! Give it some time!" instructed Lucinda. "It takes like half an hour to kick in. Besides it was good enough to send our Dean into the river, it's good enough for your sorry ass."

"Positive vibes. Positive vibes," said Roxy. "We don't want anyone fuckin' freakin' out tonight."

Lucinda shut up and smiled at Telly, who was quietly waiting for something to happen. She was glad it was a weeknight. Otherwise Virginia and Clarissa and all the other annoying summer campers would be tagging along, fucking everything up. These were the real street kids. They lived moment to moment and the pranks and antics of the mohawked Dean made their existence just a little more tolerable.

They all sat quietly, watching the city slip into evening, waiting for things to light up.

Was it too soon to go over? It was already six. Maybe she went for a drink after work with the girls from the office. Maybe she was out with one of the guys from the office. Maybe they were back at Lisa's right now, fucking. Shit! Anything could be happening.

Zak contemplated begging advice from Lenny and Cozy but they would surely tell him to go back to bed. Besides, they had their own dramas and enough of his for one day. He'd go. What was the worse thing that could happen?

Throwing on his brown leather jacket, Zak headed out of the building and toward The Greenwood. He stopped several times along the way, considering George Costanza and his opposite impulse tactic. He'd think he should just head back but then get confused, wondering if that was the impulse he should negate. Zak would do a little box-step on the sidewalk before heading to his original destination.

The Greenwood was nicer than The Eldorado, only because it was on a tree-heavy street, away from the Burnside traffic. Its Gregorian framed two stories seemed cozier than Zak's huge building. Why would Petra want to leave a place like this?

Lisa Veerman. He pushed the button next to her name.

After a minute it was Petra's voice. "Yes?" Followed by a slight panic in Zak's heart.

"It's me. I just came along to see your face." He wanted to be just a tad sad but not a tad psychotic.

"Oh, Zak..." Then silence as the intercom went dead. It was obvious that she didn't want to let him in to her Zak-free zone. "OK, hold on. I'm coming down, but just for a minute."

Zak immediately realized that he had got the impulse and the anti-impulse mixed up. Or maybe it was the impulse cubed. Whatever, it was too soon. She had only given him the "space" speech that morning.

"Hey."

"Hey."

She looked at Zak with her big dark eyes and shook her head.

"I know. I know. I shouldn't have come. I just hate this space, this silence. I just wanted to see if things are so much better on your own." He could resist saying hurtful things. Was it genetic? A tumor, perhaps.

"Please, Zak. How many times do I have to ask you? You want us to spend our entire lives together and you can't respect my need for just a little time." He couldn't tell if she was angry or sad.

"But what is a little time? My life is on hold. I thought that you would always be with me. Is that just a fantasy?"

Petra wouldn't answer, but the look in her eyes said it all. Moving out to Portland to be with Zak had gotten her so far, but now she wanted to travel in a different direction. She was breaking both of their hearts. "Time," was all she could say.

Zak was afraid. Everything he did made things worse. "It's alright. Believe me, it's alright. Just know that I'm here when you want to talk." It was the caring friend tone that he should have taken all long.

"Thanks," she said. She didn't say I love you, like Zak had hoped. Her head was too busy swimming with love and guilt and fear and pain. Images of weddings, strange men in cafés and parties at Drake & Campbell coexisted in her mind. "I need to go back in. Don't worry, I don't have a date. I'm just meditating."

Zak never got the meditating thing. As a man he was a do-er. When he wasn't doing he was thinking up plans for doing. Petra spent a lot of time thinking about her be-ing. It seemed like an alien philosophy to Zak, although he knew he would benefit from trying it once in a while. His therapist had tried to encourage him to spend more time in quiet reflection. He even bought a yoga tape once, but was too distracted by Cathy Smith and her tight leotards. Zak was too manic for be-ing anyway. There was always something to be done.

"Oh, some china showed up today. A wedding present. That's why I came by. What should I do with it?" It was a lie that worked.

"Oh, God. I forgot about that." Petra knew if she said they should send it back it would be the same as saying that there would be no wedding, which is what she wanted to say but couldn't. "Just stick it in a corner until we figure out what we're going to do."

"You mean until you figure out what we're going to do. I'm planning on being married to you but I have a feeling, you have different plans for my life. So let me know what's going to happen to me. It's alright. It's only my life."

"Zak." He wasn't listening. He wasn't being a good friend. The conversation was over. Petra gave him a faint smile and a kiss on the cheek and went back into the building. Zak looked up at the first star poking through the cloud break. Or was it a satellite?

Up on Mt. Tabor things were beginning to happen. Lucinda caught it first (she put it down to maternal insight). The lights of the city were doing more than just coming on. Each one was a little explosion of light.

218

At first it was just one thing and then the effect spread over the whole valley. The initial key was the lights on Hawthorne, Portland's Haight Street, directly below.

"Wow. Are you guys seeing what I'm seeing? Look down at the street lights!" said Lucinda.

"What? What?" asked one of the gutter-punks, who wasn't getting anything yet.

"Oh, cool," said Roxy. "Those lights are all starting to churn and run together. Wild!"

Telly wasn't getting it. The city seemed as vibrant as ever. When he thought about Elo, he couldn't imagine anything more colorful than Portland, Oregon, even on a Monday night. Maybe the drug would have no effect on him. Although that theory went out the window when he began to drink alcohol. Still, it was such a tiny tab.

"Telly, you seein' this?" asked Lucinda, her pupils dilating.

"It's beautiful," said Telly.

"Oh, man, look at that!"

One by one, the punks' mouths opened as the city's brilliance became known to them. It was as if there was a secret city behind the city, a fourth dimension Portland that no one else could see. In the 4D city, nothing was static, everything was kinetic. Each streetlight was a thousand streetlights. Roads went everywhere at once. Cars became liberated from their earthly path. Busses looked more like caterpillars. As the drug sank in, it was as if a whole new world was trying to break through.

"Fuck," gasped Lucinda. "I've never seen anything like this."

The group spent a good thirty minutes staring at the boulevard below, watching as the light show increased. Telly was the only one not fully tripping. He looked at the valley and the kids with his usual awe of wonderment, trying to figure out what they saw. Were they witnessing something more beautiful than the green, wet world?

219

"Shit! We're missing the sunset!" shouted Roxy. The kids had been so transfixed on the street scene, they were missing the sun setting behind the West Hills. The orange sunlight was bouncing off the clouds at odd angles. The West Hills had become a throbbing mound of Jello, swallowing up the sun. In the fourth dimension, the ground and sky became part of the same atomic mass, a giant plastic relief map, hand painted by third graders.

"The clouds are made of fuckin' styrofoam, dude. They're being held up with strings. I can see it!"

"No, it's paper mache and they're on fire!"

"The sun is never coming back!"

"It's a dying ember in space. It's going supernova!"

"Is this Lucy in the Sky with Diamonds?" Telly asked Lucinda.

"Oh, yeah. We are full on trippin' now." She looked over at the kid with the guitar. "Hey Ronnie, play us some music!"

The kid took his eyes off the sky long enough to swing his guitar in front of him. He made a brief pass at the opening notes of "Lucy" and then went into Pink Floyd's "Wish You Were Here." The lack of tuning sent the group into a panic. It had to sound just right! It had to sound like the record. All this out of tune shit was going to collapse society or at least drive them mad. So Ronnie tuned and the plucking notes bounced off of the hill and rolled down to the city.

Finally, to the strains of David Gilmour's grandson, the group began to branch off into their own worlds. Some walked around the hilltop, looking up at the suddenly huge trees. Others listened to the sound of the city and Mt. Tabor Park, as they became intertwined. Lucinda stayed put and focused on the world between her feet.

"Fuck," she said. There was an ant on the ground between the shards of grass. This simple ant was now the most complex creature ever invented by the gods. Its head, abdomen and thorax were each finely designed machines. She felt as if she was watching the ant through an

220

electron microscope. She could see the details on its armor and hear the clicking of its mandibles. It was exquisite! All the elaborate space stations and computers could not compare to the brilliance of this ant!

"Telly, I think this ant is talking to me." Telly scooted over a little closer.

"I'm sure it is."

The ant remained between Lucinda's feet, arching its back and twirling its antennae around. It was looking Lucinda dead in the eye. "What are you trying to say to me, Mr. Ant?"

The ant would not leave. It knew that Lucinda would not stomp on it. The two Earthlings stared at each other for almost an hour. The grass was gigantic and radiant and she was a benevolent observer in the land of the giants.

"OK, so I think that Mr. Ant and I are somehow related. He like knows me. Maybe it's Dean!" she said, with excitement.

"All living things are related," said Telly, finally taking off his sunglasses.

"It's fuckin' Dean!" shouted Lucinda.

"Dean?"

"What?"

A couple of the kids ripped themselves away from their kaleidoscopes to see what all the fuss was about.

"It's fuckin' Dean. He's been reincarnated as a fuckin' ant," she told the small group.

"Figures."

"You're fuckin' trippin', bitch!"

"Don't squash him."

"Squash him!"

Lucinda held back the gutter punks to make sure Dean the Ant was safe. She put her hand down and let him crawl on it. "He just wanted to be with us, didn't you little Dean?"

"That's some pretty bad fuckin' karma to come back as an ant. Fuck!" Roxy had joined the little ant group. "Let me hold our Dean."

"No, you'll stomp on him." Lucinda cupped her hand so Dean could safely climb inside, which he did. "Besides, Telly says all livin' things are related. This ant is life!"

Roxy was too spaced to be hostile. She sat down on the hill. "Yeah, this dude told me that we all have the genes of the first living thing on Earth. We're all, like, descendent from the first microbe. It's like our grandmother times a million."

"Fuck."

Telly smiled at the thought, the theory.

Lucinda turned over the hand with Dean the Ant in it and looked at the back. The back of her hand became something other than the back of a hand. It was a key to the genetic history of life on Earth. She could see the hair growing out of her hand. The hair on her arms was growing darker and descending toward her fingers. She was devolving.

"Shit! Look at the back of your hands! You can see the hair growing!"

The group all looked at the back of their hands and saw the same thing. The hair was sprouting out like in those stop-action films that show plants growing.

"Fuck, we're turning into apes!" shouted one kid.

"We're going to become dinosaurs!"

"No, we're gonna become ants!"

Lucinda pulled her thumbs in and pressed her fingers tightly together. "No, we are becoming fish."

"Holy fuck!" The kids all saw their hairy paws quickly transform into scaly fins.

"What's next?" asked one of the kids, looking at Telly, who figured he must have a different evolutionary path. When he looked at his hands,

222

he didn't see hooves or paddles. He saw brilliant light glowing under the skin. Finally, something.

"A jelly fish!"

"I'm gonna be a fuckin' amoeba!"

"Wow, I just realized something," said Lucinda, looking up at the sky. "If we go back to the first living thing on earth, we must go back to where that thing came from."

"What?" asked Roxy.

"Space people," she said quietly. "In school we learned that life probably came to earth on a comet. We are related to whoever that comet came from."

"Fuck."

Suddenly there was commotion up on top of the hill. It was some of the other kids on their own trip. The hillside gang were distracted from their climb back into the primordial ooze and stood up.

"Hey, you guys! Come up here! There's someone inside this tree! We think it's Dean!"

Zak's whole world was his bed. He could still smell her on the sheets. The bed equaled comfort, a safe-zone to dwell. Well, fairly safe. There were sleeping pills and a bottle of whiskey next to the bed just like in the Bad Company song.

How could he resist the impulses to go back and try to talk some sense into her? A single second was "time," right? This was going to be impossible. He couldn't just turn off his love. He should have jumped, he thought again.

The endless wondering cycle was interrupted by the opening of the apartment door. It was Cozy and Lenny, checking on their charge. They came straight into his bedroom. Where else would he be?

"Staring at the ceiling again, old man?" joked Lenny. Lenny was dusty from a day of making pizzas. Cozy, as always, was a casual angel.

223

"How you doin', boy?" she asked.

"Our love couldn't go wrong. How could I know I was only dreaming?"

"Oh, Zak. Love is hard. It's never like the movies, you know that. Besides, she's not dead, and neither are you, thank God. Just chill out for a bit." She messed up his already messed up bed head.

"I went to see her tonight," he admitted.

Lenny and Cozy just looked at each other and shook their heads. "What happened?" Cozy asked.

"She was pissed, or sad. I couldn't tell. I just wanted to tell her that a wedding present showed up in the mail."

"You just wanted to see her. She said she needs some time." Cozy knew that time wouldn't heal Petra's roaming heart. Well, maybe a decade or two, but not a few days.

"I'm just going to stay here in bed, where I can't make anything any worse," Zak said with a sigh.

"No way, dude," piped in Lenny, sitting on the bed. "We got a pick-up gig this weekend and you need to be there for the debut of the phenomenal Sort Of."

"No way! Where at?" asked Zak, happy to talk about something else.

"Friday at RJ's with P.C. Bitch. The manager came into the pizza shop today and told me that they needed an opener. It won't be huge, but it'll be a good experiment." P.C. Bitch was one of those rap-metal bands, riding on the endless coattails of bands like Korn and Limp Bizkit, who had a pretty hard-core following. The gig would be 21 and over, but if they were good, the weekly would write it up and the hip kids would catch on.

"Right on, dude. You know I'll be there." RJ's was a cozy hole in the wall that always made you feel like you were at a really good punk rock party in someone's basement. It was a good place to go when you had nowhere else to go and just needed to rock.

"Hey, where's my favorite Martian?" asked Cozy.

"Christ, I don't know. I guess he's out with his little street urchin."

"Yeah, I think I saw her yesterday. They make quite the couple," she said.

"They're probably in a temple somewhere, trying to contact the mothership."

"Well, I wanted to invite him to the audition tomorrow. He can bring her along, too!"

Zak had forgotten that tomorrow was the big day. Cozy was going to belt out some Verdi and see if she could hitch a ride to a star in the alien world of professional opera. If he had jumped, he would have never gotten to see her sing again. He'd never again witness the beautiful tones come out of the beautiful angel. "Shit, I almost forgot. Are you ready?"

"God, I hope so. I've just been drinking tea and humming all day. I need my fan club there for moral support. This is it!"

Lenny put his arm around her. He was so proud of his diva. "Afterwards we're going to get trashed. We're gonna kick out the fuckin' jams. It's a big week!" He was hoping to get Zak a bit more animated.

"Alright. Let's focus on getting Cozy that fuckin' gig. I know Telly wouldn't miss it and I'm sure his little momma will be there. Me, I'll be in the front row, screaming, 'Sing some Chuck Berry!'"

"Yeah, and you'll have a Bic in one hand, a plastic cup of Miller Genuine Draft in the other," laughed Lenny. "Hey, we're going down for a coffee. Why don't you come along?"

"Who needs coffee when you have Zoloft? No, seriously, you guys go. I've still got part of the ceiling to analyze."

Cozy squeezed his neck and got up to leave. "You're gonna laugh at all this one day, you silly boy."

"Yeah, if you say so."

Up on Mt. Tabor, things were still going strong at midnight. The gang had split into infinitely shifting subgroups, each involved in variations of navel contemplation. Lucinda was deep in trance, gazing at the lights of the city, many now flickering off. She imagined all the safe citizens, tucked in their toasty beds. She felt like she could see right into their homes. They were so warm and secure, their down comforters pulled up around their necks. She thought she might be able to fly down and join them, just find a random sleeping mom and dad and slide right in between them.

While the others were enjoying the psychedelics, the acid made Lucinda deeply introspective. After the novelty of the drug wore off she began to think about the last few years of her young life. She had been envious of the families under their comforters before. Being a female on the street was twice as tough. Being cold, wet, and hungry wasn't bad enough. You had to worry about the rapists and the killers and the users. She had traded her body for a warm bed on more than one occasion. There were times when she just couldn't take another night under the bridge or fighting for a bed in a shelter. She'd let some rancid geezer grab her tit for five bucks or get her drunk so she just didn't care. Occasionally, a fuck meant a full night's sleep in a clean bed but usually she got kicked out before the sun and the gossipy neighbors were up.

And Dean wasn't exactly an ally against this soul-numbing exploitation. Once he had saved her from some drifter. The guy was trying to rip her pants off in the bushes by I-5. Dean hit him over the head with a big stick, sending him stumbling down the hill. She was shaken and, momentarily, glad to be a part of this band of vagabonds. Then, as payment for his rescue, Dean demanded sex with her in the same spot the dirty would-be rapist had assaulted her. When she said no, he tried anyway. Add that to the times that he had stolen her backpack, beer and baby (once he hid Polly from her) and Dean was a Class A dick.

Lucinda stared down at the city, trying to climb into one of those warm beds, without moving a muscle. She looked around for Telly. He was above her on the hill, muttering some strange language, probably Yugoslavian, she thought. She pushed the image of the bed out of her head and went up, next to her friend.

"Hey man, what are you doing?"

Telly was staring up at the stars that had found a broad clearing in the sky and whispering in a vaguely Slavic tongue. "I'm just talking to a satellite," he said. "Twenty thousand miles up in the sky."

"I think it's so cool when you call someone on a cell phone, or long distance, your voice goes all the way up to outer space and then bounces back down. I'm up in space trying to talk to someone. I love the modern world." She thought that she could tell which stars were stars and which stars were communication satellites.

"I'm trying to talk to someone in space," Telly said, not removing his gaze.

"Yeah, who? Any luck?"

"Just a friend. No, no luck." As the clouds crossed over the stars, he looked over his folded arms at Lucinda. Her face seemed bigger than normal. He felt her radiance shining through her eyes and out of her nose and off her lips. He had been told that this place was like heaven and now he saw it in her gentle smile (of course, to Lucinda, Telly's face alternated between that of Keanau Reeves and a quarter horse). "Lucinda, you are very beautiful," he said unexpectedly. Under the pain, she was beautiful.

"You must be trippin'! I don't feel very beautiful. I feel like a freak."

"What do you think is the most beautiful thing in the world?"

Lucinda had no immediate answer. She twirled her finger in her two-toned hair and then looked up at the sky. The moon was high and shining directly through a cloud break. "That," she said, pointing at the picture. The clouds seemed to be breathing and inviting, like a magical landscape. "The sky when the rain stops and you see the moon. Like,

227

you've seen it a million times before, but suddenly you see it and you just can't believe how good you feel. It's always been there, even though you couldn't see it. I need moments like this to remind me that it's still there and as beautiful as ever."

"Come with me," said Telly , standing up. He reached for her hand and she took it. They walked a bit farther up the hill. Lucinda felt like something special was going to happen, when Telly stopped. "We are on a mountain top," he said.

"Yes, we are," she replied, half-expecting a marriage proposal. The limbs on the trees on top of Mt. Tabor were waving like wild arms, but things seemed calm and peaceful.

"Look out at the clouds, Lucinda," said Telly in a very soft tone. She turned around and faced westward, feeling like she was inches from the cloud ceiling. Telly put his hands on her shoulders and that's when things became even more magical.

Like a 757 piercing the canopy, she was no longer on the old volcano, but flying up to the clouds! With Telly gently holding her shoulders they ascended up to the heavens. She felt no fear, just the exhilaration of breathlessness. The space between the ground and the gossamer clouds was like being under water in the shallow end of the pool. She knew of the concrete solidity of the pool floor and the fluidity of the water, but what lay above the surface? Angels playing Marco Polo? Fish out of water!

She didn't bother looking down. She had spent enough time on the ground. Her grinning face slowly brushed against the first clouds and she could feel the moisture. She wanted to tell Telly that she knew that clouds were just water but she was just too happy, blissful, to say anything. She closed her eyes as they entered the bottom of the cloud like a wayward raindrop and disappeared into its billowy blankets. She felt warm and safe there. She could sleep wrapped in Telly's arms inside the cloud, far away from the predators of the street. But they kept rising.

Then their heads came through, into the clear black night. They were in a cottony valley, surrounded by cumulus mountains, millions of stars and the brightest moon Lucinda had ever seen.

"Oh, Telly, this is the most beautiful place on Earth," she barely uttered. She saw faces in the walls of clouds around her. Familiar faces. "This must be heaven," she whispered.

She was tempted to run and dive into the cloud-tops, as if they were piles of leaves, but dared not break away from Telly. It was a whole new world. She had never seen so many stars. Were these the stars that were always over Portland? "Look, it's the Milky Way! I can see it!" The sky was both black and full of light. The stars reached down to hug her. The clouds were a great goose-down comforter. For the first time in her life, she felt no fear, only love. Her heart was full with whatever she had always been hoping for. She felt a simple contentment magnified by the sublime vision of being above the clouds. They softly drifted into a cloud-top and it felt solid.

Lucinda looked into Telly's eyes. He had said nothing on this heavenly ascension. What could she say to him? He had carried her 10,000 feet above the ground and laid her down in a bed made of clouds. Only the stars and satellites could see them. She thought she must be dreaming, but she knew she wasn't. Telly was the brightest star that ever fell from space. If she only knew his story.

"It's alright," Telly whispered and he put his cheek next to hers.

The moon moved across the stars as they floated in each others arms. Lucinda drifted off to sleep there in her heavenly bed.

Her dreams were filled with images of security. She was living in rustic mountain house with lots of skylights beaming sunshine in. Polly was scampering around with drawings and Telly was sitting on the couch with the newspaper, smiling at Lucinda. They were married and the sheets were always clean, the refrigerator was always stocked and Polly was always safe. The view from the big bay window looked down over the

229

lush valley. It was as far away from the streets and as far away from the coast as it could be.

Below Lucinda and Telly the city slept and dreamt. Those on the streets and those in homes shared similar visions of love and security and the anxiety about its loss. The collective dream power rose up to the sky. Their dreams made up the life force, the collective dream of humanity.

Cozy was dreaming that she was a Viking wife, preparing a fire for Lenny, who was 200 feet tall. She had called him off the battlefield with her song. Lenny's dreams were more pedestrian. He was in a room surrounded by the nymphets from the cover of Kiss' *Love Gun* album. Their white faces all looked up at him with lust. Their heaving cleavages were bound in black fishnet and their spiked heels disappeared into the dry-ice fog.

In another building, Petra slept fitfully. Her dreams were a series of chase scenes. First it was some guy that she had met at a winery. He was following her down NW Hoyt Street, trying to get her to go to coffee. She got away by telling him she had frozen groceries in her backpack. She turned the corner only to encounter Ben, her boss. She tried to run away as he chased, begging for her to have an affair with him. Then there were a few more Drake & Campbell guys groping for her. To escape, she ran into The Eldorado, only to find Zak on his knees, crying. She ran out of the door only to encounter the guy from the winery and the cycle of pursuit.

Zak dreamt that he was drunk, which might have had something to do with the whiskey and sleeping pills. He was sneaking into The Greenwood to leave a note for Petra. As he approached the door, out crept Petra in a Spiderman costume. Was she sneaking out for a night of crime fighting? Was this the reason she left him? To fight the good fight? Zak followed her out onto the street. She got on one of those electric carts that fat people ride because they can't be bothered to walk.

Petra/Spiderman looked at Zak and told him that the cart belonged to Bud. Bud who? Maybe her new boyfriend. He stepped back as she puttered down the sidewalk in her superhero costume. He got a sick feeling. That he had lost his fiancé to the world of crime fighting and a fat guy named Bud. He looked up at the moonlit clouds and wondered if things could get worse. Then his teeth began to fall out.

Oh, in the heat of the night, when things ain't goin' right.

Chapter Eight:
Do Ya

Rock is God. Rock 'n' roll is king. From it's very conception it has been about the unleashing of sexuality that is an essence beyond fucking. Sure, that point of conception was in the backseat of a rocking and rolling 1954 Ford, with the AM radio snuck over to the "race music" station. And, sure a lot of those early r&b songs used clever metaphors for coitus that only the hippest white kids picked up on. But from the beginning, rock 'n' roll was about a feeling. More than the momentary orgasm, rock championed living sexually. Think about Elvis' hips, Mick's lips and Debbie Harry's tits. Think about Gene Vincent snarling, Iggy Pop crawling through broken glass and Courtney Love flashing the audience. It's been a half-century-long orgy that let men paint their faces and swing their asses and let women bang out power-chords. The phallic guitar is a crotch shield for a new kind of sex.

Rock 'n' roll is the uneasy marriage of the prideful sexuality of the negro blues and the shameful sexuality of country & western music. As soon as Bill Haley and Chuck Berry and the others unleashed it upon the Earth, the straight world panicked. There were Bible readings, record burnings, parent meetings and congressional hearings. The world, through it's primary tool of repression, religion, had tried for centuries to keep sexuality in check. It was too organic and powerful to be permitted free reign in a world where man/God needed to conquer nature. When Elvis hit the stage, the genie was let out of the bottle. The sacred love that guided pagan goddess cultures for eons was revealed. Barbara Ehrenreich once wrote that the modern feminist movement was born in the midst of

233

Beatlemania. Those young girls, screaming for John, Paul, George and Ringo, inherently knew the power of their newfound sexual voice.

The genesis of rock spun out of the violation of one taboo after another. The first to go was the myth of racial separation. There, in the most segregated parts of the South, white teens broke through their parents' apartheid to find the music of Fats Domino, Muddy Waters and Big Bill Broonzy. And there was nothing the racist parents could do about it. These kids were the first wave of baby boomers with millions to follow. Next, the big three universal sexual taboos were broken. Incest mores were shot down by Jerry Lee Lewis marrying his 13-year-old cousin. Homophobia took a blow as Little Richard pranced in full drag and double-double entendres. Lastly, monogamy bit the dust as the roaming hearts of Hank Williams and Robert Johnson gave birth to the King. The seed of free love and sexual liberation was planted in the mind of every teen with a scratchy 45 of "Let The Good Times Roll."

That parents continue to abhor teen music is not surprising. Sexual curiosity inevitably ends up as sexual repression. The power of rock music is in its simple formula that your parents must not like it. In most cultures, there are only two phases of life: childhood and adulthood, usually with some painful rite of passage between them. But in post-war America, a new category popped-up, sexualized youth.

The nebulous status of youth is the source of much drama for adolescents. How can you vote, but not be allowed to legally drink a beer? Why do you pay adult prices and the movies at twelve but aren't allowed into adult movies? What are you saying when you tell a 17-year-old to act his age? If that 17-year-old isn't allowed into the adult world, she can find solace in youth culture. He or she will use any weapon available to lock out the adult world that has locked them out. The best weapon ever invented in the history of the human race is rock 'n' roll.

There is a clear link between Elvis Presley and Marilyn Manson and it has nothing to do with Satan. Both were a vehicle for teens to flip out their parents who walked out of their kids' bedrooms, nervously shrugged their shoulders and muttered, "That's not music." Mission accomplished. Rock 'n' roll is freedom. Rock is God.

Zak was getting into the habit of getting up early. If he didn't get out of bed he would just lie there, unable to get back to sleep, and think about Petra. He'd wonder where she was, whom she had been with, what she was thinking. He'd wonder if she was sitting next to a phone debating on whether or not to call him or if she was in bed with her arms wrapped around some advertising executive. The only way out of this madness was through the distraction of stimuli. He was watching lots of TV and chatting with strangers on-line and pretending to work on his masters thesis.

Fortunately, the ever-distracting presence of Lenny Rockstar was over this morning. The two were on the futon, drinking beer and watching the *Sally Jessie Raphael Show*. It was a show about Nazis who were brainwashing their kids to be junior Nazis. The New York audience, filled with every possible race, creed or ethnic identity, was screaming their lungs out at the guests. One black guy in the back was hollering, "Come up to Brooklyn! We'll kick your ass!" and the rest cheered.

"Disgusting," muttered Lenny.

"A waste of meat and bones," responded Zak.

"Flush the whole lot."

"Sally, too. She looks like Cyndi Lauper's grandmother. What's up with that?"

"Disgusting." Lenny took another swig of beer and the two sat transfixed on the chaos, unable to turn it off.

"You know what bugs me?" asked Zak. "Here are these Nazi assholes sitting there all cool and they end up looking better than the people in the audience."

235

"Because of their smart outfits?"

"No, because the audience is feeding into their every stereotype of the 'savage urbanites.' That black guy who was saying he was going to kill them should have said, 'You should come up to Brooklyn and have dinner at my house and see how normal we are.' But instead the Nazis are gonna say, 'See what we mean?'"

"So, you're siding with the Nazis?"

"Fuck off. I'm just saying that these fucking shows have zero to do with solving the problem and everything to do with getting people riled up so they won't turn the channel and miss all the commercials." It always came back to advertising.

Lenny and Zak continued to watch the show. And Zak was right, there was no solution offered to the problem. But the Nazi kids did get a free make-over. Their Hitler comb-overs were styled and their homemade Nazi uniforms were replaced by Nazi uniforms from Abercrombie & Fitch. Maybe with the right clothes they won't need fascism, at least the kind that wants to gas all non-Aryans. The united colors of Benneton.

Two more bottles of morning beer were popped open and the pair were gearing up for *Montel*, who in the preview promised to solve the problem of willful teenagers with a day in boot camp (and a make-over) when Telly and Lucinda came in.

"Dude!" said Zak.

"Dude!" said Lenny.

Telly and Lucinda looked like they had been on a wild adventure. Zak had the brief notion that his roommate had taken the girl for an overnight trip into the cosmos. They walked in sat down on the floor next to the TV.

"Hey Lucinda. You OK? This is Lenny." Lucinda just smiled at both and then smiled at Telly. "So did you guys elope or something? You look like you just got back from Vegas."

"We've been flying through the air," said Lucinda grabbing Telly's hand, making him slightly uncomfortable.

"Oh, that was you two I saw last night," laughed Lenny. "I thought it was Ultraman and the Flying Nun."

"Dude, Ultraman is like a hundred times bigger than the Flying Nun. Sally Field could probably fly up Ultraman's nose." Zak turned to the couple fearing the worst. "OK, spill, what the hell happened?"

"Zak?" Telly had a rare smirk on his face. "I understand 'Lucy in the Sky with Diamonds' now."

Lenny and Zak looked at each other and then burst out in laughter. "Dude! You fuckin' tripped?"

"Nothing is real and nothing to get hung about," was his response.

"I saw babies dancing in the midnight sun!" added Lucinda.

"Christ!" shouted Zak. He popped open a beer for Telly, but not the under-aged girl. "Have you been running around Portland all night on acid?"

"Dude, it hella rocked!" said a wide-eyed Lucinda, sitting down at Zak's feet. "We were up on Mt. Tabor and then we were up above the clouds and everything was so beautiful."

"I guess it wasn't the brown acid," dead-panned Lenny.

"Lucinda?" Zak had to ask the question. "Um, where is your baby?"

"Oh, shit!" she shrieked.

"You didn't lose it again?" he asked, not knowing that she had actually lost Polly once, that time on the bus.

"Fuck! No, she's at the... um, a friend has her. She's gonna be fuckin' pissed that it's so late." Lucinda stood up and hugged Telly tightly, her face in his chest. "Tel, please, can we meet up later?"

Telly coldly extracted himself from her grip and tried to shake her hand, which caused Zak to roll his eyes at Lenny. "Yes, call me later today, after you have gotten some sleep."

237

"Oh, cool!" She was a little too excited. Like she knew her life was about become something completely new even if she didn't have a signed contract stating such. "Bye sweetie! Bye you guys!" And she flew out the door.

"Sweetie?" said Zak, with a sarcastic churn of his shoulders.

Lenny put his arm around Telly's neck. "Telstar, how long you been in town? You've already got yourself a little hottie. It must be that alien accent."

"She is not my girlfriend. I am just..."

"Observing her!" interjected Zak.

"Oh yeah, I wouldn't mind observing that kind of Earth action," joked Lenny.

"Dude, she's a gutter-punk. She's probably got scabies, not to mention a fetal alcohol child." Zak didn't think he was harshing any romance if Telly was, in fact, an emotionless Vulcan.

Telly had moved back to the window to catch the sight of his trip-mate running down Burnside, towards the shelter. His sadness remained, but he had just had a glimpse into something beautiful that had only taken two people to create. It was best described of as a "moment," but a moment that was beyond time.

"Don't be a dick, Zak. Can't you see our Telly is in love?"

Upstairs, Cozy was meditating on Violetta, of *La Dame aux Camélias*, the twenty-three year-old French courtesan who tragically died from consumption, of all things. The Dumas play that had inspired Verdi to write *La Traviata* was a story that Cozy could relate to, filled with melodrama and young hearts. The fact that Verdi had bashed out the entire opera in only four weeks was also kind of rock 'n' roll, she thought. Sort of like The Beatles writing "She Loves You" on a napkin during a cab ride. Brilliance comes quickly.

Cozy had been practicing her channeling of Violetta for weeks. This audition could put her on the ladder to her dream. Singing in clubs and for friends who really knew nothing about opera was one thing. It gave her a sense of power and some acceptance as an "artist." But singing professionally with long-hairs who lived and breathed the classics, now, that would be something.

Her mind slipped back to her college days when she could barely talk, let alone sing arias. People assumed she was a ballet dancer because her anorexia gave her the illusion of frail grace. But ballerinas had to smoke too much and Cozy desperately wanted to sing. The world of opera gave her a lifeline out of the super-model baited trap of starvation. The biggest divas were the best.

Cozy fell in love with Leontyne Price records. She fell in love with the passion and precision of the music. She began to eat again once she learned that beauty exists in the heart, not in evaluation by others. It had taken five years of training but now she was about to sing one of the most over-the-top pieces from the nineteenth century canon. If she pulled it off, people would love her the way she loved those Leontyne Price records.

This morning she wanted to rest her voice, so she cringed when the phone rang.

"Hey, Coz." It was Petra. "I just wanted to say good luck today."

"Aw, hun, you're not going to come?" Cozy wasn't surprised.

"Well, I'm sure Zak will be there. I don't want to distract you with our drama. Besides, I just can't see him today." Her voice was trembley.

"Pet, what's going on?"

"Same old shit. Zak's a little crazy right now and it's scary."

"Kid, he's harmless. Any guy would be crazy after your little about-face. There's something else."

Petra didn't want to spill the beans about her and Ben. That morning he had cornered her and made his intentions clear and she did

239

nothing to rebuff him. "Just have a great audition, sweetie. I want to see your name up in lights."

"Oh, I'm ready. I'll let you know how it goes. Hey, you should at least come to RJ's on Friday. It's gonna be the premier gig of Sort Of. Lenny thinks it will be a big smash." Lenny's events always seemed to eclipse her own.

"I can't. That's the Drake & Campbell Founder's Day party. I sort of have to go."

"You sort of need to see Sort Of," said Cozy, making a joke.

Petra promised that she would see Lenny's band as soon as things calmed down a bit and that she missed hanging out with them. Cozy didn't have the energy to convince Petra of her mistakes. She thanked her for the call and got back to visualizing about Violetta and Alfredo and their tangled web.

It was 2:45 and Lenny, Zak, Telly and Lucinda were finding seats in the Performing Arts center. Telly invited Lucinda in the hopes that the beauty of the highbrow of opera would lure her off of the streets. Lucinda was wary of anything so far removed from her punk-rock lifestyle. But all those days spent sitting at the bus stop, listening to Cozy's voice float out of the apartment window motivated her to give it a try. She was back in charge of Polly, who was thankfully asleep in her arms.

Zak was hoping that the joys of opera would displace his blues, but then he remembered that all operas are inherently tragic. Were there any were everyone lived happily ever after? They always end in death: Radames and Aida buried alive in a tomb, Mimi croaking from TB, Carmen, Madam Butterfly, Tosca, all dead. But he wouldn't have been anywhere else. Dear Cozy had been supportive of him and would probably single-handedly get him through this current tragic-drama. He loved her, it was true. She was so kind. Cozy would never knife him in the back the way Petra had. He knew she desperately wanted to be loved and

240

he desperately wanted to love. The gods had just put them with the wrong people. Sounded like an opera.

A few seats away, Lenny was filled with trepidation. Maybe even more than Lucinda, he was a creature out of his element. As much classical music as he listened to with his girlfriend, he was born to rock. He wanted music that moved his feet and gut and, most importantly, got a reaction from people, that polarized people and made them want to fight and feel alive. He was in awe of Cozy's talent, but was of the position it would be better displayed in a heavy metal band. That guy in Iron Maiden kind of sounded like an opera singer, right?

"Oh, this is gonna be seriously kick ass," he said.

"This seems very different from your concert," said Telly. "It is more like a church." Telly had noticed the hushed tones of the few others in the audience. They were probably friends of the other singers auditioning. The people wondering around the stage were in suits and seeming very solemn.

"Yeah, opera is all serious and shit," answered Lucinda.

"Shhh. Quiet y'all. It's about to start." Zak wasn't up for the armchair analysis game. He just wanted to see his Cozy knock the roof off of the opera house.

For the auditions, there was just a string quartet. Three men and a female cellist with stacks of sheet music took their places. And then the director of the Portland Opera and a handful of colleagues took seats in the third row.

"Alright. If each singer would please state her name and her selection," the director said. Zak figured that was so he could see how articulate they were but it was actually just so the guy could keep everyone straight.

A large, 40-ish red haired woman emerged from stage right. She had that "opera singer look." Zak was surprised that she wasn't wearing a Viking helmet and hoped that she wasn't a pro. This happened all the

241

time in "amateur" striptease contests. Usually the supposed amateurs were just strippers from other clubs, not nervous bet-losers, and ended up winning all the cash prizes. Zak hoped the same scam didn't go down in the opera world.

"My name is Amber Lavender and I will be singing, 'Si Mi Chiamano Mimi' from *La Boheme*."

"That's not her real name!" hissed Lucinda without waking Polly.

Zak shot Telly a glance that was meant to say, "Control your woman," but Telly thought it meant, "Yeah, that can't possibly be her name," although Telly didn't know why, since Amber Lavender was such a beautiful name.

The music quietly began and Amber Lavender opened her mouth. Oh, she was good. The beautiful tones filled the hall. Apparently the aria was a bit of the classic because several of the people in the crowd were singing along, out of tune. The gang from The Eldorado would have enjoyed it too, but they were there to root for Team Cozy.

"She's good," muttered Lenny, shaking his head.

"Yeah, but she'd have a hard time convincing anyone that she was Mimi." *La Boheme* was a personal favorite of Zak's. The story of young bohemians suffering for art's sake and love's sake played right into his romantic notions of self-destruction. The death scene of the young and frail Mimi always got to him.

The woman managed to capture the room and when she finished applause erupted in the various of islands of people watching the audition. The shift from music to clapping woke Polly who struggled to escape Lucinda's arms.

"Shit!" said Zak, exacerbated about Cozy's competition and Polly's noisy distraction.

"Don't get your panties in a wad, dude," fired Lucinda. She set Polly down in her lap and raised her black t-shirt, lifting her left breast into the baby's mouth. "That'll shut her up for a while."

"Right on," said Lenny, catching a glimpse.

After some paper shuffling by the quartet, Cozy walked on to the stage. She had spent hours deciding what to wear and how to do her hair. The end decision was simple yet devastating. Her shoulders were not covered by her long black gown, which had spaghetti straps, but by her beautiful black hair. She had decided against the conservative back-in-a-bun look. She was young and simple, like Violetta, the fallen woman.

Lenny and Zak gasped almost simultaneously. Telly and Lucinda sat up in anticipation. Polly just sucked.

"Hello, my name is Cozy Daniels. I would like to sing 'Addio del Passato,' from Verdi's *La Traviata*."

Lucinda was going to applaud, but fortunately looked around and noticed no one else applauding. So she just tried to send a big smile to Cozy, who she hadn't actually met yet, but who had seen Lucinda from the window.

The strings chimed in on the upbeat and a spotlight hit Cozy's eye, causing it to twinkle. The waltzing rhythms put her in the spot she'd dreamed about for years and the joy leapt for her voice, masked only by the sad story of the song. The impossible scales that she danced around caused the few dozen spectators to drop their jaws. The director whispered something to a man on his right, which Zak took as a good sign. Whispering to the right-hand man.

Telly was transported by Cozy's voice. He thought about all the misery he had seen on Earth, sandwiched between police and preachers. This tragic melody made it all worthwhile. Whatever it was, this thing so removed from his own experience, made the suffering worthwhile. In the world of pain there is beauty. He knew that this was part of his quest.

When they had entered the performing arts center, Lucinda was pretty sure that the effects of the LSD had completely dissipated. But Verdi's swirling psychedelic melody brought it all back. She let her head fall back so she could see the ornate ceiling of the hall. It was so like the heavenly skies that she and Telly had danced in. Framed by the cloud-dressed sky was Cozy's adoring face. It was clear that Cozy was the mother and Lucinda was her baby, held tightly in her arms. Cozy laid her down in a field drenched in morning sunlight. She looked down on Lucinda with her long black hair blowing slowly as if she were underwater. Cozy smiled lovingly and clasped he hand to her chest like the Virgin Mother.

Lucinda snapped back into the real world when Polly bit her nipple.

The proudest rock dude in the room was Lenny. Suddenly, he got it. He got why Cozy loved this music so much. It was more technical than an Yngwie Malmsteen solo, but had more passion than every Temptations song from "My Girl" to "Papa Was A Rollin' Stone." He got it and it broke his heart. All those times he had dismissed Cozy's tastes and quiet obsessions. Who would care about music that's not even in English, he'd taunt. He got it and he knew how lucky he was to be with this beautiful woman. Lenny didn't realize it, but tears were streaming down his face. His Cozy.

Needless to say, Cozy was a show-stopper. This girl who had hung around the symphony office and cast parties was now this stunning soprano, handling the trill and the floritura like they were high school friends. She had the confidence that Miss America contestants only achieve with methamphetamines. The sounds that came out of her mouth must have been beamed in from some alien spaceship, maybe Telly's.

When she finished the short aria the room was silent. Stunned.

"Fuck," gulped Lenny and then began to clap slowly. Soon the whole room was applauding furiously and shouting, "Encore!" like it was opening night or something. Even the milk-drunk Polly joined in with wails of her own. The director and his posse looked around the room and grinned. Cozy just smiled, not wanting to walk off the stage, feeling a bit like a star.

"Let's go!" urged Lenny. Lenny and Cozy had made plans to meet at the stage door after her try-out instead of wading through all the other auditioners, who must surely now be quivering in their opera shoes.

The four made their way across the seats and out the back of the hall into the semi-bright daylight. Circling around to the side stage door they found Cozy hopping up and down in excitement.

"Oh, what did you think?" she cooed

"Bravisima," said Zak.

"Fantastic, babe!" said Lenny.

"Awesome," said Lucinda.

"Reason for hope for the living things of the universe," said Telly.

Then Lenny remembered his manners. "Coz, this is Telly's friend, Lucinda, and her Polly."

"You were amazing, Miss Daniels."

"Oh hun, call me Cozy and thanks. I'm glad to finally meet you."

Imagine that. Lucinda had really arrived. An opera star glad to meet her! "Oh, Cozy, I've listened to you sing so many times. You are just so beautiful in person."

Cozy shot Telly a wink, as in, you've got a charmer here.

But it was Lenny who was overcome with pride. "Coz, I've seen a lot of things in my life but I never seen nothin' like you. Whether or not you got the job, you won in my heart."

It was a rare romantic turn of phrase that just propelled Cozy into his arms and they hugged while the others applauded.

"Right!" shouted Zak, not wanting the Lenny-Cozy love-fest to go on for too long. "Let's celebrate!"

"Well, I don't know if I have a reason to celebrate yet, Zak. They're going to announce who got the gig at 6."

"OK, then, let's meet at the Sandy Shack at 7. We'll either toast your new career as the Rose City diva or we'll drowned our sorrows."

245

"Isn't that a bar?" asked Lucinda, feeling like she was being excluded from the revelry.

Telly knew that Zak wasn't a big fan of his friend and resented the maneuver. "I can get you in Lucinda, but you can't drink alcohol."

"Party pooper."

A few hours later Lucinda, Telly and Zak were back at the flat, playing Santana records and watching Polly try to stand up and mambo to the music. Zak had to admit that the girl was beautiful in her own way and she was obviously a doting mother, even if she did occasionally dump the poor child with random shelter workers when she wanted to roam the streets. But he worried that Telly was falling for her. Love was a dodgy bet at best, especially when it was with an emotionally damaged 19-year-old runaway.

"Polly really likes this music. Maybe her dad was Mexican."

"You don't know?" He didn't want to be rude, but it was his home.

"Dude. Does anyone really know who their father is?" She was used to the question.

"Well, for better or worse, I look exactly like my dad."

"What about you, Telly? What are your parents like?"

Telly's face went back to its normal forlorn position. "I never knew my parents."

"Oh, how sad." Even though Lucinda hated her parents, she was glad she knew them. "Are you an orphan?"

"Something like that."

Then, with a noisy wallop, the apartment door swung upon and Lenny bounded in. Cozy was riding on his back, hooting and waving a Champaign bottle that she'd been saving.

"Woo!" she shouted, crashing onto the futon, bottle still raised. "Guess who the new company soprano is!"

"No fuckin' way!" Zak was suddenly ecstatic. "I knew you had it!" He gave her a big hug that lingered.

"We are very pleased for you," said Telly, knowing that the event was important to her.

Lucinda, who in a vision saw the singer as a loving mother, grabbed her around the waist and put her head on Cozy's chest. "I'm so happy!" she said.

"Oh, thanks Lucinda. That's so sweet." And then Cozy picked up baby Polly and twirled her in the air, causing Polly to giggle.

"Our Cozy is a regular Madame Ovary!" proclaimed Lenny.

"That's Madame Bovary," corrected Zak. "And I think you mean Madame Butterfly."

"Yeah, dude, whatever."

"I just can't believe it," exclaimed Cozy. "Especially after that broad belted out Puccini!"

"Let's hear it for Amber Lavender!"

"Hip hip hooray!"

"Let's hear it for superstar Cozy Daniels!"

"Hip hip hooray!"

Everyone plopped down on the floor exhausted from their exhuberation.

"OK, let's drink!" shouted Lenny.

"Do you think I can bring Polly?"

Everyone looked at each other, unaware of what the rule was about babies in bars.

"I'm sure it will be OK. It's still the dinner hour," said Lenny. And they all headed out to Lenny's Corolla and squeezed in.

The Sandy Shack was what patrons referred to as a dive bar. Populated by alcoholics and slumming hipsters, it was about as cozy as you could get. Dinner was whatever could be grilled up out back and the jukebox was well stocked with Sinatra and Devo.

The waitress asked everyone for ID's and Telly told Lucinda to just show her identification. All Lucinda had was the beat up drivers license that she got on her sixteenth birthday in Seaside. She held on to it even though she never drove and it proved she was under 21. But she trusted Telly. Maybe he had some deal with this waitress.

The server looked at looked at Lucinda's license and then her. At first glance she thought the birth date said "1981" but on a closer look it said "1979." "OK, what'll ya have?"

"Dom Peringon all around!" said Lenny, causing the waitress to smirk. As if.

"Beam and Coke."

"Hefenwiezen."

"A Manhattan."

"Beam and Coke."

"Just a Coke, please," said Lucinda, reluctantly keeping the bargain.

With the drink orders in Lenny and Zak raced to the jukebox with Telly in tow. They were planning on subjecting the bar to a barrage of Beastie Boys, Hall & Oates, Sinatra, Tammy Wynette, Limp Bizkit, The Beatles, Great White and whatever else struck their impulsive fancy.

"So how are things going with you and Telly?" It was a moment of girl talk.

"Great! Except I'm not sure how much he likes me. He's very strange like that. Maybe it's the custom in his country not to be open with your feelings."

"Oh, I'm sure he likes you. Look at how much time you two spend together."

"Yeah, but sometimes I feel like his science project. He just watches me and Polly, like he's wonderin' if we're worth the trouble."

Before the convo could get any farther, the three men came back to the table and landed with the drinks.

"Here's to Cozy, the diva's diva!" toasted Zak, robbing Lenny of the honor.

"Cozy!"

They enjoyed their beverages and playing with Polly, who instinctively kept trying to grab Zak's and Telly's Jim Beams. They joked about who Cozy would work with first, Pavarotti or Domingo. Lenny suggested that it was inevitable that she would be paired up with Sting, but to stay away from Celine Dion at all costs.

Before another round could be ordered, Lucinda knew it was time to leave. She didn't really fit in with this older crowd, like she did the gutter-punks. She didn't get their hip underground cultural references. But she appreciated the effort and knew she could learn to speak their language. Besides, she couldn't be out of the shelter another night. She was lucky she hadn't lost her slot already. So she had to settle for a night of bad Tuesday TV with the lung hackers.

"Hey, Telly. I kind of need to split. Polly's getting tired and I'm still wiped from last night."

"OK, let's go outside and I will get you a cab."

"Great. Thanks everyone for inviting me along. I need to take my daughter home."

"Oh, hun, thanks for coming to the audition today," said Cozy. "Come by and visit. Bye-bye, Polly!"

"Yeah. Friday," added Lenny. "I've got a show right down the street. You should come."

"I'll try. Goodnight, Zak."

"Goodnight, Lucinda."

Zak used the moment to make a break for the bar. Watching the lovey-dovey rock-opera couple and whatever Telly and Lucinda were was a bit much at the moment. The Beam had him on the first slide down the razor-blade banister. The rain was getting heavy and he needed to strike that Sinatra-after-Ava position at the bar.

"Set 'em up, Joe," he said, wishing he was in a rumpled suit and tie.

"Huh? My name is Wally."

"OK, Wally. A fine Tennessee bourbon. Make it a double." Ella was singing "Stormy Weather" which was perfect for the moment. There was an old-timer at the bar who was playing Keno, hoping to win some more drink money. He smiled at Zak's forlorn look.

"There's only one thing for sure. The older you get, the more you like toast," he said to Zak.

Taking a sip of his bourbon, Zak pondered this profundity. As you get older, do your tastebuds become so bland from life that you just don't really care? Or was it that you just get used to shit being burned and charred so much that you start to like it. Whatever the geezer meant, it hung over the bar like the riddle of the ages.

"I fuckin' hate toast," he finally said.

"Keep drinkin' that rotgut, boy. Soon enough you'll be livin' on toast. Praying for it to soak up the poison from your bowels. Soon enough." and he went back to his Keno game.

Zak listened to Ella sing about since her and her man ain't been together how it keeps rainin' all the time. He stared into his drink and wondered if the songwriters were from Portland. He surveyed the bar, head slung down low. Lenny and Cozy were making doe eyes at each other, looking like a couple of Pokémon about to be devoured. Assorted alcoholics and hipsters dotted the dark corners. A soaked Telly was coming in from what surely was a passionate goodnight kiss. Keeps rainin' all the time.

"Are you OK, Zak?" asked Telly, climbing up on a stool next to the old-timer.

"Yeah, you know."

"You are wondering where she is." He was good at that.

"Yeah. Did Lucinda get off alright?" Zak was beginning to think that she was more than a lab rat to Telly.

Telly smiled. "Let's go see how our singers are doing." The two made their way back to the table, Zak careful not to spill his drink.

"What were you doing over there, you anti-socialite?" harped Lenny. Lenny and Cozy were involved in a big discussion about the music of the 1990's and needed Zak's sociological insight. "Zak, who do you think is more representative of the 1990s, Matchbox 20 or Roxette?"

"Representative of the crap?" Of course, this was Zak's world. "You might as well say Vanilla Ice or those guys that did the Macarena."

"Fine Young Cannibals!" suggested Cozy.

"Sorry, luv. That was 1989. Look, there's a complete system to this. The two definitive albums of each decade come out the seventh year."

"Is this one of your theories?" asked Cozy.

"No, seriously. Think about it. The most important pop and underground records of a decade come out in the seventh year. Dig. 1967, *Sgt. Peppers* and *The Velvet Underground & Nico.* 1977, *Saturday Night Fever* and the Sex Pistols. 1987, *The Joshua Tree* and XTC's *Skylarking* or *Appetite For Destruction.*"

"Guns N' Roses weren't an underground band," laughed Lenny.

"There were in eighty-seven when that record came out. That whole LA glam-metal scene."

"OK, we'll give you that one. So what's 1997?"

Zak held his breath for dramatic effect. "Radiohead and The Spice Girls."

Lenny and Cozy howled with laughter and Telly just looked confused.

"Zak! You are going to sit here and tell me that the most important pop album of the 1990's was by The Spice Girls? Are you drunk?" Lenny had sold his soul for rock 'n' roll.

"Dude, just listen. The Spice Girls were the end result of all that riot grrrl girl power stuff. They took it to the masses. They had 9-year-old teenyboppers talking about feminism! Besides, don't tell me you didn't love that video, where they're in the desert, acting all comic bookish." It was a hard stand to take, but Zak wasn't going to back down.

"But, man, what about the music?"

"What about the music? It's just good catchy pop. Like The Supremes. The Supremes didn't write any songs or play any instruments. Do they get respect just because they were black?"

"Scary Spice was black," said Telly, unexpectedly.

"Those songs were great. 'Wannabe,' '2 Become 1,' 'Say You'll Be There.' Great pop songs."

"I can't believe I'm hearing this." Cozy was astonished. "The man who considers anything not reviewed favorably by *Spin* 'crap,' singing the praises of The Spice Girls. I might just faint."

"Oh, Coz, I'm just sick of the fuckin' hipsters who hate something for the simple fact that it's popular. I guarantee that by around 2007, suddenly Spice Girl nostalgia will be très hip. You'll have scenesters who were 10 in 1997 trying to squeeze into their undersized girl-power shirts. It's inevitable."

"You're probably right, professor," admitted Lenny. "Look at all the props New Kids on the Block are getting now. It's fucked up."

They went on talking about the crap of the 1990s that somehow gained credibility with age. This was even true with the pivotal 1997 single, "Candle In The Wind," a post-modern pastiche, in honor of the latest dead blonde. Very little in the nineties was actually new, except for Radiohead.

When the conversation faded away from rock-talk and back to love goo, Zak started thinking of escape. It was bad enough that Petra was lost, now his Cozy was splurging her newfound success on a newly adoring Lenny. He made a break for the door but only made it as far as the bar, right next to the old-timer.

"Ain't nothin' like a broken heart, son," he said. "It will bore a hole right through your soul."

"Another Jim Beam and Coke, Wally," said Zak, who responded a bit like Nick in *It's A Wonderful Life*, as in "where do you get off calling me Wally? I don't know you from Adam." Zak just shook his head.

The bar was filling up as the Tuesday happy hour became the Tuesday night out. Young people were escaping the banal prime-time that had sucked their parents minds out of their couch-burning asses. The booths and barstools began to fill-up with aspiring barflies as Zak sipped his drink. But Lenny had had about enough of the sulking routine. No fair that Zak's depression would dampen his and Cozy's joy. So he broke away to rescue his mopey friend.

"Dude, what's up with this bit? We're trying to celebrate over here!"

"I know, Lenny. I'm just really sad tonight."

"You're fuckin' sad every night. Just snap out of it, brother!"

"I don't think I can. I can't stop thinking about this shit." He sloshed his ice around in the empty glass and then pushed it forward, hoping the bartender would make a quick refill. "I just need someone to pull the trigger."

"Shut the fuck up!"

"I'm serious. It's just too much, man. It seems so silly, but it's like everything I ever believed in was a lie."

"Shut the fuck up!"

"Dude, you shut up. You've got it all. A beautiful woman who loves you. A great band, no debt." It was becoming more than just Cozy abandoning him. It was the expectations of his life eating at him like a handful of maggots. The expectation that he would be a good husband. The expectation that he would be a successful academic. The expectation

253

that he would inspire others to do great things with their own lives. It was all zooming in on him and it just suddenly seemed too much to bear. "Len, do you know why I've been in grad school for so long?"

"Because you're trying to save humanity from itself?"

"No, because the second I'm done, my student loan comes due. Thirty-thousand dollars. Do I look like I have thirty G? Pet's dad was going to help me with it and now I'm sure he's going to bail on me."

"So this is about money?"

"No, it's about everything. I just can't handle my life. I think I might be going insane."

"Oh, there's a newsflash," Lenny said, drolly.

"Dude, I see Petra everywhere. Every chick that is like her height or hair color I think is her. Every time I see a guy kissing a girl, I think it must be her, even if she's a six-foot blonde."

"Man, you *are* insane. Look, you're just dealing with this fucked up situation. You'll come through it and have a hearty chortle, trust me. Besides there are people whose situations are a lot more fucked up than yours. Somewhere there's a guy who's got ten times as much debt as you. His wife ran off with his twin brother and his pancreas isn't working. He's gonna survive, too."

The image reminded Zak of the homeless guy, filthy and covered in scabs. What gave him the will to live? "Yeah, I know. I just feel like I have AIDS or something. Like my immune system is completely wiped out."

"Well, well it doesn't help that you spend all your time listening to sappy love songs." Lenny turned to the jukebox that was blaring a sappy Matthew Sweet song that only Zak would have chosen. "You're torturing yourself. Play some fuckin' T.Rex for God's sake. You need a dose of rock 'n' roll."

"I'm only sad in a natural way and I enjoy sometimes feeling this way," he replied, quoting Paul Weller, the singer.

"Great. Well you and the Style Council can enjoy yourselves then. But we'd like to have some fun tonight." Lenny was right in that the vibe in the bar had picked up with the evening crowd.

Telly and Cozy, curious about the serious conversation at the bar, left the booth to join their friends.

"What's going on over here guys? Is this a private party," asked Cozy, who was starting to show the effects of her Manhattans.

"Zak was just telling me how he was only going to listen to happy music from now on."

"Zipidee Doo Da," Zak said.

At the shelter nothing much was happening. At least not compared to The Sandy Shack. Polly was getting increasingly mobile and the shelter was a safe place to let her crawl around. The other women would keep an eye on her between drags of their cigarettes, while Lucinda drifted into fantasyland. Telly and his friends lived in the world that she thought she'd be living in when she arrived in Portland. They had culture and nights out. They knew about music and had different levels of friends. Not one clique but "circles."

Her life had turned out so different than she had planned. When she was a little girl in Seaside she thought that by 19 she would be living in her very own Barbie Dream House. Instead she was homeless with a baby. Her family had vanished and her friends were transitory. Telly seemed like the only real person she had met in two years. Was he her lifeline back to society? She had learned not to put too much hope into one person. But still, she couldn't help but think his interest in her was sincere. He hadn't made the moves like most guys. He was refined and stylish. The question was, was he more than just a friend?

For now, though, it was just another night of boredom.

Telly realized he was not going to get any insights into man's fate from Zak. It was the same old heart song. Zak's dialogue was borrowing heavily from whatever song was on the jukebox and Lenny and Cozy were weary of the emotional wrestle. Telly, with his dark sunglasses propped on his head turned to the old-timer for some new stimuli.

"Your friend's got the blues," said the hard-timer, pushing his black cap off his forehead. Telly read the cap. It said, "If it don't move, chrome it!"

"Yes. He says his heart is breaking." It was a saying that Telly understood, now aware of the tendency to turn body parts into metaphors.

"Ah, hell. He's got a lot of heartbreak ahead of him. He better shore up." The old geezer put his drink down and turned to Telly. "We all got heartbreak. I used to be a night watchman in a piñata factory. There was this big donkey piñata. Well, the boss caught me on the security camera one night fuckin' that damn donkey and I ain't worked since!" He took a big slurp,

"Is that why you are heart broken? Because you are out of work?"

"Hell, no! It's because I miss that goddamn piñata! It was nice." The way he said "nice" said volumes that anyone else would have been repulsed/intrigued/entertained by, but to Telly is was an acceptable statement. "Hey, you play Keno?"

The old man proceeded to tell Telly that he was playing an "8 Spot Game" and trying to win $15,000. The objective was guess which of eighty numbers on the TV screen the bouncing ball would land on. The more you got right, the bigger the prize.

There was something in the man's eyes that told Telly that this guy's life had taken a serious detour at some point. He was wise, but stupid. It was a series of bad choices that led him to be holding up the west end of the bar at the Sandy Shack. "Nine, nineteen, twenty, twenty-nine, thirty-five, fifty-six, sixty-four and seventy," Telly said as the man

256

was deciding which numbers to fill in on the slip with a number two pencil.

"Alright, I'll play those numbers for you, my friend, but you ain't gettin' my winnings." He scratched in the numbers and handed the sheet and a dollar to the bartender.

They both sat silently, waiting for the next game to come up on the bar TV.

73, 44, 9, 19, 70, 32, 29, 55, 2, 20, 64

"C'mon sweet Jesus! I only need eight of twenty!" he gulped, eyes bulging.

14, 30, 68, 56, 13, 16, 41, 7

"C'mon, baby Jesus!"

35

"Yeah! Oh, Loooordy! Fifteen big ones! I can't believe it!"

Telly just smiled as his friends looked over, curious about the coot's howling.

"Thank ya, sonny! That next drink's on me!" The shocked bartender gave him his pay-out slip to redeem downtown and the man skipped out the door, probably in search of crack and/or hookers.

Telly returned to his friends to explain that the fellow had just hit the numbers in Keno and everyone got that look, like, damn, it should have been me.

The jackpot came right as Cozy was about to tell Zak that the way to deal with his pining was to chant an anti-Petra mantra in his head. She knew all about his intended's desire to be sexually free in the big city and thought, "She's a cruel slut. She's a cruel slut. She's a cruel slut," would be appropriate. But she never got to suggest her idea because the bar scene got one more face that Zak immediately latched on to.

Lenny saw her soon after that. "Oh, my boy. Your ship has just come in." Landing in a booth with a few girlfriends was Mia McZane in a shiny black mac and go-go boots, as rock as ever.

257

"Oh, Zak, there's your dream girl," giggled Cozy.

"Forget it. I humiliated myself with her last time. She's gonna think I'm stalking her." He turned toward his drink. "No women."

"Dude, she was probably out of it that night. Let me go talk to her." Lenny got off of his stool.

"Don't!"

"No, I just want to tell her about our gig."

Zak couldn't watch. This was so fucking high school. He stared at his drink and then stared at Telly, who was watching.

Finally, he said, "OK, Tell, what's going on over there?"

"Hi, Zak."

He turned around and there she was. Just solid.

"Mia, I think you've met Zak. This is Telly and my girlfriend, Cozy."

"Hi, congratulations Cozy. Len, just told me you won a big opera role." She said this to Cozy while maintaining eye contact with Zak.

At this point, Zak decided to roll with the bourbon. "Hey Mia, when's that new Pop Art Express record coming out?" He thought that was a safe question. Damn, she looked cool.

"We're actually mixing it right now. I've got some tracks on tape in the car if you want to come out and listen to them." It was evident that Mia was enjoying the fact that a grown man could worship her as if she were a *Tiger Beat* pin-up.

Zak's head made that sound; that sound that you only hear in cartoons. The one that Scooby Do makes when he does a triple take after seeing a ghost or the one Fred Flinstone makes when he meets Ann Margrock. The closest approximation is the sound of the coil doorstopper when it is snapped.

"Um, OK."

Who knew what happened? One minute Zak was minding his own business, staring into the bottomless bourbon. The next he was in his favorite local rock goddess' Carmine Gia, making out. The syrupy psychedelia of the Pop Art Express pounded and turned the tiny VW into a rave of two. It all happened so fast. She probably made the first move, or him, could've been either. The windows steamed up and the rain painted a white-noise backdrop.

Zak just let go. He was inside a Pop Art Express song. The booze and her arms swirled around him. If it was real he would later kick himself for not mentally photographing every second. Her blonde hair fell over her face, making it a half-unveiled treasure. He only had a glimpse before she buried her cute turned-up nose into his ear, bit his earlobe and slid her hands under his jacket.

Finally, he thought, something right. He kissed her neck and remembered how many times he had seen Mia onstage, behind her keyboards, and wished he was kissing her neck. She was taking advantage of his idolatry and he could've cared less. The music gave him permission to slip his hand under her shirt. She shrugged at the touch of his cold hand but then moaned with permission to proceed.

All the outside discussion about when a women means yes and when she means no became irrelevant. There was no need for sexual harassment contracts inside the rocking sports car. The language was a collection of parted lips, tilted necks, heavy breaths, and gripping hands that said, Go for it, big boy.

On automatic pilot, Zak's hand cupped Mia's left breast. It was warm and firm, like a cereal bowl just out of the dishwasher. He had watched these sacred breasts in motion, whether she was on the stage or in the audience. He felt evil for reducing his lust to a rather marginal body part, surely not as important as her thumbs, but then fell into the Freudian abyss that makes every little boy want to return to the bosom.

The car's levers and wheels were an obstacle course for them to navigate. There just wasn't enough space to let go. Even though the tape played a twenty-first century serenade, Zak had Bad Company running through his head, specifically, "Ready For Love." Her breasts pulsed in his hands and she rubbed her palm across his crotch. How he got so hard after all the drink and nerves, he'll never know. Maybe because none of this was real.

Mia didn't let the confines of the car get in the way of her desire. She unzipped his pants. Her hands, hot from friction slid into Zak's plaid boxers.

He should have just let things happen. It was a classic rock 'n' roll moment. But for some reason, maybe the booze, maybe the slight obsession, Mia became Petra. In his mind, he was sharing one of those mundane but fully passionate moments with his fiancé. She was there and wanted him to want her. Mia's tongue was Petra's tongue. Her hand was Petra's hand. He was fondling Petra's breasts. For a moment he allowed himself to believe that he was in the clutches of his beloved and his cheeks dimpled in joy.

He should have kept his eyes closed. But when he opened them and saw Mia, ready to advance around the bases, he became conflicted. He had thought about this woman, that he didn't know, in the abstract. His fantasies of Petra were based on actual experience. It wasn't fair to confuse the two. Maybe he could fuck Mia, but he would be thinking about Petra and that was just too complicated.

"Oh, Mia?" he said as she was about to go down on him.

"Yeah? What?"

He hesitated. "We should stop. I'm all fucked up." He must be crazy. He could've consummated a long time fantasy, but his brain was just bogged down. It still felt like cheating even though he had been dumped. His heart was his own cock-blocker. "Do you think you could just give me a lift home?""

Fortunately, Lenny had briefed Mia on Zak's situation, so she didn't take it as an insult, and in fact found it kind of sweet. She dropped him off at The Eldorado with a kiss but without a phone number.

For the next few days, Zak tried to have a life but felt farther behind the basic maintenance. Just answering his e-mails alone took up half of the day. There were grant applications to be filled out and spread sheets to be made. At home he read poetry by suicidal poets, surfed porn chat groups and stared at the box of china. That box of wedding china had transformed into the monolith from *2001*. It had some larger purpose. He would sit listening to Neil Young records and stare at the box. He contemplated taking the engraved knife, saved for cutting a certain unmade wedding cake, and carving his name into the plates and then hurling them all into the Willamette River.

He spent a lot of time wishing he hadn't stopped Mia. Maybe she actually liked him. There was potential there, as far-fetched as it was. By Thursday he had only rode by The Greenwood twice on his bike. He was too confused for confrontation. He didn't want to deal with Petra or himself. Somehow he resisted the temptation to drown in the tub or choke on a ham sandwich. He wanted to see what would happen to the box of china.

Telly and Lucinda made it to that movie. They went to see a romantic comedy, staring Hugh Grant. It was the one where he gets all bumbly when he falls in love with the woman he shouldn't be in love with. Polly was starting to make words. Lucinda said her first word was, "hello" but Telly thought it sounded more like, "Elo."

Lenny and Cozy were in their own little bliss cocoon. When not organizing opera contracts or getting ready for Sort Of's debut, they were ensconced within the arms of love. Something had clicked for Lenny after the audition. Cozy was now more than a babe who came to his gigs, she was a great artist with an anything-could-happen future. He was hers and she loved the change in him.

261

RJ's was one of those rock clubs that celebrated its seediness. Formerly a strip club, the place had years of beer and punk rock sweat soaked into the floor. The exposed wooden beams and lack of light gave it the feel of a medieval dungeon, which was perfect. The place was filled with P. C. Bitch fans, testosterone-charged white boys who wanted some simplistic rap-metal to wrestle to. There were also scatterings of Gurd's more loyal fans who had got wind of the rumor that Sort Of was the new incarnation of their band.

Telly was now feeling more at home in the rock scene. He made a b-line for the bar and ordered a round of Hefeweizens for his friends. Lucinda wanted to be there but couldn't convince anyone to watch Polly. But Zak and the clinging Lenny and Cozy were with him. Lenny had a nervous look in his eye that everyone put down to this musical experiment. He gulped his lemony beer and smiled stupidly at Cozy.

The audience was populated by people from other bands. That's the way it was in the scene. Bands only survived with the mutual support of other local musicians. Everyone was curious about Gurds' transformation. This included Mia and a couple other Pop Art Expressers.

Sort Of was second on a three band bill. Around 10:30, The Mary Tyler War hit the stage in a hard-core frenzy. Sounding like the classic LA punk bands, circa 1981, the group had the P. C. Bitch fans hurling their bodies against each other and the more mature audience members moving a few steps back.

Lenny took the music as a cue to head backstage. He and Andy grabbed a couple of pitchers of beer. "OK, gang. Wish us luck."

"Good luck, sweet child of mine," purred Cozy.

"You'll rock the house, like you always do, Len," added Zak.

"Freebird!" Telly had it almost right

Lenny and his bandmate disappeared behind the stage and Zak tried to speak over the din of the ongoing Mary Tyler War. "He seems really nervous tonight."

Cozy had noticed it too. "Yeah, I don't know why. They're just changing their name, not their sound. I think he thinks they'll loose the fan-base they've built as Gurd." Cozy noticed Mia talking to some fellow rockers. "Hey Zak, there's your girlfriend. What the hell happened the other night?"

He knew that Mia would be there but avoided making any eye contact. "I told you I don't want to talk about it. I'm just too sad to be kissing girls. It's not fair to suck anyone into my black hole"

"Man, Telly, you sure picked a winner here. You hang around with this guy much longer and your home planet is going to be toast."

The comment made Telly think, hard. It was a gamble. Maybe he should have bonded with a bubbly cheerleader or a colon cancer survivor. He was having a difficult time understanding what kept Zak going in spite of himself. His time was running out and he didn't feel like he had all the data he needed.

After some more MTW thrashing and the obligatory between-set milling, it was time for Sort Of. Without the usual theatrics, Lenny, Andy, J.E., Buren and a new keyboard player walked out onto the stage and plugged in. All five were in tight black trousers and shiny silver shirts. Usually Lenny was boundless energy on stage but tonight he was calm.

"Welcome to the first show of Sort Of. We've got some old favorites by that other band and some surprises. We're going to start off a new one. It's called 'Lost Planeteer'."

The tune began with Lenny on acoustic guitar singing about wandering the galaxy, looking for help for his planet. Cozy and Zak smiled and Telly nodded at a winking Lenny. Len had taken his Hot Cake Hideaway confession and turned into a Bowie-esque rock saga. Quite an honor.

Sort Of then launched into some more familiar Gurd numbers. Those that didn't realize that Sort Of was Gurd excitedly pushed toward the stage.

263

Then the band lowered its tone. Andy and J.E. kept the basic 4-4 rock beat going. Lenny approached the mike but broke out of his charismatic lizard king mode.

"I've got something to say now, people. There are times when you have to hang on to your Ego. But there are times in life when you have to shut up and listen to your heart. There are times when you must let go and go with the love flow!" He was beginning to do his Southern preacher bit, but pulled back. "My heart is full of love tonight. I am in love with the most beautiful opera singer on Earth. I hope I will get to hear her sing for the rest of my life. So right here, right now, I'd like to dedicate this song to her. It's called, 'Do Ya Want My Love,' and I'm hoping that Cozy Daniels will say that she'll marry me."

Before anyone could react, Buren ripped into the power chords of the new song. The drunken crowd cheered! Cozy was just shocked. Had she just been proposed to? She couldn't ask Lenny because he was onstage singing about preachers banging drums. She looked at Zak who also was shocked and screamed and hugged him.

How odd, Zak thought, that Lenny had just proposed to Cozy and she was in his own arms. He felt happy/sad. Cozy then hugged Telly and the crowd all watched her reaction. She moved to the front of the stage to watch her man and his love song. Do ya? Yes, of course!

When the song ended she jumped up on the stage and Lenny looked into her eyes.

"Of course, I'll marry you, you silly boy!"

Everyone in the whole damn place cheered. It was just like the bus in "Tie a Yellow Ribbon Round the Old Oak Tree." On cue, the band swung into King Floyd's "Groove Me," the funkiest "let's get married" song ever.

"Another hot babe bites the dust," smirked Zak.

Telly shook his head. "I know that you believe they belong together, Zak."

"Well, that's a long way away from damn sure. But they'll be fine. They fit together like a lunchbox and a thermos." His jealousy gave way to sentimentality. "Hey, Tell, I think I'm going to get out of here. You can find your way home, right?"

Zak walked west toward the river, sipping from his flask full of Jim Beam to cut against the rain. Everyone was becoming a happy pair, he thought. The movies and TV shows were filled with happy pairings. Telly and Lucinda. Lenny and Cozy. What happened to his happy pairing? Betrayed with a kiss. He didn't know about the Drake & Campbell company party going on and how his worst fears were coming true.

He found himself on the right bank of the Willamette, looking at the swift moving black water. If this was another scene from *It's A Wonderful Life*, this would be about when Clarence shows up. But there was no Clarence, with his Mark Twain in his pocket and a taste for flaming rum punches. Just Zak, alone with his sadness and a wish to be washed out to sea.

There were just too many minuses. The main one would be stumbling through life always wondering where she was and who she was with. Portland was small town. It was inevitable that he would bump into her with some slick dude and she would be happy. Happy to be away from his tortured love. Added to that were the mounting expectations of a life well lived. No matter how many songs asked, "how can you mend a broken heart?" It was a reality that few understood.

He reached into his pocket and pulled out a crumpled piece of paper. It was a short Langston Hughes poem called, "Suicide's Note."

The calm,
Cool face of the river
Asked me for a kiss.

Despite the current, the surface of the water was smooth as glass and inviting. He thought about dear Jeff Buckley floating down the Mississippi into rock infamy. It was an easy way out. Selfish, but guaranteed to end the torment. It might even look like an accident with all the alcohol in his veins. The millions of gallons passing by seemed to have their own magnetic pull, tugging at his hand.

In the middle of his fantasy of the final baptism, Zak began to laugh. He laughed out loud at all the torn lovers who were contemplating the big check out. All the losers who were a slit away from throwing away the universe's greatest gift over someone who didn't really deserve the ego boost. He thought about Telly's story about worlds on the brink of collapse for lack of any joi de vie. How silly the standing-on-the-river-bank Hamlet routine must seem to the casual observer. Another idiot climbing out of the gene pool.

Zak laughed out loud and set the Langston Hughes poem into the river, letting it float way. With one more swig from his flask, he shook his head and headed up the bank. Not tonight, he thought. He was hungry and headed home to make some toast.

Chapter Nine:
Shangri-la

Love. Just the sound of the word sends backs arching and hearts fluttering. Even the beginning of the sound of the word. Lo... Luck. Lubbock. Lust. All things that turn out bad. How many wars have been fought and lost over it? How many have plunged off Lovers' Leap or poisoned themselves or their competition? How many idiots are rotting in prison because of love? People have ripped off their ears, poked out their eyes, and sewn up their genitals, all for love. If all those Burt Bacharach songs get their way, there won't be anyone left but a handful of disfigured, half-dead cripples.

The propaganda is overwhelming. The cinemas are filled with romantic-comedies. The bookstores have shelves of books with heaving cleavages and Fabio in passionate embrace. And the radio pumps out thousands of love songs. Pick any era and it is plagued with messages of love, whether it's "All You Need Is Love" or "I Will Always Love You." Take the 1980's for example. A decade characterized by greed, Ronald Reagan's dirty wars and really, really bad haircuts. As usual, the most popular songs were love songs. In fact, 10% of all the number one hits had "love" in the title. "Crazy Little Thing Called Love," "Woman In Love," "Keep On Loving You," "The One That You Love," "Endless Love," "I Love Rock 'n' Roll," "What's Love Got to Do With It," "I Just Called To Say I Love You," "I Want To Know What Love Is," "The Power Of Love," "Part-time Lover," "Addicted To Love," "The Greatest Love Of All," "Glory Of Love," "Higher Love" "You Give Love A Bad Name," "I Just Can't Stop Loving You," "Love Bites," "Groovy Kind Of Love," "I'll Be Loving You" and the song that surely led more than one redneck to kill himself, "Baby I Love Your Way/Freebird."

Evolutionary psychologists argue that love plays a vital role in the survival of the species. Love is the lure in the snag of reproduction. Love makes us want to fuck and become parents, thus ensuring the survival and stability of the human race. But if that's the case, why are over half of children born to unwed parents? Only a quarter of American families are the traditional mom-dad-kids, and who's to say that those families are built on love?

The evidence is overwhelming that love stinks. It's like a Sandra Bullock movie. On the outset it seems like a great idea, but when it's done you feel like you've had two hours/years of your life stolen from you. The sweet songs bait us and then Delilah chops off our hair or George Jones bashes us in the head with a whiskey bottle and there ain't nothin' left but the pain. There is a multi-billion dollar industry that is built on the myth of love, and none of those movie studio CEOs, florists or balloon arrangers are going to tell you the truth.

There was one man who told the truth about love, Albert Francis Sinatra. Frank was the only man who managed to color in all the shades of the tender trap. He knew how love could get under your skin and drive you to drink, heavily. He knew it was for only the very young at heart and then came the melancholy. Both Republicans and Democrats tried to claim Sinatra, to control the truth, that love is pain and self-destruction. The young, with their unscarred rock 'n' roll hearts, were oblivious to the importance of Frank Sinatra. When he died in 1998, it was just another geezer in the death pool. But to anyone over 25, it was more significant than the demise of all those 27-year-olds. At some point in each life, everyone will need Sinatra. It is as inevitable as the lie of love.

God, Zak felt bad for bailing from Lenny and Cozy's big moment. Lenny was surely looking for some affirmation after the gig, maybe even wanting to ask Zak to be the best man. This depression had turned him into a selfish prick, like his drama was more important than anyone else's drama. He left poor Telly to make excuses, like a lame hostess whose lame husband pretends to be sick to get out of the lame bridge party.

He had been staring at his bedroom ceiling since 5 am. Ever since the shit hit the fan he had been mysteriously waking up at 5 am, as if it was significant. Eventually he figured he should go up and see the two and let them know how happy he was for them, even if he wasn't. Well, he was happy for someone. He just wasn't very happy for himself, he figured. OK, he secretly loved Cozy. Sometimes he was plagued with guilt over it during the heady days of "Zak and Petra." Now he was just confused, thinking her love might be the thing that rescued him from a life without love. He was at a point where he really needed to be loved and he felt like some was coming his way from Cozy's long arms.

He was finally shaken out of bed by the Dream Police. Telly was blasting Cheap Trick in the living room. When Zak came out of the room he found Telly sitting on the floor with the headphones on. His head was bobbing to the music and he had failed to turn off the "speakers" button. Oblivious to the noise, he was intensely trying to understand the meaning behind the music.

"Telly. Telly! Telly!!!"

His roommate was staring at the album cover. Zak tapped him on the shoulder and Telly slid off the headset, noticing the music was playing loudly in the room.

"Dude, on this planet, we turn off the speakers when we listen on the cans."

"I am sorry, Zak. I was trying not to wake you."

"It's alright. The Dream Police weren't inside my brain anyway. Something else was."

"Zak, we were worried about you last night. Lenny and Cozy wanted you to celebrate with them." Telly tried to push a comforting smile through his dour expression.

"Sorry, I was doing some stinkin' thinkin'. I just needed a good walk in the rain."

"Do you love Cozy?"

Zak didn't know the answer to that question. He knew it was a different kind of love than the way he felt about Petra. Not a deep passion, just a warm glow of contentment. "Man, I'm gonna run upstairs and give those two lovebirds a big wet kiss. Let me know if that record holds the secret of life."

Telly put the headphones back on and Zak headed out the door.

Lenny and Cozy were in the full flush of love. They might have had other things to do that morning, but they were having too much fun being goofy, cuddling and giggling. Everything was ahead of them now. Their creative projects and children and levels of understanding. They just looked at each other and smiled. Each finally got it. Just like Telly finally "got" *Sgt. Pepper's* after his little trip. Cozy got the promise of a lifetime of love and acceptance. Lenny got the final piece that says this man was not whole until he dropped the macho wall around his heart. Both got that, eventually, love breaks through personality conflicts to give much more than it takes.

"Baby."

"Baby."

"Baby, baby."

"Baby, baby, baby, I got so much love inside me," sang Lenny, doing his best TLC imitation.

Cozy giggled more. "Are you supposed to be Chili or T-Boz?"

Lenny grabbed a condom off the nightstand and held it up to his face. "Left Eye!"

270

The casual observer would have thought the two were stoned off their asses. It was just the bliss, the fleeting bliss. Amid all the neck kissing and grinning, Zak knocked on the door.

"We're in here, Zak!" shouted Cozy, beckoning him into their bed-in for peace.

"Look at you two."

"Look at you one."

"I just wanted to come up and say 'congratulations.' I think it's awesome that y'all are finally getting hitched." He sat on the edge of the bed and seemed happy.

"We think it's awesome, too!" squealed Cozy. "Now where did you go off to last night, boy? You missed the big party."

Zak didn't want to harsh their ebullient vibe. It was nice to just be in the presence of a love that worked, even if it was doomed. She was too good for him. "Oh, I just went for a walk. I had a headache."

"Yeah, right. Zak are you OK?" Cozy put her hand on the back of his neck, pulling him in like a mother would pull her crying son to her breast. "We're worried about you."

"I'm OK." But Cozy's loving concern was just too much for him. Where was Petra's loving concern? How could someone just switch her love off like that? He fought back the tears, unsuccessfully.

"Dude." Lenny didn't want to be left out of Cozy and Zak's bond. "I know you're happy for us, but ..."

"I'm sorry. I'm just having a really tough time. Surprise, surprise. I was hanging out down by the river last night. It was all I could do not to throw myself in."

"Bro, what did I tell you about that?" Lenny was trying to be helpful. "Besides, you know that the Willamette River is a Superfund clean-up sight. You probably wouldn't drown, you'd just mutate."

"Len!" Cozy preferred a different approach. "Zak, honey, you know things are going to get better. They're at their worst right now and you

271

didn't kill yourself. You didn't jump off that cliff or dive into the river. You are over the hump. It's only going to get easier from here."

"Hmm. That sounds logical, but I just don't feel it. It's not a linear thing. Like it gets a little better each day. Sometimes I'm just crippled by this, whatever it is. I just don't think I'll ever fully recover. I don't want to be scarred but smarter. I'd rather just check out now before I slide any farther." He forced another grin to his face, as if to say, isn't this all so silly.

"Boy! You have got so much to offer the world. You are the one who is going to change it. It needs you in it."

"Fuck the world. What's the use of changing things? Look at all the stupid people breeding. How can you stop that? All the idiots who end up on *Jerry Springer*. All the crack whores who spend their abortion money on dope. The skinheads who knock up dumb white girls to have more white serial killers in the world. I can't change that. The only thing that will change the world is the annihilation of 98% of the human race."

"Fuck's sake," muttered Lenny, unable to counter this tone from a friend once filled with hope and the human spirit of optimism, a regular John Lennon.

"Listen to this shit, Zak. It's not you. You stopped taking your Zoloft, didn't you?"

"It was interfering with my drinking."

"Great, so you've replaced your anti-depressants with depressants. No wonder you feel like shit!"

"Look, I don't need the drugs. It's my heart not my brain. My heart is broken. All those fucking songs are true. I can't just mend it. Everything will be lived through the shattered mirror of her loss. All my dreams were wrapped up with her. I thought there was morality in the world. You can't just tell me that I'll ever have that joy back. I'm getting out of love."

272

Cozy ran her finger through her black hair. Was this the yin and yang? One person's happiness had to be tempered with another's sorrow? Lenny got out of the bed for some distance, but she stayed close to her friend.

"You silly boy," said Cozy. Zak made that laughing sound that is really just blowing air out of your nose. "If people get over the deaths of others, you'll get over this. Your heart will go on."

Lenny couldn't resist the musical cue. "Near, far..."

"Lenny!" they screamed in unison.

Zak had already run this line through his head. "Do those people ever really get over it, really? Aren't they always fucked up? I mean, Pet never really got over her sister dying. I think all this is partially a product of that. Like if she marries me, I might die tragically." Petra and Zak had never discussed it. If he had been a better boyfriend they would have. Her sister had been killed in a drunk driving accident when Petra was 12 and he couldn't help believe it motivated her self-destructive impulses, this just being the latest version.

"Zak, you've got to get a hold of yourself. I've got a wedding to plan. If you fuck it up by killing yourself, I'm going to come down to hell and make sure they torture you with Celine Dion records."

"Near, far..."

"Lenny!"

But it was too late. Zak burst out in laughter. He felt like the happiest sad person on Earth. How many coal miners would kill to have his slack life? Maybe Celine Dion was right.

"Listen, Zak, I want you to promise me one thing. I want you to call your shrink and go talk to him. That's what he's there for. And lay off the booze, would ya?"

"That's two things."

He wanted to leave the lovers to their connubial whatever so he apologized and thanked and headed back downstairs to #110. Telly was

273

already off on a Saturday adventure. Zak put a Fionna Apple CD on and climbed back into bed, pulling the covers up to his neck.

Polly was oblivious to the rain. Spending the majority of her new life outside in Oregon it felt natural. It wasn't actually rain, but "showers" which sounds heavier than rain but according to the dopey weathermen was just the normal drizzle.

Telly was never late. Maybe Lucinda was early, anxious to have a "date" with her man. Mother and child were sitting on a wooden bench at the entrance to the Portland Zoo, watching normal-looking families doing what normal-looking families do on Saturdays all over the world, look at caged animals. Could this be her and Telly in a few years? Taking a preschool Polly to see the new baby rhino?

The improbable course of events that had brought her to this spot swirled in her head. A leering father. An acid casualty. A drunken sailor. A thousand wet nights. Snorting shit that could have been fucking anything. The day Polly was born. Telly at the bus stop. Sometimes it was so hard to remember what was real and what was dreamed. How did people write those fucking autobiographies, complete with fully transcribed conversations from 20 years ago? She could barely remember what she ate yesterday, or if she ate. What a mess. At least pretty Polly wouldn't go hungry.

Somebody probably had pointed it out to him. Telly was wearing Zak's old black leather jacket that went a bit better with the green and black striped pants than the white jacket did. Polly saw him before Lucinda. Perhaps her parrot eyes were more like frog eyes, more adapt to the rain than her human mother.

"Elo," cooed the baby.

"Hello, Polly. Hello, Lucinda. I hope that I am not late," he said as flatly as always.

"No, I'm early. You know, lots of free time. Are you ready to see the zoo?"

Telly paid for himself and Lucinda and they let Polly in for free because she just seemed kind of pathetic. Once inside, the three followed the crowd around the park. Lucinda had been to the zoo plenty of times as a kid, so the animals weren't quite as exiting as parading around with her baby and Telly, approximating some fucked up definition of normality.

The zoo was quite another thing for Telly. He was confused. Earthlings caging other earthlings for show. The chatter of the macaws made Polly giggle but it woke a deep sadness in Telly. A few of the baby monkeys cowered in a corner and chewed on their fingers. He knew they didn't want to be there, caged in the cold Oregon dank. All the animals had that look of resignation, the same look cows in the slaughterhouse have or death row inmates. What's the use of fighting? What's the point of raging against the machine when each fit of resistance just brings another cattle prod to the genitals? He knew that look. He'd seen it many times before.

"What's the matter, dude?" Lucinda just wanted to move through all the exhibits so they could go park at the snack bar or hit a coffee house.

He thought for a second, before speaking. "Lucinda, do you ever feel like one of these creatures? Caged?"

"Shit! I'm about as uncaged as you get. Why do you think I live like this? I can go anywhere at anytime." They sat down on a sheltered bench near the gorilla yard.

"But do you ever feel too tired to fight, as if your very spirit has been crushed against a stone?"

She looked down at the ground. She had no snappy answer. Why was he asking her this? She knew that he was somber, maybe even morose, which was a word she remembered her mother using to describe her. Whatever, it wasn't exactly polite conversation. She thought Zak was

275

supposed to be the depressed one of that bunch. Because she *had* been too tired to fight, almost every day. She had been too tired to face the rain, to nurse her daughter, to ask another poor person for change. It was all too much. Daily, she wanted to blink her eyes and open up in someone else's life. Someone who didn't sleep in squats or shoot smack. Someone who had their very own washer and dryer so the sheets could always be clean.

"I don't know."

"Lucinda, what is it that you want most in the world." Telly desperately needed answers but to Lucinda, it sounded a bit like a proposal was on deck.

"You mean, besides a million bucks and a blimp?"

"A blimp?" He wasn't expecting it.

"Yeah, a fucking blimp. I want a blimp to fly around in and when it gets dark I'm gonna have it say, 'Fuck you, asshole.' It'll be awesome!"

The fantasy brought a grin to Telly's face. Most people wanted a Lexus. She wanted a Goodyear blimp. "But what do you want to happen in your life?"

"Shit, I'd be happy with a place to live. Not a fucking shelter either. I mean my own apartment with a room for Polly and maybe a cool roommate to hang out with. And a self-cleaning oven. And a landlord that didn't sneak in and sniff my panties."

"And do you think you will find this place?" He was looking for clues.

"Hell, yeah! Oh, I'm not gonna be on the street much longer. If I can get a job and free day care and the deposit and phone money. No sweat. I'll be livin' large." Under the sarcasm was a strand of hope.

The unwoken fool. That's how Zak was starting to feel all curled up in bed, almost 30, his life slipping away. He had to get over this somehow. He wasn't feeble-minded. He was a strong personality who stood up for truth, justice and the Armenian way.

Music was always good medicine. Anytime things had been bad or weird or uncomfortable, there was a song for him. He climbed out of the bed and headed into the music room to comb the racks for just the right one. Aerosmith? The Cult? Drivin' 'N' Cryin'? L7? Just past The Velvet Underground he stopped and pulled out The Verve's *Urban Hymns*. Yeah, "Bitter Sweet Symphony" was a big Stones rip-off and it had been used in an evil Nike commercial, but the song always made Zak feel like a bad-ass.

Zak slapped it into the CD player and as soon as the sampled strings poured out of the speakers he felt better and strutted around the apartment. "Cause I'm here in my mode. I am here in my mode," or whatever he was singing. It was five minutes and fifty-seven seconds of ecstasy, when all was right with the world. A million different people.

But like all great pop tunes, the song faded away and the hook retreated to the recesses of the subconscious. If you don't turn off the CD in time, "Bitter Sweet Symphony" becomes the bittersweet "One Day," another poisonous paean to the inevitable reunion of lovers.

Zak plopped down on the futon, into his pre-Zoloft morning hole. There was the box of china taunting him, filled with dinner parties and Thanksgiving dinners and home-made Valentines brunches that would never happen thanks to Petra's Dr. Jekyll and Mr. Hyde routine. They were just plates but they were so much more, a box of all the happiness that had been promised to him and then snatched away at the last minute. God damn that box.

It was getting to be too much. He could feel his inner-cripple unfurl inside of him. Zak began thinking of all the things that were fucked up in his life. Maybe to put Petra in perspective. Maybe as an argument for suicide.

1) His CD burner was broken and it was too expensive to fix.

2) He had avoided all conversations with his mom since the wedding cancellation.

3) He hadn't gotten his Oregon drivers license yet, which in this state was probably a felony.

4) An undergrad was accusing him of losing his term player. But the kid was a football player who probably hadn't even written the damn paper.

5) He had a cyst on his back that hopefully was a fast acting tumor.

6) All bills were late.

7) The power windows on his Bug were failing.

8) His student loan was hovering in the dark, waiting to destroy him.

9) He might be addicted to Internet porn.

10) He couldn't go twenty minutes without wishing someone would shoot him in the head. No, actually the chest would be better. Then he would have a few seconds to get some last words off to Petra. The usual blah-blah-blah about dying of a broken heart.

But sooner or later summer would be here and everything would be beautiful and everyone would be happy and no one would be jumping off of the bridges of Portland. But wherever you are in the calendar, Christmas is just around the corner. And it would be a lifetime of Christmases without her compared to the Christmases with her. Like the Christmas where his grandfather got Pet to sit on his lap and then tried to feel her up. Or the Christmas they got stuck in a Waffle House on the way to visit relatives in Slidell and drove everyone crazy by playing the Waffle House Christmas songs on the jukebox. "Scattered and Smothered with Christmas Love."

No doubt he would be up on the bridge just like George Baily this Christmas. But stupid George Baily was going to jump because of a measly $8000. He had love. He had a loving wife and children and Zuzu's petals. Zuzu, who's real life son would kill himself later on. Dumbass

George Baily. Zak would kill for that life. Petra in the old Granville house. Ernie and Bert serenading outside the window. Zak felt like he had more of a reason to jump than George did.

But Christmas was still months off. He might get shot before then. Crime was always worse in the summer when people got sweaty. He picked up the *Oregonian* that Telly had been reading. He stopped at the top story on page A3. "Missing Eugene woman apparently committed suicide." Great. A woman that had been missing for a month was found at the bottom of a lake, wearing a backpack filled with rocks, "leaving behind a husband, two daughters and her business, a children's bookstore." To all concerned the death was a mystery, it said. But Zak knew how well you could hide depression. He knew that you could put on a front that would fool even your shrink, but on the inside you were praying for the cold hand of death to knock the shit out of you. Later people will say they saw the signs, always later.

Story about the Eugene woman caused Zak to cry. It didn't take much these days, but this story was a little close to home. Maybe he wished he'd thought of the rocks in the backpack thing. Pretty clever. If you really wanted to live, you could probably wriggle out of it. He collected himself and continued to thumb through the paper.

There was a Saturday lecture up at the university. A grad student from the school of social work named Tina Darwin was presenting her research on reducing teen pregnancy. He thought he should go since not many people went to Saturday lectures and anything that helps reduce the amount of fatherless children in the world should be supported. Maybe he would be inspired to finish his own thesis. He only had an hour so he jumped into the shower as The Verve played out.

On the way out of The Eldorado he saw the scabby homeless guy, the one that lived on for some reason. If Zak made it to the summer, he promised himself he'd take this man out to dinner and find out what his secret was.

"Telly, do you ever think about getting your own apartment," Lucinda asked out of the blue. It was possible that he might want his own place and then Lucinda could move in.

Telly hadn't discussed with anyone how long he would be in Portland. He himself didn't know, but it wouldn't be very long. The thought of his world teetering kept him from feeling too at home on the rain planet. But he could tell that Lucinda was becoming attached to him and he was beginning to covet his relationship with her, Polly, Zak, Cozy and Lenny.

The images of Bev, Fennel and Ryan crept into his head, his lost comrades. He knew he'd be lucky to get off of this planet alive and he had to work quickly.

"Polly, what if I were to tell you that you were never going to get into an apartment. That you would be homeless for the rest of your life. What would your response be?"

"That you're an asshole. Look, if I thought I was never going to get off of the street, I'd kill myself right now," she said in a pissy tone. "But I know that I am getting an apartment."

"How do you know?"

"I just do."

"Why?"

"Because, that's why?"

She didn't have an argument but Telly really didn't need one. He just needed to hear her believe in something she had no reason to believe in. They were in the snake-house, which fascinated Polly who stuck her tongue out at the reptiles.

Lucinda thought Telly was being obnoxious, but maybe it was a test. Maybe if she proved to him how much she wanted a place, he would help. He would be the cool roommate.

In one of the university seminar rooms, Zak listened to Tina Darwin give her Saturday lecture. It was all about the power of peer mentoring and how girls who were bonded to non-mother peers who had a political reason for not breeding were less likely to breed themselves. It was impressive research, but he was more impressed with the researcher herself. She had taken a simple idea, helping teen girls with their sexuality, and turned it into a major enterprise. She was driven, charismatic and beautiful. She was what Zak himself wanted to become before he was derailed by this love drama. He wanted to be a person who spent his spare mental time thinking about how to save the world, not how to kill himself or how to get Petra back.

He took notes on her facts and figures that he would probably never look at again. But in the margin he wrote, "I could love her." It was an affirmation to himself that someone better than Petra was in fact out there. His mind was reeling, thinking of various combinations and couplings. He was on a vector that he had blocked himself from, wishful thinking.

After the lecture he edged his way through the others that wanted to raise points or to thank her for presenting. He briefly mentioned his research on males and fetal alcohol kids and how their research was similar. She gave him her card from the school of social work and disappeared with her colleagues. It was a brief encounter but it changed Zak's whole frame of mind.

Outside of the school he hopped on his bike to ride down the hill toward downtown. Maybe he could get over this. Maybe there was someone out there to make him forget that Petra ever existed. The Saturday afternoon shoppers made him feel like he was back in the world of normalcy.

Just past the Pioneer Square Starbucks he saw Lenny and Cozy window shopping. They were looking at diamond rings and laughing, unable to imagine spending the money.

"Cozy! Lenny!" he shouted, pulling his bike up on to the sidewalk, next to them.

"Howdy, Zacker. My, you seem to be in a good mood." She was right, even though it couldn't compare to her good mood.

"Oh, I was just at a kick-ass lecture."

Lenny rolled his eyes. "Yeah, lectures always get me going like that. There's nothin' I like more than a nice long lecture. Who gave this lecture? Jennifer Love Hewitt?"

"Almost. This goddess. It was just right on. It put me right on track. And..." Zak pulled out her card and rubbed against his face.

"Dude! I always knew you'd leave us for a damn intellectual type," joked Lenny.

Cozy just smiled. Anything to get him out of this funk and out of the idea that Petra was anything but bad for him. Of course, it would be a really painful period, but one he would make it through. He just had to focus on the infinite possibilities.

Zak rode off on his bike, looking more like a little boy with a Toys-R-Us gift certificate than a lovesick mopester.

"He can do it," said Cozy in a low voice.

"Yeah, that's what they said to that gymnast, Kerri Strug, and where is she now?"

Exile On Mainstreet was blasting. Zak was trying to convince himself that he was cured and on his way to finishing his masters work. In the middle of the Keith Richards guitar solo, Telly, Lucinda and Polly came in to the apartment. Lucinda laughed as it seemed like she was always seeing Zak in these private moments. She had never seen *Risky Business*, but if she had, that's what she would be thinking of; Zak in his underwear with Bob Seger.

"Hey y'all," Zak said, turning down the Stones.

282

"Good afternoon, Zak. You seem happy." Telly could tell that it was somewhat forced but worth encouraging. Lucinda and her baby sat down in the armchair like they were back home.

"Telly, my main man. I think I've got your answer," he said, grabbing his roommate's arm.

"What was the question?" Lucinda was excited to be in on something.

"Why we're all here, darlin'. Or better, why we stick around." Telly was silent, waiting for Zak's take on his prime question. "One word. Chaos. Our world is in total chaos. Everything changes so quickly. One day, we're blaming epilepsy on masturbation and the next we're sending robots to Mars. Bad shit happens to good people and good shit happens to bad people. Tony Danza is a household name and Noam Chomsky isn't. It's all completely random. The polio vaccine, random. Hurricane Starla, random. Regis Philbin, random."

"And that's a good thing? I thought everything was supposed to have a purpose," said Lucinda.

"You've been going to church too much. Yeah, there is an order to things. There's lots of predictability. Tomorrow's weather will probably be like today's. Susan Lucci will probably lose the Emmy. Some crap song will probably be #1. But things are fucked up just enough that as soon as you think you've got it figured out, the exact opposite thing happens. It's chaos. You can't predict shit!" Zak was animated. This thesis had gelled in his head on the bike ride home.

Lucinda still wasn't getting the point. "So what?"

"So, if you can't predict anything, that means anything could happen. Anything! You might get discovered and become a movie star. Telly, you might save the world. I might get married to Ashley Judd. The odds are against it, but it could happen. How many people talk about their success by saying, 'Never in a million years did I think I'd be' whatever? The cards are totally stacked against us, but not all of them.

The Joker is in the deck and it could make anything happen. Remember Y2K? How there were all these predictions of chaos. Well, of course nothing happened. But the possibility that something might have happened was exciting as hell. Power outages, terrorism, the four horsemen of the apocalypse. Fun! You're not going to leave a movie before the ending, right? The unknown is worth sticking around for."

Telly thought about this. He thought about the way his friends acted when they listened to music. They were suddenly plugged into the world of possibilities. He only knew chaos as an enemy, to be conquered with order and reason. But what he saw in the churches was people believing in something unreasonable, in the face of reason. There probably wasn't a God, but there might be.

He rubbed his hands against his temples and slowly shook his head.

"Telly, hon, what's wrong?" Lucinda was concerned that Zak had upset him.

"Zak, may I speak to you privately?"

"Yeah, dude, OK." Lucinda was confused. She was in the room after all. Zak followed Telly into the music room and shut the door.

"Zak, I must ask a favor of you." His face was strained in earnestness.

"Sure, man. What do you need?"

"I believe that I will leave Portland soon."

"Dude, you just got here!"

"I may have to go home and if I do I would like Lucinda and Polly to have my room."

Zak stepped back. Despite his mood, he wasn't really into the idea of a gutter-punk and her screaming baby moving in. She probably came with a lot of grungy friends who would steal his CDs and beer.

"I know of your reservations and I understand them." It was that mind meld again. "I will give you the full rent for one year."

"Fuck, man, where are you getting this money?" Telly always seemed to have cash on hand. Were they beaming it down to him or was he just playing a lot of Keno?

"Please, Zak. She is a good person. She needs a home. Her child needs a home."

"Christ." It was a tough plea to back away from. It might be interesting. It might be interesting to Tina Darwin. "Yeah, deal. But when? Did you phone home? Are they on the way."

"No, I will go by myself. When they call."

The two went back to the living room where the untrusting Lucinda was tapping her foot. Telly wanted to wait to tell her. He might not be leaving anytime soon. There was still so much to learn.

"Your CD is over, dude." The last track, "Soul Survivor," had played out and Lucinda was sitting in silence.

"Hold on, I've got a song for us." Zak was caught up in the new optimism in the apartment. He dove into a CD stack on the floor and slipped a silvery disc into the player.

The comforting voice of Paul McCartney was unmistakable, even to Telly. It was "Hey Jude" and he was taking a sad song and making it better. It's a fool who plays it cool by making his world a little colder. Zak was singing along and hamming it up like it was a karaoke bar. A smiling Lucinda knew the song well and got caught up in singing along, even though she could only remember about every third word. Telly thought that line about the world on your shoulders was for him. And Polly danced. The scene was like a bunch of kids at a sleepover goofing to their favorite Top 40 song.

When the "na-na-na-nana-na-na" part hit, Zak picked up Polly from the floor and swung her around as if they were ballroom dancing. Lucinda giggled at the two. The song made everyone in the room feel happy for no apparent reason. Telly noticed the transformation as well. It was as if "Hey Jude" contained a magic spell. He was lucky he missed

Zak's playing of the Beatles disc earlier in the day when he just repeated "Don't Let Me Down" over and over as if in a maudlin trance.

Every time things seemed desperate there was a song. It was the same for the people in the Cathedral of the Sacred Heart singing to Mother Mary. The ones who seemed so sad coming in were lifted somehow by the music. Somehow the music channeled the chaos into definable terms. Anything was possible. The world of randomness and the world of predictability were briefly united in a tune. Here was the seed of hope. It was never too late.

After the song faded out, Zak suggested coffee. It was almost Saturday night and there was a caffeine deficit to deal with. He rang up Cozy and Lenny and invited them out. Neither had any singing to do that evening, so the promise of high-octane java scorching their throats brought them downstairs in a jiffy.

The five plus baby found a cozy indy coffeehouse on Northwest Flanders Street and settled in. Lucinda was starting to believe that these people were actually her friends now. So different from Roxy and the gang at Pioneer Square. The gutter-punks just complained about how fucked up everything was. These people talked about their projects. Lenny was planning on making t-shirts for his band that said, "Sort Of Rocks" in glittery silver letters. Cozy was starting rehearsals on Monday with the opera and would be meeting lots of new people. Zak was talking about the lecture and how he was going to finish his thesis up before July.

Lucinda didn't really have any projects other than the constant search for food, shelter and Pampers. But she remembered how she used to write poetry in her journal before she left Seaside.

"I'm writing a book of poetry!" she chimed in, startling nearly everyone. "Yeah, I thought I'd write a bunch of poems about being on the street and maybe sell it. Do you think anyone would be interested?"

"Oh, sweetie, that's a great idea!" exclaimed Cozy, happy that Telly's friend felt part of the creative process. She could tell she was trying and wanted to give her a leg up. "I think people would really benefit from knowing about your experience. I bet even the local media would be interested."

"Really? You think I could even get on TV?"

"Anything is possible in this town."

Telly sipped his latte and watched the happy group, so filled with future orientations. The pieces were starting to come together for him. The optimism had infected him as well. For the first time he thought there might actually be a chance. But it also brought sadness because he knew that if his mission was complete he would soon be leaving his good friends and would never learn how things turned out for them. He felt like he was watching the setting from a third person perspective. Friends talking and dreaming. "Let It Be" was playing in his head as he looked at the closeness between Cozy and Lenny or the bond between Lucinda and Polly. And Zak was laughing!

They began making Saturday night plans. All agreed that alcohol consumption should not be a central activity. They picked a Christina Ricci movie at the cinema-draught-house where alcohol consumption would be only secondary to film viewing.

"I think I might try to talk to Pet later," said Zak, hoping to parley his good feelings over to her so he could see that he was OK.

"Dude, are you sure? What's the point?" Cozy thought he should just give her some space. Lots of space, like kilometers.

"Yeah, I just want to say that I'm OK and that she can have as much time as she wants. I'm not going anywhere. I've been such a fucking drama queen lately. I love her so I can give her what she wants. Besides, I've got so much grad work to do. Maybe by this summer she'll realize what a mistake she's made and maybe I'll have met someone even better and she'll be shit out of luck." It was a new tone.

"You've got it all figured out, professor," said Lenny, eyebrow raised.

"I'm just tired of being sad. Seeing that woman give that lecture today just made me think about how much there is to accomplish in life. What if everyone was stopped dead by a broken heart? We'd have a pretty small population."

The line made Lucinda think about Polly. Polly broke Lucinda's heart every day. Polly was a constant reminder of what she left behind; the life of a normal teenager complete with Friday dates and final exams. Polly was the product of too many bad decisions. She was another fatherless child, "at-risk." The social worker told her that Polly would probably become a single teen mother, too. She would probably be homeless or on drugs or both. Something had to happen and Telly was the best hope she'd had since she had her baby.

After the film the gang split up. It was obvious that Cozy and Lenny were headed home to have engagement sex. They barely saw the movie and disappeared halfway through to go up to the balcony. Zak wanted to take a walk to plan what he was going to say to Petra. He had to choose every word carefully. Telly told Lucinda he would ride back to the shelter with her so she could get in before curfew. It would be a depressing end to a fun day for her, but it was better than hanging out with the dead end kids.

Once off the bus the two walked and smiled at each other. Polly was sleeping but still heavy.

"Lucinda, I have something to tell you."

Oh, God. Could this be the moment? She stopped on the sidewalk and looked up at him.

"I believe I have a solution to your housing problem." Oh, maybe.

"What? Did you win the lottery?"

"No. My time here is only brief, I am afraid. When I leave, Zak has allowed you to move into my room, rent free."

It was one of those good news/bad news things times a million. She wanted more than anything to get off the streets and have the life that her new friends had, but she wanted it with Telly.

"What? You're leaving? I thought you were staying on Portland. Is it something I did? Are you going back to Kosovo?" she fretted.

"I am going back home and it is nothing you did. I came here for a specific purpose and I believe I have accomplished it."

"So what are you, a spy?"

"Sort of." He looked to the sky but there were only clouds.

She didn't understand but she knew she was losing him. Maybe she suspected it was too good to be true. She grabbed and hugged him. "Oh, Telly, don't say goodbye, please."

He remained dispassionate, as difficult as that was. "I won't. I don't know exactly when I must leave. But when I do, you will have a home."

"Zak's gonna let me live there for free? And Polly?" He didn't seem too baby-friendly before the "Hey Jude" thing.

"The rent is paid for one year. He has agreed. Your parents can come and visit you and meet Polly." He stroked her hair.

"Oh, Telly."

It was late, but there were still plenty of lights on at The Greenwood. Butterflies flickered in his stomach as he approached the building. Just seeing her was a thrill. He had gone from seeing her every day almost all day long to barely at all. Every glimpse had to be savored, especially if he was going to back off for a while. Hopefully she would come down and talk to him.

He pushed the button by Lisa's name.

"Hello?"

"Hey Lisa. Is Petra around?"

289

"No, she's out Zak. I'll tell her you came by, OK?"

He didn't buy it. "C'mon, Lisa. I have something really important to tell her."

"Zak, I'm serious. It's Saturday and she's out."

That didn't sound good. Out, like date out? She was supposed to be contemplating her solitude. If she was out with the girls, Lisa would be there. He didn't want to know. One of the things he learned in Boy Scouts is that when you're lost, just stay put and someone will find you. He felt lost so he sat down on the curb.

The still of the night was broken by a woman's moaning. Half a block up was a white Ford Bronco. Just like the one OJ used as the getaway vehicle. The yuppie SUV was rocking back and forth like it was parked on the last row of a drive-in. Zak chuckled. Pretty bold, he thought, right there in the middle of everything.

The humor only lasted a second, until he recognized the sounds coming from the truck. He'd heard them a million times when he was making love to his beautiful fiancé. It was Petra.

He froze and felt sick to his stomach. Maybe he was wrong. Maybe that's how a lot of women sounded when they were getting off. Christ, it sounded like her. He couldn't move. Time just stopped. His heart turned to fire, about to burn out of his chest, his stomach filled with acid. His arms and legs pulsed and became weak.

It seemed like it was going on forever. He had to know. At the risk of embarrassing somebody unknown to him, he slowly walked up on the Bronco, to the passenger side. There were the boots he had bought her for her last birthday, with her panties around one ankle. The driver was on top of her, fucking his Petra, his sweet love, like she was a piece of meat. This is what she wanted.

He didn't want to see anymore. The scene already would be burned into his mind until the day he died. But he couldn't resist banging on the window. She had to know that she was killing him. He didn't know why

290

she had to know, he just beat the window in sorrow. It was the pounding of the end of the world.

Startled, Petra looked up to see Zak's contorted face. It was the last thing she suspected. She was living out a fantasy of being spontaneous and unconnected to anyone and there he was, her connection. She screamed, "No! Oh, God!" and Ben sat up. Mistaking Zak's horror for jealous rage he started up the Ford and tore off, leaving Zak standing in the middle of the street, stunned.

Reality is a frail thing. You spend your life constructing this picture of the way things are. It's an intricate painting with thousands of hues, but each one deeply embedded with meaning. It might not be much, no Sistine Chapel, but it's yours. If you're lucky, you can work on the same canvas your whole life, show the evolution of your form at each turn. Or someone can take a red-hot knife and slash it into a million pieces.

A hundred things sped through his head as he tried to make sense of what he had just seen. Maybe he was standing outside the Carmine Gia, watching the logical conclusion of Mia and himself. But he had stopped himself, out of love. His love for Petra was a life-vest that stopped him from drowning in stupidity and impulsiveness. Where was her vest?

Maybe this guy was raping her. She was drunk and he was taking advantage of it, in which case he couldn't be angry at her but could kill this Bronco-driving yuppie motherfucker. Zak thought about unleashing his anger on him until he was just a pile of meatloaf. But he knew those sounds too well. They weren't of a girl being raped. They were of a woman enjoying sex.

He had to leave. He couldn't stand in that spot any longer. That would forever be the spot where his hope died. He stumbled backward and then wandered away trying to pretend that it didn't happen. He was at home in his bed having another Petra nightmare. Anywhere was better than here.

291

Petra was frantic. She knew that she had hurt him. His face upside down through the window looked like an Edvard Munch painting. She had betrayed her tender boy. His suicidal tendencies were nothing to laugh about. Not tonight. She had to find him, to try and explain somehow.

He was likely to go to the river, maybe a club for a few stiff drinks. Her tears mixed with the rain as she ran toward downtown. She hoped that he would run to Cozy who seemed to be his crutch in her absence. She went to The Eldorado and headed up the stairs. Zak's apartment was on the first floor, but there was only Telly sitting on the window seat. He hadn't seen Zak since the movie. Petra's desperate tone made him worry, though. He had appeared in such good form just an hour earlier.

Nearly out of breath, Petra trotted up to the fourth floor.

"Hi, Pet? What's up?"

"Cozy, have you seen Zak? It's really important."

"Oh, shit. What happened?"

She couldn't tell her that Zak had seen her fucking some other guy, in a Bronco no less. She didn't want to believe any of it happened either.

"Cozy, either my subconscious just solved my problems or I just messed up royally."

It wasn't too hard to figure out what that meant. But Zak had seemed as far away from any suicidal impulses as he had been in weeks. The river was too big to search. It stretched out for miles.

"Do you want me to help you look for him?" She wasn't too keen to go on another "save me now" mission for Zak. She was finally comfortable with her man. But she knew Petra's power over him. She could build him up just to tear him down.

Petra thought for a second. There was one spot she should try first. A place they would go when the rain stopped in July to watch the city. They spent many romantic summer nights up on the roof. It was where he gave her the diamond ring she now kept in a drawer.

"Coz, can I go up your fire escape?"

Her straight brown hair against her pretty face made her look a little like Natalie Wood climbing the fire escape to meet Tony. Hopefully this wouldn't end as tragically as *West Side Story*. From the roof, the city seemed huge, reaching from the West Hills down through the river valley.

Zak was there, but not on the ledge. He was just sitting against a structure, looking out at the night, getting soaked. She drifted in.

"Zak? Honey?"

"Oh, God. Here it comes, the big Dipsy Dumpster." His sardonic tone was his only defense.

"Oh, honey, I'm so sorry. I would have done anything to prevent you from seeing that." She wanted to get close and hold him but she needed distance.

"Anything except just not do it. Who was it? Some guy from work?"

Where were the words? "Zak, I'm going through something big. I don't know what it is. I have to find out. You have to let me."

"Let my wife fuck other men?" He was shaking with anger or cold.

"I'm not your wife. I can't be. Can't you see that? I can't do it. I've changed."

"Changed? Into what? You're my Petra, my very same Petra that won my heart."

"I'm sorry, Zak. I don't want you in my life right now."

It didn't make any sense to him. Just a month ago this woman had wrapped her dreams around his. She was known to adore him. Everyone said so. A love like that doesn't just "change."

"No! I don't believe you!"

"You never believed me, Zak. That's half the problem. You never took me seriously." She was angered by the supposed male feminist who didn't know how to hear what women said to him.

"That's just a communication problem. Venus and Mars and all that. We can work that out. That's what marriage is all about!"

"It's too late, Zak. It's too late."

"That's such bullshit. It's never too late. It's never too late for something like this, like love. Look what you're throwing way." It was bullshit, the "it's too late" bit, anyway. That and "I've changed" were the things people said when they didn't have a real answer. Like when a kid asks why she can't stick a fork in the electrical socket and the parent just says, "Because." It's supposed to stop the conversation but Zak wasn't about to give up.

Petra wasn't doing a very good job of explaining herself. Maybe there was a song, she thought. Probably by Melissa Ethridge. Something about needing to break free. She wasn't thinking about loneliness or a lack of companionship in old age. She was thinking about the need to follow her young Id.

Thoughts of leaping off of the roof flitted through Zak's mind, but he held strong. He slowly approached Petra. She was so beautiful, even in this jaggered state. He would never be with anyone so beautiful. He had no song to help him this time. Just his own words.

"Petra, listen to me. All that I am as a man, everything that I have been through, every poem that I have written and every class I have taken. Every lesson that I've learned and every impossible situation that I've struggled through. Every losing battle that ever I've fought, every banner that I've carried has been because I wanted to live in a world that I could share with you. Even before we met, my life was preparing me to love you. Everything that is moral in me believes that our love is right, that us together is so much more than us apart."

She was moved. She didn't deserve such love. She was still the selfish party girl from Alabama and this kind of love would smother her. She had no response.

294

"Pet, baby, our Shangri-la is right here. You just have to say yes. We can have it all. I don't care about tonight, just come home, please. Let's start over."

The rain was indistinguishable from the tears. It seemed like Portland was always crying. That's why no one used umbrellas. The rain was camouflage.

"Zak, I've made up my mind. I'm sorry. Now I want you to come down off this roof. OK?"

"Don't worry, I'm not going to jump. Because I know you'll change your mind. You're acting stupid. Maybe not tonight, but someday you'll change your mind and I'll just wait."

"But can't you see how manipulative that is? I can't live my life knowing you're just pining way, waiting for me. I won't be guilt-tripped."

"It's not guilt-tripping. All wooing is manipulation. I want you back and I'll do anything I can to convince you."

"You have to let go, Zak. I'm not just going to wake up one day and say, 'oops!' and come back." Her complex accent, Czech and 'Bama blended, made even the harshest send off sound sexy.

"You might."

"No, Zak."

"Anything is possible."

"Just come in and get dry."

Petra led him back in through the window, so Cozy could see he was OK. No explanations were given. He was fine, it seemed. She deposited him in his apartment with a concerned Telly who was given orders to keep an eye on him.

"I'm sorry about all of this, Zak. I really am. I'll call you tomorrow and make arrangements to get the rest of my stuff." She kissed him on the cheek and faded back out, into the Saturday night.

Zak and Telly spent the entire night talking. Telly talked about the beautiful things he had seen in Portland and how they could be just as beautiful on Elo; opera, cathedrals, drinking with friends, dancing babies. Zak talked about how hard it would be to live without Petra, about the permanence of her absence. When Telly reminded him of his excitement about the unknown twists and turns in life, Zak smiled. But he had come to the conclusion that he couldn't get through it without her.

The two played records until the sun came up. Zak kept playing sad ones, like Counting Crows and Jeff Buckley, that reminded him of her. Then Telly would use his turn to play songs that would bring back his joy, like "Jumpin" Jack Flash," and "In The Basement," and "Hey Jude." But the good songs always faded away.

The bond between Zak and Telly was strong. They often seemed like two souls headed down the turnpike in opposite directions, meeting in one of those common rest areas, each looking to the other for a lifeline. The dark Telly helped Zak to see how beautiful life on Earth really was, just like Clarence Odbody, AS2. But it just didn't seem like enough. If everything was a lie, what was the point of pretending? If all you need is love was untrue, then hate and war had won. If the world was just a culmination of self-serving egotists, then why bother cherishing the few moments that weren't all about getting paid?

Zak's mind felt like it was in brain freeze. Like when the push-up stick is too cold in the middle of August and an ice spike is driven into your medulla oblongata. The image of her boots in the Bronco wasn't going away. The lie of "it's too late" wasn't going away. Her beautiful, tender face and all the memories it held weren't going away.

Something about Telly's presence made him feel better. Even though the guy was the most dead panned, dour fucker that had ever failed to light up a room, there was some reassurance that of all the places in the universe, he ended up here, with Zak.

Zak didn't remember how he got back out to Astoria. His VW was there, parked at Lynne's place, so he must have driven. All he remembered was Lucinda knocking on the door bright and early to drag Telly to church. When they went to wake him up, he was gone. There was a stack of hundred dollar bills on the table next to a note that said, "Anything could happen."

They knew that he had gone back to wherever he came from, Elo, Kosovo, Toledo. Lucinda cried openly and Zak hugged her until she stopped. But he was sad too. Petra was gone. Cozy and Lenny would probably disappear into wedded bliss. Now Telly had vanished. Beamed up. He was alone. Lucinda was moving in, but she was too young and different to have that connection that he craved.

He was on the cliff again, by Coxcomb Hill. It felt like magnetic north to him. The bluff seemed much higher in the daylight. The turbulence of the Columbia meeting the Pacific beat against the rocks below. His hair blew in the gray sea wind as he thought about all that he had lost and how hard the recovery could be.

There, right on the edge, he felt simultaneously alive and dead. He was a non-being in this world, yet every sense sparkled in the cold ocean air. He didn't want to be Sisyphus, another day, same boulder. Why try?

The rocks below had been smoothed by the sea millions of years before man arrived. New rocks would fall as the waves pounded mercilessly against the earth. They too would be claimed by the caressing hands of the ocean's daughter. The white noise of the splashing sea foam was hardly interrupted by the new earth that was being added to the rocks. Just more crashing and pounding in many millennia of the same. The sea claims one more piece of the surface world. No one would notice, it would happen so quickly.

The box of china broke apart on the way down. The dishes flew loose and struck the rocks like so many abalone shells. Some rested in crevasses. Others were carried straight out to sea by the next wave, to be ground down into sand. To be reborn. The rhythm of the waves sung it's own song. It sounded a lot like the end of "Hey Jude." Na-na-na-nana-na-na, nana-na-na, hey Jude.

Amen.

Made in the USA
Lexington, KY
23 November 2013